Rosemary Friedman's novels and short stories have been widely translated and broadcast. She has written commissioned television series' and screenplays for the UK and USA. She reviews fiction and has judged many literary prizes and awards. She lives in London with her husband, a psychiatrist.

By the same author

Golden Boy
No White Coat
Love on My List
We All Fall Down
Patients of a Saint
The Fraternity
The Commonplace Day
The General Practice
Practice Makes Perfect
The Life Situation
The Long Hot Summer
Proofs of Affection
A Loving Mistress
Rose of Jericho
A Second Wife
To Live in Peace
An Eligible Man

VINTAGE

Rosemary Friedman

POCKET
B O O K S

LONDON · SYDNEY · NEW YORK · TOKYO · SINGAPORE · TORONTO

First published in Great Britain by Simon & Schuster, 1996
First published by Pocket Books, 1996
An imprint of Simon & Schuster
A Viacom Company

Simon & Schuster Ltd
West Garden Place
Kendal Street
London W2 2AQ

Simon & Schuster of Australia Pty Ltd
Sydney

A CIP catalogue record for this book is available from the British Library.

ISBN 0-671-85342-2

Printed in France by Imprimerie Hérissey (34587)

Thanks are due to

M. Anthony Barton (Chateau Langoa-Barton), M. et Mme Daniel Cathiard (Chateau-Smith-Haut-Lafitte), Mme Sylvie Cazes-Régimbeau (Chateau Lynch-Bages), M. Charles Eve and Mme Pamela Prior (Chateau Loudenne), M. Pierre-Gilles Gromand d'Every (Chateau de Lamarque), Mme de Lancquesain (Chateau Pichon-Longueville Comtesse de Lalande), M. et Mme Sacha Lichine (Chateau Prieuré-Lichine), M. Peter A. Sichel (Chateau d'Angludet), Mme Christine Valette (Chateau Troplong-Mondot), for their help and hospitality.

I would also like to thank: Mr Matthew Breslin, Mr Nicholas Faith, Mme Deborah Geffré, Mr Adrian George, Mr Daniel Green, Ms Emily Grossman, Mr Robert Joseph, Ms Stephanie Lloyd, Mr Peter Taussig, Mme Christiane Schulyer, Mme Renée Tata, Ms Nicole Tinero, Dr Jonathan Waxman, Mr Victor Woolf, and Ms Ilsa Yardley, and Dr Dennis Friedman for his invaluable help and advice.

For
Sonia Land

Au commencement était la vigne . . .

'Ce sont les passions et non les intérêts qui mènent le monde.'

Alain.

CHAPTER ONE

The sole remaining testimony to the fact that twenty-eight-year-old Clare de Cluzac had spent the impressionable years of her life on the banks of the Gironde, in the midst of one of the finest vineyards in the Médoc, was a photographic palate which enabled her to tell a Pichon-Longueville Comtesse de Lalande from a Château Gloria at a distance of twelve paces and a tendency, when under pressure, to employ the French expletive.

Clare's birth, at Château de Cluzac, a medieval fortress, which, together with Lesparre to the north and Blanquefort to the south, stood firm against the invading Vikings (many of whom were later to be seduced by the liquid delights of the area), was greeted with only muted joy. Baron Charles-Louis Eugène Bertrand de Cluzac, and to a lesser extent his Irish wife, Viola (née Fitzpatrick), had been hoping for a son to carry on the ancient line of Barons de Cluzac, whose members included an ambassador sent to Turkey by François-er, a celebrated adviser of Henry III, a Major General of the French Army in India, the General Military Commander of the Médoc, and one of the first elected mayors of Bordeaux.

This last was Clare's great-great-great-great-grandfather and the great-great-great-grandfather of Charles-Louis Eugène Bertrand, who was today solely responsible for the wine production of Château de Cluzac, once the jewel of the Médoc and now crumbling like a damp sugar-lump in the vagaries of a climate as unpredictable as that of England.

That Clare had lost touch with her father (apart from having dinner with him at Claridge's on the rare occasions when he came to London), a handsome but autocratic playboy, was due both to the fact that her mother had left him when Clare was eight, taking her daughter back to Ireland with her, and that they had never seen eye to eye. From the moment of her birth, Clare had not been able to do a thing right.

Hopeless at sport, which she was never able to take seriously, and frequently lost in a world of her own peopled by imaginary friends, whatever she did was a terrible disappointment to Charles-Louis. He could not accept that any factor other than laziness contributed to her poor level of scholastic attainment. She became so nervous in his company that she reached the point when she was afraid to say anything at all. Even her sense of humour seemed to annoy him. Sometimes the Baron would test her on what she had learned that day at Cours Albert le Grand, the exclusive private school to which, a small and lonely figure, she was taken each day by the chauffeur. He interrogated her in such a hectoring tone that, even if she knew the answers to his questions, she found herself unable to reply. Dogged by a constant sense of inadequacy, and busting her gut to be good enough for her papa, she was unaware that Baron de Cluzac was unprepared to accept from her the mediocrity he unconsciously recognised in himself, and that what he was looking for was perfection.

Clare had not been back to the Médoc since she was eighteen, when she had decided that she was *ras le bol* both with her father's cavalcade of women and his overbearing treatment of her. Digging her heels in, she had declared that enough was enough. She still owned twenty-four per cent of Cluzac – willed to her by her grandfather, the late

Baron Thibault – which yielded half a dozen yearly cases of Château de Cluzac, with its deep loganberry colour and perfume of acacia, by way of dividends. When she was caught off guard, her vinous origins overrode the veneer of Notting Hill and St Mary's Ascot and made their way to the surface.

Dressed in black leggings, voluminous black tee-shirt and ubiquitous sneakers, her black bob framing her oval face, she was pushing her trolley round Catesbury's. As she circumvented the Wines and Spirits, a dull voice, tense with the agony of indecision – a state of mind endemic in superstores in which there was so much on offer – stopped her in her tracks.

'I don't know whether to get a Bordeaux or a claret, Arthur.'

The speaker, a woman well-honed by existence, whose comfortable figure and neat grey hair bespoke a life of accommodating others, held a bottle of Catesbury's red (£2.99) at label-reading distance of her bi-focals.

Arthur, who was pushing the trolley and had stopped docilely in his tracks while his wife made up her mind, was able to be of little help. Had he ventured an opinion it was likely it would not have been heeded.

It was strange, Clare thought, how people of precisely the same degree of attractiveness seemed always to be drawn to one another. Richard Gere and Cindy Crawford. John and Norma Major. Torville and Dean. Arthur's trousers enveloped a waist whose girth suggested an affinity to bitter rather than Bordeaux. They were held up by braces visible beneath an open anorak as colourless as himself. The little hair that remained to him, some of which sprouted from his ears, might have been cut from the same swatch as his wife's. Even their spectacles, pale and plastic, appeared interchangeable and probably, in moments of need, were.

'A Bordeaux *is* a claret,' Clare remarked kindly. She

looked at the distinctive straight-necked bottles (ideal for holding the long hard corks) for which her native Bordeaux was justly famous. Lined up like skittles, they stood between the sylph-like Alsacians and the sturdy Côtes-du-Rhône. They were, she suspected, purchased by the supermarket more for the keenness of their price than the quality of their contents.

Two pairs of once-blue eyes swung round to meet her own. The couple were struck, as people always were, by the almost indecent animal vitality of Clare's appearance, by the luminosity of her skin and the spirit that leaped from eyes the colour of the Liffey. It took a moment for Arthur and his wife, no longer as quick off the mark as they had once been, to respond to the gratuitous counsel, by which time both the moment and Clare had passed.

Filling her trolley with vegetables – she and Nicola were having friends to dinner – and making unfavourable comparisons, Clare saw in her mind's eye the abundant early-morning markets of her native France: geometrically piled stalls of polished purple aubergines, emerald-green peppers, feathered bunches of golden carrots, misshappen tomatoes and bug-ridden lettuces.

Sidonie had taught her to cook when she was a child. Not taught. Sidonie was too parsimonious with words for that. For want of anything better to do, Clare had merely hung around the château kitchens with their dented copper pans, iron stove and open wood fire filled with vine-clippings. She had learned to gauge the seasons (no hothouse tomatoes or melons in December at Cluzac) at the elbow of the château cook, her long-suffering face chiselled from granite. *Pot-au-feu* with marrow bones flavoured with juniper and fistsful of herbs meant that it was winter. Soup made from tender nettle tops and sorrel simmered in beef stock heralded the spring. Fish terrines and *tartes* of figs from the gardens marked the arrival of summer, while in the autumn, in the expectant lull before the *vendange*, Sidonie bottled scented pears in syrup, put up plums the colour of green chartreuse, preserved tomatoes, and made apple and rose-petal jelly, and *confiture de citrons* for winter use.

Clare watched attentively as she snapped off the outer leaves of baby mauve artichokes, no bigger than a child's hand, before simmering them in olive oil and wine. She stared with fascinated horror as she massaged partridges with butter, bound defenceless woodcocks with string or, wielding a heavy cleaver, skilfully jointed rabbits, disdainfully discarding flaps of skin and tips of forelegs, and cutting the back into three or four pieces. Mesmerised by the sound of the balloon whisk, rhythmically striking the sides of the copper bowl held beneath Sidonie's arm, by the pounding of veal and the pummelling of garlic cloves for aïoli or garlic soup (to assuage colds and reduce high blood pressure), she learned how to chop vegetables in the palm of her hand, to put a thick crust of bread in her mouth before peeling onions, and to clean a frying-pan with salt and a ball of crumpled paper.

It was Sidonie who had brought her up. There had been several nannies, most of them English (as was the custom among the château owners) – including a Miss McKay and a Miss Forbes – but they left, many of them in tears, a phenomenon that at the time Clare did not understand but which she was vaguely aware had something to do with her father. While the Baron was riding to hounds, shooting duck and teal, playing Real Tennis (which made good use of both his stamina and guile), or indulging his passion for vintage cars, and her mother was busy in the stables with her beloved horses, Clare was left to her own devices. She wandered like the dogs round the vineyards, played beneath the canopies of ancient cedars in the park or in the huge lofts of the château, or, like a dark shadow, attached herself to the heels of Sidonie.

Sometimes she went into the dank and shadowy semi-underground *chais* with their beaten earth floors. Almost overpowered by the dizzying fumes that emanated from the rows of oak barrels, their rotund bellies stained crimson with the lees of the wine, she sought out Jean Boyer, the Baron's cellarmaster and Sidonie's husband, and made him tell her stories. As a boy, Jean had helped the resistance fighters during the German occupation. He would show Clare the stumps of his three missing fingers, blown off by the detonator he had laid on the track to stop a Nazi troop train. Although he dared her to touch his maimed hand, she could never bring herself to do so.

Jean and Sidonie, for some reason she had never been able to fathom, had no family of their own. This, she gathered, with the perspicacity of childhood, had something to do with her father, the Baron, whom they both feared and loved. Childless herself, Sidonie occupied herself silently with Clare, allowing her to stalk her like a miniature shade, and holding her wordlessly against the upholstery of her bosom whenever there were tears.

Brought up by peasants, Clare adored peasant food. For tonight's dinner in the flat she shared with Nicola in Notting Hill, she was making a vegetable soup (almost a meal in itself). Unlike Sidonie, who with her strong right arm would have passed it lovingly through her battered *mouli-légumes*, the paint worn from its handle by her capable fingers, Clare would sling the cooked vegetables into the food-processor until they resembled baby-food (Sidonie would have had a fit), which would be mopped up with 'French' bread, to half a dozen baguettes of which she helped herself from the bakery shelves.

'Can I come?'

The young man who addressed her and whose basket contained a healthy packet of Quorn, a few carrots and some spring onions, wore beaten-up jeans and a done-to-death sweat-shirt. He was not bad-looking. Men were always coming on strong to her in supermarkets. The long aisles proclaiming Soup and Soap, Preserves and Pet Food, had taken the place of singles bars. Status was indicated at the checkout, with Mr Men Orange Drinks and squashy packs of disposable nappies being the kiss of death.

'Sorry,' Clare said amicably, moving on to the cheese counter.

'No sweat.'

She knew that she was attractive to men. Sexual vibes, over which she had no control, radiated effortlessly from her being and made them, irrespective of age, want to possess her. It was not that her body was anything to write home about. She was underweight, her collar-bones protruding beneath her long neck like salt-cellars, her arms skinny and her breasts unenviably small. The de Cluzac nose dominated her oval face, on which the heavy eyebrows remained unplucked. Her wide and open smile revealed healthy teeth which complemented the animation of her eyes. It was the sum of the parts, rather than the parts themselves, that laid her open to the advances to which she had become accustomed.

Paradoxically, her father's cavalier treatment of her as a child had equipped her to deal with men. Put down and criticised by him for as long as she could remember, a less robust personality might have been pulverised into a pale ghost of submission from which the last vestiges of self-esteem had been crushed. The Fitzpatrick gene, inherited through her mother from a line of long-lived Irish pugilists, had merely ensured that the Baron's treatment of her, her failure, as a mere girl, to receive recognition from him, had equipped her to stand up for herself.

That this assertiveness was sometimes mistaken by the opposite sex for aggression, she attributed to the male tendency to regard as contentious any degree of outspokenness which distinguished women from door-mats. It was an argument that never failed to silence Jamie.

She had been going out with Jamie Spence-Jones, a Senior Registrar in orthopaedic surgery at the John Radcliffe Hospital in Oxford, for over a year. A dedicated rugby player and erstwhile captain of cricket at Cambridge, Jamie, with his powerful shoulders and muscular legs, was as tall and well built as the Baron; but, by virtue of his good nature and equable temperament, he was the antithesis of her father.

They did not actually live together. Jamie had a fifteenth-century cottage near Waterperry which he was modernising in his spare time, and during the week Clare lived in Notting Hill.

From Monday to Friday she and Nicola, an art historian by training, ran a contemporary art gallery, the Nicola Wade Gallery, in a basement in Neal Street. Nicola was the artistic brains, sniffing out unknown painters with the unerring nose of a Luberon pig for truffles, and Clare the hustler, leaning on the bank for loans, bringing in the punters, taking charge of the marketing and arranging the private views. On Saturdays, by way of extra income, they had a stall in Portobello market, from which they sold second-hand books and 'antiques' painstakingly tracked down by them both.

Surprisingly, in the current economic climate – the art market was in the doldrums – the gallery was going from strength to strength, and they were hoping to move to a larger and more up-market basement in Albemarle Street. Clare had her eye on Millington's, where rumour had it that after thirty-five years selling fine ceramics in London, Michael Millington had had enough of the rat-race and was retiring to St Ives to set up a low-key gallery featuring work by local craftsmen. The only problem was that the bank manager had almost died laughing when she had outlined their plan, and there had seemed no way that they could raise the necessary cash.

At the supermarket checkout Clare scribbled her name on the cheque, which had been filled in for the correct amount by the automatic machine, and returned it to the cashier together with her cheque card.

'This supposed to be a *D*?' the girl stabbed her biro at the *particule* that separated Clare from Cluzac.

'Not a *D*, a *de*,' Clare corrected her, 'for the sake of which Marie-Antoinette, together with a great many of her compatriots, lost their heads.'

The girl was staring at her open-mouthed. Clare did not think it worth her while elaborating upon, or explaining, the fact that under the *ancien régime* the noblesse was actually looked up to for its sense of tradition and its spiritual and moral values and that, unlike in England, in France you can enoble yourself only if you can prove letters patent from the king and descent through the male line.

Leaving it at that, she stuffed the last of her purchases into a carrier bag, rescuing a recalcitrant lime, and staggered out through the automatic doors into the King's Road.

CHAPTER TWO

Had Clare not decided to buy a birthday present in Bond Street for her grandmother, Baronne Gertrude de Cluzac, she would not have run into Big Mick Bly and the course of her entire life might not have been changed. The Hermès scarf she had in mind was not going to endear her to her bank manager. Concerned about her personal overdraft, he had recently cautioned her about writing any more cheques, and had threatened the withdrawal of her credit card.

She was not exactly extravagant – she spent in fact very little on herself. Most of her clothes came from street markets, she wore very little in the way of underwear, and never darkened the doorstep of a hairdresser. When the ends of her hair began to straggle, she handed the kitchen scissors to Nicola. Any money she did spend – and it never stayed very long in her purse – was lavished upon others. She adored buying presents. It did not have to be a birthday. She could not pass a flower stall without buying a single rose or a bunch of violets and then thinking to whom she would give them. Her generosity extended to the human flotsam huddled listlessly in shop doorways whom she was unable to pass without making a not insubstantial contribution to their booze or drugs; it encompassed the Geranium Day for the Blind, Save the Children, and even the Royal National Lifeboat Institution. In a swift moment of empathy, as tins were rattled eloquently beneath her nose, she imagined a day without the use of her eyes, her stick-limbed self in an equatorial wasteland, or in oil-skinned peril on some uncompromising sea. Her profligacy was an aberration which played havoc with her personal account only. In her business dealings, as far as the art gallery or her antiques stall was concerned, she was as hard as nails. The artists represented by Nicola could rest assured that their works were priced fairly and according to market forces, and that they would be promptly paid. Their contracts – drawn up by Clare – were honoured, the clients vetted for solvency, and the rent for the gallery never allowed to fall overdue. It was her business acumen, combined with Nicola's flair – a felicitous partnership – that accounted for the popularity and success of the gallery.

It was not that she had any faith in the merchandise that was displayed, appropriately lit and labelled, on the gallery walls. Brought up among portraits of her ancestors painted by Steuben and Ingres, by-passing Cranachs and Gericaults each time she climbed the stairs to her bedroom – which looked out on to the vines – she was unable to tune into neo-conceptual icons made of match-boxes, bits of string and plumber's felt, or to the tributaries of dense and multicoloured paint that looked as if they had been paddled in by the dog. It never failed to amaze her that reasonably sane people were willing to part with their money for what passed for 'modern' art.

On Private View days, the clients, clutching their glasses and narrowing their eyes, would crowd round a canvas which called itself *Venice Lido* (but which seemed to her to represent nothing so much as dirty washing-up water), as Nicola lectured them on how contemporary art should be approached. She would watch open-mouthed as they succeeded, where she had failed, in 'looking into chasms and grottoes', 'building relationships with the image' and responding to 'the essence' of place.

On Saturday mornings the boot was on the other foot. Behind the trestle table lugged out of Nicola's hatchback and set out with cut-glass scent bottles, old metronomes, pewter teapots, backscratchers, tortoise-shell boxes, ivory button-hooks, Clarice Cliff toast-racks and the odd volume of Plutarch's *Lives*, Clare was in her element. Her stock was bought at country sales where prices were routinely higher than London, and bidding often became feverish. Although private buyers with no knowledge of the market outnumbered dealers, this was balanced by the fact that in old homes that had been lived in by the same family for years, objects of character were more likely to turn up, there was a greater chance of 'finds' than in the London salerooms, and items were often less accurately catalogued than in the up-market auction houses.

Often she had to bid for a 'lot' – comprising a box of assorted kitchenalia (saucepans, pyrex dishes, storage jars and jelly moulds), two dolls, a wooden bed-head and an assortment of child's wellington boots – in order to secure a copper coal scuttle (much sought after as pot-plant containers), which was what she was really after. Tracking down teacups and toast-racks among the battered fridges and electric cookers, strapping rickety tables to Nicola's roof-rack, standing ankle deep in mud with her catalogue in a Suffolk marquee, she was as happy as a sandboy.

Back in London, persuading American tourists that life without a chipped majolica inkstand or a *cloisonné* vase which had lost its mate was not worth living was right up her street. Seeing them coming, in their matching Burberry raincoats or *Oxford University* sweaters, as they darted from stall to stall fingering willow-patterned plates, peering at makers' marks, and prodding moth-eaten teddy bears, she would cast her line and, with the dexterity of an angler, rearranging the lustre and the cream ware before her, haul them in.

Sometimes she fabricated stories: the early Worcester

mustard pot, only slightly cracked, which had belonged
to George III; the pinchbeck mantel clock, property of
a titled lady. As far as the price was concerned and the
customers' determination to get the better of her, they need
not have bothered. She was not deceived by the shabbiness
of their clothes (as often as not they were dealers) or the
persistence of their bargaining – she saw them before they
saw her and adjusted her price accordingly. This time it
was Nicola, flapping her arms with cold in winter, lifting
her face to the rays of the sun in summer, and keeping a
weather eye open for an available man in all seasons, who,
trying to keep the smile from her face at Clare's fairytales of
provenance, or her testimony that the price offered was less
than that which she had paid, took the money and wrapped
the goods in old newspaper before stuffing them into used
plastic bags. She was unable to credit how anybody in their
right mind, with even the minimum of street cred, could
be beguiled by Clare's blarney, be persuaded to part with
their dosh.

Narrowly avoiding being annihilated by an oncoming
taxi, Clare, who had an hour to kill before her meeting with
Michael Millington in Albemarle Street, got off the bus
at John Lewis and nipped across Oxford Street in search
of her grandmother's scarf. It was the morning after the
dinner party and, as far as she could remember, they had
all got roaring drunk; the evening had gone rather well.

Nicola's friend Hannah, owner of *If You've Got it
Flaunt It*, a trendy clothes emporium in the King's Road,
and Seth, the artistic director of a fringe theatre currently
organising a programme of South American mime, her
current boyfriend; Zoffany, a compliance officer in a City
bank recently made redundant (with whom Clare had
been at school), and Jonathan, a barrister specialising
in company law, her new partner; Francesca Foglia the
TV cook – *Alfresco with Francesca* – and Sebastian Boyd
(with whom Jamie had qualified), a Senior Registrar in

radiology at the Middlesex Hospital, with whom they
hoped to set her up; Oleg, a sad-eyed Russian photo-
grapher, unable to find work in his own field, who
had a picture-lighting workshop in Camden Lock, with
whom Nicola was besotted but whose Eastern European
despondency she was unable to penetrate; Tony and
Clive, who ran a high-profile florist's (catering for society
weddings and extravaganzas and specialising in outlandish
table decorations comprising driftwood and bits of old
rope as well as flowers) in the New King's Road, and
who lived upstairs, and Jamie who had been delayed by a
spinal canal stenosis – at which he had to chip away slowly
to relieve the pressure on the nerves – and had shown up
only when they were on to Francesca's working woman's
summer pudding, which owed its success to the addition
of a Chivers blackcurrant jelly.

Clare had set the table with the Compagnie des Indes
china, Venetian glasses and worn, silver-gilt cutlery given
to her by her grandmother and stored, for want of space,
beneath her bed. The once-blue, drawn-thread tablecloth,
from the same source, overlapped the table round which
they had to squeeze, and had to be doubled up in the
middle. Arranging it in a pleat with the complaining
Nicola – who said Clare was off her trolley and that
she had absolutely no intention of ironing it – brought
back to Clare the linen-room at Cluzac at the top of the
François-er tower a hundred feet above the moat, a great,
dark, oval room lined with shelves and linen presses, no
longer in use, reached by a spiral staircase.

The wheels of the conversation were lubricated by a
welcoming vodka from the freezer (a crafty bid by Nicola
to make Oleg feel at home); the bottle of Rioja Francesca
had brought with Clare's soup; Château de Cluzac 1991
with Nicola's *poulet à l'orange* (a can of frozen orange
juice chucked over the appropriate number of chicken
thighs and put in a hot oven); and a Beaumes de Venise

courtesy of Tony and Clive, who had also brought a *cache-marie* composed of brussels sprouts and lavender for the centre of the table, with the summer pudding. As the evening wore on, the talk had turned from the horrors of reaching the age of thirty, an analysis (male) of sexual desire, women's tussles with the glass ceiling, the newly opened Channel Tunnel, the stinginess of the Arts Council, an exposé of ultrasound which used sound waves to image organs in real time, the mentality of serial killers and the possibility of the Duke of Clarence having been Jack the Ripper.

As Clare served her soup from the Spode tureen with Baronne Gertrude's English silver ladle, they had each been required by Nicola to say what reaching the age of thirty meant to them, while Clare – not yet twenty-nine – made mental notes.

'Relief that the twenties are over.' Zoffany tasted the soup. 'Delicious. *Félicitations a la cuisinière!*'

'Coming to terms with the fact that I shall never be a size ten.' Hannah helped herself to a large chunk of bread, which she spread liberally with butter.

'No problem, darling, the superwaif is dead!' Francesca raised her glass. 'Long live the "real" woman.'

'Maturity,' Jonathan said ponderously, although Clare doubted if he had ever been anything but mature.

'Courage to pull the plug on a relationship,' Nicola said. 'When I think of all the wankers I have put up with just because I was too immature to extricate myself . . .' She disappeared into the kitchen to attend to the chicken. 'In one's twenties,' her voice drifted through the door, 'what one is looking for is thrills. Now I can't imagine anything more exciting than to spend the rest of my life' – her tone was wistful – 'with one absolutely divine man.'

Oleg, at whom the remark was directed and who had put his soup spoon down on the drawn-thread tablecloth, did not react.

'Reaching my sexual peak.' Francesca eye-balled Sebastian.

'Women don't peak until forty,' Clare objected, sitting down. 'By which time men are definitely going off the boil.' She looked up in time to see Zoffany and Jonathan exchange the swiftest of glances and realised that the conversation had touched a nerve. Her isolated childhood had led her to be tuned into adult distress signals and she knew instinctively that if you really wanted to know what was going on you had to watch people's faces in repose.

Take Hannah, the life and soul of any party, with her apparent lack of self-consciousness and aptitude for making others laugh. When Hannah was caught off guard, when she thought no one was looking, the sparkle would fade from her eyes, her face would crumple into deep creases and her plump mouth, which she was constantly feeding, would droop at the corners. Or take Seth, who controlled the conversation as he controlled his actors, by virtue of the fact that his voice rarely rose above a whisper – you had to strain sometimes to catch what he was saying – whose face (if you paid close attention) became suffused with repressed anger if he was interrupted or crossed. Francesca was at apparent ease before the TV camera, but was betrayed by her expression of chronic anxiety when her public persona was switched off, and the supercilious Jonathan by the way he looked round the table for approval each time he spoke. Although Sebastian's diagnostic skills were unquestioned, his emotional immaturity was revealed by his often puerile jokes. Tony's mouth beneath his sophisticated moustache lapsed into a thin line of petulance and jealousy whenever Clive, a macho six-footer, paid too much attention to somebody else, while Zoffany's true self was exposed by her bitten fingernails which, when she thought no one was looking, she surreptitiously chewed. Only Oleg was a closed book except for the unmistakably sexual signals which were directed not towards Nicola but, to her great discomfort, towards Clare herself.

These were her friends and she loved them. There had been none when she was growing up.

When Jamie finally arrived, he was greeted with inebriated hugs and kisses both from Clare and her girlfriends, with whom he was extremely popular. Upending the Rioja, he proceeded to make up for lost time.

It was two o'clock in the morning before everyone had gone home, and already getting light by the time Clare had finally got to sleep. The delay was due to the fact that, having carried out the traditional post-mortem on the evening, which had turned out to be a noisy but unqualified success, Jamie had asked her to marry him.

'How would you feel about spending the rest of your life with me?'

'Sorry?' Clare, who was knackered, was almost asleep.

'How would you feel about spending the rest of your life with me?'

'Can't think of anything nicer. 'Night.'

'Is that all you've got to say?'

'Honestly, Jamie, I can't keep awake.'

Ten minutes later, Clare sat bolt upright.

'Was that a proposal?'

'You could say that. What on earth are you *crying* for?'

'It's the nicest proposal I've ever heard.'

The following two hours had been spent planning the wedding. Clare, egged on by her grandmother, had always had a romantic picture of herself as a bride drifting, in a cloud of ivory tulle, down the aisle of the Church of the Immaculate Conception in Farm Street, and Jamie, who · had something much more laid back in mind, had suggested a simple little church in the heart of Soho followed by a few drinks in a wine-bar with their friends.

They were just drifting off to sleep with the matter

unresolved when Jamie said, 'You haven't answered the question.'

'What question?'

'How would you feel about spending the rest of your life with me?'

'I'd like that more than anything else in the world.'

Still on cloud nine – Nicola, who made no secret of the fact that she thought weddings a bit naff and marriage bonds an outmoded symbol of patriarchal ownership, had nonetheless been delighted with the news and had cracked open a bottle of champagne for breakfast – Clare hurled herself at the glass door of Hermès. She almost fell flat on her face, on to the thick carpet of the emporium, as it was swung open for her by the bemedalled commissionaire.

A neat navy-blue salesperson with large gold earrings registered Clare's ankle-length skirt and sneakers. Knowing a time-waster when she saw one, she disdainfully displayed a selection of traditionally patterned scarves to do with the signs of the zodiac and horseshoes. Clare rejected the almond greens and sugary pinks, which were reluctantly opened up like multicoloured flags to subside with a silken whoosh on to the counter.

'My grandmother likes *blue*.'

Cautioning her colleagues, in rapid French, to keep an eye on her dubious customer, the woman disappeared in the direction of the stockroom, from which she eventually returned with a blue scarf garlanded with roses.

'That will do admirably.'

Resorting to her native French, Clare demanded that the box be gift-wrapped. Pulling herself up to her full height, she made out a cheque (hoping it wouldn't bounce). She had no trouble with the *particule*.

CHAPTER THREE

Baronne Gertrude de Cluzac, patrician and upright, tinted her hair, wore high-heeled shoes and had the figure of a young girl, despite the fact that she had reached the age of eighty-five.

She had been brought up by a series of governesses to put duty before pleasure in accordance with the family motto, *Ad Augusta per Agusta* (to honours through difficulties); but after so many years the line between the two had become blurred and now, more often than not, the duty had become the pleasure.

Since leaving Château de Cluzac over twenty-five years ago she had not been back to the Médoc. To say that she had 'left' the Médoc, was to imply that she had departed from her home voluntarily. After the tragic and premature death of his father, Baron Thibault, the indolent Charles-Louis – who three years previously had come down from Oxford having gambled away his allowance and failed to get a degree – had virtually kicked her out.

Baron Thibault had not only been the 'great man of the Médoc' in the heyday of the great wine-producing estates, but a great man. In every respect. Energetic and aristocratic, he excelled at sport, had a keen eye for business, was respected by his employees in whose affairs he took a personal interest, and was passionate about his vines.

On a personal level, Thibault had been a good husband

and a good father. A *bon viveur* and full of charm, with a courtesy and generosity that endeared him to everyone, and a prodigious appetite both for life and for food, Thibault liked nothing better than to head the long oak table capable of seating twenty-two, to which he brought a spirit of social brilliance and conviviality. Gertrude, herself the daughter of a château owner, this time in Sauternes, had adored him. The feeling had been mutual.

A wise woman, she had learned early on in the marriage, which had taken place when she was eighteen – not unusual in those days – that a man of such prodigious appetite must be free to indulge it. Unwilling to restrain him, to bridle him as she did her horse (she was a fearless horsewoman), she let him take the bit between his teeth and did not question him too closely when he returned from the trips abroad taken without her, or from his frequent and regular visits to Bordeaux.

From the moment they had met, at a Christmas party at Cluzac, to the moment when an ashen-faced *chef de culture* had knocked on the door of her boudoir to bring the news of Thibault's death while out hunting, they had loved each other dearly. Gertrude was not stupid enough to imagine that among the peaks of married life – it was after all an arcane and impossible institution – there would not be troughs of despair and despondency (no longer tolerated by the young), moments when she would wonder what she was doing in the larger-than-life Thibault's bed at all. These were soon dissipated by his overwhelming generosity (both of body and of spirit), his innate decency and his genuine love for her.

Charles-Louis, although similar in build, immaculately turned out, and with Thibault's impeccable manners, was a far cry from his father. Out of touch with his own feelings and impervious to those of others, he had a temper verging on the sadistic and humiliated those who crossed him, in the case of women often reducing them to tears. Gertrude was at a loss to know where her son got all his unpleasantness from. It was neither his egotistical behaviour, his arrogance, nor his frank womanising that now bothered her, however, but the fact that, after 300 years, he was not husbanding Cluzac.

In touch with the old Comtesse de Ribagnac, her contemporary on a nearby estate with whom she exchanged discursive letters, Gertrude was kept informed on a monthly basis of Charles-Louis' conduct. Despite the boomtime of the eighties, when an incredible run of great and bountiful years had driven prices through the roof and Médocain growers had ploughed back their profits, her son had apparently made no investment in the cellars, had not bothered to repair the dilapidated roofs of the château, and although his vineyards, under the expert eye of Albert Rochas, were impeccably kept, there had been little or no replanting. Making no secret of the fact that, as one of the last true landowning aristocrats, he was above the commercial fray, that he did not trust – and strongly objected to paying taxes to – a socialist government (a sentiment with which Baronne Gertrude for once concurred), Charles-Louis seemed to turn a blind eye to the viability of Château de Cluzac, the gates of which he kept firmly closed.

It was not only their inability to get on with one another that made Baronne Gertrude exasperated each time she thought of Charles-Louis, but also the fact that, unlike his father – who had taken his responsibilities seriously and devoted himself to Cluzac – her son preferred whisky to claret and had not the least dedication to wine, the making of which he supervised as necessary but did not love.

On her enforced departure from the Médoc as a reasonably young widow, Baronne Gertrude had made her home in the Pas-de-Calais, in the Château de Charleville, which belonged to her family, and in Paris where she had a great many friends.

It was there, at the British Embassy, that she had met, and ultimately married, Selwyn Donaldson, the United Kingdom Ambassador to Sweden. After Thibault's death she had not thought that she would marry again. It was too much trouble. But Selwyn, a widower, had wooed her with an English courtesy which had eventually captured her heart. The wedding had been a quiet one in the church of la Madeleine in the eighth arrondissement, and she had spent the next ten years as Lady Donaldson in the embassies and salons of Warsaw, Bonn, Washington and Rome, where she brought a Gallic style and grace to the diplomatic carousel.

They had been back at their London base, a crepuscular mansion flat facing Rotten Row, when Selwyn's pancreatic cancer had been diagnosed. It was all over within three weeks. Missing the gentle man terribly, Gertrude had considerable difficulty in coming to terms with the loss of her second husband. It was several years before, pulling herself together, she reverted to her previous title, gathered about her a coterie of friends – largely bridge-playing – and made a new life for herself in the Hyde Park flat where her existence was enlivened by the intermittent visits of her granddaughter, Clare.

The two Cluzac women had more in common than their disparate ages would suggest.

Although Gertrude had had as little as possible to do with her son since leaving Cluzac, his wife, Viola, had kept in touch with her when she had walked out on Charles-Louis and returned to Ireland with the eight-year-old Clare. Glad of something to do to mitigate her loneliness, Baronne Gertrude had devoted herself to the upbringing of her granddaughter, leaving Viola free to attend to her horses.

During Clare's schooldays at St Mary's Ascot, her summer holidays, until she was old enough to opt out, had been spent at Cluzac with her father. At Christmas and Easter, when she did not go back to her mother in Ireland, on which she was not at all that keen – they had little in common and Clare was frightened of horses – she stayed with her grandmother, from whom she learned the principles of duty and responsibility, as well as everything there was to know about sex, about which Baronne Gertrude was surprisingly relaxed.

Although the Baronne had a deep-seated and unshakeable belief that everyone was looking for one person to love, she tolerated the open-ended relationships which, like the new multiplex cinemas, had replaced the monoliths of the past, but was absolutely convinced that those who indulged in them were destined to get hurt.

Baronne Gertrude talked openly to her granddaughter about sex from the age of puberty onwards. She explained that it was a joyous experience and as crucial to life as breathing. Clare thought that she must be the only girl in London to debate with her grandmother the wisdom of losing her virginity to the first man (married and with two children) into whose arms she had fallen after leaving her convent school.

A great many men had bitten the dust since then, but although, like Napoleon in *War and Peace*, her grandmother had little time for the medical profession and did not mind saying so, the Baronne's favourite, among Clare's many admirers, was Jamie.

The fact that Jamie – who was wont to recite chunks of Shakespeare over his anaesthetised patients in the operating theatre – immediately recognised the sentiments as Tolstoy's endeared him at once to the Baronne.

After a shaky start – Jamie had failed to hold the Baronne's chair for her at dinner and had committed the solecism of cutting the 'nose' off the Brie – the two of them had got on famously. While the Baronne often entertained Jamie with tales of her girlhood in Sauternes and stories about her life at Cluzac, their shared interest was literature and they enjoyed attributing each other's quotations.

Clare and Jamie had been invited to dinner to celebrate the Baronne's birthday, for which she had given the menu a great deal of thought and her current au pair, who attended English classes in South Kensington, a hard time. Baronne Gertrude did not cook and rarely entered the kitchen, which had not been renovated since the death of the first Lady Donaldson.

Born, bred and having lived for the greater part of her life in a château, the Baronne, although perfectly capable of giving instructions to others, had very little practical knowledge of running a home. In the eighteenth century, according to her wide reading on the subject, before domestic space had misguidedly become the female prerogative, the women's quarters in the great French houses were as distant from the kitchens as the men's, an indicator that they did not have even a supervisory role over the domestic arrangements. As far as she was concerned 'home' was not by any means synonymous with 'woman' and she considered the class divide to be far more significant than that of gender.

Her formative years had been spent in a country house of which, despite the passage of time, her recollections were extraordinarily clear. They were defined by favourite and specific places. The chapel, the billiard room, the dining-room, the drawing-rooms, the library, her parents' apartments, the guest rooms and the nursery quarters, the vast, seemingly endless and sometimes terrifying corridors, the many staircases. Once Jamie had asked her how many rooms there were and Gertrude, astonished by the question, had replied that to the best of her knowledge no one had ever counted them, and that she had absolutely no idea.

All she remembered was that her childhood (from which by now the disagreeables had been filtered out) had been an unmitigated delight. Rides in the early-morning mists, homework in the nursery, games of croquet, tennis, ping-pong, fishing, bicycle rides and bathing in opaque muddy waters, spring hunting when the children – she was one of six – were left to their own devices, parties and summer weddings, and picnics by the lake.

With her needs now attended to by a single and frequently changing au pair (Louise, Chantal, Christiane, Monique), the days of butlers with their armies of footmen, valets, chefs, housemaids, gardeners (head and under) coachmen (who taught them to sit on a horse properly), game-keepers, park-keepers, mole-catchers, laundry women, ironing women, and the man who came once a week to wind the château clocks, seemed far off. It was a world to set people dreaming, which, even in the great châteaux, where the hard-pressed owners now worked extremely hard to ensure that everything ran smoothly, would not return.

Her childhood home with its marble entrance hall, its colonnades and rotunda, its mysterious attic crammed with discarded fancy-dress costumes, ball slippers, musical boxes and trunks of old papers, the smells of the waxed floors, the coolness of the hallways, the park full of dark pines and lime trees, the walks to the kitchen garden, the races to the farmhouse to fetch the eggs: her memories were written in these images. They belonged to the past.

Now she subsisted, in her Hyde Park flat, on a very small income from the estate of the late Selwyn Donaldson, augmented by her pension, which was paid directly to her bank. From it, august and austere, with her head held high and her back still remarkably straight, accompanied by the current Louise, Chantal or Monique, she made her way to Harrods' Food Hall.

This morning, expecting and receiving the same defer-ence from the white-coated assistant behind the fresh-meat counter as she had from her bygone cooks, she had purchased a gigot. Carrying the leg of lamb home (a figure of speech: it was Louise who actually carried it), together with some petit pois and carrots and a horrendously expensive slice of Brie de Meaux (*le roi des fromages*, which, as she was fond of explaining to the au pairs, had originated in the court of Charlemagne), she gave specific instructions as to its preparation before settling down to a day spent as any other.

The Baronne was a prodigious reader and the flat was filled with an eclectic collection of books, which extended in range from the latest Muriel Spark to the essays of Montaigne. In addition to being extremely well read and a not inconsiderable historian, she was an accomplished water-colourist (the spare bedroom was stacked with her paintings of trees and flowers), and with the help of National Health spectacles, which she kept hidden on occasions when she was not alone, an adept at petit point.

By the time Clare arrived with Jamie, the Baronne, assisted by Louise, had changed into a black crepe dress on to which she pinned a diamond brooch in the shape of a butterfly given to her by Thibault on the occasion of Charles-Louis' birth – and rouged her cheeks. An appetising smell of roast lamb, seasoned with garlic and a little rosemary, pervaded the high-ceilinged flat.

CHAPTER FOUR

Retracing her steps along Bond Street in search of a birthday card for the Baronne, Clare had caught sight of a book in Sotheby's window called *Caring for Antiques: A Guide to Handling, Cleaning, Display and Restoration*, which she thought might come in useful in tarting up her Saturday-morning stock.

She had been pressing her nose to the shop window, shielding her eyes from the reflection, and trying to make out the name of the author, when she felt a tap on her shoulder and heard the surprised sound of a Mid-Western voice which belonged to her past.

'Excuse me. Isn't this little Clare de Cluzac?'

Turning round, Clare looked up into the eyes of Big Mick ('the nose') Bly. At the same time she observed, from the gilt-lettered placard that stood on the pavement, that this morning there had been a sale of Fine and Rare Wines, Spirits and Vintage Ports in the auction rooms.

It was at Château Kilmartin, more than fourteen years ago, after playing tennis with her 'cousins' Pierre and Chantal (distant relatives on her mother's side), during her final summer in Bordeaux, that she had been introduced to the larger-than-life American wine writer, once seen, never forgotten.

Big Mick, founder of *Wine Watch*, a US magazine sold on subscription, was reputedly the most influential wine critic in the business ('If Bly gives it a ninety you can't buy it, and if Bly gives it less than ninety you can't sell it'). A seriously heavy man with a penchant for seriously heavy wines, he was feared throughout Bordeaux, where obsequious cellarmasters were said to keep a 'barrique Bly', a hogshead of especially potent claret, in readiness for his unannounced visits. Bly's talent was for tasting undrinkable stuff straight from the vat and predicting whether, given time, it would become a great wine. Since his numerical ratings and tasting notes were read, and slavishly followed, by readers throughout the world, Bly could make or break a grower. He had never set foot inside Château de Cluzac. No journalist ever had.

Clare took in the meticulously distressed denims, the luridly checked workshirt and the crumpled linen jacket which had most likely cost more than a bespoke suit.

'Clare de Cluzac! Just wait till I tell Toni!'

Toni, Big Mick's diminutive, polyglot wife and *éminence grise*, travelled everywhere with him, looked after his diary and set up his European meetings.

'You're not going to believe this, but Toni and I were only talking about you yesterday at the Reform Club. Stephan von Neipperg, the Tesserons from Pontet Canet, Daniel and Florence Cathiard, everyone was there . . .'

'Why on earth would you be talking about me?'

'Well strictly speaking, it wasn't exactly about you. It was about your father.'

'What's he been up to?' The enquiry was polite. Clare was not all that interested.

'Didn't you hear the news . . . ?'

Clare imagined a peccadillo involving her father, some woman or another, on the front page of *Sud-Ouest*, although, unlike the English whose appetite for prurient gossip, particularly among politicians, was insatiable, the French were generally not exercised about such matters.

'Château de Cluzac is on the market,' Big Mick said.
'On the market!'

It was as if Bly had told her that the Howard family
had put their ancestral home in a Yorkshire estate agent's
window, or that the Marquess of Bath was getting rid of
Longleat after four hundred years of unbroken occupation.

Taking her for coffee in South Molton Street, where they
sat at a pavement table, Big Mick filled Clare in with what
was happening in the backwaters of the Médoc, which
hadn't known such excitement in years. There was no
longer anything to be said about the *quality* of her
father's wine, which had been steadily deteriorating and
was now near the bottom of the league table in *Wine Watch*
('a below average wine containing noticeable flaws').
However, the unique position of Château de Cluzac,
with its eastern slopes, well-drained soil, and *sans-pareil*
vineyards, in the patch of agricultural land alongside the
Gironde river which ranked among the most expensive
in Europe, had attracted a great many private and insti-
tutional buyers, including wealthy Japanese businessmen
and Parisian bankers.

Bordeaux had always attracted corporate money and
outside investors. Very few vineyards were still family
owned and two or three of these changed hands each
year, depending on how well the market was doing.
Among those who were anxious to get their hands on
the Cluzac estate were a German financier who wanted
to convert it into a luxury hotel and conference centre,
a Swiss consortium which had plans for adding it to its
chain of exclusive health resorts, and a wealthy Californian
who aimed to create a Napa-Valley-style theme park in
the Médoc. According to Big Mick, who had his ear to
the grapevine, the Baron had seen off the more bizarre
contenders, and three prospective purchasers had made
the final running.

Alain Lamotte, on behalf of Assurance Mondiale, one

of the first major investors to run a group of vineyards as a business, was anxious to earn brownie points for himself as well as acquiring another French château for his insurance company; Claude Balard, the sole distributor of the Baron's wines who, like other Bordeaux wine merchants since the nineteenth century, was desperate to become a '*cru classé*' owner; and Philip Van Gelder, a shadowy industrialist and absentee vineyard proprietor from the Franschhoek Valley, who was *persona non grata* in South Africa.

Courteously sending her regards to Toni Bly, Clare, who was now running late for her appointment with Michael Millington, headed for Albemarle Street. She gave no further thought to Big Mick's revelation until later that evening when she and Jamie were dining with the Baronne.

Baronne Gertrude had been waiting for them in the elegant but shabby drawing-room with a decanter of dry sherry, which was all she permitted by way of an aperitif. Clare's visits, bringing with them as they did an aura of youth and vitality and brightening up the high-ceilinged rooms, in much the same state of desuetude as she was herself, were always eagerly anticipated.

Graciously accepting the Hermès box, the Baronne greeted her granddaughter warmly but formally.

Acknowledging the roses that Jamie had brought her, she allowed him to kiss her hand.

'A house without flowers is like a day without sunshine.' She tinkled the little bell that lived permanently on the table beside her chair together with her silver rosary and the book she was currently reading.

When Jamie had first been introduced to the flat in Hyde Park, he had regarded the bell – which was rung when the Baronne needed a handkerchief from the bedroom or had inadvertently spilled a drop of water on a polished table – with horror.

'Never feel sorry for a servant Jamie,' Baronne Gertrude

had told him. 'He is thinking, One day, when I have saved enough money, I shall be able to imitate that man.'

Indicating to Louise, who had come in response to her summons, that she should relieve Jamie of the flowers, the Baronne opened the Hermès box. With a practised movement she draped the scarf, the colour of the silk complementing the agapanthus blue of her still piercing eyes expertly round the neck of her dress. Chastising Clare for her extravagance (for which the Baronne, who was extremely acquisitive, was secretly glad), she dispensed the sherry and invited her guests to sit down. Precisely thirty minutes later, she led Clare and Jamie into the dining-room, where the table, with the Victorian silver candelabrum – which had belonged to the first Lady Donaldson, and was lit even when the Baronne dined alone – was set for dinner.

In honour of her birthday, Baronne Gertrude had opened a Château de Cluzac 1945, made by Baron Thibault, which she had decanted half an hour earlier.

Putting down her spoon on the consommé, which had taken Louise three days to prepare from specially selected marrow bones – simmering and clearing the broth with egg whites then simmering it again, according to her employer's precise instructions – she signalled to Jamie to serve the wine.

She watched, with a sharp eye, as he poured a small quantity into her glass, which was engraved with the Cluzac coat of arms.

'Wine is the most civilised thing in the world, and drinking almost the last pleasure that the years steal from us . . .'

'Jamie and I are getting married,' Clare said, as Jamie replaced the heavy three-ringed decanter, which added a sense of occasion to the table.

'How very sensible of you. I couldn't be more delighted.'
Holding up her rouged and papery cheek to be kissed

by both of them, the Baronne, who had tears of genuine happiness in her eyes at the thought of a wedding,
exchanged her glass, with its inch of crimson claret, for
Clare's empty one.

'Tonight, Jamie, Clare will taste the wine.'

Over the years Clare had learned from her grandmother
that what made the difference between a great wine and
an average one was its length on the palate. Picking up
the glass, and taking her time, she examined the claret
in the light of the candelabrum then sniffed it appreciatively before taking tiny sips and finally swallowing it.
Baronne Gertrude would have nothing to do with such
value judgements as 'blackcurrants' or 'raspberries' or
'audacious bouquet', which she considered an affectation.
One did not, after all, as she was fond of saying, attempt
to put into words the flavour of roast chicken or the taste
of *tarte tatin*. Every wine tasted of itself and nothing else,
and the only thing that was important was whether or
not you liked it. This one, elegant and complex, had a
softness and sweetness in which neither fruit nor oak was
dominant. Baronne Gertrude was anxiously awaiting her
verdict.

'*Superbe!*'

'Not like that rubbish your father makes. It's not fit for
a carafe in a bistro.'

When Jamie had filled the three glasses, he followed the
Baronne's gaze to Clare's left hand.

'Clare's ring won't be ready until next week. I'm having
it made for her in Butler's Wharf.'

'Butler's Wharf? Nonsense!' Baronne Gertrude indicated
to Louise, who was standing patiently by the door, that
she might serve the gigot. 'Clare will wear the de Cluzac
sapphire.'

'That's very kind of you Madame, but . . .'

'She will accompany me to the safe deposit. You can't
be too careful. Lady Folgate – we play bridge together –

had her bag snatched outside the Army and Navy Stores. In broad daylight.'

'. . . I have already ordered the ring.'

'There is far too much violence on the streets . . .' Baronne Gertrude's voice tailed off. She exchanged glances with Clare, who would have liked to have a say in her engagement ring but did not want to upset Jamie, who said:

'It *was* to have been a surprise.'

'Now that you are to be married, Jamie,' Baronne Gertrude said, changing the subject, 'you must call me Grandmaman. Where is the wedding to take place?'

'Farm Street . . .' Clare said.

'Soho.'

'Jamie! I refuse to get married next to the wind-dried ducks!'

'A good woman would lay down her life several times for her lover,' the Baronne sighed. 'Yet she will break with him for ever on a trivial point such as whether a door should be left open or shut.'

Picking up her knife and fork, she addressed the extremely small portion of food (these days she had little appetite), which looked lost on the Sèvres plate. When the gigot was finished – in the interest of her supper the following day, second helpings were not offered – she tinkled the bell for Louise.

'You will find a bottle of Cristal in the pantry, Louise. And we shall need an ice-bucket.' She turned to Clare and Jamie. 'Weddings, not to mention eighty-fifth birthdays, are few and far between these days.'

'How does it *feel* to be eighty-five?' Clare asked curiously.

'"Old age is a shipwreck."'

'Tolstoy?' Jamie said.

'General de Gaulle.'

'It's better than what comes next,' Clare said.

The Baronne eyed Jamie.

'"There's not much in dying. I shall go to sleep and it will all be over."'

'Emma Bovary.'

The Baronne nodded in approval.

It was over coffee in the drawing-room, served by the long-suffering Louise, that Clare, who was perched next to her grandmother on the uncomfortable mahogany sofa, dropped her second bombshell.

'Did you know that Papa is selling Cluzac?'

'*Qu'est ce que tu as dis?*'

'*Papa va abandonner le Château.*'

The Baronne had gone quite pale. Clare hadn't realised the effect that the news would have on her grandmother and hoped that she wasn't about to have a heart attack.

'Perhaps you would be good enough to explain.'

Repeating her conversation with Big Mick, trying to remember all the details, she attempted to comfort the Baronne.

'To tell you the truth I'm rather pleased. Nicola and I have our eye on a gallery on Albemarle Street . . .'

'You are speaking about your *patrimoine*!' the Baronne said sharply. 'You should have been informed.'

Clare knew that by her *patrimoine* her grandmother meant not only her inheritance but the defeat of the Vikings, the unbroken line of ancestors whose portraits hung on the walls of the château, the culture and customs of France. At the risk of offending the Baronne, she said, 'It's only an old house, Grandmaman . . .'

'I thought you said it was a castle.' Jamie helped himself to sugar.

'Anywhere that produces wine can call itself a château, Jamie. There are more castles in Bordeaux than there are in Spain . . .'

A distant look came into the Baronne's eyes.

'Your grandfather took me to Cluzac as a young bride.

Our honeymoon was spent in Paris. We bought a complete set of directoire furniture for the ground-floor salons and refurbished the château from top to bottom. We devoted all our time to it. It was young Pierre-Giles de Monfort who really encouraged Thibault to take the house in hand. He was a writer and politician quite famous in his day . . .' The Baronne looked at Jamie. 'I don't suppose you remember Pierre-Giles? No of course you don't. That was extremely stupid of me. One gets confused. We entertained a great many writers and politicians. Pierre-Giles joined the Free French in London. After the war he was mayor and deputy for the department. We used to hold the French carriage-driving competitions in the park. The de Cluzac coach had yellow-and-blue coachwork and yellow wheels. At the end of the championships we gave a dinner for a hundred and fifty guests. The preparations started weeks before – it was the preparations that I loved best. Choosing the menu. Trial runs. Veal Marengo served in the copper cooking pots. We used to get them out for the hunting parties. From the old kitchens. Cakes, creams, sorbets, fruit. Tables for ten covered with damask tablecloths. A hundred and fifty napkins folded by Maurice. Maurice was the butler. Fresh flowers. Asters, roses, marguerites, ivy, asparagus fronds. Great floral arrangements for the hall, and little compotiers on each table. Then there were the placements. Decisions, decisions. And the last-minute changes! After dinner musicians played in the Louis XVI salon and the real party began . . .'

Breaking off from her reminiscences and realising suddenly where she was, the Baronne looked at Clare.

'Twenty-four per cent of Cluzac is yours, Clare. Have you nothing to say?'

'No doubt Papa will get in touch with me . . .'

'Get in touch with you! *Mon Dieu!* You should have been consulted.'

'He can hardly sell the estate without me.'

'I do not understand your attitude. Cluzac is one of only three remaining châteaux to have remained for so long in the same family. To abandon it is unthinkable. Have you discussed this with your mother?'

'I haven't spoken to Viola for months . . .'

'Then I suggest it is time you did so. Your father is up to something. He is not to be trusted.'

'I'm not all that bothered, Grandmaman. I'll be perfectly happy if I get a chunk out of the château.'

'You have de Cluzac roots, Clare,' the Baronne said. 'Like the roots of the vines, they are planted deep.'

CHAPTER FIVE

Clare had never had a hands-on relationship with her mother. As she told Jamie, who had as yet met neither of her parents, she would probably have merited more attention from her had she been born a horse. She was only marginally joking.

When Viola Fitzpatrick stated that the perceptions of a helpless new-born must be raised to the highest standard, that her intellect must be cultivated, that from the day of her birth she should be encouraged to look to one for all her little wants and needs, that she should be stroked and petted and respond to the sound of one's voice and follow one around certain that one has her best interests at heart, she was talking not about her daughter Clare, but about a filly.

Raised on a stud farm, by the time the twenty-two-year-old Viola, the eldest of the four Fitzpatrick daughters, left her native Galway to spend the summer in Bordeaux, she had had no sex education at school and none whatsoever from her parents. Although she was intimately acquainted with the covering of a mare by a stallion, she was still virgo intacta and she did not equate such equine couplings with herself.

Although it was her father who mainly concerned himself with the breeding, Viola could not remember a time when she had been thought too young to witness the apparently violent and mechanical process to which the mares were submitted, usually more than once, during their summer heat.

Standing at the door of the breeding shed, she would watch as the mare in her covering boots, twitching and irritable, her plaited tail held high in anticipation, was held by one stable lad while her private parts were washed down by another. At a nod from her father, the aroused stallion was brought in and the copulation, violent and thrusting, and sometimes not without what Viola mistook for tenderness (a bite on the neck which her father said was merely to keep the stallion in position), took place. There were always four or five stallions, and in the season – Sundays included – there were seven or eight matings daily, each one hopefully representing several thousands of pounds in the Fitzpatrick coffers.

Despite the fact that at home in Ireland she had been surrounded by so much rampaging fertility, Viola's own deflowering by Charles-Louis Eugène Bertrand, Baron de Cluzac, the consequence of which was to keep her in France for the next nine years, had turned out to be not what she had expected.

The young Viola, dark and feisty, was not the first of her kinsmen to settle in Bordeaux. When the English had put paid to the wool trade in the early eighteenth century, the Irish had come up with the ingenious idea of supplying Bordeaux with home-produced salt beef, in return for which the Bordelais had satisfied the Irish thirst for claret.

The fortunes made by the Irish in Bordeaux were typified by 'French Tom' Barton, originally from Tipperary, who bought valuable estates in the Médoc (where his descendants are still to be found), and became the biggest single purchaser of claret in the second half of the century.

Of all this Viola Fitzpatrick had only the haziest idea when she was sent by her father, George Michael

Fitzpatrick – who thought it would do her good to get away from Ireland – to spend the long summer at château Kilmartin with her second cousins once removed. The Kilmartin estate occupied a prime position overlooking the wide estuary of the Gironde, and was one of the few châteaux in the Médoc to produce white wine.

It was when her 'uncle' had asked her to take a temperamental gelding and deliver it to the head groom at Cluzac, that Viola had made the acquaintance of Charles-Louis Eugène Bertrand de Cluzac, who happened to be crossing the courtyard of his father's medieval château, as she trotted confidently in over the cobbles and enquired the way to the stables.

Flattered by the admiration in the young man's eyes – he had silently appraised her wild Irish looks while ostensibly admiring the gelding and her mastery over it – Viola had not been displeased when she ran into Charles-Louis again the following morning in the course of her morning ride.

When he asked if he might join her, Viola readily agreed. The early-morning trysts, during which they often dismounted and walked along the river bank, became a regular habit to which Viola looked forward with anticipation.

Flattered by his attentions, she was not surprised when, on one blistering morning when the sun had already burned away the early mists, he pulled her down on to the grass and started to remove her clothes.

That her objections were only perfunctory was due to the fact that not only did she find Charles-Louis extremely personable – he was quite capable, when the occasion demanded it, of turning on the charm – but, mortal sin or no, it was high time she experienced for herself the pleasures so eagerly awaited by the mares on her father's stud farm.

As in the breeding shed, the business, owing to Charles-Louis' high state of arousal and his impetuosity, was quickly over. Sore and bleeding, with pine-needles stuck to the back of her shirt, and summarily deprived of her virginity, Viola allowed him to help her mount her horse for the ride back to Kilmartin, before, looking extremely pleased with himself, and without a backward glance, he cantered back to Cluzac for breakfast.

The fact that she had let down the Blessed Virgin did not faze Viola, who was too strong-willed to give credence to everything she was told by the Church. What bothered her slightly was the lack of communication between herself and her seducer. While this deficiency of form might be expected between the sexes in Ireland, she had not anticipated it in France, where, informed by the great love scenes she had witnessed in the cinema (even in their censored form), she had imagined that things would be done differently.

This did not prevent her repeating the experience, on subsequent morning rides, when Charles-Louis introduced her to a number of permutations on the sex act which were altogether outside the remit of her stallions.

When, at the end of the summer, she discovered that she was pregnant, and Charles-Louis, panic-stricken, suggested that she take the next boat home, their first real dialogue was opened up.

'Can you see me, Charlie, living in a home for unmarried mothers run by the nuns?'

Looking at her with her mane of dark hair and her milk-white body, of which he never seemed to tire, as they lay in the long grass, while the horses grazed nearby, Charles-Louis could not, in all honesty, say yes.

He was about to open his mouth with a further suggestion when Viola said:

'Anything else is out of the question as you know very well.'

'*Qu'est ce que tu comptes faire?*'

'What am I going to do? Do you think you're in Ireland

Charlie, a few jars, take a girl to bed, then run like hell? It was you gave me this baby, Charlie; what are *you* going to do?'

It was not because he was in love with Viola that Charles-Louis agreed to marry her. Having, as he perceived it, been denied love not only by his mother, Baronne Gertrude, who had left his upbringing to surrogates, but also by his father, Baron Thibault, who was more concerned with the nurturing of his vines, Charles-Louis did not know the meaning of the word love. The reason that he invited Viola to become his bride was because, as his parents never tired of reminding him, it was his responsibility to produce the son and heir who would perpetuate the unbroken line of Barons de Cluzac. The injection of good Irish blood into the attenuated French stock seemed, to all concerned, not such a bad proposition.

The marriage between Charles-Louis Eugène Bertrand de Cluzac and Viola Katherine Mairead Fitzpatrick was solemnised in the chapel at Cluzac on a beautiful spring day, which had brought out the carpet of bluebells beneath the great trees of the drive. The bride wore a dress of Indian muslin, with a high neck and long sleeves, and an embroidered white cap from which fell a waterfall of Brussels lace which successfully concealed her thickening waistline. She was attended by her sisters, Lucy, Annabel, Shiobhan and Rose. The wedding-breakfast, masterminded by Baronne Gertrude, who was not displeased with her new daughter-in-law, took place in a marquee which was hung on three sides, in the style of Bérain, with black and white lengths of cloth, which represented wrought-iron work. One side of the marquee was left transparent, which created the effect of an additional room, which looked out on to the park. The celebrations, which went on for several days, were a cross between the grandest of *fêtes champêtres* and an Irish wake. Stumbling into the wrong bedroom – given the size of the château it was a mistake easily made – during a lull in the festivities, Viola came across her bridegroom, his wedding trousers about his ankles, covering one of the more nubile guests. It was not only this discovery, but the fact that, despite Charles-Louis' pathological weakness for women (a proclivity she was yet to discover), he hated to spend the night with them, that led them, for the eight years of their marriage, to occupy separate bedrooms.

When Clare Gertrude Sophie Elinore de Cluzac was born, six months after the nuptials, Charles-Louis, having been informed of the child's gender, held her awkwardly in his arms for a few moments. He managed a brief kiss on his wife's brow, together with a few embarrassed words of congratulation, before repairing, disappointed, to the vineyards in which an exceptionally mild January had caused the sap to rise in the vines prematurely. It was left to Baron Thibault, who was delighted with his granddaughter, to make all the right noises.

Although, as an Irishwoman, Viola seemed to possess a certain insight into the character of a horse, she was not a natural mother, and her ideas about child-rearing had been gleaned from the stables.

She believed that early training was as important as a good education, and that if children were started early enough, and dealt with intelligently enough, they would become good children. In England, where the custom was to treat foals gently when first handled and ridden, they behaved like spoiled brats. They needed to feel the hand of the trainer to control and guide them, although punishment should be administered at the moment of misbehaviour and should never be too severe. They should be taught early on the habit of obedience, so that it became a second instinct, and to do what was required of them should seem as natural as to eat when they were hungry and to lie down when they wanted to go to sleep.

It was a question of the more you spare the rod the

less you spoil the child. As you bend the twig so grows the tree, and education should be as gradual as moonrise, and perceptible not in progress but in result.

The result of this upbringing had been to ensure that Clare was in awe of her mother, striving to be obedient, to anticipate her wishes and trotting to her side when called. For love and affection she had been dependent, as a baby, on the presence of Baronne Gertrude, who was besotted with her granddaughter. Following Baron Thibault's tragic death and her grandmother's summary departure – having been deprived of the attentions of nannies Forbes and McKay almost as soon as she had grown fond of them – she had relied on the comforting presence of Sidonie and the warmth of her kitchen.

Now, watching Jamie as he expertly ground spices in the cramped Waterperry kitchen – she found watching the six-foot-two winger cook incredibly sexy – Clare allowed her thoughts to turn to Viola, with whom her relationship was civil but constrained. She knew that her mother, according to her lights, was fond of her and concerned about her welfare, but, as far as feelings were concerned, none, as far as she could remember, had ever been displayed.

'How does coming to Ireland with me next weekend grab you?'

'Kindly do not distract the cook.'

'Don't you want to meet my mother?'

Jamie added the spices to the onions, which were sweating in a pan on the ancient Parkinson Cowan gas cooker, which had come with the cottage.

'On the contrary. I think it's about time I met my future mother-in-law.'

Clare laid her head against Jamie's broad back, feeling his muscles contract as he concentrated on the onions, and wrapped her arms around his waist.

'If my father really is selling Cluzac we'll be able to

go to town on this cottage. We could build a mega extension . . .'

'For the two of us?'

'I wasn't thinking about the *two* of us . . .' Clare untied the strings of Jamie's apron, which were fastened over his middle, and ran her hands provocatively down his body.

'Cut it out, will you! I . . . am *trying* . . . to make a curry . . .'

'I rather thought you might fancy making some little Spence-Joneses.'

There was a loud 'plop' as Jamie turned off the gas. Hurling his apron enthusiastically through the open window, he took Clare in his arms in a bone-crunching embrace.

CHAPTER SIX

Since leaving the cocoon of her boarding school, where she had been mothered by the nuns and comforted by the ritual, Clare had had a great many short-lived affairs. The men to whom she found herself attracted were often a great deal older than herself, and until she met Jamie she had been unable to form a long-term relationship.

Listening to Hannah complaining about Seth, who thought that his socks washed themselves and jumped back into the drawer while he lay on the sofa reading his interminable scripts, and to Francesca, who because she cooked on camera was expected by every wally she dated to knock up a soufflé every time she brought them home, and Zoffany, who was such a militant feminist that any half-way decent man ran a mile at her approach, she knew that marriage to Jamie, ten years her senior and as solid as a listed building, would be like getting into a hot bath. She would, in addition, get her back scrubbed.

A year ago Clare had been sitting in Francesca's kitchen, while the TV cook experimented with 'fool-proof pastry', which was sticking doggedly both to the table and the rolling-pin. She was moaning to Francesca that she was *never* going to meet anyone, all the men she knew were either married or gay or in meaningful relationships.

' "If you haven't got a rolling-pin use a milk bottle." ' Francesca, who was only partly listening to her, addressed an imaginary audience.

'Who the fuck has milk *bottles*?' Clare said.

It was shortly afterwards that Jamie, who had at the time been going out with Miranda Pugh, an old friend of Nicola's and the hard-hitting editor of *Amazon*, a magazine dedicated to career women, had walked into the Nicola Wade Gallery where he had mistaken her for a waitress.

In the interests of the profit margins the gallery was run on a shoestring and the overheads pared to the barest minimum. Clare had no intention of letting it operate in any other way. On Private View days, Nicola, dishing out price sheets like confetti, dealt with the press (if any), chatted up the clients, and massaged the ego of the artist, to whom the act of exposure was usually purgatory. The catering was in the capable hands of Francesca, who could be relied upon to do it economically, which left Clare to dispense the hospitality.

The first words Jamie, who was wearing dun-coloured cords and a scarlet waistcoat, had spoken to her, as she stood by the door with her tray of Francesca's mini vol-au-vents, were, 'I'm allergic to mushrooms.'

'I only have to look at a tomato and I get spots on my bottom,' Clare said affably, intending to put him at his ease.

As he shied away empty-handed, she heard his shocked voice addressing Miranda:

'Funny sort of waitresses they get these days . . .'

Later, when the Private View was at its height, the perspiring punters shoulder to shoulder, the noise level in the cellar intolerable, and the oxygen level low, Clare, busy making out invoices, felt a hand on her shoulder.

'What sort of spots?'

'Sorry?'

'On your backside. I came to apologise. I thought you were the caterer. Jamie Spence-Jones. I came with Miranda. I don't suppose you happen to have a name?'

'Clare . . .'

'Clare. I like it.'

'Clare Gertrude Sophie Elinore de Cluzac . . .'

'We all have our problems,' he said, making her laugh.

She had got as far as telling him that she was Nicola's partner and about her Saturday stall in Portobello market, when Miranda, an anorexic redhead dressed, according to the current trend, entirely in black and carrying an outsize black Hervé Chapelier bag, rudely interrupted them to say that she'd absolutely had enough and that if she had to stand the heat another moment she'd die. Ignoring Clare, and taking Jamie, who was at least a foot taller than she, proprietorially by the hand, she pulled him away.

Watching their feet through the railings – Miranda's Manolo Blahnik black ankle-boots and Jamie's Timberlands – disappear in unison down the road at street level, Clare thought that she hadn't met a man with a tingle quotient as high as that of Jamie Spence-Jones in months.

'Tell me about Jamie Spence-Jones,' she said casually to Nicola, when everyone had gone and they were counting up the red dots in the right-hand corners of the paintings.

'He's a surgeon. At the John Radcliffe.'

'I mean him and Miranda.'

'Forget it.'

'How serious is it?'

'Serious. They've been an item for years.'

'Maybe . . . ?'

'Don't even think about it! You know, it never ceases to amaze me how the paintings which one is convinced won't sell jump off the wall, and the dead certs hang about. I don't know about you, but I'm starving. I booked a table at Zen.'

A month later, Clare had been standing behind her stall in Portobello Road, when she heard a voice say, 'How are the spots?' and looked up to see Jamie, a clumsily wrapped package beneath his arm, appraising her wares.

'How's Miranda?' Her normally well-modulated voice erupted in a cross between a simper and a squeak.

'Miranda and I split up. She's going out with Barnaby Muirhead, the Formula One man.'

'I suppose you couldn't compete.'

He ignored her witticism – she always joked when she was nervous – and indicated the bundle beneath his arm.

'A pewter tankard. One of the theatre sisters is emigrating to Australia. I probably paid too much for it. Will you have dinner with me?'

The seriousness of his voice made her pack up her wares and drive with Jamie to his cottage in Waterperry. Expecting to be taken to a restaurant, she was surprised when he went into the cramped kitchen and, preparing his *batterie de cuisine* as if he were laying out instruments in the operating theatre, set about making dinner. It became a standing joke between them that, despite Jamie's best efforts, Clare couldn't remember what they ate.

'I once went out with a man,' Clare said afterwards, 'who told me, "*I've* cooked the dinner now *you* can do the washing-up." On our first date!'

'I would never do that.'

Clare believed him. Later she discovered that Jamie didn't play games. What you saw was what you got. Leaving the dirty dishes on the table, they were drawn, like metal and magnet, towards each other and had divested themselves of every fragment of clothing before they climbed the narrow stairs.

'Lucky for me you came to Portobello for your pewter tankard,' Clare said later in his arms.

'Luck didn't come into it.' Jamie kissed her passionately. 'Nicola told me where to find you.'

Clare became a frequent visitor to the cottage and to

the John Radcliffe, where her face became familiar in the hospital mess. In all her twenty-seven years she had never been so happy. For the first time in her life she felt loved.

They had been going out for six months when Jamie had taken her to Aberdeen to meet his parents, who still lived in the mock-Tudor house where Jamie and his two younger brothers had been born. His mother, a consultant obstetrician and gynaecologist at the Aberdeen Royal Infirmary, a strong-looking woman with short grey hair, the same height and build as Jamie, had to Clare's surprise been hanging out the weekly wash in the garden – Jamie explained later that she regarded it as therapy – while his father (a general practitioner who had gone into medicine for the wrong reasons and from whom Jamie had inherited his love of literature), formally dressed for a Sunday in a tweed suit and waistcoat, set the table for lunch.

Watching Jamie's mother dismember the crisply roasted capon with frightening dexterity, listening to Jamie's easy discussion with his father about the various consultant posts for which he was applying, as though they were resuming a conversation that had taken place only yesterday, Clare basked in the warmth which, despite the lack of adequate central heating, suffused the oak-panelled dining-room with its bow-fronted sideboard and inherited silver.

'I think Clare would like another potato.' Rodney Spence-Jones addressed his wife, as Clare put down her knife and fork.

'Why don't you ask her?' Muriel Spence-Jones lobbed back the ball.

Listening to the laughter provoked by what was obviously a family joke, Clare realised where Jamie got both his equable nature and his sense of humour. Although she was unaware of time passing, she was surprised to find that lunch, which had been accompanied, in Jamie's honour, by a Gevrey-Chambertin with which she could find no fault, had gone on until four o'clock, by which time the tablecloth was liberally littered with shards of walnut shell which had escaped from the nut-crackers, and the plum-patterned fruit plates were overflowing with tangerine peel.

Taking Clare into his book-lined study, on the pretext of showing her the family album, Rodney Spence-Jones looked at her with kindly brown eyes reminiscent of Jamie's.

'I never did take to that Miranda.'

Recognising it as his acceptance of her, Clare, in a spontaneous gesture, kissed Jamie's father, to his delight and embarrassment – he was unused to such gestures – on both cheeks.

Afterwards, Jamie said that according to his brothers, who had had a full telephone report, his parents had not stopped talking about her.

Now it was Clare's turn, and she was taking Jamie to meet Viola in County Kerry, where she kept a stable of seventy-odd horses. She taught them to trot and canter correctly before instructing them in elementary dressage. Finally she trained them as show-jumpers which she sold the world over.

When Viola had left Cluzac twenty years ago, taking Clare with her, there was no question of dissolving the marriage in the eyes of the Catholic church. She had not even gone through the motions of a civil divorce. Charles-Louis had not pursued the matter, and, having been trapped into her first wedding by her unplanned pregnancy, she had no intention of getting married again.

Her relationship with Charles-Louis, since her discovery of his infidelity during their nuptials, had been tempestuous. After the death of Baron Thibault and the departure of Baronne Gertrude, her role as chatelaine of Cluzac had been made easy by the fact that the new Baron de

Cluzac, unlike his father, disliked entertaining and only rarely deigned to socialise with his neighbours. Under the eagle eye of Sidonie, the Château – staffed by an army of village women who crept around like ciphers with mops and bundles of linen – more or less ran itself.

At the time of their nuptials, Charles-Louis had apologised profusely for his aberration with the wedding guest, and Viola, in her naivety, had put his behaviour down to an excess of male hormone (which she knew all about from her father's stallions), coupled with the fact that over the past three days he had had a very great deal to drink. The second episode, when she had found him in the Orangery astride one of the stable girls, had found her less forgiving.

Accepting a chestnut mare by way of compensation, Viola had once again drawn a veil over the incident, which was to be repeated, over the years, with Charles-Louis' secretaries, with the wife of one the estate managers, with a housemaid whom she had immediately dismissed, and with Beatrice Biancarelli, a young Corsican beauty who was currently the toast of Bordeaux.

Viola was disgusted not only by Charles-Louis' behaviour, but by his inability to communicate on anything but the most basic level with anyone but Desirée, the red setter bitch who accompanied him to the garages, the vineyards and the *chais*, and who never left his side. She occupied herself with her husband's stables, the running of which she assumed; she took an interest in show-jumpers, which she gradually learned to train; and she kept a watchful eye, when she remembered, on Clare.

It was when her seventeen-year-old sister, Rose, was visiting Cluzac one September to help with the *vendange* – between leaving her convent school and going to university in Dublin, where she had won a music scholarship to Trinity College – that the crunch had finally come.

Knowing Charles-Louis as she did, and recognising the

fact that Rose, with her wild auburn hair and her eyes the colour of vintage marmalade, was as full and juicy as the ripe peaches suspended from the wall of the courtyard, Viola had cautioned him.

'Keep away from my little sister, now,' she had told him. 'You so much as go near Rose, Charles-Louis Eugène Bertrand de Cluzac, and you'll wish you'd never been born.'

All had gone well until the night of the party held in the great barn to celebrate the end of the vintage. Sitting among the exhausted army of grape-pickers who came yearly to Cluzac from Spain and Portugal, Baronne Viola de Cluzac had graciously accepted the *gerbaude*, the annual bouquet of flowers, from their spokesperson and recited her statutory few words of thanks, when it dawned on her that both her husband and Rose were missing from the table.

Stopping by the stables to pick up her riding-crop, and following her intuition, she combed the shadowy grounds. She found them in the gazebo where Rose, who had partaken too generously of the carafes of château wine, was standing naked as a moonlit statue while Charles-Louis worshipped at her auburn shrine.

Yelling to Rose to get her clothes on at once and return to her tower bedroom, Viola, screaming like a Dublin fishwife, had set about her husband with the riding-crop. In an angry torrent of cliché and somewhat mixed metaphor, she had told him that this time he had not only widely overstepped the mark but had finally cooked his goose.

The following morning she had packed her bags. Accompanied by a bewildered Clare, and the hung-over and shamefaced Rose, who was unaccustomed to drinking, she had left Château de Cluzac, and returned to Ireland.

She had no hatred for Charles-Louis. During their eight years together there had been times when she had found him both engaging and amusing. He was not an ungenerous man and had left her pretty much to her own devices in the stables, which was what she enjoyed most of all; but she could no longer tolerate his philandering, which she considered, to say the least of it, immature. They communicated whenever it was necessary, usually over matters to do with the child, but there was never any talk of divorce.

Having had her fill of life in a castle and an unsatisfactory marriage, Viola Fitzpatrick (she felt more comfortable in the old shoes of her Irish name) bought a derelict property in County Kerry, which she had since made a premier centre for the training of show-jumpers. At the Fitzpatrick Equine Centre she took in the odd paying guest who wanted to learn to jump. To say that it was a hotel would have been painting the lily. Rooms were made available and let to riders by word of mouth. Apart from breakfast, which was provided, they were expected to fend for themselves. They were invited to leave the washing-up, if they could find a place for it, in the kitchen sink.

As far as companionship was concerned, Viola had taken as a lover a lecturer in jurisprudence from the University of Cork, several years younger than herself.

When Clare had written that she was engaged to be married, it had brought Viola's age home to her. It seemed no time at all since she had left Château de Cluzac, a period of her life over which she had drawn a veil; and, when she thought of her at all, she still thought of Clare as a child.

Meeting Clare and Jamie at Cork Airport, Viola kissed her daughter and, looking up at her future son-in-law, appraised him, as if he were a horse, for hands and girth.

Leading the way with Clare to the mud-spattered Range Rover in the car-park, Viola, who had assessed the situation, took her arm.

'It's good to see you. Is it Jamie brings you to Ireland?'

Clare, who favoured her father only in respect of the de Cluzac nose, which she had inherited and which could be identified on many of the portraits of her ancestors, said, 'It's really about Papa . . .'

Viola, with some difficulty, extracted the car keys from the pocket of her jodhpurs, which she wore tight as a second skin.

'I had a feeling it might be. I think Charles-Louis is up to something. He's been pestering me for a divorce. Is he still bonking everything that moves?'

CHAPTER SEVEN

Viola was more skilled on the back of a horse than at the wheel of a car. While on the hair-raising journey from Cork Airport, Clare conjectured why after all these years her father should suddenly be demanding a divorce, the object of her speculation, Baron de Cluzac, sat at the head of his solitary table in the château dining-room, with Rougemont (grandson of Desirée) at his feet, and contemplated the sale of his château.

That he had not informed his daughter of his immediate plans was deliberate. He had not as yet finalised the arrangements for the disposal of the château, the details of which were no one's business but his own, and there was time enough. She was not the only member of the family who was involved and who would be required to sign a *pouvoir* in the presence of Monsieur Long, the notary, before the sale of the estate could be proceeded with.

Although Charles-Louis himself owned forty-eight per cent of the family home, twenty-four per cent belonged to his older sister Bernadette, the Mother Superior of Notre Dame de Consolation, a Toulouse convent, twenty-four per cent to Clare, and the remaining four per cent – as executrix of Baron Thibault's will – to his estranged mother, Baronne Gertrude.

His decision to dispose of Cluzac had been precipitated only partly by the fact that, after twenty years more or less on his own, he had decided not only to remarry but, in a move practically unheard of for a château owner, to eschew the Médoc with its vines, for Florida and its oranges.

The resolution to deliver the château, which had belonged for so long to his family, and in the vaults of which many of them were buried, into the hands of strangers had been precipitated in part by the financial difficulties in which he found himself and in part by his attachment to Laura Buchanan Spray.

With a low boredom threshold, an innate restlessness and his insatiable penchant for vintage cars – in particular those American in origin, from the 1950s – Charles-Louis was an inveterate traveller.

Leaving Cluzac in the hands of his loyal and capable staff, many of whom had been in the service of the Barons de Cluzac for three generations, and who were, if the truth were told, better off without him, he shuttled frequently to Paris and Geneva, and took off regularly for Argentina, Australia and Japan. He travelled not so much on vineyard business, but to pursue his hedonistic lifestyle and augment his collection of automobiles, on which he squandered a very great deal of money.

March, when he had finished skiing in Gstaad (with his current paramour), found him at the Concours d'Elegance in Palm Springs, April at the Cavalcade of Classic Cars in Anaheim and May in Palo Alto. In June he visited the Vintage Thunderbird Club in Hannibal, Minnesota, while Pismo Beach and Lakeport, California, accounted for much of July.

He had been in Florida, tracking down an early MGA 1600 Roadster, when he had been invited by Hunter Watney, who had cornered the market in citrus (financed by the exploitation of illegally imported Cuban and Haitian refugees), to a Republican benefit dinner at the residence of Senator Hubert Spray, whose personal fortune alone was reputed to be in the region of seventy million dollars.

Charles-Louis' fastidious pedigree and title, a rare cachet in Palm Beach, assured him a seat not only at the Senator's top table, but at the coveted right elbow of his hostess, the forty-five-year-old Laura Buchanan Spray, reigning queen of the Palm Beach set.

Although Laura, dressed tonight in a tight-fitting sheath of white sequins, which reflected the light from the myriad candle bulbs of the glass chandeliers, was surrounded by some of the most pampered and elegant women in Florida, her blonde good looks and statuesque beauty were unchallenged.

Buchanan, her first husband (well, not exactly her first but she had drawn a veil over the student of architecture she had married at the age of seventeen), had been a Californian meat magnate. He had succumbed to a cerebral embolus, following triple bypass surgery, after ten years of a not unhappy marriage, leaving a widow who was extremely wealthy even by Californian standards.

Not unnaturally, the lovely, upwardly mobile Laura Buchanan, dismissing the fortune-hunters who buzzed round her like so many flies, was extremely selective in her next choice of partner. Although she had never met him, Hubert Spray, a tall, extremely handsome, sixty-five-year-old Senator (highly respected in political circles and close to the ear of the President), who, sadly, had buried his wife on the day of what was to have been their ruby wedding, seemed the ideal candidate. Having circled his picture in *Newsweek*, Laura Buchanan, availing herself of the network she had built up, applied herself to the task in hand.

Using the owner of a TV station, an admiral of the fleet and a Californian congressman – with all of whom she had affairs – as stepping-stones, she made her unerring way to her objective. Eighteen months later, a small paragraph in the *Washington Post* announced that, in a private ceremony, Senator Hubert Spray and Mrs Laura Buchanan had celebrated their marriage. The fact that the Senator was sexually impotent, owing to the inherited diabetes which he had difficulty controlling, was not mentioned.

Slinging out the comfortable furniture and 'mumsy' drapes of the first Mrs Spray from the Senator's Georgetown duplex, Laura had summoned Magda Mojinsky, the New York decorator, to 'do it over', before turning her attentions both to making her presence felt in the Senator's office (any request had to be filtered through her) and finding a second home worthy of her social aspirations.

After two weeks searching in Florida, she came up with a stone-built mansion in a prime location, designed and built – by a strange quirk of fate – in distinctive Mediterranean Revival style (with Spanish, Moorish, Romanesque, Gothic and Renaissance influences) by her first husband, whose services were now much in demand.

The U-shaped, pavilion-like house, gated for privacy and security, was entered by a flight of steps leading up into a massive, vaulted space, part hallway and part cloister. It was built round three sides of a patio, furnished with palms and an ornamental pond, and was ideal for outdoor entertaining.

The living-room had antique cut-crystal doors, was hung with Chinese glass paintings and Venetian sconces, and was entered through double columns guarded by 'Pompeiian' figures. The hundred-year-old chimney-piece was from a château in the Pyrenees, and the chandelier, suspended from the elaborate ceiling, was custom-built by Dennis-Leen of West Hollywood.

The landscaped gardens, which boasted a terrace overlooking extensive lawns, were embellished with statuary and giant eucalyptus trees. In them were a lake, fountains, rose-garden, tennis courts, swimming-pool (with stained-glass windows and a thirty-foot ceiling), and a Japanese tea house whose spiral columns echoed the motifs of the chimneys.

The entire property, which reeked not so much of the 1200 new rose bushes planted by Laura, but of new money, could have been dropped down in the 150 hectares of Cluzac and scarcely noticed. Charles-Louis, beguiled not only by its mistress (not to mention several of her exceedingly glamorous friends), but the sybaritic outdoor life and by the *Laura Dear*, an ocean-going, fully crewed yacht moored on the waterway, found it instantly appealing.

The benefit dinner, at which Laura Spray had focused the full beam of her attention on Charles-Louis, at the expense of the influential newspaper proprietor on her left, had been followed by a suggestion that the Baron feel free to make use of one of the mansion's numerous guest suites whenever he was in the vicinity. It was an invitation of which Charles-Louis availed himself frequently.

Never averse to killing more than one bird with a single stone, Charles-Louis had not only invested heavily in Hunter Watney's lucrative orange groves, but became Laura Spray's lover in the king-sized bed in the heavily swagged bedroom overlooking the rose-garden, where, although she did not, in truth, care all that much for sex, she went out of her way to please him.

When the ailing Senator, whose blood pressure was too high and who did not pay sufficient attention to his diet, suffered a fatal stroke in the Upper House, Laura Buchanan Spray's fourth husband had long been designated. Regarding the title 'Baronne de Cluzac' as the apotheosis of her stratospheric climb, after an appropriate interval she made her move.

At the time of Laura's ultimatum, marriage or 'out' (she was not one to mince words), Charles-Louis, who was not yet divorced from Viola, had not for a moment been considering taking a second wife. His decision to do so was precipitated not merely by the attractions of life in Florida, where, because of his business interests he now spent a great deal of time, but to the fact, which came as a complete surprise to himself, that he had grown attached to the strong-minded and highly decorative Laura Spray, whom he both lusted after and needed.

Although the Baron had taken Laura frequently to Cluzac, where she had, to the horror of Sidonie, been unable to resist replacing the torn and faded curtains and slinging out threadbare carpets, she made it abundantly clear that she had not the slightest intention of living in Bordeaux. Openly snubbed by the surrounding patrician families, whom she found insufferably snobbish and turned in on themselves, she could not wait to get her prospective husband away from his icy château and the damp winters, which she tolerated only for the sake of Charles-Louis, whom (rumour having reached her ears of his weakness for women) she was determined to bring to heel.

Under the watchful eye of Sidonie, who stood statue-like by the door monitoring his every movement, the object of Laura Spray's affections carefully removed the bones from his delicate *alose*, the 'rich man's fish' which appeared in the river with the melting mountain snows and whose disappearance coincided with the flowering of the vines. Helping himself to the accompanying sauce, made from parsley, onion, bayleaves, garlic and olive oil, he pondered on the forthcoming sale of the château, the complicated negotiations for which were now in their final stages.

Of the three final contenders, Claude Balard, owner of Balard et Fils (wine merchants), prominent member of the Syndicat des Negociants, and his long-time negociant, had been rejected on the grounds that Charles-Louis not only distrusted the man (conflict between growers and merchants was too ingrained for any real co-operation to be possible) but disliked him intensely, and that his ambition to own the château was based purely on social pretensions.

Alain Lamotte, the likeable young Director of Assurance Mondiale, was harmless enough – with a charming Parisienne wife, Delphine, and two exemplary children – but his offer, although extremely competitive, was, in view of the trump card held by the third contender, no longer acceptable.

Philip Van Gelder had, as a result of certain business dealings into which the Baron did not delve too deeply, been kicked out of South Africa. The only way he could liberate the funds he had tied up in the country was through a complicated, elaborate and illegal cash scheme that required him to invest them in a wine-producing estate for which he was willing to pay well over the odds. For reasons of his own, and which were mooted in private by the two men, this suited the Baron admirably.

This morning, standing beneath the 'Médoc blue' sky, among the serried vines, which were just beginning to flower, Charles-Louis and Van Gelder, unbeknown to either Claude Balard or Alain Lamotte, but watched by Sidonie as she hung out the billowing sheets in the garden of her cottage abutting the vineyards, had shaken hands on the deal.

Prompted by a conscience that did not bother him overmuch, Charles-Louis had extracted a promise from the prospective owner that he would continue to care for the loyal staff and retainers, many of whom had been at Château de Cluzac for years and had known no other home.

Van Gelder, dressed in sharp slacks and canary-yellow pullover, which bore a designer logo, had put an arm round the shoulders of the Baron's well-worn English sports jacket.

'Don't worry about it!'

Acknowledging Van Gelder's reassurance, the Baron chose to ignore the fact that the wine-grower from Franschhoek was lying in his teeth.

Bothered by a premonition that her future and that of her husband, Jean, the Baron's *maître de chai*, was in the balance, Sidonie, wearing a starched white apron and white ankle socks, her face immobile, removed the plate on which lay the skeleton of the Baron's fish and poured a little wine into the Baron's glass.

Although she watched his every movement, and monitored the comings and goings in the château and in the *chais* with the vigilance of a well-trained hawk, Sidonie rarely spoke to her employer. When they did communicate, the conversation was brief and to the point.

On this occasion, the Baron, having merely sniffed the wine, addressed her without turning his head.

'*Il est bouchonné!*'

'*Oui, Monsieur.*'

Removing the glass, Sidonie retreated to the pantry.

Although it had not been intended as a personal rebuke, the suggestion that the wine was corked offended her. She knew that the Baron's comment referred not to the fact that the bottle had been clumsily opened, but that the wine had a stale, woody smell and taste owing to oxidation. Had she not been so preoccupied with what she had witnessed that morning in the vineyard, she might have detected the foul aroma herself.

Drawing the long cork from a new bottle, she examined it carefully before returning to the dining-room where she poured the claret into a clean glass and stood stiffly to attention while the Baron tasted it.

When he had signified his approval by the merest nod of his head, Sidonie half filled the glass, turning the bottle expertly at the last moment so that no drop was spilled on to the polished table, before serving the Baron with his *côte de veau*.

Making a mental note, before the week was out, that he must visit his sister, Bernadette, at her convent in Toulouse, the Baron dispatched his customary four-course lunch in silence.

When he left the dining-room it was without so much as a glance in Sidonie's direction. Leaving the château by the stone staircase, he jumped into his car in the sunlit courtyard planted with tropical palms and hung with wistaria. With the wheels of his 1958 Plymouth Sport-Fury spinning in a cloud of gravel, he exited beneath the stone arch and set off for Bordeaux to visit his long-time mistress, Beatrice Biancarelli.

CHAPTER EIGHT

'See that!' Viola said impatiently. 'There's no point at all in deliberately placing the horse at his fence. That's the horse's job; it takes years of training and experience . . .'

Jamie had forgotten to bring a raincoat. With his hands in his pockets, his shoulders hunched and water dripping from his hair and down his face and neck, he leaned against the perimeter fence while Viola, who wore wellington boots and an anorak and seemed unaware that it was raining, pointed out to him the finer points of show-jumping, in the art of which two riders in long macs – visitors from Holland – were being instructed.

Leaving the jumping paddock, she led him across a mud-swilled path to the stables, where several horses, their faces framed by open wooden shutters, mournfully regarded their approach.

Approaching a Belgian-bred gelding with a quivering black body and a shock of hair which fell over one eye, Viola took his face between her hands. 'This is Ardargh. I bought him last week at the High Performance Horse Sales. The first horse we've *bought* in a long time. We usually breed our own. Buying at auction is nerve-racking. He should make a top three-day-eventer. He found it strange coming here. We had twelve horses in Millstreet at the International Show. This one . . .' Moving on, she reassured a feisty-looking black horse. 'Squire's Mount, top show horse in England for four years – attaboy! –

he's just been out now for exercise this morning; he's
home bred. I wouldn't get too close. This is Falstaff.
He's eleven years old. An All-Ireland Yearling Champion.
He's the foundation stallion. Out of the best line of Irish
breeding. All our young horses are by him. He's done
very well for us. So you have. He has three full brothers,
leading stallions. We keep the horses until five or six years
and then we sell them. Over here' – Viola led the way to
a barn – 'we have a trekking centre . . .'

The journey from the airport had taken them past the
Ban-Ard Cash & Carry and Mother Kelly's Beer Garden.
Their erratic progress – the Touchstone Tavern ('Hot
Lunches a Speciality'), Terh O'Connor's Funeral Service –
down narrow country lanes and over the Shehy mountains,
was impeded every now and then by flagmen on the road,
and by slow-moving tractors noisily appropriating half
the carriageway. With Viola cursing at the wheel, they
finally rounded a bend to come, without warning, upon
the Fitzpatrick Equine Centre, a low-built stone house and
outbuildings, which had once served as an army barracks,
where the appearance of the Range Rover was greeted
by the hysterical barking of what seemed to be a great
many dogs.
    Leading the way through a small garden, its low stone wall
restraining a riot of pansies, past a window looking out on
to the yard, in which were piled china ornaments, a wicker
basket, silver show-jumping cups, and an opened packet of
fig-rolls, Viola opened the front door and led the way into
the kitchen.
    Without bothering to take off her anorak, she removed a
misshapen loaf of soda bread from a stone crock and took
a slab of yellow butter, a wedge of crumbling cheese and
some baked Limerick ham (smoked over juniper berries)
from the old-fashioned refrigerator. Pulling two additional
wooden chairs, one of which was broken, up to the table,

which was covered in a red checked oil-cloth worn in some places to the backing, she indicated, with a sweep of her hand, that lunch was ready.

The rudimentary preparations were Viola's concession to her visitors. Her rough and ready style of housekeeping, in which everyone except the horses was required to fend for himself, and with which from the age of eight Clare had been familiar, contrasted sharply with the welcome of Sidonie's kitchen, the formality of the Baron's dining-room and the protocol of her grandmother's flat.

Helping herself to a piece of the cheese, which she placed between thick slices of bread, Viola held the sandwich in two hands.

'So the two of you are to be married. Is that your ring?'

Clare held out her hand with the ring from Butler's Wharf: a wide band of gold in the modern idiom, inset with a circlet of rose diamonds, turquoises, and cabochon garnets.

'It's very handsome. I thought it would be the de Cluzac sapphire . . .'

Clare gave her a warning glance, which encompassed Jamie. Viola had never been one for tact.

'Your grandmother was keeping the sapphire for you. How is the old lady? I've a soft spot for her. I hope she's well.'

Clare looked at her mother's handsome, unmade-up face – she swore by Nivea cream and used it by the gallon – which a network of fine lines was just beginning to traverse, at her rain-softened, still-dark hair, with the single grey streak which had appeared in her twenties. It flopped unrestrained over the dark brown eyes with their deep lids, which she had herself inherited. She realised that, although it rarely occurred to either of them to pick up the telephone, and that when they did speak they were rarely on the same wavelength, she had missed her mother.

Viola was one of the very few people, Clare thought, who were – to use the French idiom for which there seemed no satisfactory translation – *bien dans sa peau*. She said what she meant and meant what she said. She was totally unselfconscious either about her own appearance or the impression she made on others, and followed her own instincts rather than the dictates of society. It was little wonder that she had not lasted long in the Médoc.

'You're looking well now.' Viola let go of Clare's hand. 'A bit on the pale side but that's the smog for you. So I'm to have a son-in-law at last. Tell me about yourself Jamie.'

'I love your daughter, Mrs Fitzpatrick.'

'That much is obvious. "Viola" will do. Clare tells me you're a medical man. You'll be at home in Ireland. Doctors and poets. You must let me know when's the wedding.'

'July.'

'That's the middle of the show-jumping! And where's it to be held?'

There was silence as Jamie and Clare looked at each other.

'We're still arguing about it,' Clare said.

'I'll tell you one thing, Jamie – I'll make a pot of tea, not that poor stuff they have on the other side – Clare always gets her own way. Since she was a child. She makes up her mind and it's hard to dissuade her. There are horses the same. You'll find common sense will do much, kindness more, and coercion very little.'

Accustomed to a mug and a tea-bag, Jamie watched fascinated as Viola brought freshly drawn water to a brisk boil before warming the teapot ceremoniously, putting in four teaspoonfuls of Darjeeling leaves, and setting it on the table to brew.

'I can be a bit bloody-minded myself,' he said.

'Then there's trouble ahead. I remember once, she must have been about six . . .'

'Mother!' Clare said.

'He'll want to know what kind of woman he's taking on.'

'He's not "taking me on". I'm in charge of my own life.'

Viola sat down again at the table. She was not to be deterred.

'Her father bought her a three-wheeler. He forbade her anywhere but in the grounds. She'd been gone for two hours before we realised. We thought she was riding round the courtyard. Albert Rochas brought her home on the back of the tractor. She was half-way to Kilmartin to visit her cousins and toppled over into a ditch. Show Jamie your hand, Clare. She bears the mark to this day.'

Obediently holding out her palm, Clare pointed to the long white line which snaked from the base of the thumb to the wrist bone where the skin had been lacerated by the gravel. It was not by the cicatrice that she remembered the incident however, but by the indelible scar which the aftermath of the accident had left on her mind.

It had been the first occasion on which her father had raised his hand to her. It was certainly not the last. Not only was the sharp slap delivered by Charles-Louis in 'her best interests', but, as if the humiliation were not enough, he actually expected her to be grateful to him for the punishment meted out to ensure her future compliance with his edicts.

His paternalism, his need to be in control, was that of the political demagogue, the omnipotent physician: do as I say and you will live; go your own way and you will die.

When Charles-Louis, beside himself with anger, assured his six-year-old daughter that the blow to the side of the head, which caught her ear and left her deaf for days, hurt him more than it hurt her, she believed him. It was several years before she had realised that her father had been lying.

Viola, who had herself been on the receiving end of his temper, did not concur with her daughter's punishment. She could see no real difference between a young child and a colt, both of whom were impulsive and ready for mischief. She never blamed a horse for its shortcomings, the responsibility for which lay with its teacher. If any punishment were necessary it should be explanatory and at the moment of misbehaviour. It should certainly never be brutal.

That Clare, unable at the age of six to cope with the pain of his betrayal, idolised her father – whom, from the perspective of childhood, she regarded as strong, handsome, and charismatic – was due to the silent bargain struck by the tyrannised with the tyrant: if she obeyed her papa, if she tried very hard to live up to his expectations of her and to do as he said, he would tell no one about her wickedness, he would keep her worthlessness to himself. It was many years after the tricycle incident before the realisation came to her that the frequent punishments she attracted were not 'in her own interests' at all, but that her father had in fact been abusing his parental position of power and treating her with contempt. It looked very much as if he was doing so again.

'Did Papa tell you about Cluzac?'

'He was too busy trying to get round me for the divorce. I shouldn't wonder he wants to get married again. I feel sorry for the poor soul, whoever she is . . . What about Cluzac?'

'The château is on the market.'

'But that's impossible. Where did you hear it?'

'From Big Mick Bly. The American wine writer. I met him in Bond Street.'

'Your father's crazy. What does he want to sell it for?'

'I've no idea.'

'You should have been consulted. Twenty-four per cent is down to you. What income have you been getting?'

'I haven't been getting an income at all.'

'Nothing?'

'A few cases of wine.'

'He can't dispose of the estate without you.'

'He seems to be having a good try.'

'You have to sign a paper. What exactly is he up to, I wonder?'

'Nicola and I want to buy the lease of a new gallery and Jamie and I are going to renovate his cottage . . .'

'Watch out he doesn't screw you. Milk and sugar?' Viola addressed Jamie.

'Both,' Clare said.

'Talk to the butcher and the block answers.'

Viola took an apple pie in a foil plate and a bowl of yellow cream from the fridge.

'It's not exactly *tarte tatin*. I bought it at Dunne's. Will you pass your plate, Jamie? I was born and bred in Ireland. My great-grandfather was Flemish. As a young boy he was involved in the Belgian war of Independence. Served with a battery of field artillery. His job was to capture the riderless Dutch horses. He was thrown from his horse under a gun carriage and injured. Afterwards he was unable to ride. He married a girl from Galway. That was my great-grandmother, Dymphna; I'll show you the album. He spent his time buying strings of Irish horses for the Belgian remount. My mother's people were foreigners, Normans, Cromwellians. They managed to remain Catholic . . . Are you a Catholic Jamie?'

'I'm afraid not.'

'There's too much fuss made over religion. People died every day in Ulster because they worshipped in the wrong church or lived in the wrong street. When's the last time Clare's been inside a church I don't know. What about the children?'

'I'm afraid we haven't got that far.'

'They'll be on you before you know it. Even today. I

was never much good at it. Mothering. My line's more horses, Clare'll tell you. It's always been horses, something to do with my great-grandfather. Did I tell you Declan was coming for supper? There's a stew in the pantry. Declan's my fella. Lectures at the university. Jurisprudence. You'll get on fine. Beef in Guinness. Eileen made it. She comes in to do breakfasts. I've only the two staying. They're from Neimegen. I've told Declan about you. He's dying to meet you.'

After lunch Clare had gone up to the bedroom they had been allotted. It looked out on to the lawn, rough with daisies, and the jumping paddock. From the window, breathing the sweet air through the rain, which was now coming down in stair rods, she watched her mother now, more at ease with strangers than with her own flesh and blood, talking to Jamie.

'There's no such thing as a genius in riding,' Viola was saying as her assistant patiently put the Dutch riders through their paces. 'Prodigies in mathematics, in music, in chess, yes. Riding must be learned the hard way. The correct way. I don't take on anyone who's not learned to ride properly. Who can't trot and gallop without stirrups and reins. No diver in his right mind would jump from the top board without first knowing how to swim. It's the same with riding. We use the cavalry school method. Two thousand years of experience. There are no short cuts. Tell me, what kind of a doctor are you?'

'An orthopaedic surgeon.'

'We could use you here for the horses if you're ever out of a job. Clare's very fond of you. You've only to look at her. She's not had a happy childhood. Her father wanted a boy. The two of them were always fighting. He's a difficult man. Very autocratic. He tried to break her spirit. He didn't succeed. She's bold and hardy, like the Irish horses. Are you getting wet, Jamie?'

Later, over supper, when Jamie started to sneeze, Viola plied him with whiskey and countered Clare's accusation that she had kept her beloved standing in the rain with the remark that Irish rain, unlike the stuff they went in for in England, never did anyone any harm.

Not only had the kitchen been transformed, but Viola herself. Clare presumed it was in honour of Declan Bailey rather than herself and Jamie. Her mother, taking no time at all over the exercise, had changed from her jodhpurs into a flattering red trouser-suit, piled her hair on top of her head, and put long ruby earrings, a present from Charles-Louis, in her ears. Although her face still bore no sign of make-up, her skin glowed and there was a softness to her which Clare had not seen before.

The beef in Guinness was accompanied by a Minervois, to which the Baronne would not have given house-room, which Declan had bought from the off-licence. The talk, into the small hours of the morning, ranged from the tenuous peace agreement in the north, to the respective merits of Anglo-Arab and Anglo-Normand mounts, to Irish literature at the turn of the century.

The evening ended with a recital of '. . . Away, come away: Empty your heart of its mortal dream . . .' by Declan, after which Clare and Jamie tactfully excused themselves and went upstairs.

'Your mother's great,' Jamie said as they got undressed.

'She likes you.'

'Did she say so?'

'I would have heard all about it by now if she didn't . . .'

Flinging his trousers on the floor, Jamie put his arms round her, lifted her, as if she were weightless, off her feet and covered her neck with love bites.

'Jamie, what *are* you doing?'

'It's all this talk about stallions.'

CHAPTER NINE

From the window of her boutique, Beatrice Biancarelli looked out on to the deluge that descended from the threatening sky on to the canopy of the deserted café opposite. Behind her, in the tiny cubicle, the plump Marie-Paule Balard struggled into a turquoise satin sheath, one size too small, which she had set her heart on wearing for the forthcoming Fête de la Fleur, the great party given by the château owners to celebrate the June flowering of the vines.

The rain that fell on to the deserted Allées de Tourny, to bounce off again in watery stalagmites, was not like the soft rain of Ireland, which, as Viola had assured Jamie, was not really rain at all but a gentle and welcome precipitation which softened the skins and greened the meadows of the Irish. The *cordes* which plummeted relentlessly into the grey Garonne – capable not only of rising but of flooding dramatically – made a wide river of the Esplanade de Quinconces, with tributaries in the running gutters, swelled the basins of the bronze fountains with their chariots drawn by sea-horses, and transformed the Friday market, lined with flower booths and stalls of symetrically hung hams, into a sea of coloured umbrellas.

Although it was almost twenty years since Beatrice Biancarelli had eloped to Bordeaux with a handsome tenor (who had left her stranded outside the Grand

Théâtre when the final curtain came down on *Turandot*),
she still had not come to terms with the climate.

In her native Corsica, where she had spent the first
fifteen years of her life, summer, fierce and blazing, had
been summer, and winter – despite the fact that the island
had the best weather in all of France – winter. One knew,
at least, where one was.

The poverty of her childhood had left its indelible
mark. Reluctantly switching on the lights in the shop,
Biancarelli, for thus she was known in the town and by
her many lovers, examined her reflection in the cheval
glass. It passed the time while she waited for Madame
Balard, an exceedingly demanding customer, to emerge
from the cubicle.

'*Puis-je vous aider, Madame?*' Biancarelli trilled automatically, lest Madame Balard, doing battle with the
turquoise satin, should think herself forsaken.

The enquiry was merely polite. Biancarelli knew, as of
old, that assistance with buttons and zip fasteners was
not what Madame Balard required. Only when she had
arranged herself to her own satisfaction and emerged, all
sixty-six kilos of her, would she want to be reassured that
she looked, at the very least, like Isabelle Adjani or Claudia
Schiffer, for which some positive reinforcement would be
required.

Examining her face dispassionately in the mirror,
Biancarelli thought, with alarm, that it was showing
distinct manifestations of its approach to the dreaded
fifth decade. The emerald chiffon scarf she had wound
round her hennaed hair not only accentuated the deep
green of her eyes – which could have a man at her feet
in thirty seconds and in her bed in as many minutes – but
revealed a few almost invisible lines which traversed her
forehead. At the first signs of crow's feet around the eyes,
or, worse still, bags beneath them, it would be off to the
cosmetic surgery clinic.

Beautiful herself, with taut brown skin, strong legs and good bone structure, not to mention a lively and volatile personality, Biancarelli hated anything that was not beautiful. For this reason she was not anticipating, with any sort of eagerness, the sight of Marie-Paule Balard emerging from the cubicle, squeezed into the turquoise dress which she had warned her was a size too small. With youth and beauty, the attributes that had transported her from the granite hell-hole of Bonifacio to the green pastures of Bordeaux, as her trump cards, she liked to look upon youth and beauty. The only exception she made was for her lovers, in the main old and ugly, who provided the means to the end.

Tilting her chin and half closing her lids in order to get a better view of herself, she wondered what Madame Balard, now doing battle behind the curtain, would have to say if she knew that less than an hour from now, when she had handed the boutique over to her vapid assistant, Danielle – who rarely managed to sell anything at all but whose discretion could be relied upon – Biancarelli would be in bed with her husband.

Claude Balard was not her only regular lover. In addition to her several *petits-amis* who came and went with the seasons, Biancarelli had another daily assignation, this time in the early afternoon, with the Baron de Cluzac. Although the arrangement had been going on for several years now, and her address was used as a poste restante for both men when the occasion arose, neither of her two protectors had any idea that she was bestowing her favours upon the other. Claude Balard being a self-opinionated egotist of the first order, and Charles-Louis de Cluzac an autocrat *par excellence*, such a thought would not have occurred to either of them.

Both Claude Balard and Charles-Louis treated her extremely generously, each taking it upon himself to 'look after' her both in financial terms and in respect of trips to the Côte d'Azur and to Paris. Claude Balard had even promised her a little house by the sea in Arcachon when his current plans came to fruition. Biancarelli did not make herself available either to them or her other paramours, however, solely for the money. She loved sex and she loved men, although making them happy, indulging their little ways, never quite filled the vacuum of the aching void within her. Unaware of the identity of her father, and abandoned by her mother, she had been brought up in an orphanage from which she had escaped to make her own way in the world. Her only assets had been her figure, which was fully developed by the age of thirteen, a lively if untutored mind, and a definite way with clothes.

Lying about her age, she had wheedled her way into service in a small hotel in Bonifacio built into the ramparts of the citadel. Making the beds and cleaning the rooms, the walls of which were covered with scarlet fabric, gave her a taste for luxury.

Although she had already been sexually abused by the superintendent of the orphanage – a situation which she accepted, as she did the physical punishment and frugal meals, as par for the course – she had no idea, until she was taken in hand first by the *plongeur*, a hot-blooded young man who sweated, stripped to the waist, cleaning dishes in the kitchens all day, and later by a middle-aged male guest (when his wife was out shopping), of the fascinating potential of her own body. Like a musical instrument, it was, she discovered, capable of playing a great many variations on the same tune.

It was from the Italian tenor, however, who had picked her up in a nightclub in Ajaccio and spirited her away to Bordeaux, where he swore to make an honest woman of her, that she had learned the true art of making love. It was only the Italians, as she was later to learn, who were capable of taking the exercise seriously. The Germans were too fastidious, the French preoccupied with their stomachs, and the English had no idea about women. The Italian tenor, a short and overweight man with a pock-marked face, had initiated her into the finer points of lovemaking, in which his artistry was consummate. Devoting himself, regardless of time, entirely to her pleasure, he had increased it tenfold by the judicious placing both of pillows and himself, while simultaneously instructing her how best to augment his own enjoyment.

When the singer had abandoned her to return to his wife and children in Paris, she had used her newly acquired knowledge to divert the afternoons of a Bordeaux jeweller. When the jeweller decamped to Abu Dhabi, he had set her up, among the chic fur shops, in the boutique in the Allées de Tourny, in gratitude for the happiness she had given him.

Claude Balard, a greedy and avaricious man, was dissatisfied with his marriage to Marie-Paule, who would have nothing to do with her husband's sadistic fantasies. He used the willing Biancarelli, herself a victim both of her abandonment by her parents and her upbringing, as a vehicle for the acting out of his hostility towards women. During their afternoon sessions, he subjected her to a variety of indignities, including tying her to the bed and spanking, which was not altogether playful.

Charles-Louis, on the other hand, isolated, self-centred, and far removed from reality, looked to the boutique owner to provide him both with the reassurance that he was loved, and the warmth and affection that had been missing from his early life. When the time came to *faire l'amour*, he could do so only when her back was turned.

Much of the time with the Baron was spent talking. This afternoon, taking Biancarelli into his confidence and using her as a sounding-board, he had told her that the forthcoming sale of Château de Cluzac had been ratified by his handshake with the South African, Van Gelder.

Biancarelli was upset that her post-prandial lover would shortly be leaving Bordeaux for Florida. She was going to miss the Baron. Despite his quick temper – which he arrogantly considered a mildly funny extravagance – and his occasional bullying, to which she paid little attention, she was fond of Charles-Louis. In the privacy of her cosy boudoir, in her non-judgemental presence, he reverted to the habits of his childhood and exhibited the touching dependency of the son she had never had.

The *appartement* above the shop in the Allées de Tourny was not Biancarelli's only confessional. The ladies of Bordeaux relied upon her for their *tailleurs* and their gowns, and she bore each one of them in mind as she attended the *prêts-à-porter*. Gossiping freely as they riffled through the garments on her rails, the ladies were secure in the knowledge that any indiscretions on their part would go no further.

Drawing back the curtain of the cubicle, Marie-Paule Balard emerged into the showroom. Biancarelli regarded her client's turquoise reflection in the mirror.

'*Magnifique!*'

It was a lie of course. Although it was not in her nature to dissemble, there were occasions on which it was necessary to be sparing with the truth both to her ladies and her lovers. She did not like to hurt people, to puncture their often frail egos. Where was the point? If she could make them feel better about themselves by perjuring herself a little, she was willing to do so.

You had, of course, to know your customers. An intuitive knowledge of psychology, of the weird and wonderful processes that made people tick, was Biancarelli's stock in trade. It accounted for her success both in business and in bed.

Little Madame Balard held the turquoise satin skirt,

which was far too long for her stunted figure, in both hands and pirouetted before the mirror.

'*Qu'est-ce que vous pensez, Madame Biancarelli?*'

Biancarelli, pins in her mouth, fell to her knees. Grasping the superfluous material at the hem of the beaded dress, which flowed on to the grey carpet, she turned it up expertly.

'*Elle vous va très bien,*' she said. It suited her.

Marie-Paule Balard smoothed her plump, beringed hands over her stomach where the turquoise satin, pulled tight, was wrinkled.

'Shall I tell you a secret?' Biancarelli's mouth was full of pins. She inclined her head. 'You've heard that Château de Cluzac is for sale?' Biancarelli nodded. 'Monsieur Balard is buying it!'

Biancarelli removed the pins from her mouth. '*Vraiment?*' She knew perfectly well it was untrue.

'Negotiations have been going on for some time between my husband and Baron de Cluzac. You mustn't mention it to a soul.'

Biancarelli, indicating that her client should turn, made the sign of the cross to indicate that her lips were sealed.

'Château owners! And what a château . . .' The little body quivered with excitement. 'Badly neglected of course. Can you imagine?'

Deciphering the sub-text, Biancarelli knew that what Madame Balard was trying to tell her was that no longer would the Balards be subjected to the intermittent myopia of the château owners at the Fêtes de la Fleur, no longer would she be humiliated, but would be able to humiliate in her turn.

The hem completed, Biancarelli stood up and put her hands on the back of the dress where the material strained over Marie-Paule's hips. She was not required to comment on Madame Balard's secret. Refraining from disillusioning her about the sale of Cluzac, she stuck a pin, as an indication to her seamstress to let it out as much as possible, into the seam of the turquoise dress.

'*Un petit centimetre ici . . .*'

It would need a great deal more than a centimetre. She hoped that there would be sufficient material to accommodate Madame Balard's ample hips, not to mention her bosom.

'*Voilà!*' She stood back.

'I'm not *quite* sure about the colour . . .'

It was time for the psychology, for the strong reassurances which would not only convince Marie-Paule that she looked svelte and elegant, but that the turquoise satin, although arguably a little tight, was the most suitable dress in the shop. She had already, on several visits over the past week, tried on all the others. The scarlet halter-neck was too revealing – her arms were not her best feature – the floral chiffon too diaphanous, and the long pleated skirt with the tailored silk jacket made her look like a lampshade. It was make-up-your-mind time, the distasteful acceptance of the fact that the hoped-for miracle would not, on this occasion, be wrought.

The recognition that she would never be Isabelle Adjani was followed, as night followed day, by the inevitable doubts.

'You haven't sold this model to anyone else?'

'Of course not.'

'It's very expensive!'

Biancarelli caressed the fabric. 'It's the finest slipper satin.'

'A small discount, perhaps . . . ?'

Biancarelli shook her head. Madame Balard did not possess the ladylike qualities of a château owner. Besides, it was too early in the season to start slashing her prices.

'Well, if you're quite, quite sure, Biancarelli, I suppose it will have to do.'

'With Madame's pearls and some satin shoes . . .' Biancarelli moved in for the kill.

'I already have a turquoise evening bag . . . ?'

'Perfect. I'm sure Monsieur Balard will like it.' She knew very well that Monsieur Balard couldn't give a damn.

'The alteration will be completed in good time?'

'But of course . . .' Biancarelli moved to the desk. 'You will bring your shoes to the fitting.'

Madame Balard tottered towards the cubicle.

'You won't tell anyone what I'm wearing? You'll keep it to yourself?'

Biancarelli was making out the bill.

'Rest assured, Madame!'

The fact that Madame Balard was wearing turquoise satin for the Fête de la Fleur was not the most earth-shattering of her secrets.

Helping her client out of the dress, so that she would not scratch herself on the pins, she averted her gaze from the salmon-pink corselet from which the pallid flesh bulged both above and below.

Suddenly aware of the silence, Biancarelli realised that outside in the street the rain had stopped. Holding the turquoise dress over her arm, she turned off the lights in the shop, which was filled with light so bright that she would have to wind down the blinds to protect the display in the window.

'The rain has stopped,' she trilled to Madame Balard, smiling and lifting her face to the sun, her life's blood, which streamed in through the window. In the café opposite, the waiters, napkins beneath their arms, were mopping the wet tables.

' "*Après la pluie le beau temps*!" '

CHAPTER TEN

After a tedious morning spent in the company of tax inspectors Monsieur Huchez and Monsieur Combe, who over the past few years had been hounding him regularly, Baron de Cluzac was glad to take his red Aston Martin DB6 MK1 sports coupé from the garage, and set out for the Convent of Notre Dame de Consolation in Toulouse to visit his sister Bernadette.

It was the custom of the *fisc* to assume, unless convinced otherwise, that in any industry profits were being made. Aware of the fact that during the eighties Bordeaux wine sales had practically doubled (one estate had earned pre-tax profits of 62 million francs), and informed of the Baron's turnover by his negociant, Claude Balard, Monsieur Huchez and Monsieur Combe had come to enquire, for the umpteenth time, after the French government's substantial slice of the cake.

The amount which, according to them, the Baron now owed the government in back-taxes was both ludicrous and astronomical. It had been an extremely irksome morning and, having seen the two *fonctionnaires* off (until their next visit), he was relieved to get out on to the open road. Having informed Bernadette of the forthcoming sale of Château de Cluzac to Philip Van Gelder, he would, in the fullness of time, get in touch with Clare.

Although his sister Bernadette, who had taken the vow of poverty, was not permitted to possess so much as a pin or a piece of paper, he had no doubt that the convent, always in need of funds, would put her share of the proceeds to good use. He wished he had similar faith in his daughter.

Thinking about her, an exercise that never failed to jack up his blood pressure, he allowed a BMW driven by a woman to overtake him, which irritated him even further. Putting his foot on the accelerator in order to regain his superior position on the road, he recalled his last meeting with Clare.

He had gone to London to attend a car auction at the Royal Air Force Museum in Hendon, where he had his eye on a chocolate brown Buick Riviera Custom Stretch with an unusual quarter vinyl roof. Having visited his tailor in Savile Row, ordered some shirts in Jermyn Street and, to his chagrin, been out-bid for the Buick, he had diplomatically left the wife of the cabinet minister (with whom he was having an affair) to attend a soirée at Number 10 with her husband, and taken his daughter for dinner at Claridge's.

The fact that Clare had marched into the foyer, where he was on his third whisky, half an hour late, wearing a duster round her head, a cheesecloth dress which had seen better days, and sneakers, and carried several iridescent green Marks and Spencer's bags, did nothing to improve his mood.

Had Charles-Louis produced a son, as big and powerful as himself, he might possibly have respected him. Contemptuous of women, whom he lusted after but regarded as sexual conveniences, he had never paid any attention his daughter's needs and feelings, never actually listened to what she had to say, and never regarded her as anything but permanently inferior.

Having categorically refused to try for a place at Oxford, all she could manage to do with the education he had bestowed upon her was to waste several years at drama school. This had resulted in a stint as stage manager, followed by several TV commercials, a couple of appearances

at the Edinburgh Festival (in fringe theatres), and a spell
as a flamenco dancer. After this she had set herself up in
a London street market as a *brocanteuse*. The truth of the
matter was that Clare was indolent. She underestimated
herself. Born into the French nobility – an advantage
which she had no hesitation in throwing away – the best
she had been able to produce by way of a boyfriend, at
least on the last occasion they had met, was a percussionist
in a band.

Sitting opposite her at his habitual table in the restaurant, where both his title and his presence ensured the most
attentive of service, Charles-Louis had almost choked over
his terrine of quail.

'A drummer!'

Accustomed to the ill-temper and impatience with which
her father had always put her down, unless of course she
happened to fit in with his plans, Clare applied herself
equably to her smoked salmon mousseline.

'Graham plays with the Orchestra of the Age of Enlight-
enment . . .'

'Never heard of it!'

Charles-Louis was saved from further comment by the
arrival of wine which he had ordered from the list on
which Château de Cluzac – thanks, he presumed, to
Claude Balard – was not included. Taking his recently
acquired half-glasses from his top pocket, he checked the
label, which, to the tutored eye, revealed the calibre of
the contents.

By reading the information clockwise, it was possible
to deduce the name of the growth, the *appellation*, the
volume, the degree of alcohol, the vintage, the exporter,
the name of the bottler, and whether the wine had been
bottled at the château – in this case the nearby Château
Talbot – where it had been produced. When he had
satisfied himself, the Baron indicated to the sommelier
that he might remove the cork from the bottle.

They sat in uncomfortable silence while Clare thought of, and immediately rejected, things to say. Her father didn't like gossip, was not an intellectual, never read books, had few political views other than a conventional affiliation with the right, was embarrassed by personal contact, and was not terribly bright. She knew that it was useless trying to recount to him anything interesting or amusing which had happened in her life, because, judging by past form, if he actually managed to let her get to the end of the story without interruption, he would insist on careful rephrasing until all the joy and spontaneity had gone out of the account.

While they waited, her father's fingers tapped impatiently on the white tablecloth in a familiar gesture. Managing to make the apparently innocent question sound like an insult, he asked Clare how old she was.

Decoding the enquiry, Clare understood that the information her father was seeking concerned not so much her age, but what she intended doing with her life.

'You know perfectly well how old I am, Papa. I shall be twenty-eight next birthday.'

'Isn't it time you settled down?'

'I have settled down . . .'

'When are you going to get married? Find yourself a decent job?'

'I've got a job, Papa. Two jobs.'

'You know very well what I mean, Clare. Not as a market trader . . .'

'Managing the Nicola Wade Gallery is not exactly a jobette! Have you any idea of the work that's involved? Dealing with the artists, with museums, with collectors, with corporate buyers, entertaining foreign clients? I do all the marketing and exhibitions, we have to work several months in advance, the printing and production – brochures, catalogues, press releases, literature, you name it – take care of the insurance, plan the advertising and artwork, cold-call the clients, tap into business from a totally different point of view. Take last night. I put on an event at just about the biggest firm of corporate lawyers in the City. I managed to persuade them that, if the retinas of their staff were stimulated by hanging art on their walls, increased brain activity would mean increased productivity . . .'

'A door-to-door salesman! Look at you.'

Charles-Louis mentally compared his daughter's appearance with that of young Olympe d'Hautebarque – with whom he had had a brief liaison – whose father's estate, Château le Maréchal, abutted his own. Thinking of Olympe's suits in pastel colours, her elegant shoes, her fashionably dressed hair and her discreet jewellery, he managed, on this occasion, to prevent himself from giving voice to his thoughts. He was, as usual, more concerned about his own gratification than with any right Clare might have to please herself. She was saved from the familiar lecture about her appearance and lifestyle, which she knew by heart, by the arrival of the main course.

The sommelier poured a little of the claret into the Baron's glass and waited anxiously until the Baron signified his approval. As soon as he had withdrawn, Clare tasted the Talbot.

'Leave it a while,' Charles-Louis ordered, indicating that she should put down her glass.

'Why?'

'You know perfectly well why.'

'I'm not bothered. Robert Browning used to put ice in his red wine.'

'Are you trying to provoke me?'

'Not at all. Did you know that Thackeray drank Burgundy with his bouillabaisse? And Keats liked *his* claret "cool out of a cellar a mile deep".'

'Where did you hear that rubbish?'

'Grandmaman . . .'

Charles-Louis refrained from commenting.

'. . . People have been drinking wine for thousands of years, Papa. There are no rules about it. Nothing written in stone. You can't even say one wine is "better" than another, any more than you can say your lamb is better than my beef. Taste is purely subjective . . .'

'There is such a thing as accumulated wisdom.'

'Grandmaman says that all that is needed is a perception of smell, a sense of taste and an eye for colour,' Clare said loftily. 'She says that for this reason, and because they're used to buying scent and soap, women are better at tasting than men. Grandmaman says I have a photographic palate.'

The evening, as the Baron recalled, had, as usual, ended decidedly coolly. Having kissed his daughter formally, he had put on his felt trilby and set out for Pall Mall and his club, while Clare, clutching her plastic carriers (which had been handed over with great ceremony by the hall porter in exchange for the Baron's *pourboire*), made for Oxford Street and her bus.

Apart from the statutory exchange of cards at Christmas – the Baron's, with its etching of Château de Cluzac, sent by his secretary – Charles-Louis had neither seen nor heard from his daughter since. Dismissing her from his mind as he approached the outskirts of Toulouse, he concentrated on his forthcoming meeting with 'Bernadette' whom he had known as a boy, as his fun-loving sister Sylvie.

He had been ten years old when the incident that had led to Sylvie's withdrawal from the world, and the abandonment of her earthly name, had taken place. Although the repercussions had shaken not only Château de Cluzac but the entire Médoc, he had had, at the time, only the vaguest of ideas what it was all about. Later he had managed to fit together the various hints and innuendoes like the pieces of a jigsaw puzzle, and come up with Sylvie's story which was never directly referred to.

Headstrong as her brother was timid – which as a child, in awe of his father, Baron Thibault, Charles-Louis had once been – Sylvie's exuberant presence had breathed life into the château. It was Sylvie who had organised treasure hunts, who had dared him to steal apples from the neighbouring orchards, who had frightened geese and chickens, and made lifelike effigies out of snow. The fun, much of which had taken place in the vineyards, where the children spent a great deal of time, ended abruptly when Sylvie was fifteen.

Charles-Louis had been confined to his room with *la rougeole*, and Sylvie, for whom the gloomy house had little interest but who loved to roam the shady woodlands, to follow the paths that wound between the trees and to clamber over walls, had taken out her bicycle to ride to the nearby Château de Marianne to visit her friend, Charlotte.

Cycling through a deserted field, she had been stopped by one of the vineyard workers, a well-built lad of eighteen who had lagged behind his fellows and had asked her if she had the time.

Getting off her bicycle, Sylvie had consulted her new watch, a birthday present from her father, which the *vigneron* had duly admired. Taking her white hand in his own earthy one the better to examine the enamel face, he had been overcome by the girl's proximity and was unable to resist pulling Sylvie into his arms. Sylvie – or so the story went, and Charles-Louis could well believe it, for even in adolescence his sister had been both extremely well-developed and curious about sex – had not objected when their lips had met in a kiss. Pulling away from Lucien, for that was the boy's name, she had bent over to retrieve her bicycle, which was lying on the ground. Her body, clearly outlined beneath her flimsy summer skirt, had inflamed Lucien, whose intelligence was decidedly limited. Grabbing Sylvie, he had flung her roughly to the ground, and, stopping only to unbutton his trousers, hurled himself on top of her.

He was, according to the story, which had, very much later and little by little, been extracted from Sylvie, extremely drunk. His breath, at any rate, reeked of alcohol. Be that as it may, he had ripped off Sylvie's clothes and subjected her to a rape so vicious, so violent and so protracted that after the alarm had been sounded and Sylvie was found by the *chef de culture*, unconscious and bleeding, she had been unable to speak for several days. When she did finally manage to communicate it was no longer Sylvie who spoke. The ordeal had robbed Charles-Louis of his sister and replaced her with a stranger from whom the *joie de vivre* had been extinguished and the will to live doused.

That Sylvie had not given in without a struggle was evident from the tattered state of the shirt with which Lucien had returned home. It had been exhibited in the court, which had found him guilty and sentenced him to ten years in prison, together with a report of injuries which included lacerations to his face and back, inflicted by Sylvie's desperate nails, and a broken nose. This last had been caused by her shoe, which she had managed to slip off and with which she had succeeded in hitting him repeatedly with all her not inconsiderable strength. It was a Pyrrhic victory.

Sylvie, putting her head round the door of his sick-room to say she was going for a cycle ride, was the last Charles-Louis had seen of his erstwhile playmate. The Sylvie who survived, to haunt the château like a shadow of her former self, was another Sylvie.

By the time she was eighteen, Sylvie had recovered, or so they all thought. Her engagement to the young Comte de Fustel de St Médard was announced. On the day of the wedding she left her beloved standing at the altar to become the bride of Christ.

Parking his red Aston Martin in the forecourt of the convent, alongside the 2CV driven by the nuns, Charles-Louis put on his jacket and tugged at the iron bell-pull which hung at the side of the oak door beneath the outsize bronze replica of the Virgin Mary.

The Sister, whose face beneath her coif regarded him through the iron grill, recognised him at once. Charles-Louis was a frequent visitor.

Greeting her respectfully as she swung open the door and motioned him to come in, he followed her down the corridor and through the cool cloisters until he came to the room set aside for the Mother Superior.

CHAPTER ELEVEN

'Loulou you are up to something.'

Despite the fact that Charles-Louis was in his fifties, and Sylvie (now Bernadette), five years his senior, she still addressed her brother by his nickname. The childish appellation made him feel that she both loved and cherished him, which was perhaps why he liked visiting Bernadette, although he could not pretend to understand what appeared to him to be his sister's futile renunciation of everything that made life worth living.

They were seated, Bernadette beneath the crucifix which occupied the place of honour, in her large, comfortable room. Shafts of coloured light from the stained-glass windows criss-crossed the Baron's grey flannel trousers and made geometric patterns on the wooden floor.

The furniture in the room was simple, but in accordance with the rank and position of the Reverend Mother. Like many who had gone before her, Bernadette would have preferred to inhabit an ordinary cell. Since she no longer belonged to herself however, but to God, her personal wishes had been set aside. Her pleasant room was accessible both to her daughters and to strangers. Holy poverty was relegated to her bedroom, situated through a door behind her writing-table, which was appointed much more simply. It had wooden shutters at the windows, and a bed with a coconut-hair mattress beneath an unframed sepia picture of Saint Theresa. Another door, behind a

thick curtain, led to the chapel where she attended the
Offices daily and on Sundays, and Festivals at the high
altar. The chapel, panelled with carved oak and hung
with rich fabric, was adorned with works of art such as
were fitting to the Saviour, whom Bernadette consulted
frequently in prayer, and who dwelt in the Tabernacle.

In his sister's pleasant office, in which Charles-Louis
was always surprised to find himself affected by the
pervasiveness of its spiritual tenor, many a doubt had
been set at rest, many a guilty conscience appeased, and
many an overburdened heart granted the consolation it
was seeking. It was here that beginners were initiated into
the sacred principles of religious observance and vocations
were confirmed. Here that the novices were received or
tactfully sent back to a more suitable existence in the
outside world. Here that itinerants were instructed in
the ways of monastic life. Here that, during the course
of a cheerful conversation, the Mother Superior not only
revealed to visitors the hidden beauty of the religious order,
but sowed in their hearts a tiny seed that might one day
bear fruit.

Looking at Charles-Louis as he sat, in his green checked
shirt and green pullover, opposite her on the wooden chair,
Bernadette noticed that he was waggling one foot, in its
hand-made shoe, in agitation. It was a sure sign that he
had something on his mind and that his visit was not
purely social.

Her little brother – she still thought of him as her
little brother – was her only contact with the family
she had renounced. Baronne Gertrude had not spoken
to her Sylvie (as she then was) since she had fled from
the altar leaving her mother to cope with the disbelieving
guests, a cornucopia of crystal and silver by way of
wedding presents, and a banquet which had taken many
months to organise. It was to have been the wedding of
the year and Baronne Gertrude, who from that day had

erased her daughter from her mind, had never forgiven her. Bernadette prayed for her soul daily.

The bridegroom she had deserted was more forgiving. She had written him a letter of apology in which she had explained that the purpose of her life, which had changed so dramatically on that summer day in the vineyard, had in a flash of revelation become clear to her. She was devoting what remained of it to helping others and to God.

The Comte, an affable if somewhat spineless young man, lured to Château de Cluzac by Baronne Gertrude for the precise purpose of forming an alliance with her increasingly reclusive daughter, had written her a long letter, which she still had. It chivalrously declared his undying love for her and affirmed the devastation she had caused in his heart, from which he was unlikely to recover. Six months later her had married her friend Charlotte.

The Order which Sylvie de Cluzac had joined, Notre Dame de Consolation, required her to keep the Rules. By the daily and hourly sacrifice of everything she loved, she vowed to make the striving after a more perfect walk with God the one object of her life. As a novice, she had had her waist-length hair cut short and she had put on the scapular of penitence, the cord of chastity and the sandals of obedience, although she had not then been required to separate herself from the world either by dress or by enclosure.

When she finally entered the Order, kneeling before the altar to take her farewell of earthly joys, the sisters had come, with lighted tapers, to kiss and embrace their new sister. '*The wise virgins took oil in their lamps; they went in with Him to the marriage, and the door was shut.*' The chant was followed by the symbolic slamming of the door, a sound that would ring for ever in her ears.

Sister Bernadette Magdalena de la Charité, for this was the name she had been given, had henceforth devoted herself to good works and manual labour. The life she had chosen expressed the subjection and penance of the body, humbled the spirit and taught her to follow the example of her Lord Jesus Christ.

In the convent of Notre Dame de Consolation, the sisters were not ashamed to work in the house and in the garden, to hew and carry wood, to make hay and to dig potatoes. Following the example of St Margaret, Dominican nun and daughter of King Bela of Hungary, they swept the convent, washed the dishes, cleaned out the dirtiest places, and took upon themselves the very lowliest of offices.

Bernadette's particular occupation was the administration of the kitchen garden, an aptitude for which she had learned from Monsieur Louchemain (who was responsible for supplying the Château with vegetables at Cluzac), and running a restaurant for the homeless, La Couronne d'Epines, the crown of thorns, in the old quarter of Toulouse. The restaurant was supplied, at her insistence, with barrels of *presse* wine by her brother Charles-Louis.

Much as Bernadette enjoyed her work in the restaurant, however, she had no desire whatever to return to the world. It always surprised her to discover how many discontented people there were, out there in the street, and it was with a feeling of relief that she came back to the convent.

Bernadette's thoughts were interrupted by a light tap at her door. As the Reverend Mother Superior, she held responsibilities not only to God and to the poor and needy, giving them food and drink and clothing them in winter. She devoted herself also, day and night, to her children in the convent, consoling them in sickness, supporting them in their struggles, and closing their eyes at the hour of death. At their service night and day, she was, like any other mother, frequently interrupted to share in their joys and their sorrows, their labour and privations.

She bid the supplicant enter. It was the Prioress with the day's post which, with downcast eyes, she laid upon

Bernadette's table. Later, when Charles-Louis had gone, she would read it out to the Revered Mother and together they would deliberate as to the answers. Business matters and requests for aid, which were granted, or refused with regret (if the sisters were overburdened), would all be dealt with. There might be letters from aspirants begging for admission to the Order about whom enquiries must be made, accounts to be looked at, visitors to accommodate. Decisions could not be made without permission from the Mother Superior, who had to correct abuses, preserve order and maintain the due observance of the Rule. In the course of a single hour, she might be called upon to bestow a blessing on a sister setting out to visit a sick person, approve sketches and designs submitted from the artists' studio, give strangers leave to look over the convent, bestow permission on students to spend a few days in spiritual exercise, counsel a novice, hear medical reports of the sick who had been visited, and monitor the progress of a sister in the infirmary.

When the Prioress had gone, leaving a pile of letters such as would have daunted any business executive, and she was alone with her brother, Bernadette addressed Charles-Louis.

'What do you want to tell me, Loulou?'

'What makes you think that I have come to tell you anything?'

'You never could keep a secret. Remember when we used to play *cache-cache*? When it was my turn to find Victorine or Charlotte you always told me where they were hiding. I only had to look at your face.'

'I am selling the château.'

Bernadette crossed herself.

'*Seigneur Dieu*. Château de Cluzac? You're not serious?'

'I'm selling up. Going to Florida. Investing in orange

groves. Miles and miles of them. They're quite a sight. I wish you could see them.'

'I don't have to go to Florida to see the beauty of God's creation.'

'You'd see another aspect of it.'

'Am I lacking as a person because I haven't been to Florida? What's her name?'

'Whose name?'

'It has to be a woman.'

'Laura Spray.'

'Does she know about Viola?'

'I'm working on Viola.'

'Have you found a buyer for Cluzac?'

'A South African.' Charles-Louis took some papers from his briefcase. 'I shall need your *pouvoir*.'

'How much money will there be?'

'Enough. What had you in mind?'

'A new roof for the chapel. When it rains we have to put buckets behind the altar. What about my homeless, Loulou? Where will I get their wine?'

'I shall speak to Van Gelder.'

'Do you remember Miss Bloo?' Bernadette's face had taken on a faraway look.

Charles-Louis cast his mind back to their English governess.

'Muffins . . .'

'And Oxford marmalade.'

'I can still hear Maman's voice: "Don't go in the billiard room, the floor has been waxed." "Papa is in the library." And when she taught you to say, "May I have this dance?" before we went to a party. Do you remember the Mass of St Hubert before the hunt, when the priest blessed the forest and the pack? Little did I know . . .'

'And old Monsieur Lebrecht . . .'

'. . . who came to wind the clocks.'

'And the kennels and the Orangery . . .'

'And swimming from the landing stage . . .'

'Do you remember the time you pushed me in the river? *Et l'heure du gouter* . . .'

'Chocolate cake and *fanchonnettes* with redcurrant jelly on the top.'

'Shall I tell you a secret? The only longing I still have regularly is to walk through the vineyards . . .' She caught Charles-Louis' eye as they recalled what had taken place there and was never spoken of.

That evening of long ago, when the setting sun had cast long shadows from the rows of ordered vines, that had changed the course of her life, was never far from her mind. A lifetime of penitence would not assuage the guilt. The incident had become the leitmotiv of her thoughts ever since. Had the event taken place yesterday, rather than forty years ago, the memory of it could not have been more vivid.

She blamed no one but herself. At fifteen she had been preoccupied both with unbidden thoughts and the increasing unfamiliarity of her own body. Satisfying the burgeoning desires, which she regarded as shameful, through her forbidden reading purloined from Baron Thibault's library, she looked upon the world with wonder and in particular upon the opposite sex. She had noticed Lucien in the vineyards. Passing by on her bicycle she had surreptitiously admired his luxuriant black hair, his strong arms, his deep barrel of a chest which she had imagined pressed hard to hers. Looking up as she passed, on more than one occasion, their eyes had met.

When he waylaid her on that fateful evening she had known very well that it was not the time that he wanted from her. She had *wanted* him to kiss her. An unfamiliar essence emanated from his body and created chaos in her own. Immediately he had touched her she had become frightened. Her fear had communicated itself to the boy. What happened afterwards, and which was seared into her memory, had been beyond her control but she had been the instigator. It was because of her guilty desires that a young man, not all that bright, a young man who needed not punishment but tender loving care, had been deprived of his freedom, that he had been locked away.

'What does Clare have to say?' Bernadette dismissed the recurring thought.

'Clare's not interested in Cluzac.'

'Nonetheless . . .'

'All in good time.' Charles-Louis indicated the papers. 'These must be signed in the presence of a notary. I can arrange it if you wish.'

'That won't be necessary.'

Charles-Louis picked up his briefcase. There was a young lady in the Place St Georges who was expecting his visit.

'Still up to no good?' Bernadette said.

Charles-Louis blushed as his sister divined his thoughts.

'I shall pray for you.'

Charles-Louis kissed her affectionately. 'Save your breath.'

At the same moment as Charles-Louis folded himself into his Aston Martin and drove away from the convent, his daughter, six hundred miles away, was leaving Millington's in Albemarle Street. Clare had never met Bernadette. Curious about her aunt, she had from time to time tackled Baronne Gertrude on the subject, but Grandmaman had refused to be drawn.

'There are matters best not talked about,' Baronne Gertrude said. 'Things better left alone.'

That Bernadette followed Clare's progress, that she always enquired fondly from Charles-Louis about her well-being, her niece had no idea. She imagined the Reverend Mother, whose name she was not allowed to mention, as an austere and distant figure of unshakeable faith and devoid of doubts, desires and insecurities; as someone who had found God, rather than someone in constant search of him; as someone who lit up the dark lives of the poor and sick with a self-righteous sense of purpose.

In the Neal Street Gallery, to which she had hastened with the result of her meeting with Michael Millington, Clare found Nicola, who was about to hang an exhibition of naïf nudes, surrounded by naked women. She had the telephone receiver tucked beneath her chin, and was trying to eat a smoked-salmon bagel from a brown paper bag.

'For you.' Taking a bite from the bagel, she handed the receiver to Clare. 'Kettle's Yard.'

When Clare had finished reassuring the curator of the Cambridge museum about a tour she was setting up for Moti Aron, an Israeli artist, in the New Year – they always worked at least six months ahead – Nicola crumpled the empty brown paper bag and threw it accurately into the bin.

'Well?' She was dying to hear the results of the meeting.

'Which do you want first, the good news or the bad news?'

'I'll take the bad.'

'Millington's needs completely gutting. I don't think the old boy has touched it since he took the lease. We'd need a budget for renovation. Rewiring, replumbing, lighting, new loo, new kitchenette, additional staff. I don't think we'd be able to manage with one part-time student. Then there's the rent, Eighteen K a year payable quarterly with rent reviews at two and seven years, and rates. The rates will blow your mind, the premium on the lease – fifty thousand pounds is going to go nowhere . . .'

'OK. I get the message. What's the good news?'

Clare stared at a particularly unattractive nude whose pudendum was displayed in graphic detail and was putting her off her stride. She turned the canvas towards the wall.

'I've told Michael Millington we'll take it.'

Nicola's jaw dropped.

'Where are we going to find fifty thousand pounds?'

'Easy. My share of Château de Cluzac.'

'It's only a *rumour*, Clare. How can you be sure that your father's really going to sell?'

'I can't. I'm going to Bordeaux to find out.'

CHAPTER TWELVE

On the strength of the (unsubstantiated) news about Château de Cluzac, Clare had agreed to purchase the remainder of Michael Millington's lease, and had shaken hands on the deal. She had managed to get round Jamie to reschedule what was supposed to be his study leave, and to come with her to Bordeaux.

Hiring a car at Mérignac, they had headed northwards on the Route des Châteaux, which ran up the eastern side of the triangular peninsula between the Atlantic Ocean and the Gironde river, known as the Médoc, the largest and most important red wine district of Bordeaux.

The laws of Appellation d'Origine Contrôlée which divided the area into eight, concerned the suppression of fraud, and applied to cheese and chickens as well as to wine. Local wine-growers were restricted to certain grape varieties, were required to plant their vines at specified distances, prune according to regulations and pick only when the authorities allowed them to. Any failure to adhere to the AOC system – which was France's pride and joy – and their wine would be demoted to substandard *vin de table*.

On either side of the road, eye-catching signs – Château Gloria's in the form of a mammoth wine bottle – invited visitors to tour the cellars of such celebrated châteaux as Giscours, Prieuré-Lichine and Palmer, as well as to taste their wines.

Driving through the neat vineyards in which the vines, arms extended, straddled support wires stretched taut between wooden pickets, Clare heard the sound of hammer upon wood as they were knocked into the ground, which had heralded the spring in her childhood.

'According to Grandmaman, there's no better sight than a well-kept Bordeaux vineyard.'

'I must say they're pretty impressive. What are those things for?'

Taking her eyes momentarily off the road, Clare followed Jamie's pointing finger.

'The blue tags mark the young vines. Bunches from vines less than five years old aren't allowed to be included in the *grand vin* . . .'

'Look out!'

Clare slammed on the brakes, stopping short of a flock of sheep which, beneath the watchful eye of the shepherd, were making their bleating way towards them.

'"*L'agneau de Pauillac revient tous les ans à la saison du renouveau.*" They come back to graze every year.'

'No wonder Grandmaman is so fond of her gigot.'

'Wait till you taste the Pauillac lamb, fed on their mother's milk and cooked on a salamander.'

Jamie stroked the coarse grey wool of a friendly sheep which had put its inquisitive nose through the open window.

'I've decided to become a vegetarian.'

Setting off again, they passed through the sleepy villages, Arsac, Arcins, Cussac, and the now dull flatlands of mostly mediocre wine which lay between Margaux and Beychevelle. Keeping to the road, which wound its way north until it reached St Julien, which boasted more *crus classés* than any other commune in the Médoc, Clare, who was nodding off in the heat of the midday sun, almost missed her narrow turning.

Pulling up sharply, she swung the car into a minor

road, narrowly missing a large Citroën in which sat two black-clad figures, which was coming towards them.

'Château de Cluzac!' Clare put an excited arm round Jamie's shoulders.

'Where's the sign?'

'There isn't one. Papa wouldn't dream of putting up a *pancarte*. There's no way he would allow the public – not a category in which he includes himself, incidentally – anywhere near his patch.'

As they followed the bumpy track for half a mile, she experienced a sinking feeling, like Alice falling down the rabbit-hole. She swung the car round again, this time into a long drive bordered on either side by birch trees. The naked trunks faced each other, like chorus girls about to burst into song.

Overcome by jumbled recollections of things long past, she idled beneath the ramparts and brought the hired Peugeot to a halt, next to the Baron's Aston Martin, in the shadows of a forbidding castle of crenellated walls and octagonal towers circumvented by a neglected moat.

'You've got to be kidding!' Unfolding his lanky frame from the car, his shirt stuck to his back with perspiration, Jamie, his hands on his hips, looked round him with amazement.

A large red setter bounded across the sunlit courtyard, closely followed, down the steps of the château, by his master, Charles-Louis, Baron de Cluzac.

'*Viens ici!*'

At the sound of the Baron's imperious voice, the dog, his bushy tail waving, stopped dead in his tracks.

'Rougemont,' Clare said. 'He follows Papa everywhere.'

Approaching her father, Clare kissed him dutifully.

'This is Jamie Spence-Jones, Papa . . .'

'How do you do, Sir?' Meeting the Baron's appraising eyes, which were level with his own, Jamie held out his hand.

'*Enchanté!*' The Baron's frigid tone belied his greeting.
'Jamie and I are engaged to be married . . .'

The Baron was saved from further comment by the appearance on the steps of an emaciated blonde whom Clare took at first to be the same age as herself. She sported an immaculate linen trouser-suit – the cream jacket of which was draped with apparent nonchalance around her shoulders – and had expensively streaked hair, which was tied into a ponytail secured with a black ruffle more suited to a teenager.

As the Baron escorted his elegant companion down the steps, Clare, who had been about to open the boot of the car, realised that although the woman had obviously been extensively nipped and tucked, closer inspection of her neck proclaimed her to be considerably older than she looked.

'Laura, this is my daughter, Clare and . . .' his voice trailed insolently off.

'Jamie Spence-Jones,' Clare said clearly.

'Mrs Laura Spray, from Florida.'

'Welcome to Château de Cluzac.' Laura held out her hand.

Clare barely touched the extended fingers with their red tapered nails. Noticing a lemon marquise diamond of at least twenty carats on Laura Spray's other hand Clare had no difficulty guessing why her father had been pestering Viola for a divorce.

'I've heard so much about you.' Laura took charge of the situation.

'I'll bet you have,' Clare muttered beneath her breath as she reached for her duffle bag.

'Now, if you'll excuse us, your father was about to show me his new hunter. Sidonie will look after you. Luncheon . . .' She squinted at the tiny face of her watch. 'Is sharp at one.'

Arm in arm, watched by an open-mouthed Clare, and

followed by an obedient Rougemont, the couple disappeared, without a backward glance, in the direction of the stables.

In the cool entrance hall of the château, to the contrasting gloom of which their eyes, slow to accommodate, gradually became accustomed, Clare's real welcome was waiting. Standing on the black-and-white tiles, all of them worn and some of them badly chipped, like the faithful servant in a Flemish painting, Sidonie held out her arms to greet her wayward child. Her pleasure at seeing her erstwhile charge, who had not set foot in Château de Cluzac since she was an adolescent, could be gauged by the unbidden tears that sprung to her eyes and by the suffocating warmth of her embrace.

When Sidonie had released her, Clare introduced Jamie.

'*C'est mon fiancé*!'

Sidonie dropped a little curtsey.

'*Monsieur*.'

'You can call him Jamie.' Clare knew that Sidonie would do no such thing.

'*Monsieur Jamie*.' Sidonie took Clare's bag from her. She looked doubtfully at Jamie. '*Les chambres sont déjà prêtes* . . .'

'One room will do.' Clare laughed. 'I want to show Jamie my old bedroom before lunch. I want to show him everything . . . Good grief, what's that?' She stopped at the grotesque sight of an enormous urn of formally arranged, oversize flowers, such as usually graced the foyer of a grand hotel. It stood at the foot of the stone staircase, with its iron balustrade, which was lined with oil paintings of her ancestors.

'*Il y a eu beaucoup de changements, ici*,' Sidonie muttered, trying unsuccessfully to wrest Jamie's bag from him. '*Quels changements, Mademoiselle Clare!*'

Sidonie insisted on unpacking for her as if she were still seven years old. Leaving her in the first-floor bedroom she had prepared – with its walnut *armoire*, damp patches on the ceiling, old-fashioned wash-stand, and four-poster bed – Clare, unable to wait, climbed the narrow steps of the tower with Jamie in her wake.

Opening the door to a dusty octagonal room with the peeling and faded remains of fleur-de-lys wallpaper, in which a collection of broken chairs that would have fetched a small fortune in Portobello Road seemed to have been abandoned, she crossed the threadbare carpet and flung open the windows.

The sea of vines which greeted her and which sloped down to the river – vines, in order to thrive, should be able to look at the water – brought an unexpected lump to her throat.

'Not exactly your Notting Hill.' She leaned back against Jamie who, putting his arms round her breasts, slipped her vest-top from her shoulder.

'Jamie! It's almost lunchtime.'

'*Qu'est ce que tu préfères, manger ou faire l'amour?*'

She was torn between the Scylla of her father's wrath and the Charybdis of Jamie's manifest desire. As her long sack-cloth skirt fell to the floor together with Jamie's chinos, his damp shirt, the gilt clock on the marble chimney-piece, flanked by its garniture, chimed the three-quarter hour. Clouds of dust rose from the narrow bed – which was covered with a hand-worked quilt – as Clare's view of the ceiling, with its plaster rose from which hung a drunken lampshade and the fabric-covered screen behind which she had washed as a child and the crucifix above the bed where she had offered up her prayers, revolved.

Afterwards, the silence in the room wrapped them in its somnolent pall. The clock chimed fussily. *Une heure et quart.*

Reaching for his trousers, Jamie kissed her naked shoulder.

'I don't think your father likes me. What am I going to talk to him about?'

'I wouldn't worry about it. It's not possible to have a conversation with him, unless you happen to be an aristocrat or a gillie . . .' Clare scrambled into her clothes and ran her fingers through her hair. 'He can't seem to get to grips with the middle classes.'

Charles-Louis and Laura Spray were waiting for them in the library. There had obviously been words. The Baron looked pointedly at the clock.

In the *salle-à-manger*, at the table set with its antique *couverts*, monogrammed glasses, and silver salt cellars garnished with miniature clusters of grapes, Clare made for her usual place opposite her father, to be pipped at the post, as in a silent game of musical chairs, by Laura Spray. Meeting her father's eye she moved away grudgingly and sat down facing Jamie.

'*Qu'est ce que vous faites dans la vie*, Jones?' Attempting to discomfort him, the Baron, who never spoke other than in English when English speakers were around, addressed Jamie in French.

'I'm a surgeon, Sir. At the John Radcliffe Hospital in Oxford . . .'

'I know where the John Radcliffe is.'

'My brother's a paediatrician at the Cedars of Lebanon.' Laura unfolded her napkin and nodded to Sidonie to serve the hors d'oeuvres, a dish of avocado fans, tomato with basil leaves, and slivers of poached fresh salmon.

'Jamie specialises in orthopaedics.'

'*Un charpentier!*' A carpenter.

Clare ignored the insult. 'He's an accredited Senior Registrar and is applying for consultant posts . . .'

'*Madame d'abord!*' Interrupting her, the Baron frowned at Sidonie as she approached Clare with the hors d'oeuvre dish.

Tight-lipped, Sidonie backtracked and offered the dish

first to Laura Spray. Laura made the servant wait while she pushed aside the fish and helped herself to a sparrow's portion of tomato and a few leaves of what she referred to as 'baysil'.

'I had stones in my gall bladder.' She put a confidential hand on Jamie's arm. 'They showed them to me on the ultrasound.'

'Did you have them removed?' Jamie asked politely.

'Keyhole surgery. You can hardly see the scar. I was out of the hospital in four days . . .' Laura broke off in horror as Charles-Louis reached for the bread.

'Charles!' she removed the bread-basket and smiled sweetly at Clare. 'I've put your father on a diet. No bread with main meals. French beans, tomato, Swiss chard, eggplant, celery, cauliflower, side salad . . . Bread means nothing but trouble.'

Remembering the oppressive meals of her childhood at which she had been afraid to speak, Viola had curbed her ready tongue and the servants had trembled, Clare could not believe that anyone at her father's table was actually telling him what to do.

She wondered at the hold that Laura Spray – who had passed on the Cluzac wine with its facsimile of the medieval château on its label, and was sticking to water – seemed to have over him.

Looking round the dining-room, which had once been the armoury of the fortress, she noticed that the familiar faded curtains, which had been at the deeply recessed windows ever since she could remember, had been replaced with stiff floral chintz, vibrant with poppies, which trailed on the floor and was tied back with co-ordinating braid. She addressed Laura Spray.

'What have you done with the Toile de Jouy?'

'Threw them in the garbage. They were in rags.'

'Is it true that you're selling Cluzac, Papa?'

Laura and Charles-Louis exchanged glances. Sidonie's face, as she waited to clear the plates, was impassive.

'What gave you that idea?'
'I met Big Mick Bly in Bond Street . . .'
The Baron glanced at Jamie.
'I suggest we discuss it later.'
'Jamie and I are getting married, Papa.'
'And you, Clare, are a de Cluzac. A fact you seem to have forgotten.'

CHAPTER THIRTEEN

'What do you think of the French intervention in Rwanda?' the Baron asked Jamie over the roast duck from which under the eagle eye of Laura Spray he removed every morsel of skin, feeding them to Rougemont who, judging by the way he licked his lips, must have thought that it was Christmas.

'It's a war between classes . . .'

'Nonsense!'

'An attempt to eradicate an entire caste . . .'

'Genocide?'

'It's as near to genocide as makes no difference.'

'The consequence of ethnic chauvinism is not necessarily genocide. The French army . . .'

'With all due respect, Sir, the French army have behaved atrociously . . .'

'They have gone in to *protect* the Hutu.'

'Who have butchered seven hundred and fifty Tutsis in the last three months with the help of French arms! It's a good thing Rwanda has no ocean border or we'd have the Americans in there as well.'

'It's the biggest humanitarian disaster since the United Nations came into being . . .' Laura Spray had been reading her *Herald Tribune*.

Jamie looked up sharply. 'What about the millions of Chinese under Chairman Mao?'

'More than one million refugees have fled to Zaire.'

Laura Spray chose to ignore the interruption. 'Surely, Jamie, you don't propose we just leave them to starve?'

'Unfortunately, Mrs Spray, foreign aid is not always the best answer. Particularly in Africa. Look at the Sudan, look at Ethiopia . . .'

'Perhaps Dr Jones has another solution, Laura.'

'"*Mr*",' Clare said. 'And anyway his name's Jamie.'

'The only realistic solution is to send the refugees home. It's up to the RPF government to restore peace between the Hutu and the Tutsi. It cannot be done by the UN, by the South Africans, by Save the Children, or by the Red Cross. First aid is charity. Second aid is dependency. Third aid is war . . .'

The conversation was like a table-tennis match during which Jamie gave as good as he got, refusing to let the Baron wrong-foot him. It continued until the plates were cleared away and the cheese was brought in, accompanied by glistening salad leaves in an oversized Limoges bowl, which brought back memories of mealtimes which, like the present one, Clare fervently wished to be over.

The pudding, a strawberry sponge which miraculously concealed Sidonie's vanilla ice-cream, was waved away with a disapproving shudder by Laura Spray, who pointedly helped herself to two grapes.

In the green salon, with its neo-Renaissance furniture, its family portraits and woven carpets, their design of branches now threadbare, into which would fit the whole of Nicola's flat, Laura Spray presided over the coffee pot.

Jamie, who, like the Baron, never sat when he could stand, wandered round the room examining the pictures. He peered at a sombre painting of a brown-and-white retriever holding a pheasant in its mouth.

'Haven't I seen that somewhere before?'

'Possibly,' the Baron said. 'The copy is in the Louvre.'

Putting her lips to her tiny porcelain cup, Clare almost choked.

'Decaffeinated. Special Brew,' Laura Spray said. 'I bring it from Florida . . .'

Clare was saved from further comment by the chiming of the monkey clock, a present from Baron Thibault to her grandmother.

Swallowing his Special Brew, Charles-Louis replaced his cup on the silver tray. Beatrice Biancarelli would be waiting.

'If you'll excuse me.' He looked at Laura.

'Of course, Charles. I'm going to take a nap.'

'I need to talk to you, Papa.' Clare put down her undrunk coffee.

'Later.' Charles-Louis looked evasive.

'It won't take long.'

Leaving Jamie, his head on one side, to look at the books in the ebony bookcases, which were lined with yellowing ivory, Clare followed Charles-Louis into the adjacent room, where he liked to work. He stamped his foot imperiously on the floor whenever he needed his English secretary, Petronella Townsend, whose office was situated directly below. Sitting down at the long table, on which was a white ring-file bearing a Château de Cluzac wine label, and putting the width of it between himself and Clare, he waited for his daughter to speak.

'What exactly is going on, Papa?'

'What is it you would like to know?'

'Firstly, what is that woman doing here?'

'I see your manners have not improved. Laura and I are getting married.'

'Excuse me. I thought you were married to my mother.'

'Arrangements are being made.'

'Those dreadful curtains! She will make a pig's ear of Cluzac . . .'

The Baron let the insult pass.

'We shall not be living at Cluzac. I intend to make my home in Florida.'

'So you *are* selling Château de Cluzac?'

Casting a surreptitious glance at his watch, the Baron nodded impatiently.

'Don't you think, Papa, that I should have been consulted?'

'Consulted! *Mon Dieu!*'

'I do own twenty-four per cent of the estate.'

'You would have been informed in due course.'

'Have you "informed" Tante Bernadette?'

'She is delighted. A new roof for the chapel, more money for her riff-raff, her bills will be paid . . .'

'Who is buying the château?'

'A South African.'

'Does he not have a name?'

'Van Gelder. Philip Van Gelder.' The Baron was irritable. He was anxious to get away. 'Does it make any difference what his name is?'

'It's a matter of courtesy.'

'You'll get your share of the money. A not inconsiderable amount. I trust you are not going to let that carpenter get his hands on it.'

'Jamie is a *surgeon*, Papa. He is a Fellow of the Royal College of Surgeons. He also has an MD . . .'

'How long do you intend staying?'

'Jamie has to be back next week.'

'The notary is drawing up the *acte de vente*. It will be ready in a few days. We shall need your signature. It's the Fête de la Fleur on Saturday. At Château Laurent. The *arrivistes*. You and Jones will be my guests . . .' As he stood up, the Baron's eyes appraised Clare, from the vest-top, which was slipping from her thin shoulders, to her sneakers.

'*Va chez Biancarelli*. Get yourself some decent clothes. Tell her to send me the bill.'

When her father had gone, Clare pulled the ring-binder, marked confidential, towards her and opened it. Château de Cluzac. Information Memorandum. 'The sole purpose of this memorandum is to assist recipients in deciding whether they wish to proceed with an investigation with a view to making an offer for Château de Cluzac . . .' She flicked over the pages.

Château de Cluzac is situated in the district of St Julien Beychevelle in France, approximately 32 km (20 miles) north of the city of Bordeaux. The property consists of Château de Cluzac (the castle itself) and the vineyards. The castle, which has four turrets, one in each corner, is impressive. It was erected in 1661 and major renovations were carried out in 1871. The interior has a wonderful atmosphere and, although in need of decoration . . .

The understatement of the year. Pulling up a chair, Clare sat down at the table.

. . .The size and splendour of the castle means that it could be used for many different purposes such as education (corporate training, seminars etc), wine tasting, or it could even be divided into several attractive, spacious flats. In addition to the castle there are a number of other buildings . . .

Curious to see how her father had been managing the estate, Clare turned to the summary of the wine.

Château de Cluzac produces and sells wine under her own name which can use the classification Appellation d'Origine Contrôlée (AOC). Château de Cluzac has produced wine since 1650 and is one of the largest properties in the Médoc. Annual production is targeted at 420 thousand bottles which are sold throughout Europe and in a few overseas markets . . .

Now thoroughly absorbed, she studied the income state-
ments and the breakdown of the costs, which revealed that
the Château de Cluzac wine seemed to have been sold at
an extremely modest price for several years. As far as she
could see, no profits had been recorded. It was hardly
suprising that all she had received from her father by
way of dividends were a few yearly cases of wine. In
the circumstances, although the château – according to
Big Mick Bly – seemed to have attracted a great deal of
attention, she assumed that her father was extremely lucky
to have found, in Philip Van Gelder, a suitable buyer.

Replacing the document exactly where she had found
it, she went to rescue Jamie from Laura Spray, who was
giving him a detailed account of her laparoscopic surgery.
She wanted to show him round the estate and introduce
him to Albert Rochas, the *chef de culture*, who looked
after the vineyards.

The Rochas family, like many others of the Baron's
staff, had served the de Cluzacs for several decades. Albert
himself had been born on the estate. Starting work as
an apprentice, he had later had become a fully fledged
vigneron, and finally the all-important *chef de culture*,
with overall responsibility for the seventy hectares of
Chateau de Cluzac vines. Now in his early sixties, he
looked forward to retiring peacefully on the land.

The *chef de culture*'s seasonal work, on which the crop
depended, began on 1st November and ended on 31st
October. First came the pruning of the vines. This was
a delicate operation, which consisted in cutting off the
twigs, or *sarments*, which would later be collected by the
women for their fires or to give to friends in a traditional
social gesture. Keeping those branches that would bear the
next year's grapes, Albert prepared the wood that would
be the framework for the following year.

The pruning called for a sharp eye. It occupied most of
the winter months, and was followed by the trimming of

the vines and the replacing of the pickets. It accounted for only one of the sixty-odd times the entire vineyard was gone through in the course of a single year. Albert Rochas, and his team of twenty *vignerons*, also had to take cuttings to be used in the vine nursery, fight an ongoing battle against couch grass and attend to the hedging and ditching and shifting of earth at the end of the vine rows. They had to find precious time for ploughing, spraying against fungal diseases (at least seven times a season), weeding – particularly important during the summer months when the weeds extracted precious water and nutritious elements from the soil – and the myriad other vineyard jobs which varied from year to year.

The quality of the wine produced at Château de Cluzac, as at any other château, depended on four vital elements: the climate, the soil, the vine and human skill. If the first two were right, the difference between a *vin médiocre* and a *grand vin* ultimately evolved upon selecting the correct *cépage*, or grape variety, based upon detailed soil analysis and the climate in each part of the vineyard. In a temperate climate, such as Bordeaux, the vines had to counteract the vagaries of frost, hail and summer rain, as well as minor deviations brought about by the sea and moon. The grape variety had to match the style of wine eventually required, and remain within the choices legally permitted. In most châteaux this vital selection was made by the owners. At Château de Cluzac, in the face of the Baron's lack of commitment to his vineyards, it was made by the *chef de culture*, to whom fell the equally important task of deciding at which precise moment to start picking the grapes.

To be a winemaker in the Gironde, which in winters of severe frost had seen the mercury fall to a catastrophic minus twenty degrees centigrade, needed nerves of steel. Albert Rochas, renowned throughout the Médoc for his cool head and his sound judgement, was no slouch in that direction.

Taking off his cap at Clare's approach, Albert, whose rugged good looks were worthy of a movie star, was inspecting the vines for the enemy in the shape of insects, mites and moths.

Greeting Clare in the rough accent of south-west France, he appraised her companion, every detail of whose appearance he would relay, over his evening *soupe*, to his wife Matilde.

Albert had known Clare since her birth. It was he who had built her her first swing and allowed her, under his supervision, to help with the *vendange*, although her father had strictly forbidden her to fraternise with the grape-pickers. Clare was at her ease with the handsome *chef de culture*, regarding him almost as an affectionate uncle. She got the impression that Albert was not his normal, cheerful self.

Speaking to him in French, Clare introduced Jamie and enquired how things were going in the vineyards, which were not only Albert's pride and joy but his *raison d'être*.

'*Ça va.*'

'*Et les vendanges?*' She asked about the recent harvests.

'*Exceptionelles!*'

'*Et cette année?*'

Albert shrugged. He did not wish to tempt a providence on which he was dependent.

'*Si nous n'avons pas de pluie. Pas de coulure . . .*'

'When it rains during the flowering season, the petals drop, the grapes don't always set, and you get the patter of tiny grapes,' Clare explained to Jamie.

'*. . . pas de millerandage.*'

'Poor flowering conditions means faulty fertilisation of the grapes. *Comment va Matilde?*' she asked Albert, releasing a catalogue of daily inconveniences which stemmed from the inroads of Matilde's arthritis. '*Et comment vont vos enfants?*' she said when the saga was finished.

'*Ils vont bien.*'

'*Avez-vous des petits enfants?*'

Albert proudly admitted to seven grandchildren. It was the first time he had smiled.

Pointing to a space, the width of several vines, many more of which she had noticed, Clare said, 'What are all these gaps?'

Albert returned to his examination of the flowering vines on which the grapes would eventually appear. Clearly she had said the wrong thing.

'The vines were old . . .'

'Why don't you replace them?'

'Your father does not wish them replaced.'

'Have you asked him?'

Albert nodded.

'What did he say?'

'No mon-nay! No mon-nay! Monsieur does not allow me to buy the right treatment for the grapes. *Excusez moi, Mademoiselle, Monsieur. Je dois continuer mon travail.*'

Looking back at Albert as, leaving him to his work, she continued on her walk with Jamie, Clare had the uneasy feeling that all was not well at Cluzac, as if a cloud were were hanging over it. She wondered if it was Laura Spray.

Taking Clare's arm and matching his step to hers, Jamie looked at the tidy soil, at the vines – as carefully tended as if they were in a garden – which stretched in their symmetric rows into the green distance.

'All this to make a few bottles of grape juice!'

CHAPTER FOURTEEN

The honour of hosting the annual Fête de la Fleur, which was held in June, and the September Ban de Vendanges, which enabled the wine-growers and people from the trade to get together and for which everyone took tables to entertain their guests, was always keenly fought over. The château owners were not only anxious to celebrate their good fortune in living in Bordeaux – the largest quality wine-producing area in the world, which generated 12 billion france in turnover, supported 13,000 producers and 550 wine merchants and brokers – but vied with each other in using the occasion to cultivate the market. Although the form taken by the fêtes varied from château to château, the festivities rarely ended before dawn.

Last year the honour of holding the Fête de la Fleur had fallen to Médaillac, which had mounted an oriental fantasy in which champagne flowed, tropical palms sprouted from the floor of the cellars, orchids were flown in from Asia – as were the musicians and entertainers – and guests from all over the world had danced the night away in what was, by day, a prosaic bottle store. It was an extremely hard act to follow.

For Marie-Paule Balard, the Fête de la Fleur marked the high spot in her calendar. This year most of all. It was to be the last, or so she thought, that the Balards, Claude, Marie-Paule herself, their son Harry, and their daughter

Christiane, would make their appearance as a family of negociants rather than château owners.

Year after year, firmly corseted, painstakingly groomed, her figure constrained by her evening gown as if by a mould into which it had been poured (and overflowed), hung about with the family diamonds (her family), which she had warily carried home from their hibernation in the bank, her plump feet tight in their satin shoes, her dimpled hands manicured, her hair firmly laquered, she would sit at the round table. Holding tightly to the anchor of her evening bag, and smiling for all she was worth, she would make animated conversation with those on either side of her, while inside she seethed at the sight of the svelte women in their little black numbers – which scarcely covered their *poitrines* and often did not reach to their knees – who occupied the *places d'honneur*.

Like many others in Bordeaux, Marie-Paule Balard disliked her husband, a bombastic man, frequently overcome with rage and always on the lookout for a scapegoat upon whom to vent it. Since it was his wife, more often than anyone else, who was around when the paroxysms of anger overtook him, it was on Marie-Paule's long-suffering head that the negociant's wrath generally fell.

Selling luxury drinks had always been as much a matter of social contacts as of the inherent quality of the product. It was she who was blamed when visiting importers and foreign visitors were not entertained assiduously enough, or if the hospitality she bestowed upon them was not up to standard and they were allowed to slip through the net. It was her fault – despite the fact that she was always ready long before Claude – if they were late for dinner or the opera, if it rained unexpectedly, if they took a wrong turning in the car, or a button detached itself from his shirt. After twenty-five years of marriage, if he lost an order to a competitor, the *bourse* fell, the roof leaked, or a holiday turned out to be a disaster, Marie-Paule knew that the fault must be hers. She accepted her role as whipping boy. She was used to taking the rap.

Like many men whose outward behaviour was overbearing and filled with sound and fury, Claude Balard was still a small boy unable to manage without his mother. While he took his resentment at this out on Marie-Paule, he was at the same time dependent upon his wife. The fact that he had been handsomely paid by Marie-Paule's father to take his homely daughter off his hands was neither here nor there. He compensated for his ambivalent feelings towards her by his assignations with Beatrice Biancarelli, on whose favours he was equally dependent. Dismissing the reality that he was deceiving his wife with his mistress and his mistress with his wife, the *chartron* deluded himself that he was faithful to them both.

The *chartrons* – the wine merchants of Bordeaux – took their name from the tall grey façades of the warehouses of the Quai des Chartrons where, since the seventeenth century, the *aristocratie du bouchon* had carried out their trade. The Quai des Chartrons, once the finest suburb in France, now run down and decaying, ran for two kilometres on the wide banks alongside the Garonne.

Originally, the *chartrons*, an influential body of merchants, had purchased direct from the growers *sur souches* (before the grapes were picked), or *en primeur* (immediately after the wine was fermented). Responsible for bottling it themselves, the merchants had cherished the wine like a new baby and, like foster parents, brought it up. As a result of their efforts there were frequent disputes – like those between opposing schools of child psychology – as to whether it was heredity (the vines, the grapes and the fermentation) or environment, the care lavished upon the wine in the dark of the *chartronnais'* cellars, which was responsible for its character.

When the growers finally decided to nurture their own 'children' until they were ready to be sent out into the world, the *chartronnais* were no longer needed as adoptive parents and were deprived of their former glory. They were forced to undertake a less charismatic role and simply bought and sold wine (usually to the wholesalers), which had already been bottled by the château owners.

Wines sold under the label of a particular negociant varied from generic blends to high-class bottles from individual châteaux. In some cases, these châteaux were themselves owned by the negociants. Like many Bordeaux wine merchants, such as the Guestiers and Bartons before him, Claude Balard's overweening ambition, in which he was supported and encouraged both by Marie-Paule and Harry, a partner with his father in Balard et Fils, was to become a classed-growth château proprietor.

Although he was a member of the Syndicat de Negociants de Bordeaux, Claude Balard, unlike the majority of his colleagues, who were pillars of Bordeaux society, was both corrupt and corruptible. His devious nature had been inherited by Harry, a young man exempt from the common laws of politeness, who had more than once been in trouble with the police. By not only paying less than the market price, but selling twice as much wine falsely labelled 'Château de Cluzac' as he had bought from the Baron (to markets such as Japan, cruise ships and the less reputable airlines), Claude Balard was able both to line his own pockets and finance the extravagant habits of his son. His ultimate triumph over the Baron would come when he was himself installed as owner of that much coveted jewel of the Médoc, the Château de Cluzac.

The Balards occupied an elegant, high-ceilinged *appartement* in the tree-lined Cours Xavier-Arnozan, which ran at right-angles to the dilapidated Quai des Chartrons, where Balard et Fils had their cellars. They were not the only Bordeaux family who were looking forward to the Fête de la Fleur.

The turquoise satin gown, a mute reminder of the

forthcoming evening, which would begin with a massed band of welcome on the drawbridge of Château Laurent and end with a display of fireworks over the vineyards, hung on Marie-Paule's armoire. Another dress, neither turquoise nor satin, but fashioned, what there was of it, of café-au-lait lace, provided an equally trenchant cue.

While Marie-Paul's creation had come from Beatrice Biancarelli, the fashion guru of Bordeaux, Delphine Lamotte had been shopping in Paris, the city of her birth.

Delphine, whose husband Alain was pinning *his* hopes on adding Château de Cluzac to his portfolio, was also waiting anxiously for the Fête de la Fleur. With the aid of the little lace number from Givenchy, she hoped to persuade the Baron, notoriously susceptible to the charms of women, to look favourably on Assurance Mondiale, of which Alain was the Président-directeur Général in Bordeaux. Unlike Marie-Paule Balard, Delphine had been brought up in the Boulevard Courcelles, where her family was '*trés snob*', and her aspirations were not social but material.

Shopping, for herself, her individual home, in which there were always fresh flowers, and her two delightful children – the eleven-year-old Amélie and the three-year-old Joséphine – was her north, her south, her east and her west. Her tastes were simple: she liked only the best. Alain, who took pride in his wife's looks and doted on her bubbly sophistication, liked nothing more than to indulge her.

The acquisition of Château de Cluzac meant not only an additional feather in Alain's cap, but that he would be rewarded with a considerable bonus and commensurate rise in salary. It would provide the *résidence secondaire* after which Delphine hankered, and would hopefully cover more than one yearly visit (usually at the time of the *soldes*, when the previous season's models were disposed of more cheaply) to the house of Givenchy.

Of all the young couples in Bordeaux café society,

Delphine and Alain Lamotte, together with their impeccable home and their beautiful and talented children, were
the most envied. The fact that Alain had graduated from
'Sciènces Po' and was clearly destined to rise like a meteor
in his chosen field, and Delphine, bored with lessons, had
left school at seventeen, after which she scarcely opened a
book other than *Elle Décoration* or *Marie-Claire*, did not
detract from their almost perfect relationship.

A devoted mother, Delphine chauffeured her daughters
to school, to music, and to elocution and dancing lessons,
monitored their reading, escorted them to museums to
improve their minds, took them on outings, and entertained their friends. Dressed in the latest and most expensive juvenile fashion (much of it brought back from her
visits to Paris), looking, even when playing in the garden,
as if they had just stepped out of a bandbox, the two girls
were clones of their mother.

Delphine's dedication to her children did not prevent her
from being, to all intents and purposes, an exemplary wife.
While she chattered away vivaciously in company, often
about nothing at all, the good-natured Alain regarded her
with silent admiration. They not only thought alike, and
frequently talked alike – as if their opinions had been
rehearsed – but had common interests, in bridge, tennis,
and sailing on the Gironde. The only arena in which Alain
Lamotte experienced the slightest dissatisfaction was the
bedroom, where Delphine, so profligate with her energies
as far as their home and their children were concerned,
seemed unaccountably to lose her enthusiasm.

When Marie-Paule Balard had returned to Biancarelli to
fit the turquoise frock, she had run into Clare de Cluzac,
whom she had not seen for more than ten years. She had
followed her progress since Clare had been a baby, when
she had cherished the romantic notion that when she was
grown up she would, despite the fact that she was five
years older than her son, be a suitable wife for Harry.

To date, Harry had shown no signs of marrying. Marie-Paule presumed that he had girlfriends. He spent nights away from home – sometimes several in a row – to which he returned more disagreeable than ever and looking decidedly the worse for wear. The sight of Clare de Cluzac at Biancarelli's reinforced her determination to persuade Harry to accompany his parents to the Fête de la Fleur, where the girls to whom he would be exposed would at least be from the appropriate drawer.

Looking at Clare, as she rummaged through the rails of Biancarelli models, Marie-Paule Balard, who had recognised her immediately, was not at all sure that she had grown into the fairytale princess she had once envisaged as her daughter-in-law. Unlike the marriageable young women of her acquaintance, who paid as much attention to their appearance as did their mothers, Clare de Cluzac, in her black vest, her black ankle-length skirt, her hooped earrings and her plimsolls – she looked, Marie-Paule thought, more like some vineyard worker than the daughter of a château owner – seemed to have little regard for protocol.

Standing before the looking-glass, preening herself in her final fitting for the turquoise dress, Marie-Paule Balard watched Clare from the corner of her eye as Biancarelli knelt at her feet to check the hemline.

'*Que pensez-vous de la vente du château, Mademoiselle?*' Marie-Paule addressed the Baron's daughter.

'*Ca m'est indifférent.*' Clare extracted a handful of scarlet crepe from the rail and saw that it was liberally adorned with buttons and bows.

'Monsieur Balard has dreamed of becoming a château owner for a very long time . . .'

Clare, who knew that Cluzac had already been promised to the South African, met Beatrice Biancarelli's eyes in the mirror and was aware, although she had no idea how, that the boutique owner knew too.

'A *cru classé* estate has always been Claude's ambition
. . . When do you think your father will make his decision?'
Marie-Paule fingered the satin stretched tight across her
chest doubtfully.

Beatrice Biancarelli sighed.

'*Madame a une belle poitrine.*'

Proud of her bosom – the de Cluzac girl did not seem
to have one worth mentioning at all – Marie-Paule ran
her hands over the bolster of turquoise satin.

'That Assurance Mondiale is after the estate is common
knowledge,' she said. 'Alain Lamotte wants Cluzac for his
company, but to run a château properly you have to live
the life. *My* husband would take a *personal* interest . . .'

That Madame Balard was spitting in the wind was not
Clare's business. She let her rattle on about how advan-
tageous the move would be for Harry, and how satisfying
for herself to move from the Cours Xavier-Arnozan to an
even more prestigious address.

Looking through the garments on the rails, not one
of which she would be seen dead in, Clare was not all
that interested. She wondered how Beatrice Biancarelli
knew about Van Gelder, and let the negociant's wife
rattle on.

When Marie-Paule had left the shop, Beatrice Biancarelli
apologised for keeping Clare waiting. Madame Balard and
her ilk were her bread-and-butter; she had a duty to her
regular clientele. Reaching above Clare's head she drew
the curtain, on its rattling brass rings, over the rails of
garments.

'*J'ai beaucoup mieux pour vous.*'

Vanishing into the back room, Biancarelli reappeared
with a narrow black sheath, supported by shoulder straps,
with a side split to the knee. Draping it against herself and
adopting a model's pose, she put her head on one side and
regarded her mirror image.

'I was keeping it for myself.'

Clare noticed the keyhole bodice, which would expose her breasts.

'Papa is not going to like it.'

Indicating the changing-cubicle and holding out the dress, Beatrice Biancarelli shrugged. She would deal with the Baron.

'*Tant pis!*'

CHAPTER FIFTEEN

Halliday Baines, his athlete's body finely tuned, kneeled on the beach on the Marlin Coast of Queensland, a few kilometres along the Cook Highway north of Cairns. He was building a castle for his five-year-old son Billy, well away from the cream foam of the breakers.

Filling his bucket with sand, the little boy, his narrow chest as brown as his father's, looked longingly at the deceptively inviting ocean, which he knew very well he was forbidden to enter, even to cool off, except from the safety of the netted area farther down the beach.

'Tell me about the stingers, Dad.'

'*Chironex fleckeri*.' Halliday gave the stingers their Latin name as he had many times in the past. The little boy loved to hear the story of the box jellyfish that infested the waters, on the edge of which stood the neat house, its wide verandahs overlooking the eucalyptus trees and the deserted shore, in which he had been born.

'Why "box" jellyfish, Dad?'

Billy waited for the answer, which he knew by heart.

'Because they have a four-sided bell . . .'

'"A kind of box . . ."' Billy patted the sand in his bucket.

Halliday smiled.

'A kind of box.' He raised his arms and advanced menacingly towards Billy.

'With tentacles three metres long hanging from each corner,' they said in unison.

'With enough poison in them to kill hundreds and hundreds of prawns, not to mention three or four human beings!' Halliday put his arms threateningly round his delighted son.

' "Takes three minutes to die . . ." ' Billy had not the least idea what he was talking about but he liked the sound of the words. 'The pain's terrible. The venom . . . The venom . . . What does the venom do, Dad?'

'Arrests your heart, nukes the red blood cells, and destroys the skin tissue. Upend your bucket, lad. We'll just finish this castle then it'll be time for tucker.'

'Mum said we could have a barbecue.'

'Coral trout or barramundi?' Halliday had been fishing earlier in the day.

'Barramundi.'

'Get your togs on then, son.' Halliday stood up and flexed his muscles.

'Mum says you're going away.'

'I'm always going away, Boy-oh!'

'Mum says you're not coming back.'

'She did?'

'She says we're going to live in Katoomba.'

'Katoomba's a great place. Fantastic scenery, gum trees. You'll have your Uncle Chris . . .'

'Where will you be, Dad?'

'I'll be in France. All over. I'll be back to visit. Don't you worry. I'll tell you about the jellyfish.' Halliday raised his arms. 'With the long tentacles . . .'

Billy did not smile.

'Mum says you're not going to live with us any more.'

'Not exactly.'

'Who's going to fix the barbecues?'

Halliday looked out at the ocean. It was a good question. *The* question from the standpoint of a five-year-old.

The split had been coming for a long time. Halliday could not entirely blame Maureen. The fact was that he was never at home.

He had met Maureen at Sydney University, where she was reading for an arts degree and he for a degree in agricultural science. Not long after their graduation and marriage he had reluctantly left Maureen – who not only hated to travel but had a flying phobia and had never been out of the country – to spend six months in France examining the country's wine regions. It was there that he developed an interest not only in wine but in climate, and in particular the effects of temperature and humidity on wine styles, which he brought back with him to Australia.

His pragmatism, unfettered by tradition, led to his rapid grasp of methods and technology, which were now doing for the wine trade what the Japanese had once done for the motor industry. By flouting the most hallowed convention of French wine, that of *terroir* – the belief that a vineyard's soil is unique, and capable of shaping a wine's flavour – together with that of the Appellation Contrôlée system which supported it, he demonstrated that competent wine farming, combined with the closest attention to high-tech detail in the *cave*, was all that was required.

A maverick who believed that a good machine was better than a bad team of harvesters, Halliday Baines preferred to gather his grapes with giant tractors which straddled the vines and beat them with rubber arms which shook off the bunches. He was the doyen of a growing band of itinerant oenologists who were reshaping winemaking methods all over the globe. With a technique all of his own – *le style Baines* – he was widely acclaimed by wine writers in both the northern and southern hemispheres, by whom he was recognised as a star winemaker with a big reputation.

Halliday worked not only in Australia, where the grapes had sometimes to be shipped distances the equivalent of that between southern Turkey and Bordeaux, but in vineyards all over the world, some of which were twenty hours' flying time away.

The initial reaction of the Bordelais to the presence of the pugnacious Australian was resentment. His technical expertise, plus his natural affinity for the soil, which they could ill afford to dismiss, eventually won them over. Halliday Baines now acted as consultant oenologist to half a dozen classed growth Médoc châteaux, where from August to October – his lack of French notwithstanding – he advised the château owners about fermentation temperature gradients, clone numbers, yeast strains, and the exact proportions of free-run juice versus what came out of the press.

His long absences from home, plus the fact that his sensitivity was more often than not reserved for his vines rather than the needs of his wife and family, had – not surprisingly – had a deleterious effect on his marriage.

Maureen, a schoolteacher, had, he supposed, been patient. Although Halliday had, since his university days, loved her for her quiet good nature, her efficiency as homemaker and the fact that she was a wonderful mother to Billy, they had actually spent very little time in each other's company. It had never occurred to him, because of her full-time teaching job (she was now Head Teacher of a Cairns primary school) and the demands of their son, that Maureen might be bored.

When he had arrived home from Argentina on their wedding anniversary, with a gold bangle he had grabbed from the Duty Free shop in Buenos Aires, to find her with her metaphorical bags packed, he was totally unprepared.

'You're not going to like *my* anniversary present,' Maureen, who had never beaten about the bush, said as he embraced her on the verandah where she had been awaiting his arrival. 'I'm leaving you, Halliday.'

Although there was a strange feeling of trepidation in his entrails, he had tried to make light of her pronouncement.

'You've been watching too many movies.'

'I'm serious.' Maureen pulled away. 'I thought it better to give it to you straight.'

Halliday couldn't believe that he was hearing what he was hearing.

'You've never said anything.'

'You were never here.'

'I thought you liked it that way. I thought you didn't mind.'

'You never thought.'

'Look, Maureen, I'm sorry, I'll try to spend more time at home. We'll take a trip . . . ' He couldn't remember the last time he had taken Maureen away.

'It's too late, Halliday. There's somebody else.'

It was that which had done for him. He didn't know if it was the jet-lag or the shock of her totally unexpected pronouncement but he had lost his rag.

'Bitch!'

He was surprised to find tears in his eyes.

Maureen had slapped him sharply across the face and gone indoors leaving him to stare at the blurred green and gold of the ocean as he attempted to analyse his reaction to the fact that his wife had been unfaithful to him. The energy and drive that enabled him to run a world-wide business, do the work of three men and cope with different time zones and lack of sleep, had contributed to his own (technical) infidelity with women in various quarters of the globe who, captivated by his outdoor charm and his charisma, had flung themselves at his feet. While enjoying their company however, he had, paradoxically, never – not even in imagination – pictured himself as anything but firmly committed to Maureen. Patently he had been living in cloud-cuckoo-land.

Later in the evening, after Billy had gone to bed, Maureen had apologised for the slap, which was due to her overwrought state, and revealed, to his amazement, that Chris Owens, a TV producer who lived in Katoomba in the Blue Mountains, had been her lover for the past five years.

'What did you expect me to do, Halliday?' Maureen said, surprised at his amazement. 'Spend the rest of my life cleaning the house, going to work, and picking up Billy from school? I'm thirty-five years old!'

Looking at Maureen, in her brief shorts, radiant with the unmistakable glow of a woman in love, he wondered how he could have been such a damned fool.

'Is that it then?'

'I'm afraid it is.'

'Not a chance?'

'You've blown it.'

'What about Billy?'

Five years, Maureen had said. He suddenly grew frightened. As usual, Maureen read his thoughts.

'I met Chris when you first took off for Chile. Billy was three months old . . .'

'I *am* going to see Billy . . . ?'

'Whenever you like. You're his father. Billy loves you.'

'What about Billy's mother?'

'You didn't give me much of a chance.'

'I've been a damned fool. Look, Maureen, what if I stayed around more . . .'

'Halliday Baines? The big-shot winemaker.'

'Christ, Maureen! Give me a break.'

The conversation with Maureen had taken place more than a week ago, since when Halliday had moved his kit downstairs and slept in the den. Now, watching Billy put on his tee-shirt, pick up his bucket and his spade, he thought his heart, to which he had never paid the slightest attention, would break.

In answer to Billy's question as to the fixer of future barbecues, the preparer of coral trout and barramundi, Halliday replied, 'Uncle Chris.'

'Uncle Chris doesn't do barbecues.'

'What *does* Uncle Chris do?'

There was silence as Billy walked ahead of him up the beach. His five-year-old was already well drilled in the art of diplomacy. He added the pain of Billy's unfamiliar reticence to the other hurts he had totted up during the past week.

The barbecue was to be the last evening the three of them would spend together. Although Maureen set a special table on the verandah and they opened a bottle of Penfold's Grange, with 'vintage' Coke for Billy – a joke at which nobody laughed – it was not a resounding success. In the absence of hunger, invariably the best sauce, the barramundi, white and succulent, was only messed with, and Maureen threw most of the fish away together with the pavlova she had made – Billy's favourite dessert.

After dinner, while Maureen, who had tactfully left the two of them alone together, was indoors stacking the dishwasher, Halliday and Billy sat side by side on the hammock, its motion, propelled by Halliday's foot, in harmony with the waves.

'Do the Four Kings, Dad.'

Ever since he could distinguish the pictures on the cards, Billy had been mesmerised by his father's card tricks. As he grew older, whenever Halliday was at home, he had entertained him with stories about magicians. He told him about the water-spouter who could shoot half a dozen jets from his mouth, and the stone-eater who could swallow thirty pieces of gravel. He told him about Johannes Brigg, a German entertainer who had no legs and only one hand, but could simultaneously juggle with umpteen cups and balls and play several musical instruments.

Sending Billy indoors to fetch the cards, Halliday thought that this would be the last time. Doing the Four Kings in the presence of 'Uncle Chris' would not be the same.

Extracting the four kings from the deck that Billy

brought him, Halliday fanned them out so that each one slightly overtopped the other and showed them to his son. Sliding them together again, he turned them face down and placed them on top of the pack. Slowly and deliberately, watched closely by Billy on the hammock, he dealt the four top cards on to the table.

'Don't take your eyes off them for a moment!'

Dealing four more cards from the pack he laid them, one by one, next to each of the kings.

'Alligator, alligator, alligator!'

Chanting the magic words, Halliday told Billy to inspect the cards on the table. The four kings had miraculously disappeared.

'How'd ya do it, Dad?' Billy's question was always the same.

So was Halliday's answer. 'Tell you when you're grown up.'

Tonight the response stuck in his throat. He put his arm round his son, feeling the slightness of his body through his pyjamas. 'Come closer, I'll show you.'

Holding the boy tight, he explained how, while he was drawing the four kings from the pack and fanning them out in his hand, he had surreptitiously positioned four *ordinary* cards beneath them. Having shown Billy the four kings, he had pushed them together in such a way that when he replaced them the four ordinary cards were on top of the pack. These were the first four he dealt on to the table. The second four were the kings.

'Gee, Dad. Show me how to do it!' Billy's eyes were alight.

Taking the small fingers in his own, Halliday helped them manipulate the cards. Repeating the manoeuvres over and over, until his eyelids were heavy and it was growing dark on the verandah, Billy finally mastered, albeit clumsily, the moves of the trick. Trying it out on his father, he was delighted with the result.

'Am I grown up now, Dad?'

The pride in his small voice knocked Halliday for six. He took the boy in his arms.

'Time for bed, son.'

'Do you *have* to go away tomorrow?'

''Fraid so.'

'Where are you going?'

'All the way to France.'

'To make some more wine?'

'As a matter of fact I'm going to a big, big party.'

'Whose birthday is it?' Billy snuggled into his lap.

Putting away the cards for the last time, Halliday said, 'It's not exactly a birthday party, son. It's called the Fête de la Fleur.'

CHAPTER SIXTEEN

Wearing the black dress she had bought at Beatrice Biancarelli's, Clare entered the *petit-salon* with its marquetry bookcases and ancient Savonnerie carpet. Noticing with relief that the faded green hangings of Genoa velvet had as yet been spared the attentions of Laura Spray, she crossed to the window and looked out on to the evening park.

The few days she had spent in Bordeaux had gone quickly. She had enjoyed showing the place where she had grown up to Jamie, but she had had enough of Laura Spray, with whom there had been daily confrontations. She would not be sorry to get home to the more prosaic delights of Notting Hill.

Although Viola had had her suspicions that Charles-Louis was up to something, Clare saw no grounds, apart from her father's infatuation with the American socialite, for her mother's misgivings.

True, there were rumblings, both in the *chais* and in the vineyards, concerning the Baron's cashflow problems. The vineyards were full of holes and, given the superb quality of the grapes which the remaining vines produced year after year, Albert Rochas had a problem accepting that the Baron could not afford to replant.

In the cellars, where Clare had introduced Jamie to her erstwhile companion the cellarmaster – although Jean Boyer had been even less forthcoming than the *chef de culture*, whose preoccupation was the vineyards – the old man had seemed equally malcontent.

Owing to the nature of the soil, the *chais* at Cluzac, in common with those of many of the other châteaux, were built partly above ground and partly below to provide insulation. They were not, in the traditional sense, cellars at all. The long low, wistaria-covered outbuildings, their thick walls pierced only by small windows closed with painted shutters, stood below their tiled roofs on the north side of the courtyard. These outbuildings housed not only a succession of vast and intercommunicating dark dank bays, where the barrels in which the wine was matured were stored on wooden chocks, but also the administrative offices, which were under the care of the estate manager, Monsieur Boniface, whose drooping moustache, neglected teeth and lugubrious appearance belied his name.

Unlike most of the other châteaux in which 'inox' – stainless steel vats in which temperatures could easily be controlled – had been installed, no effort had been made, or money been spent, on keeping the Cluzac *chais* up to date. At vintage time the grapes were fermented, macerated and dumped indiscriminately in old wooden *cuves*, idle for eleven months of the year, which had to be scraped and disinfected before they could be used again.

After shaking hands politely with Jamie, the bow-legged Jean Boyer, whose credo it was that 'one barrel of wine could work more miracles than a church full of saints', had, to Clare's surprise, abruptly turned his back on them. Swaying, in his darned red jersey, between the neatly aligned barrels, which stretched far into the distance, he disappeared into the crepuscular depths of the cool *chai*.

Following him, Clare explained to Jamie that the capacity of each of the *barriques bordelaise* was officially designated at 225 litres. The shape, circumference and number of iron bands were also specified, and each barrel yielded 25 dozen bottles.

For the first two months after they were filled, the barrels remained upright, allowing the carbon dioxide from the fermentation process to be dissipated more easily. They had to be topped up two or three times a week for the first year. Once the level remained constant, the casks were turned *bonde à côté* ('three-quarter bung') for approximately four months. Three times in the first year the wine had also to be 'racked on its lees' or carefully transferred from one cask to another, leaving behind a deposit of vinous sludge, after which it was clarified or 'fined'.

The making of a claret required meticulous care on the part of the cellarmaster, whose job it was to control the softness and sweetness of the wine so that neither fruit nor oak predominated. It was the tannins imparted by the wood that helped to give wine its character.

Catching up with Jean, Clare asked how *his* wine, which he blended and assembled and about which he was fiercely proprietorial, was coming along. Her innocent question, intended to open up their usual dialogue, if only about his wartime exploits and his missing fingers, provoked an unexpected diatribe aimed indirectly at her father.

'*Il me faut des barriques!*' Jean waved his arms over the innocent rows of red-bellied barrels. '*Il me faut des barriques.*'

This statement was followed by a rapid explanation, which Jamie had some difficulty following, not only of how, in order to maintain the quality of the de Cluzac wine, Jean desperately needed to replace at least one-third of his barrels, but that the vat house was in urgent need of reroofing, and the petrol pump in his old Renault needed changing.

'*Avez-vous demandé à Papa?*' Clare asked, attempting to calm the cellarmaster down.

Jean Boyer rolled his eyes expressively and spat contemptuously on the beaten earth floor.

'*J'en ai ras la bol de demander.*'

'What does he say?'

'*Il répond toujours la même chose. Impossible. Impossible. Impossible . . .!*'

Standing at the window of the *petit-salon* as she waited for Jamie to struggle into the dinner suit he had hired in Bordeaux for the Fête de la Fleur, and for her father and Laura Spray, Clare trusted that the problems of the estate which so exercised Jean Boyer and Albert Rochas would hopefully be resolved by the new South African owner.

'You're not going out like that!'

Charles-Louis, who had appeared in the doorway of the *petit-salon*, looking extremely distinguished in his midnight blue tuxedo, was staring at the swell of Clare's breasts, visible through the keyhole opening of the black dress.

The coldness and disapproval in his voice took her back to her childhood, when, denigrating her best efforts, her father had voiced his opinion of her school work, attacking his daughter for being a failure, rather than simply upbraiding her for not getting twenty out of twenty for her composition.

She faced her father. She was no longer eight years old.

'*You* told me to go to Biancarelli, Papa,' she said innocently. 'Surely you don't want me to cover up three thousand francs' worth of Versace.'

The Baron was saved from replying by the entrance of Laura Spray. She wore a tangerine silk suit, with an ankle-length knife-pleated skirt and long jacket. This was topped by a flowing chiffon scarf in the same colour, which was wound nonchalantly round her neck (presumably to disguise its scrawniness) and flowed like an orange tributary down her back. The basically simple outfit, which had, without doubt, cost an arm and a leg, would not have been too bad had it not been garnished with the lemon marquise diamond, matching drop-earrings, three rows of – presumably priceless – pearls fastened with an outsize emerald clasp, a ruby-encrusted lapel brooch and a beaded orange and diamanté evening purse. Any analogy with a Christmas tree would have been unkind to the Christmas tree.

Unable to see clearly without her spectacles, and too vain to wear them, Laura appraised Clare's revealing dress (already voted ravishing by Jamie) and the gash of crimson lipstick which provided the only distraction in her ensemble.

Jamie's sentiment was apparently endorsed by a great many of the men, married and otherwise, who – mesmerised by the luminosity of the flawless skin Clare had inherited from Viola, not to mention the dramatic scarlet and black of her appearance – gravitated towards her in the vast and brightly lit marquee which had been erected in the grounds of the eighteenth-century *chartreuse* (a hermitage built in the shape of an unequal quadrilateral) that was Château Laurent.

The entry of Baron de Cluzac, with Laura Spray on his arm and closely followed by his daughter, could not have caused more of a stir in the 'ballroom' – which had taken several days to erect and was modelled upon that at Versailles – had they been royalty. Charles-Louis rarely showed his face among the Médocains; Laura Spray, whose designs on the Baron were ruminated upon at Bordeaux dinner parties and circulated, *de bouche à l'oreille*, among the château owners, was the subject not only of gossip but of speculation; Clare de Cluzac had not been seen in France for a great many years, and her escort not at all.

The Rothschilds had bought Lafite with money from banking, and the Agnellis an interest in Château Margaux with the profits from Fiat cars. Milli and Mathias Mercier had sold their successful clothing business five years ago to buy Château Laurent for an undisclosed sum.

With the help of Halliday Baines, the enthusiastic young couple, newcomers to the area, had carried out an ambitious renovation programme, which included new bottling plant and ultra-modern vat stores and computerising the management system of the château. Their ambition, apart from dedicating themselves to wine rather than blue jeans, was twofold. To restore Château Laurent second-growth claret to its former glory, and to host the Fête de la Fleur. The latter they thought, mistakenly, would set the seal on their arrival in the Médoc.

No sooner had Charles-Louis and his party been welcomed by a decidedly apprehensive host and hostess, than they were waylaid by a sweating Claude Balard, his white dinner jacket straining across his belly.

Momentarily taking Balard's outstretched hand, and greeting his negociant's turquoise-clad wife and seventeen-year-old daughter, Christiane, briefly, without presenting them to Laura Spray, the Baron continued his progress across the room. Eschewing the reception area, in which the champagne flowed and a string quartet played softly, he made straight for his place of honour at the top table.

'A tu vu ça?' An affronted Marie-Paule addressed her husband, wondering whether the Biancarelli dress, to which she had painstakingly matched her satin shoes, had been a waste of money. Christiane Balard, a girl as sweet at her brother Harry was boorish, wore a simple white figure-hugging shift with a single row of seed pearls. She took her parents by the arms.

'The Baron has only just arrived, Maman. I'm sure he'll talk to us later. Was that Clare de Cluzac? And who is the lady in orange?'

Humiliated in the sight of everyone – in the immediate vicinity alone she picked out Comte and Comtesse Laterre from Château Laterre, Natasha and Alexandre Rostov from Prieuré Gélise, and Julien and Stephan Castinel, twin brothers from Castinel, a Palladian château in the heart of the Médoc – Marie-Paule ignored her daughter's attempt to defuse the situation. Staring after the Baron's party, with the same resentment with which the Russian insurgents had regarded the families of the Tsars, she put Charles-Louis' behaviour down to the fact that she was only the wife of a negociant, rather than to the fact that she was unappealingly plain and unbelievably boring.

'Next year they will be laughing on the other side of their faces!' She was referring to her husband's bid for Château de Cluzac and her own misplaced belief that it would be successful.

Determined to drown her sorrows, Marie-Paule led the way to the flower-decked bar, at one end of which stood Halliday Baines, already a little the worse for wear, and at the other Big Mick Bly, his neck as thick as mortadella, who towered above the sycophantic group who surrounded him as they hung on his every word.

While the Baron and Laura Spray – revelling in her role as First Lady and comparing it favourably to her elevated status in the Palm Beach set – seated one on either side of Milli and Mathias Mercier at the top table, played King and Queen, Clare and Jamie were seated at the other side of the room with Christiane and Harry Balard (in an embroidered silk waistcoat and yuppie wing-collar), and Alain and Delphine Lamotte.

The months of preparation had almost resulted in a *crise de nerfs* for Milli Mercier. She was determined that the Château Laurent dinner, which celebrated the harvesting of the grapes approximately a hundred days hence – on the successful outcome of which most of the guests depended for their livelihood – would not only outshine the Fêtes de la Fleur of her rivals, but would long be remembered in the annals of the Médoc.

These days it was unnecessary to peruse the repertoires of the *grands chefs*, such as the notorious Vatel, who was said to have committed suicide when, at the banquet he had prepared for Louis XIV, the fish had not arrived on time. After lengthy consultations with a couple of *traiteurs* and a top Bordeaux restaurateur, Milli had come up with a suitable menu to which Mathias, consulting his cellar books, had matched the wine.

Keeping a nervous eye on the slow progress of the dinner (the first course of which had not been served until well after ten o'clock) in the marquee, which she had festooned with ivory silk imported specially from Thailand, Milli Mercier herself did not touch a thing.

At the Balard table, Marie-Paule, who had eaten too much and by the time the coffee was served could scarcely keep her eyes open, was dreaming about the Venetian Carnival, complete with Doge's Palace, which *she* would create for the Fête de la Fleur at Château de Cluzac. At the young people's table, Alain Lamotte, for whom the night was still young, was waving away the smoke from his cigarette and outlining for Clare his ambitious plans for her father's estate, when a gavel was banged and silence called for, for the speeches.

After Mathias Mercier, pride illuminating his face like that of a schoolboy who had succeeded in his *Baccalauréat*, had replied to the toast to the host and hostess (now more of a nervous wreck than ever), and resumed his seat, Baron de Cluzac, guest of honour and Président de l'Union des Grands Crus, rose slowly to his feet.

Short and to the point, delivered with a charm and panache which cut no ice with Clare, his few and uninspiring words were received with as much enthusiasm as if they had been the American Declaration of Independence. When he sat down, to sustained applause and a public embrace from Laura Spray, who had been gazing raptly at him during the whole of his performance, it was the cue for the serious part of the evening's entertainment to begin.

While the tables were being cleared and the first of the

two bands, which Milli Mercier had brought from Paris, tuned their instruments, the guests, some of whom were clearly overcome by the heat, strolled out into the grounds. Christiane Balard was bored out of her mind with the long drawn-out dinner and the interminable speeches. She was chatting animatedly to Clare as they made their way – ahead of Jamie, Harry Balard and the Blys – between the tables, when she was stopped in her tracks by the sight of Halliday Baines.

Clare followed her gaze to where the thick-set Australian, his hair to his shoulders, stood with his back to them at the bar waiting for his glass to be filled.

'Halliday Baines.' Christiane dropped her voice. '*Je suis folle de lui* . . .'

'Who's Halliday Baines?'

Christiane raised her eyebrows. Everyone in the room knew Halliday Baines, the flying winemaker. '*L'oenologue.*'

'The guy no self-respecting viticulturist can manage without!' Big Mick's voice was heavy with sarcasm.

The pint-sized Toni, darkly chic in her white trouser-suit, put a restraining hand on her husband's arm.

'They hate each other's guts.' Harry Balard moved in on Clare, at whose décolleté he had been staring insolently all evening. 'Baines and Bly. The egoist and the evangelist of wine.'

'My grandfather never had an oenologist,' Clare said.

'Well said, young Clare,' Big Mick boomed. 'Bordeaux has been producing *grands crus* for more than two hundred years. Good-quality grapes crushed and fermented. Control the temperature and keep it clean. It's dead simple . . .' Looking mischievously towards the bar as they made their way to the gardens, he raised his voice further. 'You don't have to go to university to learn that!'

Leaving the bar, and holding his glass of claret by the foot, Halliday Baines, his gait unsteady, approached the wine guru.

'Are you being deliberately offensive, Bly?'

'*Le style Baines*!' Assuming an effete voice, Bly mocked the younger man. '"Lightly extracted and truly exquisite . . ."'

'If the big fat wines *you* rate so highly had half the elegance of your lovely wife here . . .'

'Cut it out, Baines,' Bly said sharply, his large bulk 'accidentally' jostling the Australian, making him spill his claret down the front of his starched white shirt.

Christiane Balard, glad of an excuse to get near Halliday, dabbed at the spreading red stain with her lace handkerchief.

'*Excuse* me!' Bly's voice was disdainful.

Taking Halliday's empty glass from him, he moved towards the bar. 'What'll it be, Baines, another glass of claret? Or would you rather have a Fosters?'

CHAPTER SEVENTEEN

The traditional wine-tasting, held by the Baron's negociant on the morning after the Fête de la Fleur, was primarily for those in the trade. Clare's invitation, which had been issued by way of a challenge, had come from Claude Balard himself.

Despite the fact that they had had little or no sleep, many of the journalists and wine buyers, curious to discover the outcome of a wager made at Château Laurent, managed to make their bleary-eyed way to the Quai des Chartrons where, stretching back for half a mile beneath the pavements, lay the cellars of Balard et Fils.

By the time Clare and Jamie had returned to Cluzac after the Fête de la Fleur, it was getting light. Clare had been unable to sleep. Careful not to wake Jamie – which, judging by the stertorous way he was breathing, would have been extremely difficult – she had got out of bed, pulled his sweat-shirt over her head, picked up her plimsolls and gone downstairs. Making her way over the stone floors and through the draughty passageways, she unbolted the door of the kitchens and let herself out into the damp and misty grounds.

Walking by the moat, with its swans and water lilies, the shimmering reflections and deep, weed-filled mysteries of which had so fascinated her as a child, she went over in her mind the evening at Château Laurent, which in the event had turned out to be surprisingly enjoyable.

Having opened the ball, at the request of his host and hostess, with Laura Spray – clearly a classy dancer – the Baron had made his farewells. Escorted to his yellow Dale Earnhardt Chevrolet by a disappointed Milli and Mathias Mercier, and without the hint of an excuse for his summary departure, he had driven away from the château.

Clare, who had already taken the floor several times with Jamie, insisted that he dance with Christiane Balard, who was sitting self-consciously by herself, while she was escorted to the bar by Alain and Delphine Lamotte.

Running his hand along the neatly aligned bottles, Alain – who was having some difficulty in focusing on the labels – had selected a claret.

'Malescot St-Exupéry.'

Taking the glass from him, Clare sniffed it tentatively before shaking her head.

'I'd say Cos d'Estournel. Still rather hard. Probably eighty-six . . .'

'Don't argue with the lady, Lamotte.' The mocking voice was Claude Balard's. 'Rumour has it she has a photographic palate. *Si c'est vrai* . . . ?' He shrugged. 'I very much doubt.'

'I don't believe I've had the pleasure.' Halliday Baines' gaze was focused unsteadily on the front of Clare's dress.

'Clare de Cluzac.'

'The one fortress I haven't succeeded in penetrating.'

Ignoring his outstretched hand, Clare turned her back.

'In your condition I doubt you ever will.'

'Give him a break.' Alain Lamotte poured oil on troubled waters. 'His wife's just left him.'

'I'm not surprised.' Clare was about to walk away when Claude Balard caught her arm.

'How about a blind tasting?' The negociant's face was red. 'We'll soon see about this photographic palate.'

'I'm not that bothered.'

Clare caught Halliday Baines' cynical eyes.

'Midday tomorrow . . .' Claude Balard threw down the gauntlet. '*Chez Balard et Fils.*'

Clare's plimsolls were soaked with the dew from the couch grass in which she had been walking, and she was beginning to feel both cold and hungry. Nodding to Monsieur Boniface, who had just arrived in his car and was walking across the courtyard towards the *chais*, and pulling the sleeves of Jamie's sweat-shirt over her hands, she wrapped it round herself more tightly and made her way back into the château, where, in the kitchens, the lights were now on.

Sidonie, who always rose at dawn, was giving Jean his breakfast before he started work. Sitting at the wooden table, the cellarmaster acknowledged Clare with a grudging '*Bonjour Mademoiselle*', before breaking off a length of misshapen baguette which he dipped into his bowl of coffee.

Sidonie, who hadn't given up the habit, hugged Clare.

'*Que vous avez froid*!' she said solicitously, fussing round her as if she were six. Throwing a log on to the fire, which she had started with vine twigs, she poured another bowl of coffee from the chipped enamel jug, and pulled out a chair at the table on which a tray, with a drawn-thread traycloth and flower-sprigged porcelain, was set for what Clare presumed was Laura Spray's breakfast – fresh raspberries and a jug of hot water – which would be taken up by one of the village women who came in daily to help Sidonie.

Without a word, and without finishing his coffee, Jean left the kitchen.

'What's up with him?'

'*Les hommes*!' Sidonie shrugged. 'They're all the same. You'll find out soon enough.'

'It's not just Jean,' Clare said. 'I can hardly get a word out of Albert. Something's got up his nose.' Putting both hands round the bowl to warm them, Clare sipped her coffee and looked speculatively at Sidonie, who disappeared into the pantry, from which she emerged with an enormous basket of redcurrants. Spreading a newspaper on the table, she took a colander from its hook and started expertly to separate the redcurrants from their stalks with the help of a fork.

Reaching for another fork, Clare said, 'Let me help.'

'*Attention à vos mains*!' Sidonie's concern for Clare's hands belied her expression. It was like old times. She was not displeased.

'Is Jean upset because the château is being sold?' Clare watched the berries fall haltingly into the colander. She was not as expert as Sidonie.

'We were born here. This is our home.'

'It will still be your home.'

'That's not what they say in the village. Jean and Albert hear things. *Au café*.'

'Mr Van Gelder will need you . . .' Clare's voice was reassuring. 'His family may own vineyards, but from what I hear he doesn't know a vine from a bonsai tree.'

'*C'est cette dame! Madame Spray!*' The cook's voice was contemptuous. 'Monsieur has lost his senses since she came.'

'You can't blame Laura Spray, Sidonie – although as far as I'm concerned she's a pain in the arse – Château de Cluzac is an anachronism. It's falling to pieces. It hasn't made money for years.'

Sidonie looked up sharply.

'*Et alors!*' Her voice was sceptical.

'I've looked at the sale document, Sidonie. Those figures must correspond with the books.'

'Books!' Sidonie sniffed. 'Books!'

'Sidonie . . .!' Clare got up from the table, put her arm round the older woman and her face against the worn cheek. 'Are you trying to tell me something?'

Sidonie looked at the grandfather clock in the corner of

the kitchen. It was not yet seven. The Baron was out riding and would not return for at least an hour. Laura Spray, concerned for her beauty, was certainly still asleep.

Getting up from the table, Sidonie wiped her hands on her apron and made conspiratorially for the door.

'*Suivez-moi, Mademoiselle Clare. Suivez-moi!*'

To Clare's surprise, Sidonie led her up the stairs to the first floor, along a corridor and up a short flight of steps to what was known as the Baron's Room. Clare associated her father's private sitting-room – largely taken up by a day bed above which hung a portrait of the first Baron de Cluzac, and a huge cylinder-top desk – with chastisement. In it, on many occasions, as she stared stubbornly out of the window, she had been read the riot act as a child.

Crossing the threshold into the room, the octagonal walls of which were covered with familiar once-red damask, Clare stopped in horror. In place of the faded Aubusson rug of no determinate colour was a fitted tartan carpet – still smelling of new wool – strident with squares of blue and yellow. She exchanged an appalled glance with Sidonie; there was nothing to say.

Mystified, Clare waited while Sidonie closed the door and crossed to an alcove where, on an Oeben table, stood a silver-framed photograph of her grandfather, Baron Thibault, dressed for the hunt. The Louis XV mechanical table, heavily decorated with ormolu bronzes and inlaid marquetry depicting scenes of classical ruins, was one of her father's favourite toys.

'*Ouvrez-la!*'

The table contained several hidden compartments and some nests of small drawers. On the rare days when Clare had pleased her father she had been allowed to operate it.

Watched closely by Sidonie, she opened cupboards large enough to admit only her hand, and sprung open drawers containing her grandfather's medals from the First World War, old letters and photographs. Pressing a hidden button, she watched as a rectangular central section rose slowly from the base of the table. While Sidonie looked tactfully out of the window, she located the panel behind which was a cupboard, small but deep. In it was a single, worn, leather-bound volume, *Mémo de Chasse*, Hunting Diary, embossed in what had once been gold.

Opening the diary curiously, Clare realised, to her surprise, that the *Mémo* had not to do with hunting but with wine. She was beginning to understand why Sidonie had brought her here.

Sitting at her father's desk, a thing she would not have dared to do when she lived at Cluzac, she became so engrosssed in deciphering his handwriting on the flimsy gilt-edged pages, that she was unaware that Sidonie had left the room. It was hard to believe that she was reading what she was reading.

Neat columns had been ruled in the diary in which had been entered figures which went back several years. The figures, clearly written in ink, disclosed the prices realised from the sales of Château de Cluzac wine, which was nothing extraordinary. What blew her mind was a second set of figures, pencilled alongside each entry, showing a very much higher price. From her dealings with the Nicola Wade Gallery, she knew enough about book-keeping to recognise *double* sales figures when she saw them. The higher, pencilled price, meant that Château de Cluzac had in fact, for several years now, been making hefty profits and that someone – could it have been Claude Balard – must have been issuing false invoices. She wondered where the money, twenty-four per cent of which was hers, had gone, and what the hell was going on!

Jamie was still snoring softly when she got back to

the bedroom. Climbing into bed beside him, profoundly shocked by the secrets yielded up by the mechanical table, by her discoveries in the Baron's Room, she insinuated herself into his sleeping arms.

The wine-tasting took place in the three cellars, connecting one with the other, in the warehouse that was Balard et Fils. Jamie, who had never been to a wine-tasting and was out of his element, stayed close to Clare.

'Who are all these people?'

Harry Balard, who had overheard the question, pointed out a not unattractive young woman in a floral skirt and red shoes who was unmistakably English.

'Julie Smith, wine buyer for Catesbury's. Richard Simpson' – he indicated a suave young men in a Garrick tie – 'the London Wine School. Nick Masters – supplies the shipping companies. Hypolite de Nevers, *Paris Soir*. Paulette Pauling' – he pointed towards a formidable-looking grey-haired lady wearing her spectacles on a cord round her neck and carrying a notebook – 'doyenne of wine correspondents, author of several books. And our very own Halliday Baines . . .'

'We've met.' Halliday nodded to Clare. 'What's a pretty girl like you doing in a place like this?'

'Where I come from such remarks are no longer considered politically correct,' Clare snapped. Sometimes she heard herself talking like her father. It came as a surprise.

'A de Cluzac to the bone.'

'The chap behind the table,' Harry Balard continued, 'is Bernard Groise, the new winemaker at Escampet. He'll be giving a short talk later. There's our host and hostess from last night . . .' He turned to greet Milli and Mathias Mercier, leaving Clare and Jamie on their own.

Jamie looked at the trestles, each with its white cloth and laden with its uncorked bottles of claret, behind which stood the various château owners and staff from Balard et

Fils ready to supply information about the wine that was on offer.

'What's the form?'

'Just help yourself.' Clare pointed to a table in the centre of the room on which were clean glasses, bottled water to cleanse the palate and a plate of crackers. 'Take a glass and hang on to it.'

Jamie made his way to where Halliday Baines, in blue jeans and work shirt, was leaning nonchalantly against a trestle, and poured some red wine from a jug into his glass.

'That's the *dregs* jug, mate.'

Taking two clean glasses from the table, Halliday proceeded to explain to Jamie the time-honoured rules of wine-tasting.

'Number one. The glass. Large enough to allow the scent to collect above the liquid. Number two. Clear. To show off the "robe". Never use a small glass and never fill it to the brim. Not even at home. Here endeth the first lesson.'

Pouring a not insignificant claret from one of the bottles on offer into the two glasses until they were one-third full, he handed one of them to Jamie.

'Right, mate. Hold your glass over a white surface, keep it still, and take a dekko at the colour. There's nothing quite the colour of red wine. Not even in nature. Wines are like women, as they age they lose their vivacity . . .'

Meeting Clare's eyes he allowed his voice to tail off.

'Little by little the red gets browner, with maybe a touch of orange. When wine gets old the pigment precipitates out of it. Wines which have little tannin in them will not age. If the wine's purple, it's down to molecules combining and piling on top of one another, like building bricks. These drop down and form the sediment. Sediment in a bottle of wine is not a fault. It's a sign of authenticity and age. Sediment in a young wine – three or four years old, say – is another story. That's down to technical error. A twenty-year-old claret *without* sediment . . . I'd be very suspicious.'

He swirled his wine round rapidly.

'This releases what we call the volatile elements. Increases the smell up to ten times. A concentrated, fat, alcoholic wine will form clearly visible "legs" . . .' He showed the glass to Jamie. 'Which linger before sliding down. Try it.'

Jamie twirled the wine in his glass.

'Now hold it to your nose.'

Halliday watched as Jamie did so.

'What you're getting there is the "bouquet". Not to be confused with aroma. Aroma refers to young wine. OK. Now, whistle the wine in and let it fan out over your tongue . . .'

Jamie, who was beginning to enjoy himself, did as he was bidden.

'Keep it there, ten or twelve seconds, long enough to allow it to express itself, establish its personality. Wine's not like lemonade. It's not for quenching your thirst. As the first sensations diminish, other flavours reveal themselves. If these remain in the mouth for some time after the wine has been swallowed or spat out, we say that it has 'body'. What remains after you've swallowed is called the *persistence*. A pleasant aftertaste is good. If it's bitter or acid the wine's not well balanced. Some wines leave nothing. They may be *good* but they won't be *great* . . .'

'So the longer the aftertaste the better the wine?'

'Right! And when you're all done . . .' Halliday pointed to an urn in the corner filled with wood shavings. 'When you're all done, mate, you spit the stuff out!'

'Three cheers for Crocodile Dundee!' Harry Balard led a round of applause as Balard senior approached Clare.

'*Et bien, Mademoiselle, vous êtes prête?*'

'Quite ready.' Clare's voice was equable.

Clare, accompanied by Jamie and Halliday Baines and a few curious onlookers, followed the negociant into the adjoining cellar where a table on which several half-filled glasses, two notebooks and two pencils had been set up for the blind tasting. With an exaggerated bow of politeness, Claude Balard handed Clare the first glass of unlabelled wine.

CHAPTER EIGHTEEN

Clare tapped on the door of Laura Spray's bedroom.

'Who is this?'

Clare entered the room. She had a letter in her hand.

Laura was sitting in front of the mahogany toilet mirror, with a crepe bandage round her hair, rubbing something into her face with the tips of her fingers.

'I'm looking for my father.'

'You'll find him in the office with Monsieur Boniface. A couple of guys from the tax office stopped by.'

'The *fisc*? What are they doing here?'

'I really don't know. Can I help?'

Clare looked at the letter.

'I don't think so.'

'You know, this light is driving me crazy. And the size of this looking-glass! Everything about this *chat-oh*. It gives me the creeps. I shall be glad to get back to Florida. My vanity unit runs the entire length of the bathroom. I mean bathroom. Not this antiquated number across the hall with a tub that takes for ever to fill. Did this cream hit the UK yet? Glycolic acid? Dead cells beneath the skin are bound together by a kind of cement which holds back the growth of new cells. What you get is a traffic pile-up . . .'

'Believe that you'll believe anything.'

'Glycolic acid dissolves the cement, the dead cells come to the surface, slough away, and the skin is left smooth. It slows the ageing process.'

Clare thought that they could have used Laura Spray in the cosmetics hall at Harrods.

'It's made from naturally occurring fruit acids . . .'

'Cleopatra used asses' milk. It didn't do her any good.'

Ignoring the remark, Laura held out the jar to Clare.

'Care to try some?'

'How long do you think my father will be?'

'Not too long, I guess. We're going to the opera.'

'I'll come back later.'

'If you don't mind my saying so, Clare, it wouldn't cost you to be polite to me. Your father and I *are* getting married.'

'My father is already married.'

The glycolic acid was returned to the dressing-table.

'Am I hearing you correctly?'

'My father is already married. To my mother.'

'They were divorced years ago.'

'Fine.'

'Weren't they?'

'Why don't you ask him.'

Leaving Laura to her rejuvenation, Clare climbed the stairs to her old bedroom. Propping the letter, addressed to her father, beneath a Zurich postmark, on the chimney-piece next to the chiming clock, she lay down on the bed where only a few days ago she had made love to Jamie.

The blind tasting at Balard et Fils had gone better than expected. Putting her trust in her first impressions, eliminating the impossible, and working her way through the wines from the Loire to Savoie, she had brought into play not only her three senses but all the summers she had spent at Cluzac in the company of Jean Boyer, all the holidays she had spent with Grandmaman, who had introduced her to a wide variety of wines from the *caveau* she had brought with her from France and kept in a store-room beneath the building. Over the years Clare had built up her repertoire. Once tasted, never forgotten. It was not difficult.

A small crowd had gathered to watch the contest between Clare de Cluzac and Claude Balard. Picking up a glass, observing – the more violet a red wine and the more green a white, the younger it was – then smelling (a brief sniff could put you on the track of the grape variety) before swirling the wine unhurriedly round her mouth, Clare was immediately able to place many of the samples. Among the reds she identified a minor château from the Graves, and – crafty touch this – a 1989 claret from her father's château; among the whites, a crisp Pouilly Fumé made from Sauvignon grapes, a generous Pouilly Fuissé from Chardonnay, and a maverick hock from the Rheingau.

She stuck on only two, and, when the papers were handed to Paulette Pauling for assessment, she had scored twenty-one points over Balard's eighteen. Big Mick Bly, who had arrived wearing cowboy boots and a stetson, had – only half joking – offered her job on *Wine Watch*. Harry Balard, siding with his father, had turned his back on her. When she looked round for Halliday Baines, for his approval, he had gone.

'You did great.' Jamie hugged her.

'I wasn't going to let that shit get the better of me.'

'Wait till he knows he's not getting Cluzac. He'll really have egg on his face.'

At the mention of the Château, Clare's eyes grew thoughtful. She had not discussed the *Mémo de Chasse* with Jamie. Not out of any feelings of loyalty to her father, but because she needed time to work out for herself the significance of what she had found in the mechanical table.

After lunch in Bordeaux, she left Jamie to find his way to the Musée des Beaux-Arts and arranged to pick him up later at le Régent, where it was fashionable to hang-out, for the drive back to St Julien.

Setting off along the Rue Charles Bonnier, down the Vital Carles, across the wide Cours de l'Intendance (so named after the architect responsible for the remodelling of Bordeaux), dodging the traffic that raced round the Place de la Comédie, she made her way to the the Allées de Tourny.

By the time she got to Biancarelli's – where she had the distinct impression that she saw Claude Balard leave the boutique and disappear into the crowd – she had bought a selection of silver wine labels in various shapes and sizes, an only slightly broken nineteenth-century child's pull-along horse, and a wine-taster the *antiquaire* had tried to kid her was Louis XVI, all of which would go down nicely in Portobello Road.

'I hear you're getting married,' Biancarelli said, as Clare tried on the 'smoking' she had altered.

'Who told you that?' Clare's voice came from behind the curtain.

Lulled out of her usual reticence, Beatrice realised that it was Charles-Louis who had let slip the news about his daughter's forthcoming wedding.

'One hears things.' Beatrice perceived she must watch her tongue. She sighed nostalgically. 'It's a long time since a man has swept me off my feet.'

'Jamie and I have been going out for some time.' Clare emerged from the cubicle. 'I'm hardly swept off my feet.'

Biancarelli looked at herself in the mirror.

'*Je ne suis plus mariable*. No one will marry me now . . .'

'There's nothing wrong with you, Biancarelli.'

'*Je sais*. It's men that are the problem.'

'Not Jamie.'

'Even the "new" one. They go to the *supermarché*, they make the dinner, they change the diaper . . . Pfui! Underneath nothing is changed. Turn round, please. I check the trouser. Are you in love with Jamie?'

'Of course I love him.'

'*J'ai dit* "in love"?'

'What's the difference?'

'*C'est comme une maladie.*'

Clare laughed. 'An illness!'

The trouser-suit was perfect.

While Clare put on her own clothes, Beatrice Biancarelli, her glasses on the end of her nose, made out the Baron's bill at her large, untidy desk. Painstakingly folding the black trouser-suit in sheets of pristine tissue paper, she went to the back of the shop to look for a carrier bag large enough to hold it.

Coming out of the cubicle, Clare, staring idly at the desk and the amount of her father's bill, caught sight of an unopened letter addressed – quite clearly – to Baron de Cluzac, care of Biancarelli. Before she had time to think, and acting on impulse, she picked it up and slid it into the deep pocket of her skirt.

Looking at the envelope now, with its Swiss postmark, propped up on the chimney-piece in her old room at Cluzac, she wondered what had possessed her to appropriate it, what flash of intuition had prompted her, uncharacteristically, to steal.

According to the time on the gilt clock, she had been lying on the bed for over half an hour. With a bit of luck her father would by now have returned from the *chai*. It was time to find out.

Picking up the letter, she ran downstairs to knock once more on Laura Spray's door. Rougement lay across the threshold. Terrified of germs, Laura Spray would not permit him inside the room.

'Just a minute!'

Rougemont looked at Clare dolefully.

'Come in!'

Laura had insinuated herself into an electric-blue dress

with a ridiculously short skirt which her father, still in his sports clothes, was zipping up.

'Can I have a word.' Clare addressed her father.

Laura glanced irritably at her watch.

'What is it?' Charles-Louis said.

'In private.'

'We're due at the theatre, Charles . . .'

'You can speak in front of Laura.'

'Have it your own way.' Clare took the letter from her pocket. 'I see you've been using a poste restante . . .'

Charles-Louis was all attention.

'Where did you get that?'

Clare looked at Laura.

'Where do you think?'

'Well kindly hand it over.' The Baron held out his hand.

'Not until I know what's in it.'

'Aren't you being a little impertinent?'

'Is that letter addressed to your father?'

'You keep out of this!'

'If you're going to be insulting to Laura, kindly leave the room. That letter is not your property.'

'How can I be sure?'

'Meaning?'

'Meaning there is something fishy going on round here.'

'We're going to be late, Charles. Can't this discussion wait?'

'I'd like to know exactly what is in it.'

'Give it to me . . .'

'When you tell me . . .'

'It's no concern of yours.'

'I want to know why it was posted in Switzerland. Why it is addressed to . . .'

'That's enough!'

Clare recognised the flashing eyes, the thin lips, the mounting colour in the cheeks. She stood her ground.

'If I give it to you will you let me see what's in it?'

'*Absolument pas*!'

'Then I shall open it.'

'Clare . . . !' Laura was horrified. She looked at Charles-Louis, who was now extremely angry.

'*Tu n'as pas le droit. Je te le défends*!'

At the sound of the raised voices, Rougemont became restless. He scratched at the door, his howl adding to the cacophony.

'*Trop tard!*' Clare tore open the envelope.

The Baron let the dog into the room.

'Charles!' Laura was distraught.

Coming up behind Clare, Charles-Louis tried to snatch the letter but Clare, who had already removed a folded sheet of paper from the envelope, was too quick for him.

'It's a bank statement! The Banque de Genève.'

'Then it can't be for me.'

'It has your name on it, Father.'

'*Ce n'est pas possible*!' The Baron was pacifying Rougemont, while Laura looked as if she was about to be sick.

'On the envelope.'

'*Exactement!* There is a mistake.'

'I don't think so.'

'If my name is not on the statement, then it is not for me.'

'There *is* a name on the statement. I presume it is a code name. You know as well as I do, Papa, that Swiss bank accounts are numbered. They never disclose the identities of their clients.'

'What your father says is right. Anyone can make up a code.'

Clare shook her head.

'Not this one.'

At the dressing-table Laura fastened a lapis-studded bracelet over her wrist. 'What is it?' she said curiously.

Charles-Louis, followed by Rougemont, made for the door. 'I think we had better continue this discussion downstairs.'

'Too late. The code name is "Rougemont", and the statement . . .' Clare cast her eye over the telephone numbers in the right-hand column of the account, over the millions and millions of francs.

'No wonder you've been buying orange groves . . .'

Charles-Louis and Laura exchanged glances.

'No wonder Cluzac hasn't been showing a profit.' Clare's voice rose. 'No wonder I've had nothing in the way of dividends except for a few lousy cases of wine. You've been ripping me off for years!'

'Can we postpone this little discussion until later?' Laura picked up her wrap.

'This is not a "little discussion", Mrs Spray, and the answer is no, we cannot.' She faced her father. 'You have been lying to me, Papa.'

'Everything is in order.' Having recovered from the shock the Baron had regained his cool. 'Maître Long, the *notaire*, will be here in the morning. He will explain everything . . .'

Clare played her trump card.

'Even the *Mémo de Chasse*?'

A silence, which lasted for several seconds, was palpable in the room. It was Clare versus her father. Laura Spray had disappeared.

'Who told you about the *Mémo de Chasse*?' The voice was crisp, businesslike.

'How long has it been going on?'

'I told you. Everything can be explained. Van Gelder is waiting. Tomorrow you will sign the *pouvoir*. You will get your share of Château de Cluzac. You will get your twenty-four per cent.'

'Twenty-four per cent of what? I'm not exactly stupid, Papa. I know it pleases you to call me a *brocanteuse*

– yes I do like selling junk – but I also run a serious business in London, a fact which you conveniently ignore. Twenty-four per cent of what you say Château de Cluzac is worth, or twenty-four per cent of what, according to the *Mémo de Chasse*, it is really worth? And there is someone else to consider. What about Tante Bernadette and her homeless? You have been robbing both of us.'

Taking Rougemont by the collar, Charles-Louis walked to the door of the bedroom. His voice was icy.

'Your Aunt Bernadette has agreed to the sale. Papers have been drawn up. Your signature is a formality. There is nothing you can do.'

At every attempt of her father's to intimidate her, Clare's courage always rose. She thrust the incriminating letter into her pocket.

'*On verra*!'

We shall see.

CHAPTER NINETEEN

It was with some trepidation that, following the showdown with her father, Clare drove to Toulouse to visit Tante Bernadette.

As a decidedly lapsed Catholic, she had not for a long time communicated with either God or his earthly representatives, with whom she was not only out of sympathy but out of touch; a long time since, as one of the 900 million other Catholics across the world, she had dutifully repeated the decades of the rosary or told her beads in the hope of promoting spiritual growth through contemplation.

The only rosary she saw these days was the silver one her grandmother kept on the table beside her chair. It brought back the ivory rosary of her childhood, and the black beads of her schooldays which, in moments of boredom, she had transposed in her imagination into a musical instrument on which every Hail Mary was a tune.

Forsaken but not forgotten. The words of the credo were still lodged firmly on some back burner in her head. 'In the name of the Father and of the Son and of the Holy Spirit Amen O God come to our aid O Lord make haste to help us I believe in God the Father almighty creator of heaven and earth I believe in Jesus Christ his only Son our Lord He was conceived by the power of the Holy Spirit and born of the Virgin Mary He suffered under Pontius Pilate was crucified died and was buried He descended to the dead

On the third day he rose again He ascended into heaven and is seated on the right hand of the Father . . .'

As faith had given way to the reservations of adolescence, to be rapidly followed by the certainties of maturity, she remembered her confrontations with the patient sisters at St Mary's. The main sticking-point had been venial sin, a grave violation of the law of God committed deliberately, knowing it to be wrong. OK. Fair enough. Although it was hard to get through the day without committing one. Why must we confess every mortal sin to a priest? Because every mortal sin offends God and wounds his church, and he imparts his forgiveness by means of the Church and through the ministry of the priests. How come the priests have the power to forgive sins? Christ breathed on his apostles who possessed the fullness of the priesthood and said 'Receive the Holy Spirit. If you forgive the sins of any, they are forgiven; if you retain the sins of any they are retained.' How do the priests forgive? By listening to a person's confession, giving him a penance and absolving him in the Name of the Trinity.

She recalled the solemn words of the absolution. 'God the Father of mercies, through the death and resurrection of His Son has reconciled the world to himself and sent the Holy Spirit among us for the forgiveness of sins; through the ministry of the Church may God give you pardon and peace, and I absolve you from your sins in the Name of the Father, and of the Son and of the Holy Spirit.'

She had frequent discussions with Grandmaman about the Church's attitude towards women, which was rooted in fear. Like most men who thought themselves infallible, the Pope – Vicar of Christ, the Successor of the Apostles, Pontifex Maximus of the Universal Church, Patriarch of the West, Primate of Italy, Archbishop and Metropolitan of the Province of Rome, State Sovereign of the Vatican of God's City, Servant of Servants – wanted to keep women in a subordinate capacity, wanted them only to say 'yes' and 'amen'.

Although Grandmaman, who regularly attended mass at Brompton Oratory, where she took Holy Communion, claimed that Christ had allowed both married men *and* women to come with him and form a Church, she argued more out of habit than from belief in the absolute truths of the last great absolute monarch. At the age of eighty-five, she was too old to change, now that the words of the rosary had become part of her. Using the beads like a mantra, not so much to ask the blessed Virgin's intercession as to set her mind free for contemplation, she practised cafeteria Christianity, picking and choosing to suit herself.

Following a long telephone conversation, during which she had brought her grandmother up to date with recent events at Château de Cluzac, Clare had called the Convent of Notre Dame de Consolation to ask permission to visit her aunt. She had been taken aback when the Reverend Mother herself had answered the telephone.

'This is Clare de Cluzac, daughter of Charles-Louis . . .'

Clare thought she heard a chuckle.

'I know perfectly well who you are.'

'There is something I would like to discuss with you, Tante Bernadette.'

'*La semaine prochaine, peut-être . . .*'

'It is rather urgent.'

'Tomorrow I shall be at my restaurant in the Rue Valade, La Couronne d'Epines . . .'

'Restaurant?'

'For the homeless. Come at one o'clock and be prepared to roll up your sleeves.'

Leaving Jamie to browse in Baron Thibault's library, she had driven to the pink-brick city of Toulouse, which she hadn't visited since her childhood. Negotiating the narrow streets with difficulty, she found the Rue Valade and parked on the pavement outside the Couronne d'Epines.

Entering an inconspicuous doorway, set deep into the wall, above which a porcelain Jesus Christ wore a chipped crown of thorns, she gingerly descended a steep flight of dark steps. They led into a noisy cellar in which a rag-bag of misfits sat shoulder to shoulder at oilcloth-covered tables on which were baskets of bread and steaming tureens of soup.

'So this is Charles-Louis' daughter!'

The voice came from a grey-clad figure bearing aloft a tray perilously loaded with steaming plates.

The first thing Clare thought of was that they could have been mother and daughter. Beneath the coif, the contours of the flushed face, moist with perspiration, were those which Clare regarded in the mirror each morning. The same aquiline nose, identical hooded eyes.

'*Une carafe d'eau, ici,*' Tante Bernadette shouted over the hubbub. '*Il faut du vin a cette table!*'

Among the many part-time jobs she had taken after leaving school, Clare had been a waitress. The Couronne d'Epines was a far cry from the Hammersmith pub with its lecherous manager. As she followed Bernadette and her team of sisters, squeezing her way between the benches, answering requests for water or for bread, she became so involved with removing the deep white plates wiped clean of every vestige of *navarin* of lamb, with serving the cheese and the thick wedges of *tarte aux abricots* of which Sidonie would not have been ashamed, that she almost forgot why she had come.

It was after four o'clock by the time the last of the homeless had made their reluctant way up the steep steps and out into the afternoon sunlight.

The dishes were washed in what had once been a dungeon, in a stone sink with a single cold tap. Rolling up the sleeves of her grey habit, Bernadette handed Clare a pristine linen tea-towel, brought from the convent and embroidered with a cross, and plunged her arms up to the elbows in the greasy water.

'*Je peux faire ça*!' Clare protested, wondering irreverently if Tante Bernadette shaved her head beneath its *serre-tête*.

'I'm used to it, child. A little prayer . . .' She scrubbed at a plate. 'Our Lord's detergent. It does wonders with the grease. Now, while we have a quiet moment, tell me why you came to La Couronne d'Epines.'

'It's about my father.' Clare picked up a dripping plate.

Tante Bernadette worked away with a brush with clogged bristles as if she were actually enjoying it. She smiled into the grey sludge of the washing-up water.

'What else could it be?'

Maître Long was already ensconced amid a sea of documents at the head of the table when Clare – summoned by an agitated Petronella who had hammered on the door of the bedroom where she and Jamie were still in bed – presented herself, still only half awake, in the Baron's office.

'I gather, Mademoiselle, that you are acquainted with the facts,' he said, when the introduction had been effected. 'Your father, Monsieur le Baron, is selling Château de Cluzac to Mr Philip Van Gelder, from South Africa, for a sum of . . .'

Pacing the room, Charles-Louis cut the notary short.

'What we need, Clare, before you go back to London, is for you to sign your *pouvoir*.'

'Making over . . .' Maître Long, stick thin, with a sharp nose, receding hair, and a powdering of dandruff on the shoulders of his shiny suit, took it upon himself to complete the Baron's sentence. 'Making over the twenty-four per cent of Château de Cluzac which belongs to you, to your father.'

Clare sat down, facing the lawyer at the far end of the table, although no one had invited her to do so.

Maître Long searched among his papers.

'We shan't keep you more than a few moments, Mademoiselle. *Alors!*' He located what he had been looking for and marked some crosses in pencil upon several sheets of printed paper. 'We require your signature here . . . and here . . . and here . . . *et, encore une fois* . . .' he turned over a leaf, 'here. Clare Gertrude Sophie Elinore de Cluzac.' Taking the lid off his fountain pen, he took the papers courteously to the other end of the table. Indicating the first cross he had marked, he proffered the pen to Clare.

Ignoring him, Clare, now wide awake, turned to her father, who was tapping the window pane impatiently as if trying to attract someone's attention, which she knew he was not.

'Suppose I refuse to sign?'

The tapping stopped.

'What do you mean "refuse"?'

'Suppose I do not give you my *pouvoir*.'

'Don't be childish, Clare. Château de Cluzac is being sold to Philip Van Gelder. The terms of sale have been agreed. What remains are the formalities. Under the terms of your grandfather's will we need your signature. That is all there is to it. You have nothing to say.'

'On the contrary, Papa, I have plenty to say. For starters, how it is that Château de Cluzac has shown no profits? How is it that I have been living on a shoestring? Why have I seen nothing whatsoever by way of dividends for several years?'

Charles-Louis breathed a sigh of relief. Pulling up a chair next to Clare, he switched on the charm. She could understand why women were drawn to him. Once, she had asked her mother why on earth (apart from the fact that she had been pregnant at the time) she had married such a complete *con*, to which Viola had replied, a trifle wistfully, that 'even shits have charm'. Now her father was directing the full force of his magnetism – the winning smile, the seductive eyes beneath their straight dark lashes – in her direction.

'You are quite right to be concerned about the château. There is a very good reason, as Maître Long will confirm, why you have received nothing. There has been nothing to receive.'

Unable to remain in one place for very long, the Baron got to his feet and put his hands in the pockets of his English worsted trousers.

'Times, you see, Clare,' he went on reasonably, 'have changed, I'm afraid. In common with the rest of France, indeed with the whole of Europe, Bordeaux has a serious economic crisis on its hands. Our claret, against which all other red wines were once measured, now has to compete with the very real challenge of the New World.'

'I think you are forgetting,' Clare said, 'that I have seen the *Mémo de Chasse*.'

Maître Long raised his eyebrows. He was getting lost.

'The *Mémo de Chasse* is neither here nor there,' the Baron said, the veneer of charm slipping. 'Let me explain. A situation has arisen whereby I owe several million francs in back-taxes to the French government. For reasons of which you are now aware, I am unable to bring back into the country any money which . . . I may have elsewhere. In short I am in trouble with the *fisc*. I cannot afford to turn down Van Gelder's offer.'

'And I can't afford to throw away my inheritance. You know perfectly well that Château de Cluzac is grossly undervalued. Why should I hand over my twenty-four per cent, so that you can scarper off to Florida on the proceeds?'

Ignoring her question, Charles-Louis exchanged confidential words with the lawyer before moving to the door.

'Your signature would have made things very much simpler, Clare. We can, however, proceed without your consent. Bernadette has already agreed.'

'I went to see Tante Bernadette. She has changed her mind about giving you her *pouvoir* . . .'

Charles-Louis' hand gripped the brass door-knob, assiduously polished by Sidonie. The lawyer held open the lid of his briefcase. She had their full attention.

'I told her about the *Mémo de Chasse*. She wasn't too impressed with the fact that you have been ripping off Notre Dame de Consolation. She requires half a million francs to repair the roof of the chapel, which is in danger of collapsing.'

'The roof of the convent chapel is not high on my agenda.'

'I have also discussed the matter with Grandmaman. She is absolutely appalled at the thought of the château being sold.'

'Your grandmother has nothing to say in the matter.'

'Grandpapa left her four per cent of Château de Cluzac because he wished it to remain in the family. Have you no feelings?'

'Feelings do not come into it.' The Baron looked at his watch. 'You're wasting everybody's time.'

'Then let it be wasted.'

'Have you come into a fortune by any chance? Are you thinking of buying me out?'

'That was not what I had in mind, Papa. I was born at Cluzac, I grew up here . . .'

'I must say you've taken very little interest in it.'

'I refuse to let you get away with throwing away my *patrimoine*, for which Grandpapa worked so hard. I want you to withdraw Château de Cluzac from sale.'

'Impossible.'

'Impossible?'

'If you insist on making trouble Clare, the château

will be sold over your head. I shall take the matter to a tribunal.'

'If you go to a tribunal I will inform them about your account in the Banque de Genève . . .'

'You wouldn't dare.'

'Try me. The French government takes an extremely serious view of these things. If you attempt to get the money out of Switzerland the police will stop you at the border. The account will be frozen. Forget Laura Spray. Forget Florida. You will go to jail.'

'You really are a monster, Clare.'

'I had a good teacher.'

'If I don't raise the capital on the château, Monsieur Huchez and Monsieur Combe will have something to say. How else do you suggest I pay my back-taxes?'

'I'm afraid, Papa, that's your problem.'

Through the window Clare could see Jamie, in his running gear, setting off round the vineyards with a loping Rougemont at his heels. Trying to control the banging in her chest, she faced the Baron.

'From now on Château de Cluzac will be efficiently – and legally – run,' she said.

'I am already committed in Florida. Who, may I ask, will run it?'

The words that escaped from Clare's lips came as much of a surprise to herself as they did to the Baron.

'I will.'

CHAPTER TWENTY

The announcement that Château de Cluzac was no longer on the market, and that young Clare de Cluzac was taking over the estate from her father, ran through the Médoc with the speed of a forest fire. To some the news was as welcome as the plague of phylloxera, which at the end of the 1870s had attacked the vines and wiped out seventy-five per cent of the harvest.

It was Harry Balard, who had the information from the golf club, who brought home the news that dashed his sister's romantic hopes, shattered his mother's aspirations and spiked his father's guns.

For Marie-Paule it was the end of a dream. Her marriage to the handsome Claude Balard had turned out to be a disappointment.

The first major indication that all was not well had come with the birth of their son Harry, conceived on their honeymoon. Marie-Paule had been led to believe that a new mother was a blessed Madonna whose image must be worshipped; a fragile human being, pushed to the edge by childbirth, who was in desperate need not only of tender loving care but of understanding from her spouse.

Contrary to her expectations, any compassionate feelings towards her which her husband had previously harboured, and which had been expressed beneath the covers of the *lit matrimoniale*, had, at the moment of Harry's birth, been snuffed out like a candle. After a brief glance at his son, Balard had handed the bundle back to Marie-Paule and allowed her to get on with it, which she had done, more or less, ever since.

From that moment on, the marriage had started to fall apart. That it held together at all was due to the fact that Marie-Paule put her husband's displeasure with the way she looked (pregnancy did nothing for her), and with the manner in which she ran the house, down to deficiencies in herself rather than his own disposition. Despite her best efforts, there were times when she was unable to please him. If she chattered, he wanted to be left alone. If she said nothing, he wanted to know why she wasn't talking to him. If she laughed, it was too loud. If she dominated the conversation she was diverting attention from him. Either she said the wrong thing, or she said the right thing, but in the wrong way. Blaming *her* thoughtless words or ill-chosen remarks for his bad moods and his frequent retreat into a silence that cast a pall over the household and sometimes lasted for days, she felt obliged to make excuses for him. When he returned to his normal indifference, it was as if a load had been removed from her shoulders, and the resumptions of their conjugal duties was like sunshine after rain.

To avoid confrontation (it was not worth the candle) Marie-Paule had learned to acquiesce with her husband, to defer to his authority at all times, and to allow any will or opinion which had not already been knocked out of her by his bullying to be consumed by his. It was a cross she accepted, the weight of which she had to bear.

The burden was made more tolerable by the presence of Harry, upon whom she doted, unable to refuse him anything, and whom she protected from his father. That this was not too difficult was due to the fact that, like many other *chartronnais*, her husband was so busy peddling his wines at home and abroad that she saw him only at mealtimes.

While his run-of-the-mill clients were wined and dined in one of the many Bordeaux restaurants, those of importance were subjected to an excruciatingly formal dinner, *chez Balard*, at which English was invariably spoken. Other than on these, fortunately rare, occasions for which she was directly responsible, Marie-Paule's time was taken up with charity work and there was even a local clinic which bore her name.

By contrast to Harry, Christiane was her father's girl. From the moment that Balard had glanced into the crib at the end of his wife's bed, he had been instantly captivated. He babbled and booed at her, swung her upside down, clapped his large hands (startling her out of her wits), and sang to her in his coarse and tuneless voice. Later he bought her toys. Pull-along ducks that quacked cacophonously and dogs which did somersaults. Despite Marie-Paule's disapproval, he indulged his own appetites vicariously, and stuffed the child with sweets and cakes.

Despite her father's insensitive parenting, Christiane Balard, who was not over-endowed with brains, grew up to be not only good-looking but sweet-natured and gentle. Although her father was putty in her hands, she rarely made demands upon him, and as the only member of the family to be excluded from the paranoid circle, in which nothing they did was right, Christiane could do no wrong.

Harry's pronouncement about the sale of Château de Cluzac, made over lunch in the gloomy dining-room with its heavy Provençal furniture and collection of plates inherited from Marie-Paule's mother (dismissed contemptuously by Balard as *ramasses nids à poussières*, although he did not have to dust them), did not have quite the explosive effect upon her husband that Marie-Paule might have expected.

Putting down his spoon on the *potage au cresson* – the current cook was not inspired – which he rudely dismissed as *Bouillie Bordelaise* (the 'Bordeaux Mixture' specific against mildew and potato disease), he accused Harry of lying.

Marie-Paule, as usual, sprang to her son's defence.

'How could he make up such a terrible thing, cheri? Why would he wish to do so?'

Commanded to do so, Harry, whose transient stammer was exacerbated by the presence of his father, reiterated the news that the château on which his father had set his heart had been withdrawn from the market and would henceforth be run by Clare de Cluzac. His pronouncement shattered the tranquillity of the family mealtime, not exactly an oasis of peace at the best of times.

'Idle gossip,' Balard said, as if the vehemence with which he delivered his comment made it true.

Harry shrugged. 'Everyone in the clubhouse was talking about it . . .'

'Someone in the English Bookshop was saying that the Baron had already sold Château de Cluzac to a *South African* . . .' Christiane Balard ventured.

'Another silly rumour!' Balard looked at Harry, taking him down a peg. 'The next thing we'll be hearing is that Asterix has bought Château de Cluzac. These stories have been circulating for months.'

'Fine!' Harry said insolently, looking at his watch – he had a date in Bordeaux.

'Surely the agents would have let you know, *chéri.*' Marie-Paule poured oil on troubled waters. 'Surely they would have written to you . . .'

Ignoring his wife, and picking his teeth assiduously – a habit that irritated her intensely – Balard, who was unable to repudiate Harry's pronouncement entirely, turned to his son.

'Who is it that's been spreading this malicious gossip?'

'Pierre Kilmartin . . .'

'And where did young Kilmartin get it from?'
'Clare de Cluzac.'

The fact that her husband was not snoring like a pig
meant that Balard was awake. At the risk of having her
head bitten off, of being accused of waking him up, of
introducing controversial subjects when he was about to
go to sleep, of meddling in things that did not concern
her, of voicing an opinion on matters she knew nothing
about, Marie-Paule, unable to sleep herself at the thought
of the prize she had craved for so long being snatched
from beneath her nose, decided to take a chance.

'She doesn't even live in France.'

The fact that her husband knew immediately what she
was talking about, that he didn't taunt her with her
inability to make herself clear, gave her an indication
that all was not well. She decided to push her luck.

'Clare de Cluzac a château owner!' Her voice was scornful. 'Did I tell you that I met her *chez Biancarelli* . . . ?'

Balard pricked up his ears.

'My *femme de ménage* has a better idea how to dress.'

Turning over suddenly, and without warning, Balard
flopped down like a great porpoise coming to rest.

'You are Charles-Louis' negociant,' Marie-Paule said
soothingly, wondering if she should put a reassuring
hand on her husband's shoulder. 'He would not have
done anything without telling you . . .'

'Charles-Louis is capable of anything.'

'Maybe you should telephone him . . .'

'At three o'clock in the morning!'

'If it is true,' Marie-Paule said, now near to tears, 'I
will look a complete fool. I have told everyone that
we were buying Château de Cluzac. A Venetian Carnival . . .'

'Venetian Carnival?'

'The Fête de la Fleur. A Doge's Palace. I had it all

planned. I shan't be able to look my Baby Home committee in the face again.'

'If Clare de Cluzac thinks she   n run a château,' her husband's voice boomed from the depths of his vinous belly, 'she's mistaken. It's not like dabbling in an art gallery. You have to make financial choices. It's more like being in charge of a bank. It's like owning a racing stables – you win one race, then you lose four more. Anyone can make good wine in a good vintage. It takes years to learn how to deal with a difficult vintage, to know when to keep a reserve and when to release it. Photographic palate! What you see in your glass is a very small part of the story. It starts in the bare fields in winter, with the wet summers, with knowing how to cope with the *contrariétés*. When we want rain we get drought. When we want drought we get rain. You have to make decisions. Decisions that make the difference between an average wine and a great one. You have to know the weather. And when to start picking. Are you going to wait? If you wait, will it be raining? How will you handle the rain? Can you pick the grapes fast? Will the petit verdot ripen? What does Clare de Cluzac know about sanitation in the vineyards – I used to carry her on my shoulders when she was a baby – about fermentation? Has she even heard of the malo? Is she aware that the Cluzac *chai* is archaic, that the equipment comes out of the ark? A vineyard is a business. With seventy hectares under cultivation it is *big* business. Every day is a battle. What does she know about it? The girl must be as mad as her mother. She must think that running a vineyard is some kind of game . . .'

Balard's voice was getting louder. He suffered from high blood pressure, he was not supposed to get excited. Marie-Paule switched on the light.

'What are you doing?'

'Doctor Hébèque said you shouldn't get excited . . .'

'I am not excited! I am trying to tell you something, woman, and all you do is interrupt.'

'I am going to get you a pill!'

'I do not *want* a pill!' Balard was sweating profusely. He was dangerously red in the face.

'Then I am going to fetch Harry . . .'

'I forbid you . . .' Balard said.

But Marie-Paule was half-way down the passage. Calling Harry by name, she knocked and, without waiting for an answer, opened the door on to his empty room. Sitting down for a moment on the neatly made bed with its simple cotton quilt, she was overcome by a wave of maternal jealousy. Tracing an outline of Harry's head on the pillow, she pictured him in some Bordeaux disco dancing with another woman.

Nothing could have been farther from the truth. Although Harry was in Bordeaux, although he was in fact in a disco, although his partner wore the highest of heels, the shortest of skirts and sported the most luxuriant of eyelashes, he was not dancing with a girl.

Having not only been christened with a fashionable English name, but sent away to a fashionable English boarding school – against his mother's wishes – Harry Balard had grown up somewhat confused about his sexual orientation.

He was waiting to go up to Oxford when Julien Gilles, the tennis coach at Primrose, had, on more than one occasion, put his arms around him ostensibly to monitor his stroke. Together with an impressive backhand, and a service that was virtually unreturnable, the tennis coach had subsequently indoctrinated his pupil with skills other than those having to do with the game.

The sight of Julien's massive thighs in the showers, of his broad shoulders and muscular arms as he lathered his chest with soap, had provoked a response from Harry's body hitherto associated with the girls, optimistically introduced to him by his mother, with whom he danced, played tennis, took sailing on the Garonne, and only occasionally to bed.

In love, for the first time, with a man old enough to be his father, Harry Balard was introduced by his protector to the underbelly of Bordeaux.

In a moment of typical braggadocio, Harry had taken Julien home and introduced him to his mother. Marie-Paule, not immune herself to the indisputable charm of the bronzed athlete, had innocently enquired how Harry's tennis was coming along, and, when the two of them remained closeted in Harry's bedroom for an unconscionably long time, assumed that Julien was demonstrating to her son the finer points of the game.

When Harry deceived Julien (who was scuba-diving in the Red Sea) with Apollo Durand, a young man whom he picked up in a gay bar, the shit had hit the fan. Julien made every threat in the book, from killing himself to denouncing Harry to his family, but it was too late.

By the time Harry went up to university, from which he came down speaking French with an Oxford accent, he had discovered the delights of bisexual promiscuity. Fearful of AIDS, he did not permit his brief and indiscriminate male encounters – which belied his fastidiousness in all other respects – to include penetrative sex.

Failing to find Harry in his bedroom, Marie-Paule went to wake Christiane in her room across the passage, which was as cluttered and revealing, with its frilled cushions, miniature scent bottles, pictures of rock idols and cuddly animals, as Harry's was secret and stark.

She was unable to bring herself to rouse Christiane from what appeared to be an extremely deep sleep. With a wistful sigh at the sight of the youthful body exposed to the heat, Marie-Paule caressed a strand of her daughter's fine hair, streaked golden by the sun, which strayed across the pillow, and tiptoed out of the room.

Returning to the master bedroom, she found Claude, lying in the middle of the bed and spreadeagled over two thirds of it, breathing stertorously through his open mouth, and fast asleep.

Making herself as small as possible, she climbed in beside him. Alone for once with her thoughts – even when he was not actually controlling her, Balard's wires were in her head – she made her own plans for Château de Cluzac; plans which she was not going to give up without a struggle, and for which she would enlist Harry's willing help.

CHAPTER TWENTY-ONE

Delphine Lamotte heard the news in the hairdresser's. When she had paid her bill, taking care, as she returned her credit card to her wallet, that she did not smudge her freshly varnished nails, she had tucked Bijou, her miniature poodle, under her arm and, by dint of nonchalantly bouncing her Volkswagon Golf off the bumper of the car parked in front of her and backing into the car behind, extracted it from its parking place. Driving straight to the headquarters of Assurance Mondiale in the Rue Vauban, she swept into her husband's office, where she found him yoked, as usual, to his computer.

'Alain!' Delphine put Bijou on the leather sofa.

'*Chérie*!'

Pressing the save button, Alain Lamotte, impeccable in his impeccable white-on-white shirt and elephant tie (a Christmas present from Delphine), stubbed out his cigarette in the already overflowing ashtray and got up from his desk. Although he was always happy when his wife dropped in on him unexpectedly, he was surprised to see her. Putting his arms round her, he kissed her on both cheeks and ruffled her hair affectionately.

'*Attention mes cheveux*!' Delphine put a hand to her hair. '*Sais-tu les dernières nouvelles, chéri?*'

'News?'

Alain sat down again at his desk. He assumed that Delphine had had one of her *petits petits accidents* in the car, that Amélie or Joséphine had been sent home from school sick, or that there was a problem, a blocked filter or a *surplus de chlore* in the swimming-pool.

'Clare de Cluzac is taking over Château de Cluzac from the Baron!'

Alain glanced involuntarily at the Château de Cluzac sale document which for the past six months had been his bible. The list of liabilities to be taken over by a new owner: the long-term loans (buildings and stock as security), the short-term bank credit. He could recite, like a litany, the reported income statement for the past four years (Exhibit 3, Page 15), the sales, the gross income, the profit before depreciation, interest and tax. He was *au fait* with the volume of wine production of the Château, with the sales and distribution, with the 'adjusted' profits and the currency exposure. He patted the dossier as if to reassure himself, and looked at his wife.

'I don't understand.'

'The Baron has handed over the château to his daughter. It has been withdrawn from the market.'

'It's not possible. The Baron is already deeply committed in Florida.'

'I heard it *chez Alexandre*.'

Alain grinned. His teeth were white and even except for one in the front, which was slightly askew. The aberration produced a small gap which added to the attraction of his boyish smile.

'*Eh bien*!' he said dismissively. Like many men imbued from the cradle with *idées reçues*, he equated beauty-parlour gossip with fiction.

'Laura Spray was in the next chair.'

A light went out on Alain's face. Delphine had seen that expression before. When the news had come from Paris that his father had died; when she had miscarried their third child, a boy.

'Laura Spray *told* you?'

'She didn't *exactly* tell me. She was shooting her mouth off to Alexandre.'

Delphine had been reading about the latest exploits of Princess Di (she wondered what the magazines would find to write about without her) while she waited patiently – it was not a bit of use looking at your watch – for Alexandre, who was blow-drying the hair of a client in the adjacent chair. Alerted by the transatlantic accents, she had looked in the mirror and realised that the raised voice belonged to Baron de Cluzac's American fiancée, who was shouting to make herself heard.

'I wouldn't live in that old castle if you paid me,' Laura Spray had said as she helped herself to mineral water from the bottle on the dressing-table. 'You can't get the staff. It's falling to pieces. It needs renovating from top to bottom, and it's impossible to heat . . .'

Now paying attention, Delphine realised that Laura Spray was talking about Château de Cluzac, for which Alain had put in a sizeable bid on behalf of Assurance Mondiale, and over the acquisition of which he had had many sleepless nights.

'There's something very funny going on if you ask me,' Laura Spray confided, unaware that the salon had gone quiet. 'The Baron had everything settled. Mr van Gelder, the new owner, had gone back to South Africa to wind up his affairs. The next thing I hear the sale is off. Off! Cancelled. Finished. When contracts were about to be signed. It doesn't make any difference to me one way or another. I believe . . .' – she lowered her voice – 'that the Baron is being blackmailed by his daughter. That she has gotten some kind of hold over him. She hasn't set foot in the place for years. According to her father she's some sort of junk dealer and doesn't know a vineyard from a Van Go. To cut a long story short, the last few days have been hell. I was worried the Baron would have a coronary. Cluzac has been withdrawn from sale and Clare – she could do with your attentions, Alexandre, you want to see what she looks like – is taking over. The Baron wants us to stick around for a while, tie up a few loose ends. Frankly, I wouldn't care if I never saw another vineyard again. The sooner I can get him away to Florida . . .'

It was at this point that Delphine, who for the last few minutes had been stuck on a picture of an anorexic *Princesse Di* looking ravishing in a low-cut black dress, stopped paying attention. She was vaguely aware of Laura Spray buttering up Alexandre, asking would he come to Florida and do her hair for the wedding – which sounded as if it was going to have everything except an Aztec sacrificial fire dance – and why didn't he open a salon in Palm Beach (she could fill it for him in no time), when the full impact of what she had heard, with all its ramificaticns, had sunk in.

Ten years ago, Assurance Mondiale had decided to balance the long-term liabilities from its insurance business with long-term assets. It was one of the first major outside investors to run a group of European vineyards as a business, with a computerised database. Despite the vicissitudes of nature, these vineyards aimed to deliver an average return of at least three per cent plus asset appreciation. Those that failed to do so were sold.

Like Alcatel at Gruaud-Larose and Axa at Pichon-Longueville-Baron, Assurance Mondiale had set its heart on acquiring a premier Bordeaux vineyard. For the past six months the potential addition of Château de Cluzac to its portfolio had brought the gentle simmer of life at the Moulin de la Misère, the Lamotte residence near Villandraut, to an excited boil. Alain's plans for the modernisation of the estate, which included the latest in bottling chains, capable of filling 2,000 bottles an hour, were known even to the little girls.

Alain had done his homework. While, like an ageing courtesan, the château itself was crying out for a facelift, the eastern aspect of the sloping vineyards, warmed gradually by the morning sun and cooled gently in the evening, allowed the grapes to ripen to perfection. The property sat arrogantly, between two tiny villages, on the most coveted *croupe* in the Médoc. Of its 150 hectares of gravelly topsoil (which not only reflected the heat but prevented the soil from drying out), stony subsoil (with its minute traces of minerals, which enhanced the subtlety of the wine) and iron foundations, 75 hectares were legally plantable. Thanks however to Baron de Cluzac's neglect, only two-thirds of these were actually planted. Bringing the vineyards up to their 10,000-vines-per-hectare maximum (as laid down by the Appellation Contrôlée) would mean that there was the very real possibility of doubling the production – and by extension the market value – of the estate in under ten years. Alain had already put too much work into the project to allow such a potentially worthwhile investment to slip through his fingers.

Delphine did not like to be the bearer of bad tidings. Possessed of more than his fair share of energy and drive, and with a well-earned reputation for delivering the goods, Alain was programmed for success. He did not take kindly to failure, which he attributed to some deficiency in himself. The last thing she wanted was to prick his balloon.

'It doesn't make sense,' Alain said. 'Everyone knows Charles-Louis can't pay his back-taxes. There is no way he would have chucked away fifty million francs . . .'

'There's something else, *chéri*.'

Leaning back in his leather chair, Alain waited.

'According to Laura Spray, the Baron had already made a deal . . .'

'With Claude Balard?'

'With a South African . . .'

'A South African?'

'Charles-Louis, it appears, has been double-crossing both of you.'

By the time Clare had left the Baron's office after giving him her ultimatum, leaving her father and a stunned Monsieur Long to pick up the pieces, Jamie had set off on his morning run. He had completed his first circuit of the vineyards and, followed by Rougemont, was setting off for the second time, when Clare caught sight of him.

'Jamie!'

'Hi!'

'Jamie, wait. I've got something to tell you.'

'Later.'

'It's important.'

'So is this.'

Catching up with him among the vines, and lunging at him in a rugby tackle, she brought him to the ground, while Rougemont, who had no idea what was going on, barked hysterically.

Jamie pulled Clare down on top of him.

'It had better be good.'

'How would you feel about postponing the wedding?'

'Postponing it?'

'Say January?'

'I've two conferences in January. *Locked Intermedullary Nailing* in Rome . . .'

'We could always get married in St Peter's . . .'

'And *Cement Techniques* in Barbados . . .'

'Or on the beach.'

'I'm reading papers at both of them.'

'I've just told my father I'm going to run the château.'

'You *what?*'

'I don't know what came over me. When I thought about what Papa was doing, what he had been doing for years, I just flipped.'

'He agreed of course!'

'He had no choice.' While Rougemont, who had now quietened down, licked the sweat from Jamie's face, Clare gave him a résumé of what had taken place.

'You don't know the first thing about running a château.'

'I can learn. It's better than being ripped off.'

'What about us?'

'Think what we'll be able to do with all the dosh.'

'That's not what I meant.'

'Say the word and I'll sell the estate to the South African. Let my father get away with swindling me for all these years . . .'

'When will I see you?'

'It's only for six months.' Clare interspersed her words with kisses. 'Bordeaux's . . . not . . . very far . . . away.'

'Clare, everyone can see us!'

'Only Rougemont, and he won't tell.'

CHAPTER TWENTY-TWO

A rusty pick-up truck made its jolting early-morning way along the potholes and came to a halt by the ditch at the junction of the Route des Châteaux and the narrow and anonymous road that led to Château de Cluzac.

Lowering the tail-gate and jumping out of the back, half a dozen hefty, blue-overalled workmen exchanged pleasantries in the flat accents peculiar to the region.

Climbing down from the cab, where she had been sitting next to the heavily tattooed driver, Clare de Cluzac, wearing shorts, a tee-shirt and plimsolls, walked round to the back of the truck to supervise operations.

She watched apprehensively as the team, issuing brusque instructions to each other, gruntingly manhandled a metal sheet covered with old sacking out into the roadway. Regarded with idle curiosity by the early-morning *vignerons* pedalling their slow way to work on ancient bicycles, the men laid down their burden, cursing colourfully as they strained against its weight. Returning to the truck, they emerged with batons of carved and painted wood, iron chains, mallets, tool-chests and rattling boxes of what seemed to be several hundred assorted nuts and bolts.

Realising that it was going to be a long job, and that for the moment she was not needed, Clare crossed the tarmacked road, already shimmering in the early-morning heat. Ignoring the fact that the heavy dew had not as yet been dried off by the sun, she sat down among the poppies and the thistles and picked a thick blade of the long coarse grass. Arranging it between her two thumbs, she put it to her lips and whistled, a trick learned twenty years ago from Albert Rochas.

Ever since she had been a child she had tended to act first and think afterwards. When she had told her father, a month ago, that it was her intention to run the estate, nothing had in fact been further from her mind. She had always regarded the château as belonging to her father (the two were indivisible), and her ultimatum had come as much a shock to herself as it had to Maître Long and the Baron.

Charles-Louis had been the first to recover.

'Van Gelder's family has owned vineyards in the Cape for generations. Apart from being an experienced wine-grower, he is also a businessman. I think you will find that under his stewardship Château de Cluzac will be "efficiently run".'

'You're not hearing me, Papa.'

'Understandably, you are interested in your dividends . . .'

'Read my lips.'

'I've had enough of your impertinence, Clare.' The Baron looked at Maître Long. '*On y va!*'

'If you're going to try to get round Tante Bernadette,' Clare said, 'don't waste your time.'

After dinner, when he had finished his nightly game of piquet, the finer points of which he had tried to explain to Jamie, Charles-Louis had taken Clare aside. In the Baron's Room, mellow with post-prandial Armagnac, he had motioned her to a seat and taken his chequebook from the cubby-hole of the desk. Putting on his tortoiseshell half-glasses, he unscrewed the cap of his fountain pen.

'How much did you say you need for this new gallery of yours?'

'Fifty thou.'

Making out a cheque for £50,000, the Baron had smiled patronisingly.

'You always were headstrong. It's the Irish in you. You take after your mother . . .'

'Perhaps I take after you, Papa. Because you happen to be a de Cluzac, you think everyone is for sale. Everything can be bought. Perhaps you're right. Perhaps you have always been right. Until today, when I suddenly realised that over half the money in the Banque de Genève belongs by right to Tante Bernadette and to Grandmaman and to me, and that for years you have been – not to put too fine a point on it – *stealing* from your own flesh and blood. That you were no better than a common thief. I don't know the first thing about running a vineyard. That much is obvious. I know it will be difficult but I'm willing to learn. Van Gelder will have to wait. I intend to stay long enough at Château de Cluzac to put the estate on a proper commercial footing. It can then be sold for its *true* market value . . .'

'Excuse me, I understood you were getting married?'

Ignoring the interruption, Clare glanced pointedly in the direction of the Oeben table.

'I owe it to the Convent of Notre Dame de Consolation, I owe it to Grandmaman, and I owe it to myself. There is nothing you can do to stop me, unless you want to spend the next five years in jail.'

Clare leaned forward and picked up the cheque from the table.

Breathing a sigh of relief, the Baron took off his glasses and put them back into the case.

'That's that then.' He chuckled. 'I trust Laura and I will be invited to the wedding.'

Ignoring the comment, Clare stood up, folded the cheque and put it into the pocket of her new 'smoking'.

'This will go to Tante Bernadette. For the chapel roof. I too am a de Cluzac, Papa. I am not for sale.'

As she tried to explain later to Jamie, when she had challenged her father with his years of outright dishonesty, with his disdain for Cluzac, with the contempt with which he had treated both Baron Thibault's carefully husbanded legacy and her own *patrimoine*, with the Swiss bank account, something inside her had snapped. As she had looked out of the window at the sea of vines among which she had been brought up – such bringing up as there had been – it was as if she had become a vine herself, as if she were rooted to the spot. When the Baron, convinced as usual of his own superiority, of his own pre-eminence, from which pinnacle he believed that no one below had the least knowledge of the world, had enquired superciliously who she imagined was going to run the château along the lines she had described, her response had been unpremeditated. It was the incomprehensible feeling that she was defending the medieval fortress, in whose parks she had once played and in whose moat she had once swum, against the onslaught of the invading Vikings – rather than from the ministrations of a South African entrepreneur – which had provoked her reply. She was as ill equipped to administer a wine-growing estate as she was to mastermind a space station.

'Would you really have shopped your father?' Jamie said later as, with his arm round her shoulders, they strolled back through the vineyards.

'I don't suppose Papa considered for one moment the fact that he was double-crossing me or that he was doing anything illegal. He simply didn't want to pay his taxes.'

'Answer the question. Would you have shopped him?'

'At that moment, yes.'

'And now?'

'It's what he deserves. Don't let's talk about my father.'

'What shall we talk about?'

Clare put her head on his shoulder.

'If I do stay here for six months, will you still love me?'

Jamie dropped a kiss on her forehead.

'It will take more than a few lousy grapes to come between us.'

A great deal more diplomacy had been needed to win over Nicola than it had done to get round Jamie.

'Bordeaux!' she had said when, back in London, Clare had broken the news to her. 'I thought you and I were supposed to be in partnership?'

'We are.'

'Has it not occurred to you that you might be letting me down?'

'It's only Bordeaux. I'm not disappearing from the face of the earth. Look at it this way. Six months from now the Nicola Wade Gallery will be able to go into business in a big way. We'll set up a gallery in Paris, one in New York.'

'I thought the idea was to get out of Covent Garden . . .'

'In the fullness of time.'

'If you really want to know, I think you're a rat! Not to mention a head case. What do you know about grapes?'

'Less than nothing. There are people . . .'

'Have you considered the possibility that "people" might like to see you fall flat on your face.'

'No doubt they would.'

'What does Jamie have to say?'

'Jamie was OK once he'd got over the shock. He's going to come over whenever he can.'

'What about the wedding?'

'We've postponed it until the end of February.'

'Farm Street or the wind-dried ducks?'

'Neither, as a matter of fact. Jamie's parents want us to get married in Aberdeen . . .'

'You can twist Jamie round your little finger . . .'

'I wouldn't be so sure.'

'Don't expect me to be so accommodating. What am I going to do about the Moti Aron exhibition? What am I going to do about Kettle's Yard?'

'Why don't I ask Zoffany if she's interested? She's a bit over-qualified but I don't think she's found anything in banking yet.'

'Suppose I don't want to work with Zoffany?'

Getting up from the desk, on which stood the vase of sweet peas she had brought Nicola as a peace offering, Clare put her arms round her partner.

'Don't be like that, Nick. I feel badly enough about skiving off. Imagine it was *your* father screwing you.'

'My father is a dentist.'

'You wouldn't let him get away with it.'

'Michael Millington's not going to be at all pleased.' Nicola ran her fingers through her Nicky Clarke hair-cut as Clare put her jacket on. She was due at her grandmother's.

'I have enough problems of my own right now. I can't take Michael Millington's on board,' she had added.

Watching the men erect the heavy metal sheet at the side of the road, manoeuvring it into place and securing it against the wind with wooden struts, Clare went over her conversation with her grandmother, which had taken place among the elephants and rhinoceroses in the Natural History Museum – a short walk from where she lived – which was the Baronne's second home.

'I said your father was up to something.'

'You were right.'

'He's lucky that you let him off so lightly. If what you have told me were to get out it would be Cruse all over again.'

She was referring to the scandal of the 1970s, when the greed of the wine-growers, combined with the severe shortage of decent claret, had reduced many Bordeaux negociants to desperation.

By some bureaucratic oversight, the detachable coupons of the tax slips (*acquits verts*), which enabled suitably approved shippers to move a load of wine from one country to another, indicated neither the colour of the wine involved nor its *appellation*. This loophole allowed shippers to *buy* ordinary red wine and AOC white, then switch certificates so that they were *selling* ordinary white, but AOC red. By this simple trick they lost 10 per cent on the white wine, but gained an illegal 300 per cent by upgrading the red.

All that was needed to perpetrate this deception was a supplier of good red wine that could pass as claret, and front men such as the highly respectable, if commercially ruthless, Cruse et Fils Frères.

Tankers arriving at the Cruse cellars carrying wine from the Midi (equipped with an *acquit blanc*), were issued with an *acquit vert* and directed to another of the Cruse warehouses. This manipulation of the tax slips was a licence to print money. When the Tax Office got wind of what was going on, the 'Winegate' affair that followed referred to a 'fraud big enough to make a wine-grower blush'. Everyone in Paris, including *Le Canard*, was curious to find out the precise nature of the banana skin that had caused 'the best known shippers in Bordeaux' to slip up.

The Cruses were charged with criminal practice and tax avoidance. After a trial lasting several weeks and involving 10,000 pages of evidence, they were given suspended sentences with their businesses to be kept under strict legal surveillance. Protesting their innocence to the last, they were also ordered to find a ruinous 38 million francs to satisfy the taxman's demands.

Unable to face the ignominy of the trial, old Hermann Cruse, a respected director of the firm, which had been foolishly persuaded to turn the law to its own advantage, had thrown himself from a bridge into the Gironde. The guilty parties in the case were subsequently pardoned, but the reputation of the Cruse family never recovered.

Although it was no secret that Baronne Gertrude held no brief for her son, she had no desire to see the de

Cluzacs similarly discredited, nor to tarnish the good name of Bordeaux.

Entering the Whale Hall with its grotesque suspended skeletons, the Baronne took her granddaughter's arm.

'You were always a law unto yourself. Do you remember when you cut all your hair off, when you were thirteen?'

'It was so long I could sit on it.'

'Such beautiful hair. It was a long time before I forgave you. I only wish I had seen Charles-Louis' face when you confronted him with the *Mémo de Chasse*!' The Baronne had looked at Clare shrewdly. 'Being chatelaine of Château de Cluzac will give you a worthwhile job to do.'

Sitting by the roadside now, with her back to the Château Martin vineyards, in which the July grapes were setting in promising green clusters, Clare considered her grandmother's words and prayed to a God with whom she was unfamiliar, both for guidance and for strength.

As the workmen completed their task, and the canvas shrouds were ripped from the *pancarte* she had had made, she was faced with the first hard evidence of what, in an unconsidered moment, she had so rashly undertaken.

Bold black letters on a scarlet ground, which dominated the earth-colours of the surrounding countryside, were embellished with arrows pointing in the direction of Château de Cluzac. The legend on the sign declared that the cellars of her ancestral home were now open to the public, and that, for the very first time in the history of the estate, its prestigious *deuxième cru* wine was to be sold to the *hoi polloi*, at the door.

CHAPTER TWENTY-THREE

The ongoing effect of Clare's showdown with her father touched the lives not only of Jamie and Nicola in England, but also of a great many exceedingly disgruntled people in France.

Marie-Paule Balard came as near as possible to murdering her husband without translating her thoughts into action. The homicidal fantasies that occupied her mind night and day precipitated a visit to the doctor in the Cours de Verdun for an *ordonnance* for tranquillisers.

Claude Balard was glad to get out of the house. Furious at losing Château de Cluzac, he already had enough on his plate without his wife's constant reproaches, as if what had happened between Clare and the Baron were his fault. When, on his way to the Maison du Vin in Pauillac, he suddenly caught sight of the monstrous new sign at the roadside, where before there had been only the vista of vines, he felt his blood pressure shoot up. As he fumbled in his pocket for one of his pills, the car swerved in the path of a lorry, and there was very nearly a nasty accident as he brought it to a halt.

The sign, its ox-blood-red-painted metal set against a white wooden frame, proclaimed in unequivocal black lettering:

Château de Cluzac
GRAND CRU CLASSE EN 1855

VISITE DES CHAIS TOUS LES JOURS
VENTE DIRECTE. OPEN EVERY DAY

Although the *pancarte was* offensive, it was not this that caused the negociant's apoplectic reaction. Neither was it that, after three centuries of cobwebbed obscurity, the cellars were to be open – 365 days a year – to the scrutiny of every Tom, Dick and Harry. The public proclamation that, according to the renowned classification of 1855, Château de Cluzac had been declared a *deuxième cru* did not bother him either.

The French were by disposition categorisers. Prince Napoleon, organiser of the Paris Exhibition, anxious to display the splendour of the Third Empire, had invited the *courtiers* (brokers) attached to the Bordeaux *Bourse* to prepare a hierarchical list of the region's most prestigious wines. The Chamber had sent back an inventory based on historic prices paid, with the wines in the different classes arranged in alphabetical order.

Dissatisfied with this, the Prince insisted on an entirely 'new' division. By tasting the Médoc wines, more or less conscientiously, and placing them in order of merit within the classes, the brokers arrived at the immutable 1855 classification which (*pace* Château Mouton-Rothschild, which had been declared a first growth in 1973), had tormented the Bordeaux growers ever since.

What Claude Balard objected to, and what had brought a pain like a tight band, as if he were about to be suffocated, to his chest, was the statement that, although he, Claude Balard, was in possession of an exclusive ten-year contract, signed by Charles-Louis himself, to distribute Château de Cluzac wines, they were being blatantly offered by the Baron's daughter for sale at the cellar door.

The wine trade, like any other business, was subject to its fair share of skulduggery. The Baron was fully aware that, as with generations of *chartrons* before him,

the price which Claude Balard charged the wholesalers
for the wine was twice as much as that which he had
paid for it. While, for obvious reasons, this arrangement
suited the negociant, it also prevented the Baron from
making any official revenue in France and left him with
a handsome profit margin to be salted away in the Swiss
bank account.

Disregarding his appointment at the Maison du Vin –
first things first – and thinking that this time Marie-Paule
really would kill him, Balard, who had overshot the bill-
board, which quite outdid in vulgarity any other *pancarte*
along the Route des Châteaux, made a clumsy three-point
turn. Facing in the opposite direction to that in which he
had been going, he drove down the bumpy road towards
Château de Cluzac, where, despite the fact that it was
still only ten o'clock in the morning, Clare had been in
her office for several hours.

Facile dictu, difficile factu: easier said than done. The
truth of the Latin tag, drummed into her by Sister Agnes
at St Mary's, had been brought home to her during the
four weeks in which she had been in charge of Château
de Cluzac.

'Good-quality grapes crushed and fermented. Control
the temperature and keep it clean. It's dead simple.'
Remembering the words of Big Mick destined to needle
Halliday Baines at the Fête de la Fleur, Clare reckoned
that the wine, asleep in the cellars beneath the experienced
eye of the *maître de chai*, was the least of her problems.

A farewell supper at Hannah's, for which Francesca had
made a vat of her 'killer curry', had marked her rite of passage from the Nicola Wade Gallery to Château de Cluzac,
from Notting Hill to Bordeaux. The warm send-off given
to her at the party, to which Jamie's ex-girlfriend, Miranda
Pugh, had taken her handsome racing driver, Barnaby
Muirhead, had brought home the isolation that lay ahead.

They had all been pretty smashed when Sebastian, who fancied himself as a raconteur and who had been propping up the wall and discussing the use of ultrasound in osteomyelitis with Jamie most of the evening, had told a French joke to make Clare feel more at home.

'There's this honeymoon couple . . .'

'I hope it's clean!'

'. . . who find that their hotel in the Dordogne is full. The young man parks the 2CV in a country lane where they spend the night under the car . . .'

'Disgusting!'

'In the morning they're woken up by this *gendarme*. "'Allo, 'Allo . . . !"'

'What was Inspector Clouseau doing in the Dordogne, Sebby?'

'Do shut up Seth,' Hannah said.

'"'Allo, 'Allo . . ."'

''Allo, 'Allo!' Imitating Sebastian's phoney French accent, they all fell about laughing.

'Quiet please! "'Allo, 'Allo! What eez going on 'ere?" the gendarme says. "I'm s-s-sorry officer," the young bridegroom stammers. "But I was just repairing my motor car." The gendarme shakes his head sadly. "Non, M'sieur. I do not sink you were repairing your motor car." "Why not?" says the young man. "Zere are three reasons why not . . ."'

They were all quiet now.

'"One"' – Sebastian raised a finger. '"Your toes are pointing in ze wrong direction . . ."'

'Ooooh!'

'"Two: zere is a crowd around you shouting 'Bravo! Bravo . . . !'"'

'Aaaagh!'

'And three?' Barnaby Muirhead asked.

'"Three . . ."' Sebastian made them wait. He twirled an imaginary moustache. '"Three: someone 'as stolen ze car!"'

The party had ended in tears, as they said goodbye to Clare thrusting farewell presents into her hand: eau-de-toilette from Nicola (who still had not forgiven her), a gilt pill-box from Zoffany, a copy of a fifteenth-century necklace from the V and A museum shop from Hannah, decorated writing-paper from Tony and Clive, and a photograph frame from Francesca.

Saying goodbye to Jamie at the airport, Clare had almost changed her mind.

'What if I make a fool of myself? What if I can't do it?'

'If you can sell paintings sweetheart, you can sell wine.'

'I wish you were coming with me.'

'I'll be with you all the way.'

'Will you keep an eye on Grandmaman?'

'Grandmaman and I are going to have dinner every Tuesday.'

Clare took a handful of Nicola's pink tissues from her pocket. Her voice was unsteady.

'Mind you don't cut the nose off the Brie.'

Taking the tissues from her, Jamie lifted her chin and wiped her damp face.

'You'll be all right, darling. All beginnings are hard.'

'Tolstoy?'

'Jamie Spence-Jones. You're going to miss your plane.'

'I don't think I quite realised how much I love you . . .'

'"Absence makes the heart grow fonder."'

'Jamie Spence-Jones?'

'Anonymous. Let me see you smile.'

'I don't feel like smiling.'

Clare wound her arms round Jamie's neck.

'I'll call you every night.'

The first thing she had done on taking over Château de Cluzac was to set up an office for herself. Appropriating one of the large disused rooms in the *chais*, she had thrown out the ancient *armoire* stacked with yellowing papers, the worm-eaten table and the rickety chairs. Doing a 'Laura Spray' on the administrative building, she had transformed it into an efficient bureau, with glass doors and windows, through which she could both be seen and see into the sunlit courtyard. Hanging up a sign of welcome '*Accueil: Bureau de Vente*', she installed herself on a black leather chair, which contrasted with the gleaming white tiles of the floor, behind a vast chrome and ebony desk.

The fact that the renovations were done on credit, underwritten by her name, and that no funds were available to pay the bills, incurred the opprobrium of Monsieur Boniface. When she visited the estate manager in his dusty and adjoining office, with its faded plan of the château and its vineyards attached with drawing-pins to the wall, he informed her that the cash crunch, which had led the Baron to put Château de Cluzac on the market, meant that there were no funds available either to meet the monthly salary cheques or to ward off Van Gelder and keep the show on the road. He did not trouble to hide his resentment at Clare's presence at the château, a resentment that was shared not only by many others on the estate, but paradoxically by Sidonie.

Clare's first priority was to set up a meeting with Monsieur Guilleret at the Crédit Lyonnais in the Cours de l'Intendance. The bank manager, who had accommodated the Baron to the limit, received his daughter with suspicion. He was not moved either by Clare's declared intention to promote the Château de Cluzac label, known to few people outside France, to international prominence, or her plans to make the château into a viable proposition which would take it into the twenty-first century. Doubting her ability to transform the estate (his views on women were decidedly *vieux jeux*), and painfully aware that there were already too many dodgy loans around, he turned down, in the nicest possible way, her request for a loan.

On her way out of the bank Clare almost collided with

Alain Lamotte, whose rendezvous with Monsieur Guilleret
followed her own.

'Lamotte.' He held out his hand. 'Assurance Mondiale.
We met at the Fête de la Fleur.'

'I'm so sorry,' Clare sympathised with the young man,
in his penguin tie, who had set his heart on Château de
Cluzac.

'No hard feelings.' Alain Lamotte glanced at his gold
Rolex as he swung his briefcase towards the stairs. 'Look,
if you need any help . . .'

He was the first person to proffer assistance rather than
obstacles.

Swallowing her de Cluzac pride, Clare clutched at
the offer.

'As a matter of fact . . .'

'*Bon*. I'll call you.'

By the time Claude Balard drove like a demon into the
courtyard at Cluzac and burst in upon her in her new
office, Alain Lamotte, true to his word, had not only called
on Clare but taken her to lunch at the Lion d'Or. She was
badly in need of friends. Judging from the look on his
face, Claude Balard was not going to be one of them.

The transformation, not only of the *chais* but of Clare's
appearance, took a modicum of wind out of the negociant's
sails. What was it his wife had said? The Cluzac girl looked
more like a vineyard worker than the daughter of the
Baron. Despite the fact that she was tucking into a piece
of bread with Sidonie's coarse pâté (made from chicken
liver, sausage meat, unsalted pork fat and cognac), this
was no vineyard worker that faced him coolly across the
wide expanse of ordered desk.

Having transmogrified her life to that of château owner,
Clare had decided to act the part. Aided and abetted by
Beatrice Biancarelli, she now had a wardrobe of sharp
business suits – all of them trousered and most of them

black – with which to impress her prospective clients. Even her plimsolls had been temporarily consigned to limbo, and shaped heels on elegant shoes completed the seamless switch to her French persona.

'*Cette pancarte* . . . !' Monsieur Balard, red in the face, greeted her before they had even shaken hands.

'Won't you sit down?' Clare, who had been half expecting the negociant's visit, indicated a chair.

'*C'est illégal!*'

'Illegal? I don't think so. Have you not seen the other signs? Château Margaux, Château Lynch-Bages, Château Prieuré-Lichine.' She deliberately misunderstood.

Claude Balard looked at Rougemont, who was lying at Clare's feet, and returned the dog's baleful glare.

'Where is your father?'

'He left for Florida a week ago. Didn't he say goodbye?'

'*I* am the Baron's negociant.'

Clare nodded. 'So I understand, Monsieur.'

'There is a contract. It designates Balard et Fils as the sole distributor of Château de Cluzac wine.'

'My father informed me to that effect.'

'Then how can you put that monstrous sign . . . ? I have never in my life seen anything so hideous . . .'

'You have to admit, it's eye-catching. It certainly caught yours!'

'So tasteless . . . But that is quite beside the point. Your father's wine . . .'

'*My* wine, Monsieur Balard.'

'As you wish, Mademoiselle. Château de Cluzac wine. You have no right to sell it.'

'Business is business. You pay me only fifty francs a bottle. I can get a hundred or a hundred and twenty at the cellar door.'

'But you are not empowered to do so.' The girl, Balard thought, was stupid. 'There is a binding contract.'

'I must ask you to release me from it.'

'Not a chance. There is still two years to run. The contract was signed by your father. Until you remove that sign you are in breach of it. I shall take you to court.'

'Not a good idea.' Clare was unruffled.

'Try to stop me.'

'I wouldn't dream of it.' Clare stood up as the negociant made for the door. 'The Syndicat des Negocians, however, might take a somewhat different view . . .'

Balard stopped in his tracks.

'What has the Syndicat to do with it?'

'From now on Château de Cluzac will dispense with the services of Balard et Fils. Any attempt to enforce your contract will be reported to the Syndicat, together with the information that for several years now you have been issuing my father with false invoices . . .'

'Your father told you that?' Balard was flabbergasted.

'On the contrary, Monsieur Balard, by the elementary strategy of putting two and two together, I managed to find out what has been going on, for myself.'

CHAPTER TWENTY-FOUR

Clare's statement to Claude Balard, that she had discovered his perfidy for herself was not strictly true. Whereas when she had examined the *Mémo de Chasse* she had had her suspicions about her father's red-faced negociant, it was Alain Lamotte – who had carried out his own extensive checks on behalf of Assurance Mondiale – who confirmed that for some time the negociant had been lining his own pockets.

Lunch at the Lion d'Or at Arsac, with Alain Lamotte in his white shirt (testimony to Delphine's fastidious house-keeping), Dunhill jacket, and tie decorated this time with multicoloured babushkas, had to Clare's surprise lasted well into the afternoon. It was only when she looked round the little restaurant, one wall of which was lined with bottles of the local château owners' finest vintages displayed in wooden showcases, that she realised theirs was the only table still occupied and that little Monsieur Barbier, who three hours earlier had welcomed Alain and his guest so enthusiastically, was now politely waiting for them to leave.

Lamotte appeared to bear her no ill will for snatching Château de Cluzac from under the nose of Assurance Mondiale. He had gone out of his way to be helpful. Despite the brash glass-and-chrome image of the shop-front Clare had created, she had been nervously feeling her way. By the time she left the Lion d'Or, she had not only revised her opinion of Alain – whom she had unjustly pigeonholed as less of a brain and more of a pretty face – but had a better idea of what she was doing and funds with which to do it.

Alain Lamotte, company man and investor rather than wine buff, nevertheless had the château business taped. Before the first course was finished, Clare knew more about running a vineyard than she would have found out for herself in a month of Sundays.

Talking non-stop, his normally reserved tongue loosened by passion for his work, and with frequent recourse to the cigarettes by his side, Alain, who turned out to be a walking database, blinded her with figures. He informed her not only that Bordeaux produced some 660 million bottles of wine (one quarter white) annually, generating sales of 11.4 billion francs, but that over the past decade his own company, Assurance Mondiale, had spent over one billion francs to become the biggest single investor in Bordeaux wines.

'In the old days we invested in the stock market or in real estate. Then we bought forests. Now we believe that the most useful way to diversify our portfolio is to switch at least one per cent of our clients' assets to vineyards.'

'You must have been pretty mad at losing Cluzac.'

Alain said nothing. She could see from his face that he was angry.

'You *are* mad at losing Cluzac.'

'You win some, you lose some. I must admit I did a hell of a lot of work on it.'

'If it hadn't been me it would have been Van Gelder.'

Lamotte shrugged. 'I'm not bothered about foreign competition. They can't pack up the land and take it home with them. Tell me about your plans.'

'I'm going to throw the whole shooting match open to the public . . .'

'Picnic areas and a safari park?'

'That might come later. Right now I'm trying to fix up my *visites* to the cellars – if I can get Jean Boyer to co-operate. At the moment he's being exceedingly bolshie. The groups will assemble in the courtyard, then start with a tour of the château and work their way to the *chais*, which I'm in the process of cleaning up. Afterwards they will come upstairs to the "shop", where they will be able to buy *objects de vin, cahiers de cave* and books on Bordeaux, as well as honey, pot-pourri and other knick-knacks. Hannah – a friend of mine – is organising some "Château de Cluzac" T-shirts. The tour will finish in a room off the *Bureau d'Acceuil*, where there'll be tastings of drinkable, affordable wine.

'The *visite* will start in the daylight and gradually, and dramatically, get darker, ending with the descent into the *cave* – which will be lit like a grotto – into almost total darkness. Later on they can spend time in the vineyards and stroll round the gardens. Like everything else at Cluzac, the gardens have been sadly neglected. With the help of Monsieur Boniface, who is also being unbelievably uncooperative, I am planning to lay out new flowerbeds and put in some fountains . . .'

'Sorry to interrupt.' Alain Lamotte stubbed out his half-smoked cigarette. 'But it's a rule of thumb in my company that the modernisation of winery equipment, and the restoration of buildings, is carried out before anything is done to the grounds. I'm wondering just how wise it is, Mademoiselle de Cluzac . . .'

'Clare.'

'. . . Clare, to run before you can walk?'

'Not wise at all. But since the whole thing will probably be blown sky high by the *fisc* any day, probably none of it will ever happen.'

'What has the *fisc* got to do with it?'

'My father owes a small fortune in back-taxes.'

'Call them up.'

'Are you kidding?'

'Seriously. There's no one more greedy than a tax man. Tell the *fisc* what you've been telling me and they'll back off in the expectation of all the millions of francs which will be coming their way when you've put Château de Cluzac on the map.'

'What I really want to do,' Clare said, warming to her theme, 'is turn the *Orangerie* into a *salle de reception*, for weddings, conferences, that sort of thing. Jamie's going to sound out the drug companies. I want to pull negociants, businessmen, restaurateurs, wine buffs, people who will really appreciate the privilege of being in such surroundings, as well as tourists, from all over the world. I want to create a rural embassy for great wine.'

Alain Lamotte refilled his glass with wine from one of Assurance Mondiale's châteaux.

'An efficient retail operation is going to eat money. How do you propose to raise the necessary cash?'

'Have you any suggestions?'

'Your father kept a large bottle stock.'

'Bottle stock?'

'It's always been standard practice for leading châteaux to sell off the total *récolte*, with the exception of a small percentage for later sale or for drinking, within a year of the vintage. This is to finance the next year's crop. Your father's policy, possibly to spite our friend Balard, was to hold back a substantial proportion even of the more modest vintages. Possibly he had his eye on the increasing number of "collectors". Those rambling cellars of yours must hold fifty thousand bottles at the very least – representing every vintage produced on the estate – many of them lovingly cared for by your grandfather. Releasing a judicious quantity of your bottle stock would go some way to financing you . . .'

'Could you repeat that in words of one syllable?'

'OK. What you want to do is to put some of your wine

into a Christie's fine claret sale. London is still the wine capital of the world.'

'How do I go about that?'

Alain extracted a business card from his wallet. 'David Markham is a personal friend of mine. Have a word with David and tell him exactly what you've got, and how much you're willing to put on the market.' Alain signalled for the bill. 'Selling your bottle stock, however, is not going to cover the capital cost of new winery equipment. I would like to lend you the money . . .'

'You!'

'For one year. With a two-way option . . .'

'Meaning?'

'If at the end of the year you can pay back the loan, all well and good. If you can't, Assurance Mondiale can buy Château de Cluzac at the market price.'

'You mean go into partnership with Assurance Mondiale?

'These days family ownership is not always in a wine-grower's best interest. Suppose we say twenty-six per cent?'

'Why are you doing this?'

Alain could hardly explain to Clare that by lending her money, which, despite her grandiose plans for Château de Cluzac, he thought it extremely unlikely she would be able to repay at the end of a year, he might yet secure the estate for Assurance Mondiale. He leaned across the table.

'Let's say because your eyes are *extraordinaire* . . .'

Taking the young PGD seriously, Clare said, 'Cut it out!'

Driving back to Cluzac, she wondered how she could have been so crass as to imagine that Alain Lamotte, who had talked about nothing but Delphine, the children and Assurance Mondiale throughout the meal, was interested in anything but the 150 hectares of her prime wine-growing land.

Turning left at the Château de Cluzac *pancarte*, on

which Alain Lamotte had congratulated her, she thought
how her father – who looked upon himself as a landowner,
rather than a businessman, who believed in aristocratic
segregation and in keeping himself and his affairs to
himself – would have been shocked beyond belief at the
mere sight of it.

Fortunately he had not stayed around long enough to
see the flagrant arrows of the sign, indicating the once
well-guarded citadel of his ancestral home. Three weeks
from now, when he returned from Florida to arrange for
the transport of his cars, would be time enough.

Charles-Louis' leavetaking had been anything but harmo-
nious. A long session with Van Gelder had led to the South
African's storming out of the château swearing eternal
vengeance. Clare, who had been closeted with Monsieur
Boniface in his office at the time, had looked out of the
window and almost felt sorry for Papa.

'A handshake is a handshake.' Van Gelder's raised voice
could be heard across the courtyard. 'That's not the way
we do things in South Africa.'

Having presumably said as much as he was prepared to
say to the disappointed would-be purchaser of Château
de Cluzac, Charles-Louis, who had never been one to
explain, did not reply. Stony faced, hands in his pockets,
he accompanied Van Gelder to his car.

'This place has cost me money, Baron. A great deal of
money. My lawyers are not going to like it. Don't think
for one moment you're going to get away with this . . .'

Watching impassively as Van Gelder slammed the door
of his Mercedes and drove angrily away, Charles-Louis,
followed obediently by Rougemont – to whom Laura Spray
categorically refused to give houseroom – strolled towards
the stables, where Clare suspected that her father had his
eye on a curvacious new groom.

Laura Spray, wearing a pink pantsuit and matching pink

Alice band and almost asphyxiating Clare her with her liberally applied scent, had taken Clare's arm confidentially during a stroll round the moat as she attempted to make her see sense.

'How could you do this to your father?'

'I rather think,' Clare said, 'that the shoe is on the other foot.'

'I am trying to tell you something. Don't try to be smart. Charles-Louis wants out of this place. Frankly, he needs the money. He has a lifestyle to support . . .'

'He'll get his money. We'll *all* get our money.'

'You are doing this to your father out of spite.'

'If you say so.' Clare was not going to get involved with Laura Spray.

'I suggest you take your share of the sale and go back to England. Forget the whole thing. You've made your point.'

'And I suggest you mind your own business, Mrs Spray.' Withdrawing her arm, Clare turned towards the Orangerie for the renovations of which she held rough drawings in her hand. 'Stop meddling in things you know nothing about.'

'You've upset Laura,' Charles-Louis said later over his whisky in the library. 'I will not tolerate rudeness to my future wife.'

'Then tell your "future wife" to keep out of my hair.'

'I'll thank you to act in a civilised fashion towards Laura until we leave.'

Standing on the château steps amid a sea of Laura Spray's Louis Vuitton luggage, while the local taxi driver loaded the station wagon, on the day of their departure, Charles-Louis had kissed Clare coldly. Any emotion was kept for Rougemont who, looking more depressed than usual, as if he knew what was going on, clung like a limpet to his side. Having shaken hands with Sidonie, who dropped the Baron a brief curtsey, he squatted on his haunches and put his arms around the dog.

'We're going to be late, Charles!' Laura tapped her foot impatiently, pushing Rougemont away roughly as he tried to follow them into the car.

In a moment of panic, as her father vanished through the archway, leaving her alone with her bravado, Clare turned to Sidonie, in her white apron, for solace as she had done as a child.

For the first time that she could remember, Sidonie avoided her gaze. Turning on her heel and leaving Clare alone, a solitary figure on the moss-covered steps, the cook disappeared through the portico, to be swallowed up by the gloomy interior of the château.

CHAPTER TWENTY-FIVE

Sidonie's grandfather, Fernand Malbec, had joined the estate as a coachman and carter in 1910. Her father, originally an apprentice *tonnelier* (in the days when the barrels were constructed on site), had later changed direction and eventually become *maître de chai*. Her two older brothers, Marcel and Arnaud, had worked as *vignerons* for Baron Thibault, and later for Charles-Louis. Sidonie herself had been employed in the château since she had been a girl of fourteen.

The tragic death of Baron Thibault, the departure of Baronne Gertrude for the Pas-de-Calais, and the taking over of the reins of the château by the young Baron de Cluzac, had had little effect in the kitchens, where the menus, which faithfully echoed the seasons, continued to be sent upstairs as before.

Charles-Louis had been down from Oxford for only a few months, when Sidonie – who thought that, with his thick brown hair and his roving eyes, he was the most attractive man she had ever set eyes on – realised that her employer was looking at her in such a way, each time their paths crossed, that she thought she had forgotten to put on her clothes. When he waylaid her in the linen-room – where he had no business – pinned her against the wall and began to fumble with his trousers, she was too terrified to protest. As the young Baron withdrew his thrusting body from her own rigid one, she thanked him politely, before

running out of the house and into the orchard, where she
flung herself on the ground among the bruised and fallen
apples, and burst into mortified tears.

Six months later, after the linen-room incident had
been repeated on several occasions and she began to
look forward to it, she found she was *enceinte* with the
Baron's child. She had been conveniently married off to
Jean Boyer – who had had not only his fingers but his
testicles blown to pieces during the German occupation
– then a young apprentice in the *chais*. When the child,
a boy whom she had planned to christen Fernand (after
her grandfather) was born with the cord round his neck
and buried on the estate, Sidonie, never very articulate, had
retreated into taciturnity. She did not blame Charles-Louis,
who even now, in her eyes, could do no wrong, but
took her hostility out on her long-suffering husband, and
unloaded her maternal feelings on to Clare. Irrational as
it was, Sidonie blamed her erstwhile charge – rather than
Laura Spray and the fact that the estate was to be sold
– for the Baron's precipitate departure from Château
de Cluzac.

Sidonie's was not the only stone wall Clare found herself
up against. Calling on her neighbour, the Comtesse de
Ribagnac, at the behest of Baronne Gertrude, and taking
tea on her stone-balustered terrace, with its magnificent view over the Gironde and its islands, she had
noticed hordes of pickers moving in dark lines through
the Ribagnac vineyards. They appeared to make a careful
study of each vine from which they assiduously removed
surplus bunches of unripe grapes.

'*La vendange verte*,' the old Countess said, following
Clare's gaze. 'Summer pruning. It costs my son a small
fortune but it ensures the maximum concentration of
flavour and gives us the best wine.'

By dint of keeping her eyes open, as she drove up

and down the Route des Châteaux chasing builders and craftsmen in pursuit of the various innovations she had planned, Clare was surprised to discover that the vines of Château de Cluzac were the only ones of note from which a proportion of the tight bunches were not being removed.

Seeking out Albert Rochas, who made no secret of his lack of confidence in his woman boss, and seemed miraculously to disappear, with his team, deeper into the vineyards each time Clare put in an appearance, she finally caught up with the *chef de culture* as he was ploughing for the fourth, and last, time to remove the summer weeds.

Shuffling her feet to shake the freshly turned earth from her shoes, she put a hand to her eyes to shield them from the midday sun, and looked up at the cabin of the vibrating tractor. Pulling on the handbrake, Albert Rochas stared down at her.

'*Bonjour Albert.*'

'*Bonjour Mademoiselle.*'

'Could I have a word?'

Albert stared. Clare stood her ground. She was not going to stand for any nonsense.

Switching off the engine and wiping his hands on a rag, the vineyard manager, in his heavy, dust-covered boots, climbed down from the cabin reluctantly.

'Ribagnac is carrying out a *vendange verte*, Albert.'

'The Ribagnac vines are young. These are old. *Comme moi.*' He allowed himself a wry joke.

'You're not thinking of pruning?'

'*Non, Mademoiselle.*'

'Aren't there too many bunches?'

'No more than the Appellation Contrôlée will permit.'

'I thought a lower yield meant higher concentration. This year the vintage has to be special.'

'*Oui, Mademoiselle.*'

'Château de Cluzac has to make a genius wine. We cannot afford to be pipped at the post.'

Albert stared at her. Everything he stood for was being impugned.

'We will carry out a *vendange verte*.'

Despite the fact that no love had been lost between himself and the Baron, Jean Boyer, *blessé de guerre*, a troglodyte in his own cellars, was even more resentful of the new chatelaine than was the *chef de culture*. Oblivious of what was going on in the vineyards, the *maître de chai* spent his life in the semi-darkness among his vats and his barrels, which represented the most important moments in the clandestine life of the wine.

The new wine was stored in the first-year cellar, where the cellarmaster carried out the numerous rackings (transferring the wine from one cask to another), and finings, which were necessary to remove the unstable elements. After twelve months, during which the barrels were regularly topped up, and turned 'three-quarter bung', the wine was transferred to the *chai de conservation*, the second-year *chai*, where it was left on its own to mature for anything up to eighteen months.

The *maître de chai* was responsible for these and many other important procedures, as well as the eventual *assemblage* of the wine. Calling on his expertise, and taking wine which had come from different parts of the vineyard, he blended and mixed it like colours on a painter's palette.

Jean Boyer, wearing a blue plastic apron, and ankle-deep in discarded egg shells, was in the first-year cellar carrying out the *tirage au fin* (the second fining), which had occupied him and his assistants for several weeks, when Clare sought him out. Watching the cellarmaster, as he stood with his balloon whisk in his mutilated hand, carrying out the traditional technique which would preserve the integrity of the wine, took her back to the time when he had first shown her how, with a flick of the wrist, to separate the yolks (later to be discarded) from the whites of the eggs. These whites would be poured through a funnel into the barrels where, spreading out like the filaments of a spider's web, they would sink slowly to the bottom, drawing down with them the unwanted impurities in the wine.

'What's for dinner, Jean?' Clare teased him, as she had done when she was a child.

'Mayonnaise with fifteen hundred egg yolks!' had been his habitual response. Today none was forthcoming. Under the stewardship of Charles-Louis, Jean Boyer had been in sole charge of both the *chais* and the *assemblage*. He did not take kindly to interference.

Clare decided to take the bull by the horns.

'I have ordered some new vats, Jean.'

For a long moment all that could be heard in the gloom of the cellar was the regular thump-thump of the wooden whisk upon the time-blackened bowl beneath Jean's arm.

'There's nothing wrong with the old vats.'

'Temperature-regulated inox . . .'

The whisk went faster. 'We have our own style. We don't need to imitate others.'

'Château de Cluzac has to move into the twentieth century. It needs a more modern system, an analytical laboratory. We have to get the right balance between tradition and technology . . .' She heard herself echoing Alain Lamotte.

'Technology!' The whisk stopped. Jean Boyer tapped his head with his two remaining fingers. 'Here is my technology, Mademoiselle Clare, my analytical laboratory. The next thing, you will be making your *grand vin* by *informatique* . . .'

'Don't you think I know as well as you do, Jean,' Clare addressed the cellarmaster's back as he pointedly removed the bung from a barrel into which he would pour the whipped egg whites, 'that a great wine, like a great symphony, cannot be made by computer?'

Jean Boyer in his cellars, Albert Rochas in his vineyards, Sidonie in her kitchens, and the pining Rougemont who refused to leave Clare's side, were not the only ones to miss the Baron. When Clare had taken the cheque for the chapel roof to the Convent of Notre Dame de Consolation, it was to find that her aunt not only harboured no bitterness towards Charles-Louis for the fact that he had tried to cheat her, but had even made excuses for her brother's reprehensible behaviour.

'I'm sorry my father has done Notre Dame de Consolation out of so much money, that he has double-crossed you,' Clare said, giving the Reverend Mother the money Charles-Louis had given her, ostensibly for her art gallery.

'He hasn't double-crossed us, child. The wine market collapsed so your father had no cashflow. The poor man was unable to pay his taxes . . .'

'Only because he'd salted all the profits away in Switzerland.'

'If Loulou had brought the money *back* from Switzerland,' her aunt said reasonably, 'he would be convicted of fraud. They would put him in jail. Charles-Louis was *caught*, you see!'

Clare was thinking of Tante Bernadette (and the charitable scenario her aunt had superimposed upon the Baron's actions) with some amusement, as she drove out of the château gates and bumped over the potholes towards the main road. In response to an urgent need to get away for a while from the hostile atmosphere that pervaded the château, she was going to Bordeaux to call on Beatrice Biancarelli. After visiting the boutique she would spend a couple of hours in le Gaumont in the Georges Clémenceau where, no matter what was showing, she would forget her troubles in the darkness of the cinema.

As she approached the junction and turned her head automatically to admire the new sign, she did a double take. Where before had stood the giant *pancarte* which had so distressed Claude Balard, there was an uninterrupted view across the Château Martin vineyards.

Slamming on the brakes, she wrenched open the door of the car and jumped out. On the grass verge lay a heap of broken wood and twisted metal. The words VENTE DIRECTE and OPEN TO THE PUBLIC had been obliterated by angry daubs of virulent yellow paint. They were no longer legible.

Picking her way over the wreckage and stumbling as she did so, she was uncertain whether the tears that poured down her face were due to anger or to the pain from a gash caused by a spur of jagged metal, from which the blood was flowing down her calf and into her shoe.

'*Merde! Merde! Merde!*'

As she hopped on one leg, rubbing her eyes with a blood-stained hand, the driver of a jeep, which had taken the bend too fast, came to a screeching halt by the carnage.

A long whistle of disbelief at the multicoloured shards on which the words CHATEAU and CLUZAC could still be distinguished, made Clare look up.

'Need any help, mate?'

At the wheel of the jeep, wearing a reversed baseball cap over his shoulder-length hair, and naked from the waist up, sat Halliday Baines.

CHAPTER TWENTY-SIX

Taking a taxi from the station, Clare let herself into the low-ceilinged, book-lined sitting-room of Rose Cottage. The familiar sight of Jamie's discarded running shoes and his *Journal of Bone and Joint Surgery*, open at 'Supracondylar Fracture', propped up against the stone marmalade jar on the gate-leg table, made her realise just how much she had missed him.

She hadn't told Jamie she was coming. She hadn't even known herself. Upstairs in the tiny bathroom with its sloping floor, the scarlet kimono with its dragon motif, which Jamie had brought back for her from a conference in Singapore, was still on the hook behind the door. Flinging open the window she looked out, not on to vines, but on to Jamie's sweet-smelling English garden in which criss-crossed sticks formed a guard of honour for his profusion of runner beans, and the nicotineana she had planted for its night scent was coming into flower.

It had taken Jamie three years to modernise the fifteenth-century cottage, which he had first rented when he started working at the John Radliffe, and later bought. Good with his hands and brilliant with machinery, he had rewired and replumbed it. The cottage now boasted a bathroom, with a functioning hot water system, as well as central heating where it mattered. Lacking the necessary funds to extend it, for which he had already obtained planning permission, he was now ready to re-tile the roof.

Going downstairs again, Clare made coffee for herself and curled up on the Victorian sofa, which faced the inglenook fireplace, neatly stacked with logs sawn by Jamie. Opening the *Tatler* she had picked up at the station, she flipped idly through the pages, paying special attention to the anxious brides, flanked by interchangeable grooms and attended by matching bridesmaids, pinned on to the glossy page like so many satin-clad butterflies. Glad to relegate the problems of the Château de Cluzac to a back burner, she thought what a relief it was to be home.

As far as her vandalised sign was concerned, she felt as if she herself had been assaulted. She was convinced that it was the work of the Baron's frustrated negociant, although she was unable to prove it. The violent attack had turned out to be only a foretaste of the resentment, made abundantly clear by the staff, which her presence at the château provoked. Claude Balard was by no means the only one out to get her.

The unexpected appearance of Halliday Baines at the scene of her humiliation had not improved her temper . . .

'Who the fuck could have done this?' She had contemplated the crumpled remains of the *pancarte*.

Halliday Baines, in the driving seat of his jeep, put his hands over his ears in mock horror. Taking in the situation, he said, 'Selling at the door, are we?'

Clare kicked at the rubble.

'That *was* the general idea.'

'Someone in these parts doesn't approve of little girls meddling in things they know nothing about . . .'

'Don't be so bloody patronising.'

'I hear Château de Cluzac is doing a *vendange verte*.'

'Who told you that?'

'News gets around. I'll keep my fingers crossed.'

'What for?'

Halliday shrugged.

'All things being equal you should be OK,' he said. 'Not that I know too much about your place, except the cellars are deadbeat. I'll be over to Ribagnac on Wednesday. Want me to look in?'

'If you like.'

'It's down to you.'

Clare swallowed her pride. Halliday's reputation as an airborne oenologist had gone before him. She needed all the help she could get.

Taking her silence for consent, Halliday switched on the ignition. 'Cheers then! I'll come for lunch.'

Looking back over his shoulder as he began to move away, the bumptious Australian gave Clare a cheery wave before leaving her among the rubble.

'I'd let Doctor Hébèque take a look at that leg if I were you,' he shouted above the noise of the engine. 'Reckon you could do with a tetanus jab. And it might be an idea to inform the *gendarmerie*!'

Doctor Hébèque, medical adviser to many of the château owners and keeper of their secrets, not only gave her an injection against tetanus, but put half a dozen stitches in the semicircular gash in her leg.

'It was a fine *pancarte*,' Doctor Hébèque commiserated. 'I remarked it when I called at Ribagnac to give the Baronne her B12. Bordeaux is a small town, with small-town attitudes. It is not London or Paris.'

By the time Halliday Baines called at Château de Cluzac, Clare had had another inquisitive visitor. Lured by the news that the estate had thrown open its gates and there was no longer the Baron's frosty reception (for those who did manage to get past them) to contend with, the curious, anxious to see for themselves what was actually going on, were – on one excuse or another – if not exactly flooding, then trickling in.

Clare received them in her office. She had seconded Petronella, her father's erstwhile secretary, to help her with the *visites* and to be her assistant. Given her father's record, she presumed that he had at one time had an affair with the willowy Sloane Ranger, who was on the run from a disastrous relationship and a career in picture restoration.

Clare was on the telephone in her *Bureau d'Acceuil*, her leg bandaged beneath her black trousers, impressing upon the director of the firm responsible for replacing her sign that he must process her order before, rather than after, the tourist season began, when a copy of *Wine Watch*, slung on to her blotter, made her look up into the eyes of Big Mick Bly.

'Well well!' The tall wine guru dwarfed the tall Petronella who was drawing up a chair for him. Seeming to fill the office with his presence, Big Mick appraised Clare's transformed appearance. 'Don't you look the part. If your claret's half as smart as your front desk, young Clare, you're on to a winner!'

Another patronising bastard, but not one she could afford to antagonise. She finished her call and replaced the receiver.

The ratings awarded in *Wine Watch*, which employed a 50–100 quality scale and were backed by Big Mick's reputation, were taken extremely seriously both by wine-lovers and those connected with the trade.

Three months of his year were spent travelling, with Toni, tasting up to a hundred wines a day. The remaining nine months were devoted to more tasting, and to writing about wine. His findings reflected an independent assessment in which neither the price of the wine nor the name of the grower was allowed to affect his decision.

Big Mick preferred to taste from an entire bottle, in properly sized and cleaned professional tasting glasses. The temperature of the wine had to be correct, and he reserved the right to determine the amount of time allocated to each sample.

The numerical ratings he gave were a guide to what he thought of each wine *vis-à-vis* its peer group. More than 85 meant very good to excellent (few ever made over 90), 70–79 average (an everyday table wine), while anything below 60 was both the kiss of death and an indication of wines to be avoided.

Big Mick's detractors protested that a hierarchy was unsuited to a drink that had been romantically extolled for centuries, and that he made no allowance for individual preferences. His defence was that with wine, as with any other consumer product, there were specific standards of quality, recognised only by full-time professionals, as well as certain acknowledged benchmark wines against which all others could be measured. With this proviso, he allowed that there was no better arbiter than one's own palate, and no better education in wine than tasting it oneself.

While Big Mick's wine ratings carried a biblical authority, his tasting notes were worthy of its prose. A Bourgogne Blanc ('a beauty to be drunk over the next year') offered an 'in-your-face, alcoholic, round, expansive style', a Riesling *Spätlese*, a bouquet that was the 'essence of wet stones and minerals', while the excessive acidity of an Estate Riesling ('a poor example of generic wines aimed at commercial restaurants') rendered it 'thin, tart and nearly undrinkable'.

Wine Watch had given the 1992 Château de Cluzac a 75. This rating was accompanied by a downward-pointing dagger which indicated that the quality of the Baron's wine was declining. It was followed by the comment that it had become excessively astringent and was lacking in fruit and depth.

'I had lunch with Van Gelder,' Big Mick said. 'I visit his place in Franschhoek. He makes quite a respectable Cabernet. I gather that Mademoiselle de Cluzac is not exactly flavour of the month . . .'

'I seem to have got up quite a few noses round these parts.'

Big Mick chuckled. 'If you can't stand the heat you should keep out of the kitchen.'

Clare, fifty per cent Fitzgerald and fifty per cent de Cluzac, shook her head. 'Not my style.'

Escorting Big Mick round the cellars, she outlined her plans for the computerised analyses and inox, which Alain Lamotte had already set up as a matter of the greatest urgency.

As the only wine writer who had ever been allowed into Château de Cluzac (and that only because he had been accompanied by Claude Balard) Big Mick was a familiar face to Jean Boyer who grew visibly nervous at his approach.

Big Mick cast an experienced eye over the barrels.

'What you really have to do here before the *vendange*, if you want to do the job properly, is to buy sixty per cent new casks. I've been telling your father for years.'

'What do you suggest I use for money?'

'I'm afraid that's your problem, young Clare . . .'

'Please don't call me that.'

Big Mick ignored the reproof. He was only interested in wine. 'New barrels will "complete" the taste. Improve your flavour level. Let you fine-tune your tannins. All I can do is advise.'

Accepting a glass of wine drawn by the cellarmaster, who awaited his verdict with anguish, Big Mick stuck his nose into the glass.

'Don't look so worried, Jean. Bad wine never did me any harm.' His big voice reverberated round the cellar. 'You know why . . .?'

The cellarmaster didn't understand a word Big Mick was saying.

'It never gets past my nose!'

Having examined the claret by the light of Jean's candle,

taking his time over tasting it, and finally spitting it out, Big Mick dabbed at his mouth with a red-spotted handkerchief, which he replaced in the breast pocket of his linen jacket, before taking out his notebook.

Back in the bureau, Petronella, instructed by Clare, served him a glass of Château de Cluzac '70 to which, in its heyday, *Wine Watch* had awarded a 96.

The wine writer faced Clare across the desk.

'Why don't we cut the bullshit. It's my job to seek out the world's greatest wines and the world's greatest wine values. In the process of ferreting out those wines, I have never once shied away from criticising a producer whose wine I have found lacking. Just as praising overachievers encourages them to maintain their high standards, so constructive and competent criticism forces underachievers to improve the quality of their wine. I guess you know what I'm going to say to you Clare . . .'

He explained to her, as Alain Lamotte had done, that the old wooden vats created sanitation problems, made it difficult to control the proper fermentation temperature, both in cold and hot years, and were partly responsible (the name of Claude Balard was not mentioned) for the slump in quality of the château wine. If she used her 'feminine' intuition – he ignored Clare's glare – and kept to a lighter, more elegant, style when bottling her existing wine, there was every chance that, while waiting for her new, modern cellars, she would recoup some of the château's losses.

'I shall be keeping an eye on you.'

'So will everyone else in the Médoc.'

'Jealousy! The last thing they want is to see Château de Cluzac's reputation restored. Remember, *Wine Watch* is constantly on the lookout for any improvement, and Big Mick always gets in before the crowd.'

Big Mick looked at his watch and heaved his bulk off the chair.

'Médaillac next stop. Toni doesn't like me to be late for my meetings. See you around.' He looked around the chrome and glass of the office with its black-and-white photographs of the surrounding countryside, copies of which she was hoping to sell to visitors. 'You've done a great job, kid . . .' He caught Clare's eye. 'I'm sorry!'

Halliday Baines, as small and compact as Big Mick Bly was large and bulky, arrived, true to his word, in time for lunch.

The 'flying winemaker' had been around since the late 1980s when someone had had the bright idea of bringing New World techniques to the under-exploited areas of France, many of which had been making wine since medieval times. The first representatives of this Australian airborne division were dismissed as mavericks, with technology where their taste buds should have been, by those who had forgotten what cheap wine used to taste like. The idea caught on, however, and the role of the *oenologue* was becoming increasingly important.

Those who considered winemaking an art, regarded the unquestionable 'well-made' wines of the New World as wines without soul, wines without identity, wines without heart, wines that could be made anywhere. They looked down upon the new breed of winemakers, deriding what they considered to be the homogeneous nature of their wine, and the fact that they dared to question the received wisdom that quality and quantity were incompatible.

Current thinking, however, demanded that the control of the natural phenomenon (by which sugar was converted into alcohol), as well as a better understanding of the glucids, protids, lipids, vitamins, enzymes, minerals and trace elements, was essential to the final product.

Halliday Baines, who had a PhD in viticultural research, recognised that, owing to the challenge of New World wines, claret now had to be competitively marketed. He had little time for Big Mick Bly, a school dropout, who, armed only with a pen, a notebook and a few bottles of wine, had established himself as a guru.

'I hear Big *Mac*'s been here,' he said over lunch, making Clare choke on her sorrel soup.

'At least *he* endorsed my summer pruning. He said it complied fully with the Appellation Contrôlée regulations . . .'

'When God created the soil of the Médoc, he wasn't thinking of the AOC regulations.'

'He also said I needed to replace sixty per cent of my barrels . . .'

'*I'm* the *oenologue* round here,' Halliday said, helping himself to bread with which to clean his plate. 'If you want me to help you – and you're going to need my help – I'll tell you what you have to do.'

CHAPTER TWENTY-SEVEN

Waiting for Jamie to return from the hospital, Clare thought that although she was not short of willing advisers to guide the Château de Cluzac ship through, what were for her, uncharted waters, most of them were male chauvinists. Halliday Baines was their apotheosis.

Halliday had contemptuously dismissed Big Mick's suggestion that she replace sixty per cent of her barrels. Although it might be true that the flavour of new oak, like the addition of certain spices to a dish when cooking, added character to the wine – in this case a sweet vanilla flavour – which might possibly make it more saleable in the USA, the additional cost of so many new barrels needed to be taken into consideration and the exact proportion of new oak extremely carefully assessed.

Halliday's judgement was based on the findings of the Institut Oenologique at the University of Bordeaux, which had carried out a study for the ageing of red wine in barrels. It was his considered opinion that to replace only twenty-five per cent of her casks was the correct approach.

'Big *Mac* doesn't know the first thing about *barrels*. All he know about is *bottles*, tasted on neutral territory, with no reference to the producers, and dishing out marks based on his highly questionable palate.'

'Is that so terrible?'

'It's highly dangerous. The American wine trade reacts

to the number of points he gives like sheep, rather than deciding which wine their customers will *like* and what they want to sell. The French understand the culture of the grape. They judge their wines in a far more civilised way.'

Inspecting the fermentation tanks in the *chai* – after two helpings of Sidonie's ice-cream pudding – Halliday, instantly the professional, noticed that most of the old vats were time-expired and than none of them were up to scratch.

'I'm putting in new inox,' Clare said.

'I hear that Alain "the Mutt" is backing you.'

Clare laughed at the Australian's corruption of Alain Lamotte's name. 'Who told you?'

'"Any resemblance between Alain Lamotte and a tailor's dummy is purely coincidental!"' Halliday stepped over a hose on the freshly sluiced floor. 'Word gets round.'

'I can hardly underwrite inox on my own.'

'There'll be a lot of people trying to muscle in.'

'I'm perfectly capable of running the château.'

'It wasn't the château I was thinking of.'

'I can look after myself.'

Having spent more than two hours in the cellars, using his basic French to suggest to Jean – to whom current scientific concepts such as pH, oxidation-reduction and colloids were a closed book, but who listened to the oenologist with respect – that new vats would be the first step in putting Château de Cluzac on the map in the shortest possible time, and personally getting to work with the hose, Halliday told Clare that what she really had to do was to declassify part of her 1993 vintage.

Clare hadn't the foggiest idea what the oenologist was talking about. He explained that, since she was strapped for cash, the choice was one of financial responsibility, and this would be eased considerably by the creation of a 'second' wine. To do this she would have to make use of her 'reserve'; take wine from the main blend and mix it with that which had been dumped, not because it wasn't good enough but because it would have spoiled the balance.

'Balance?'

'When the constituents are in the right proportions the wine is well-balanced – good fruit flavours and a positive after-taste or "finish" in the mouth. Not enough fruit and your wine's too dull: too much fruit and it's too simple or "jammy". Insufficient sun means acidic "green" tannins. Too much sun and not enough rain, you get cold stewed tea. A good winemaker will use his equipment and his palate to compensate for the shortcomings of nature.

'Your château wine matures in the bottle. Your second wine will be for early drinking. Balance it from the start and you can do what you like with it. Sell it on the Place de Bordeaux, stick it in quarter bottles with screw caps and flog it to the airlines. Your neighbours will kill you. You can't sell it under the Château de Cluzac label. You'll have to find another name for it.'

'How about Château de Cluzac Inférieure . . . ?'

'It won't be *inferior*. Just different. Not made to last as long. Even the most fastidious airline will fall over themselves to buy it. What you decide to call it is a mega decision. Just remember that the English have black belts in snobbery when it comes to wine. The top ten best sellers are bought not on quality but on the name on the label and the price.'

'And the French?'

'The French just get on with it. Seventy per cent of what they drink is bought in supermarkets; they take no pride in their wines. Give your average Pom a wine list and it's a different story. Ri-oja, Lam-brusco, Chi-anti, Val-pol-i-cella, Pouilly-Fuissé, Pouilly-Fumé – they can't even tell the difference – Gewürz-tra-miner, Puligny-Montrachet,

Chassagne-Montrachet, Châteauneuf-du-Pape ... They like the way it *sounds*.'

'Am I *allowed* to declassify?' Clare asked, as they came out of the gloom of the cellars into the sunlight and, accompanied by a subdued Rougemont, walked through the iron gate towards the formal gardens where Aristide Louchemain, son of old Monsieur Louchemain, was tending the miniature orange trees, which spent their winters under canvas, in their square white tubs.

'You can do anything you damn' well like. There's a whole new generation of wine drinkers out there. Bordeaux means nothing to them. It means less than nothing. They'd just as soon drink wines from the Midi, from eastern Europe, from the New World. Heavily promoted "bargain basement" wines don't do anyone any favours. The retailer makes nothing, the producer gets shafted, and the consumer goes more and more down-market. We call it "the supermarket effect". As far as Bordeaux is concerned, the expensive stuff is over-priced and the sub-five-pounds claret market is stuffed with lean, green wines you wouldn't wish on your worst enemy. A "second" wine from a second growth Bordeaux château – under a fiver – and the supermarket buyers will be beating a path to your door.'

'Why hasn't Château de Cluzac declassified before?'

'From what I hear, your father would have died first.'

Halliday picked up a yellowed tennis ball which lay on the path and tossed it from hand to hand.

'Ever been to Australia?'

Clare shook her head.

'We make some great wine.'

'I've heard.'

'Two per cent of the world's output and seventy-five per cent of the world's know-how. We've just signed a two-hundred-page agreement. Took five years to draw up: Australia to stop using European wine names – champagne, burgundy, chablis, port, claret and so on – and the

EU recognises our winemaking techniques and renounces the right to geographical names such as Coonawarra . . .'

'No more Coonawarra claret?'

'Right, mate.' Stooping, Halliday rolled the tennis ball along the tended path, where it was studiously ignored by Rougemont.

'What's up with him?'

'He still misses my father.'

'In Australia we arrange our wineries differently. It doesn't make any sense to build the same high-tech processing plant in a dozen different locations, so we truck our grapes – hundreds of miles sometimes – for pressing. It's like trucking the grapes from Burgundy to Bordeaux. Only back home it's not illegal.'

'You travel a lot?'

'You could say I collect a good few air miles. It's damned hard. Ill-equipped locations, five time zones, not much sleep, no weekends off, no lunchbreaks, a workforce that doesn't speak the language . . . August I'm in California for the early white sparkling wine varietals, then it's back to Europe for the long vintage sessions. I usually finish up in Germany with the late-harvested November grapes. With the northern hemisphere wrapped up by early December, I'll take a Christmas break. January, I'll start again with the southern hemisphere. Fortunately the South African harvest is in March. Wines in other parts of the world may have bigger extractions, stronger flavours, more powerful body, but none of them has the elegance of Bordeaux.'

'What exactly do you do?'

'Fly in before the harvest. Tell the growers how, when and in what order the grapes are to be picked. Clean out the winery, supervise the vinification, maturation and bottling.' Taking a coin from his pocket, he spun it in the air before catching it and turning it over on the back of his hand. 'Most growers look for safety. The winemaker takes risks.'

'You really like making wine.'

'It's a good job. Wine makes people happy. It's like fine food, good music, a beautiful painting. Tell you a secret, Clare. I've just bought myself a half-share in a vineyard in Chile . . .'

'Why Chile?'

'Five thousand kilometres of coastline to temper the sun and keep the rainfall low. No restrictions, no Appellation Contrôlée, you're free to express your ideas. It's always been my dream . . .'

Taking his wallet from the back pocket of his sun-bleached jeans, Halliday took out a bunch of business cards and gave one to Clare.

'Any problems, send me a fax. Barossa will know where to find me . . .'

The oenologist was as condescending with his doubts about her ability to cope as was Big Mick with his 'little Clare'.

'Hang on.' Clare stood stock still. 'I just thought of something. How does "little Clare" grab you?'

'"Little Clare"?'

'"Petite Clare". Château de Cluzac's second wine?'

'Brilliant! Clare. Claret. Couldn't be better. Now all you have to do is market it.'

As Halliday replaced the rest of the business cards in his wallet, Clare caught a glimpse of a small boy's face, mischievous eyes peering out from the photograph slot.

'Your son?'

'Billy. He's just turned five. I've taught him to do card tricks. He could read a newspaper when he was four.'

'He looks like you.'

'More like his mother.'

'You must miss him.'

'You can say that again.' The wallet was snapped shut.

Clare changed the subject.

'When's your next visit?'

'I'll be in and out. I keep a pad in Bordeaux. The Rue Ferrère. I'll be here for the marathon . . .'

'Marathon?' Light on his feet, Halliday looked like a runner. There had been no marathon in the Médoc when Clare was a child.

'Châteaux du Médoc et des Graves. Beginning of September. Pauillac, St Julien, Beychevelle, St-Estèphe . . . Last year there were more than six thousand runners. I came fifth.'

'I must tell Jamie.'

'Tell him if he wants to run he has to register.'

Little by little, feeling her way, taking one day at a time, Clare was coming to terms with the château. Conscious that she was surrounded by cynics such as Halliday Baines and Big Mick, by several jealous neighbours who preferred the status quo, and by declared enemies such as Claude Balard and Philip Van Gelder, her once micro-thin skin, susceptible to every pinprick from her father, was becoming as thick as that of the grapes.

By dint of her working in her new office from 6.30 a.m., beating Monsieur Boniface to her desk, and very often not crossing the courtyard to her bed before the small hours of the following morning, everything at Château de Cluzac was now ready to receive visitors. She confidently expected the coaches, carrying tourists from Europe, the United States and Scandinavia, which would shortly be criss-crossing each other on the Route des Châteaux, to relieve her cashflow problems and swell the severely depleted Cluzac coffers.

The new *pancarte* had been erected, this time protected by barbed wire. A section of the park had been designated an '*aire de pique-nique*' (to the dismay of Monsieur Louchemain) and was furnished with litter bins as well as wooden chairs and tables. The room adjoining her office, under the supervision of Petronella, had been set up as a shop, and she was going to call on Hannah to collect the 'Château de Cluzac' T-shirts. The cellars, Jean Boyer notwithstanding, were ready for inspection. She had her own spiel ready. And the moat, home previously only to swans and water lilies, had been stocked with trout for paid fishing.

In the calm before the storm, for she would not be able to get away again before the harvest, she had come back to England not only to see Jamie and to visit Grandmaman, but to talk to David Markham, a senior director of Christie's, about including several lots of Château de Cluzac among the Château Mouton-Rothschilds and the Château Pétrus, in the next fine wine auction.

By the time Jamie opened the door of the cottage, the *Tatler* had slipped on to the floor, and Clare was asleep on the sofa. She was dreaming that Claude Balard had vandalised her sign once again and was threatening to drive her out of the Médoc. When Jamie put his lips to her forehead, she screamed and pummelled him in the chest.

'Steady on!' He grabbed her hands.

Clare sat up.

'It's you. Sorry darling. I thought I was in Bordeaux.'

'Who were you hoping to kill?'

Before they had said hallo, Clare unburdened herself to Jamie about Claude Balard, and about Big Mick and Halliday Baines, and her trouble with the sign, and her troubles with her staff, and her cashflow problems, the true nature of which she had only indicated to him during their nightly telephone conversations.

'Sorry to dump on you.'

'That's what the man's here for.' Squatting in front of the fridge in the kitchen, Jamie removed a bottle of Chardonnay.

Watching him, through the open door, Clare said, 'If I see another bottle of wine I'll scream . . .'

'Not again!'

Pouring out two whiskies, Jamie brought them over to the sofa.

'Why didn't you tell me you were coming?'

'I didn't decide until this morning. It's the last opportunity before the *vendange* . . .'

'I'm not complaining . . .' Jamie outlined the contours of her features with his hand before pulling her face to his own. 'I ache with missing you. It's the best surprise in the world. I must make a quick phone call. I promised Miranda I'd be at Quaglino's at nine. It's Barnaby's birthday . . .'

'Barnaby?'

'Barnaby Muirhead.'

Remembering the Formula One driver for whom Miranda had left Jamie, Clare picked up the pieces of her past.

'It's only quarter to seven.'

'I thought you looked too knackered to party. Wouldn't you rather go to bed?'

Removing Jamie's glass from his hand, Clare put it on the tiled hearth together with her own.

'We can do that before we go.'

CHAPTER TWENTY-EIGHT

Barnaby Muirhead, recently headline news over his dispute with the Formula One authorities concerning pit-stop refuelling equipment, not only held sway over the premier table in Quaglino's (once the haunt of Edward Prince of Wales but now a media mecca), but drew clandestine glances from other diners who recognised the popular racing driver from his pictures in their daily papers.

By the time his birthday cake, a Benetton-Ford in appropriately coloured icing bearing thirty-one flickering candles, was brought in, on the shoulder of a waiter, his guests were decidedly merry and making a very great deal of noise.

Regarding them all – the red-headed Miranda inhaling the smoke from a slim cigar – Clare realised not only how much she had missed Jamie and her friends, but the tremendous strain that she had been under during the past weeks in Bordeaux.

Relieved temporarily from her responsibilities, she had thrown caution to the winds, together with her Château de Cluzac persona, and was rapidly becoming more than a little drunk.

At one end of the long table Barnaby was explaining how, following Ayrton Senna's fatal crash into the concrete wall of Imola's Tamburello curve, a short wooden plank bolted to the underside of grand prix cars now prevented them from cornering at G-forces for which most circuits were not designed. Clare, at the far end, encouraged by an equally drunk Jonty Griffiths, Barnaby's alter ego and fellow Formula One driver, unravelled the mysteries of wine.

'Wine . . .' Her voice was only slightly slurred. 'Wine, Jonty, is like people. There are tall people and there are short people. There are thin people and there are fat people. There are big people, and there are little people. Not that you can judge by appearance. Wine has to have character. Some wines have good character. Some wines have bad character. Others have absolutely no character at all. When a wine is very young' – she was getting into her stride – 'it has a dark purplish colour . . .'

It was Jean who had explained to the eight-year-old, sitting on an upturned barrel in her father's *chai*, that the appearance of wine was defined by four elements: *limpidité*, the absence of deposit; *intensité*, the all-important density; *nuance*, the evolution of the colour from the blue of fermentation to the brown of extreme age; *brillance*, the refraction through the wine of light.

'After anything from five to ten years,' Clare went on, 'the wine reaches maturity and can continue to improve for anything up to fifteen years. A touch of brick colour at the rim . . .' She held her glass of Nuits St-Georges up to the light and tilted it slightly. 'A touch of brick colour at the rim is a funda . . . fundamental sign that it is ready to drink.'

'What I'd like to know,' Jonty Griffiths said as she proceeded to do so, 'is why, when you consider the cost of a bunch of grapes, any half-way decent wine has to cost an arm and a leg.'

Picking up the bottle of the most expensive Burgundy Barnaby had been able to find on the wine list, and watched with pride by an amused Jamie, Clare said, 'You're not talking South Africa or Portugal here, mate. You're not talking your Liebfraumilch or your Lambrusco.

Early-drinking wines that can be bottled and sold young
– that's ninety per cent of your reds – are many times
cheaper to make than wine which has been matured in
small oak barrels, which are not only expensive to buy
but ext ... extreme ... very costly to maintain. I'll let
you into a secret ...' Clare now had the attention of
the table. 'A top-quality, new, French oak barrel – none
of your oak *chips* – amortised over three years' harvest,
can add between thirty and sixty pence to the price of a
bottle ...!'

Hearing Alain Lamotte's patient voice in her ears as
he went over the costs involved in wine production,
and moving her chair (its design said to be inspired by
the contours of Betty Grable's buttocks) closer to the
blond young racing driver, who was getting more than
he bargained for, Clare leaned towards him.

'First of all your "bunch of grapes", my dear Jonty,
has to be grown. A well-tended vineyard is like a well-
tended garden. It takes an experienced vine worker the
entire winter to prune only thirty thousand – out of a
total of maybe seven hundred thousand – vines, each
of which bears anything from ten to fifteen bunches,
which eventually have to be picked, bunch by bunch,
by a whole army of pickers, who have to be housed
and fed. Take your production costs. In addition to cellar
techniques, which involve expensive labour and equipment
...' Holding up her hand with the gold engagement
ring, she enumerated on her fingers. 'You've got the
basic cost of your wine. You've got your bottling and
packaging. You've got your transport. You've got your
retail margin. You've got your duty. You've got your
VAT ...'

'You've got no more fingers!' came a voice from the
other end of the table.

'You've got your marketing to consider.' Clare was
undeterred. 'And finally, in the case of a restaurant,

you've got your mark-up, in some cases up to three hundred per cent!'

Leaving Quaglino's well after midnight, Barnaby, who got his kicks both from living dangerously and being constantly surrounded by a crowd of admirers, insisted that everyone join him and Miranda for a glass of champagne and some music at Annabel's. While the rest of the party, pleading weariness or work, declined, Clare, who was now getting her second wind, persuaded Jamie, who was so happy to see her that he was unable to refuse, to accept the invitation. Banged up, day after day, in her *Bureau d'Acceuil* at Château de Cluzac, it seemed an age since she had let her hair down.

Dancing with Jamie – although it was more a case of ambling round the packed floor of the nightclub, the lowered lights of which helped protect the anonymity of its members – her arms entwined about her fiancé's neck, Clare felt his body, warm against hers.

'All moving parts in working order.'

'Don't go back to Bordeaux.'

'I thought you were behind me.'

'I need you.'

'I need you too. You want me to let myself be ripped off?'

'Does it really matter?'

'Not in the grand order of things.'

'You've made your point. Why don't you call it a day?'

Clare thought about it.

'I have to show Papa.'

Taking the floor with Barnaby, as exhibitionistic on the dance floor as he was on the racing circuit, Clare kept a jealous eye on Jamie who, entwined in Miranda's freckled arms, was dancing with his ex-flame.

Egged on by an inebriated Barnaby, Clare was stamping her feet, clicking her fingers and gyrating uninhibitedly in time to the Lambada music, when she happened to glance up. In place of Jamie and Miranda, who had returned to the table where they were engaged in conversation, she saw her father, stiff and upright, in a midnight-blue dinner jacket, shuffling his feet disdainfully, while an exotic Latin American, wearing an exquisite emerald necklace, moved her hips provocatively by his side.

'Someone you know?' Barnaby followed her glance.

'You could say that. Will you excuse me for a moment?' Clare edged her way across the tiny floor.

'*Bonsoir Papa*!' The hooded eyes regarded her without surprise. '*Je t'avais bien vu.*' Clare indicated his partner who was gazing at the Baron adoringly. '*Tu me présentes à ton amie?*' she asked.

Her father stared at her. He had no intention of making any introductions.

'How's Laura?' Clare said.

The Baron's lips tightened in a familiar gesture of annoyance.

'She's well.'

'Perhaps you and your . . . friend would like to join us?' It was the champagne speaking.

'Thank you.' Charles-Louis' manners were impeccable as usual. 'Some other time.'

The next thing Clare remembered was waking up in her old bed in Nicola's flat in Notting Hill, with Jamie bending over her.

'How did I get *here*?'

'I carried you. Over my shoulder. You were obscenely drunk.'

'Rubbish.' She noticed that Jamie was fully dressed. 'Where do you think you're going?'

'I'm going to work.'

'To work! What's the time?'

'Six-thirty.'

'Aren't you coming to bed.'

'I've been in bed all night.'

'You could have fooled me.'

'I certainly could. You took one look at your father and polished off the entire bottle of Bolly.'

'My father makes me puke.'

'Give him a break.'

'Are you telling me I should feel sorry for him?'

'I'm telling you I have to go.'

Clare recognised the expression on his face as he slid a hand beneath the duvet.

'Come back to bed.'

'Tempting as it is I have a heavy operating list this morning.'

Jamie had his working face on. He was already at the John Radcliffe. It was not surprising that he couldn't summon up much enthusiasm for her father's peccadilloes or the problems of the Château de Cluzac vines.

'See you tonight. At Grandmaman's.'

'Love you.'

'Love you too.'

Calling on Hannah, who lived above her shop in the King's Road, to collect her first batch of Château de Cluzac tee-shirts, Clare found her fat friend taking a lentil-and-saffron bath and massaging her head with unguents made from chillies and hot oil.

When she'd finished her beauty treatment, Hannah held up an outsize tee-shirt. Across the front in leaf-green lettering was '*Au commencement était la vigne* . . .' (In the beginning was the vine . . .), above a facsimile of a gnarled and twisted vine and the de Cluzac coat of arms.

'I think they've turned out rather nicely.'

'Hannah, it's gi-normous!'

'I see no reason why the well-endowed should be marginalised. Most of them are medium and large. You can flog the extra-large to the Germans.'

Before her meeting with David Markham to arrange for

the sale of some of her father's bottle stock, Clare went to Neal Street to make her peace with Nicola, who had already left for the gallery by the time she had finally woken up.

Nicola purported to be more interested in hanging an exhibition of paintings by a young man who lived among the communities on the shores of Lake Atitlan, than in Clare's problems at Château de Cluzac.

She pointed to a canvas of thickly daubed oranges and reds, and explained how the artist, assaulted by the impact of colour, had explored it in an intense sequence of abstract compositions, while Clare spoke of the hostility she was encountering at the château and recounted in detail the episode of the vandalised sign.

'He also produces miniature paintings, scaled down from his larger work,' Nicola said, 'to make pendants and bracelets, which he frames in cast silver, in homage to the people of Guatemala.'

'Fuck Guatemala. Aren't you interested in Château de Cluzac?'

Nicola picked up a cobalt-blue canvas and held it tentatively against the wall.

'Not particularly.'

'Is Zoffany coping all right?'

'She's OK.'

'Look, I'm really sorry I left you in the lurch. Getting Château de Cluzac on its feet is something I have to do.'

'Did you hear me complain?'

'Nicky . . .'

'For God's sake don't call me Nicky.'

'I want to ask you a favour.'

'Go ahead. I'm listening.'

'I want you to mount an exhibition for me at Château de Cluzac. Find me some artist who's done paintings of vineyards – France, Spain, it doesn't have to be Bordeaux – anything to do with the grape. With the coachloads of tourists I'm expecting, paintings, and posters, should sell like a bomb. I'm also going to flog *objects de vin*: old labels, funnels, tasters, corkscrews . . .'

'Talking of corkscrews,' Nicola said.

Opening a drawer in the desk, she took out a brass-and-ivory corkscrew and held it out to Clare.

'Victorian. I picked it up in Portobello.'

Recognising it as a peace offering, Clare put her arms round her friend.

'It's been shit miserable without you,' Nicola said. 'Not to mention the fact that that odious Oleg has shacked up with an Estonian poet.'

'Why don't you come to Bordeaux . . . ?' Clare thought of Halliday Baines, deserted by his wife. 'I could introduce you to a nice young man?'

Nicola was not displeased with the idea. Her words belied her expression.

'I have a gallery to run, remember?'

CHAPTER TWENTY-NINE

Although Clare was at home in two languages, she was ambivalent about which culture she owed allegiance to. When she was in England she thought and dreamed in English, but no sooner had she set foot in France than her unconscious switched, unbidden, into French.

Suspended, or so it seemed, on a sunlit pillow of cloud, at an altitude of 33,000 feet, between the two countries, she was uncertain where she belonged.

While the mantle of Château de Cluzac, with its moat and turrets, where she had spent her formative years, sat easily on her shoulders, across the Channel, where she had her friends and Jamie, was home.

Pondering the question, she wondered if the answer was that, because she belonged everywhere, she really belonged nowhere (on the grounds that, when 'everybody is somebody, nobody is anybody'); and, as she stared at the tray of food that had been set in front of her, the voice of the stewardess asking what she would like to drink made her dismiss her metaphysical thoughts and prick up her ears.

'*Du vin, s'il vous plait.*'

Clare surveyed the quarter bottles of wine ranged like miniature soldiers on the loaded trolley.

'*Du rouge ou du blanc?*'

'What is the red?'

Picking up a screw-capped bottle, the girl peered at the label.

'La Balardine.'

One of Claude Balard's concoctions. Filling her plastic glass with the thin purplish liquid, Clare held it to her nose in a futile attempt to detect the floral scents of rose, of violet, of broom; the fruity aroma of raspberry, cherry or peach; or the pungent perfumes of spice. Putting the glass to her lips, and letting the wine run over her palate and the sides of her tongue, which reacted to its acidity as if it had been stung by a thousand needles, she shuddered.

According to Halliday Baines, it was a mistake to believe that all French wine originated in the ancient cellars of some distinguished château. Over half of it was primitive stuff, produced in communal wineries where the quality of the end product was equal to the lowest common denominator of the grapes that were tipped into the press. While some local *vignerons* took pride in their smallholdings, others were less meticulous, and many co-operatives were not very good at making wine.

With the decrease in wine drinking in France (together with the rest of Europe), and the fact that there was absolutely no international market for *vin ordinaire*, many of the small growers were now being paid by the government to rip up their vineyards, which they were doing to the tune of 100,000 acres per year. Already there were 19 billion bottles of plonk in the European wine lake. Stored as industrial alcohol, it would end up in perfume bottles or be used to make subsidised car fuel. By the year 2000, according to Hallliday, over a quarter of French vineyards would, literally, have gone up in smoke.

Taking out her pocket calculator, Clare estimated the number of seats on the plane, multiplied it by the number of flights per day, then, with the help of the in-flight magazine, attempted to work out the number of journeys made by the airline to its various destinations in the course of a single year. The results were astronomical.

When Halliday Baines had suggested that she declassify

part of her '93 vintage and sell it cheaply to an airline, she had
been secretly affronted by his suggestion. The unequivocal
figures on the tiny liquid crystal display in front of her
prompted her to revise her opinion of the *oenologue*, and
take the idea of Petite Clare more seriously.

It was perfectly true, as Halliday had pointed out, that
there were two markets for wine as well as two distinctive
consumers: the *cognoscenti* who wanted a high-quality
wine – which they were willing to pay for – and the majority, who now regarded wine as an everyday beverage and
were perfectly happy with a bottle of Château Catesbury's
to accompany their evening meal. Most supermarket wine
was purchased by women and was consumed on the same
day it was bought.

Petite Clare would bring an affordable second-growth
wine to the shelves. Properly marketed, and at the right
price, it would be a welcome replacement for the vinegar
she had just tasted, which was deemed fit to accompany
the airline food. She was not bothered by the fact that
the quarter-bottles would have screw caps, rather than
the traditional corks without which the consumers would
feel short-changed; they had little more than snobbery to
commend them.

Sniffing a cork, as sommeliers in the more upmarket
restaurants tended to do, told them little about the condition of either the cork or the wine. A good *look* at
the cork, on the other hand, would reveal whether it
was wet and crumbly and likely to have imparted the
unforgettable 'corked' odour capable of snapping one's
head off. The fact that the corks were punched from the
bark of the cork oak, which was often left lying around
in pretty basic agricultural conditions, in contact with the
soil and other undesirable substances, had prompted the
New World pragmatists to make use of the unromantic
screw-caps for their bottom of the range wines.

*   *   *

Halliday Baines notwithstanding, Clare could not imagine screw-topped bottles being allowed anywhere near the King Street auction rooms where she had met the senior director to discuss the proposed sale of a quantity of prestige claret, destined to appeal to the discriminating end of the market.

David Markham had greeted her with open arms.

'You could not have come at a better time, Mademoiselle de Cluzac. Six months ago the market was positively awash with mature Bordeaux. Suddenly, what we call "collectable claret", for which people are willing to pay quite grotesque prices – thirteen thousand pounds for a dozen Château Latour 1929; ten thousand pounds for a rare *bottle* of Yquem – has virtually disappeared. Disappeared!' He put his elbows, in their navy-blue chalk stripes, on the mahogany desk (which Clare, casting a practised eye over it, recognised as George III) and his manicured fingers together.

'All that I have left today are some undistinguished wines from the better recent years, one or two big names from the frankly uninspiring eighty-seven vintage, plus an exceedingly large number of eighty-sixes and eighty-eights, about which I have my suspicions. I would be far more tempted to gamble on them if they were cheaper, and if I did not have the nagging feeling that a lot of far more attractive bottles were eventually going to emerge from the woodwork.

'To be perfectly frank, I am so short of claret that I have transferred all this month's lots to a subsequent auction, which could fit in very nicely with what you have to offer. Tell me Mademoiselle de Cluzac . . .' A gold pen, with a gold nib, was removed from an inside pocket and a pristine sheet of the firm's letterhead laid in eager anticipation on the pristine blotter. 'What exactly is it you wish to sell?'

'I haven't a clue,' Clare said. She would have to enlist

the help of Big Mick or Alain Lamotte to help her make her selection. 'I'll let you know.'

Hiding his disappointment that she had not come armed with her cellar list, David Markham re-capped his fountain pen. Sliding a previous sale catalogue across the desk, he ran through the terms under which private stocks of top-quality claret – preferably in the original wooden cases, and excluding large formats, such as imperials and jeroboams – were accepted for sale.

Bidding was per dozen bottles (irrespective of how many bottles there were in the lot), lots consisted of multiples of a dozen, and incomplete dozens were invoiced pro-rata. Commission was charged to sellers, at from ten to fifteen per cent of the hammer price, and purchases could be shipped, by Christie's contract shippers, to destinations anywhere in the world.

Shaking hands with David Markham, who eagerly awaited her instructions, and promising to get in touch with him as soon as possible, more for her own sake than for his, Clare left the auction rooms and made her thoughtful way up Duke Street to Fortnum and Mason to buy an extravagant cashmere twin-set for Sidonie.

True to his word, Alain Lamotte had advanced her the five million francs he had promised. Out of this she had paid for the inox, which the suppliers had promised to work day and night to install. The rest of the Assurance Mondiale loan had been eaten up by wages, by day-to-day running costs, by incidentals, and by the renovations to the *Bureau d'Acceuil* and the Orangery.

The purchase of new casks – be it the sixty per cent stipulated by Big Mick (which represented 480 barrels) or the twenty-five per cent (200 barrels) advocated by Halliday Baines – was out of the question. Even if her innovations at the Château proved to be financially successful, there was no way she was going to raise the capital sum of around 600,000 francs, which both Big

Mick and Halliday agreed was indispensable for a vintage that would restore Château de Cluzac to its former glory.

Outlining the changes she was instigating at Château de Cluzac to Grandmaman, she had surprisingly encountered the same wall of suspicion and resentment that had greeted her efforts in the Médoc.

'A "bouncy castle!",' Baronne Gertrude had said. 'A "bouncy castle". *Qu'est ce que c'est que ce* "bouncy castle"?'

When Clare explained that beneath the ancient cedars of the park, where she had installed her picnic chairs and tables, an inflated plastic fortress, complete with towers and turrets, had been erected, which would hopefully keep the children amused while their parents spent their money in the shop or in the cellars, she thought that her grandmother was about to have a fit.

'*Vraiment*, Clare! I am beginning to think that we might have been better off with the South African. I thought that you were serious. I thought that you were going to run the château as it should be run. What is the point of all this . . . this bouncy castle nonsense?'

'To make money.'

At the Baronne's table – which was where Clare and Jamie were sitting over their tournedos, cooked, in accordance with the Baronne's wishes, to a rare blueness – although no subject, including that of sex, was taboo, any discussion of money was considered the mark of the parvenu.

'Let's be realistic, Grandmaman . . .' Clare ignored the Baronne's warning glance towards Louise, who was not the least interested in the conversation, and was circumventing the table with the *gratin dauphinois*. 'If Château de Cluzac is to be rehabilitated, if I am to get its name known, and respected, throughout the world, I am going to need money. I'm going to need pots of it. And I'm going to

get some of it, I can't help it Grandmaman – in the form
of *liquide* . . .'

Baronne Gertrude shuddered at the mention of cash.

'Hopefully from passing trade.'

As Clare outlined her plans to run the estate on a
strictly commercial basis, the Baronne's eyes grew misty.
She saw the wrought-iron gates of the château outlined
against the Médoc sky, the vista of the great lawn on
which the pagoda seemed to float, heard the ringing of
the chapel bells at Christmas time summoning the family
to Midnight Mass.

'*Tout passe, tout lasse, tout casse.*' She waved Louise,
with her dish, away. 'Crowds tramping round the de
Cluzac cellars. Your grandfather took such pride in them.
Trout-fishing in the moat! Bouncy castles on the lawn! Let
us discuss the wedding.'

'I was reading a magazine on the plane,' Clare said.
'There was this amazing gold dress, with an embroidered
Nehru suit for Jamie . . .'

'I'll choose my own suit!' Jamie snapped. He had had
a heavy day.

The Baronne looked from one to the other.

'I'm sure you will both look absolutely splendid. My
dearest wish is that I shall be around to see it.'

Jamie helped himself to potatoes.

'I see no reason why you shouldn't be.'

'Fantasies of staying the hand of mortality, Jamie,' the
Baronne said sharply, 'are incompatible with the best
interests of our species. You should know that.'

'We refuse to get married without you,' Clare said.

'It is useless vanity to attempt to fend off the certainties
that are the necessary ingredients of the human condition,
Clare. Far from being irreplaceable, it is right and proper
that we should be replaced.'

'You are being unnecessarily morbid, Grandmaman.'

'Not at all. Death comes easiest for those who during

their lives have given it most thought. One must always be prepared for its imminence.'

'"The utility of living"' – Jamie had recovered his composure – '"consists not in the length of days, but in the use of time; a man may have lived long . . ."'

'". . . and yet have lived little."' The Baronne completed the quotation.

As the airline lunch trays, with their empty screw-topped bottles, were swiftly and efficiently cleared away, and the Airbus began its bumpy descent through the clouds to Bordeaux, Clare thought how hard it had been to leave Waterperry and Jamie, who had an interview at the Middlesex Hospital coming up and was on call at the John Radcliffe for the next three weekends.

In the arrivals hall at Mérignac, Clare found herself behind a familiar checked sports jacket and a slim, tanned figure in a sleeveless linen dress, hung about with shiny carrier bags emblazoned with designer names.

'Alain?'

Alain Lamotte spun round at the sound of her voice.

'Clare.'

'We've been to Paris,' Delphine said superfluously.

Alain took in Clare's hand baggage.

'Do you need a lift?'

'No thanks. I've got the car.'

Alain put a protective arm round Delphine as they made their way towards the baggage claim.

Clare had left the car in the long-term car-park. Slinging her grip on to the back seat, she got into the driver's seat and switched on the ignition. Lowering the visor against the setting sun, she put the car into gear. The car lurched drunkenly forward as if it were out of control. Realising that something was wrong, she got out and walked round her father's yellow Renault. The cause of the problem was obvious. Had she not been thinking about Alain and Delphine Lamotte and what a handsome couple they made, she might have noticed. Beneath the bumpers, as if they had been attacked by a madman with a machete, all four tyres had been viciously slashed.

CHAPTER THIRTY

Marie-Paule Balard sat in Doctor Hébèque's waiting-room waiting for her name to be called. It was Harry, who had accompanied her to the Cours de Tournon and who sat in the chair next to her reading a motor magazine, who had persuaded her to make an appointment with the doctor for the malaise, the precise nature of which she was unable to put her finger on, which had been making inroads into her life for some time and which had finally overtaken her.

The crux had come at a soirée given by the Balards in honour of Mr Timo Toivonen and Mr Kari Mkila, two important wine merchants from Finland, a country that was just beginning to find its feet as far as French wine was concerned. During dinner, Marie-Paule had retreated into a world of her own. She had addressed not one word to the guests, whom her husband was hoping to entice to the cellars of Balard et Fils. When Balard reprimanded his wife publicly for her lack of enthusiasm about Finnish life (the second highest suicide rate in Europe) and customs (a liking for a jolly session in the sauna, followed by a roll in the snow before dinner), Marie-Paule had burst into tears and left the *salle-à-manger*, leaving them all to get on with it.

It came as no surprise when, angrier than she had ever seen him, Balard reported that as a direct result of her behaviour, which had left a cloud over the Provençal table – which was not all that dazzling at the best of times –

Mr Toivonen and Mr Mkila had taken the business of Alko, the state-owned alcohol company (the Finns were renowned for excessive drinking, and in view of their long dark winters who could blame them?) to the rival Gastinet Frères.

The row that followed went on all night. It was overheard by Christiane and Harry, who could not help but be a party to it, as well as by those passing along the tree-lined Cours Xavier-Arnozan beneath the open shutters. The aftermath of the débâcle *chez Balard* was a series of repercussions which were as carefully orchestrated as the movements of a symphony.

The overture covered the old ground of Marie-Paule's lack of co-operation as far as her husband's business endeavours were concerned. To this hurtful accusation – was not her entire life devoted to supporting both Balard and his endeavours? – she did not at first deign to reply. Finally goaded, not only by the most recent charge, but by a catalogue of long-standing grievances dredged unjustly from the past, the confrontation deteriorated into a slanging match which took place in the master bedroom, during the course of which voices were raised, copious tears shed, and even *objets* thrown.

This cacophonous prelude was followed by a week of monosyllabic silence, as the master of the house made his displeasure felt. His wrath was exacerbated by a visit to Château de Cluzac – which according to Harry had something to do with the de Cluzac wine contract – after which his face, which was seldom very agreeable, was terrible to behold.

The silence was broken by a flurry of activity on Balard's part, comings and goings punctuated by a series of urgent telephone calls, which culminated in the negociant's returning home in the small hours of the morning, his handkerchief bound round a bleeding cut on his finger, and his leather jacket streaked with acrylic yellow paint.

Whatever it was he had been up to seemed to cheer him up considerably. The negociant's silence gave way to malicious laughter, although his wife, for the life of her, could not see the joke.

This apparent amusement, hard on the heels of the yellow paint (which the dry-cleaner had been unable to remove from Balard's jacket), heralded a return to the more or less untroubled waters as the household relaxed and its bourgeois routine was resumed.

That her husband's unpredictable behaviour was due to his disappointment over losing Château de Cluzac, coupled with the serious drop in income he expected as a result of no longer being its negociant, Marie-Paule was well aware. That her own indisposition derived from the same source, she had absolutely no idea.

All she knew was that she no longer wanted to get up in the mornings. Getting out of her bed at noon, she could not wait to return to it, and she retired for the night, often before Balard had left for *l'Union*, increasingly early. Like a preremptorily deflated balloon, the bounce that once had sustained a daily round of unremitting activity, had gone out of her. She stood mesmerised before the counter in the *boucherie*, vexing the other customers as she vacillated between the *entrecôte* and the *faux filet* (as likely as not changing her mind again once she had decided); sat silent and withdrawn at committee meetings convinced that she, who had never been short of an opinion, had nothing useful to contribute; let the dust gather, and the mattresses remain unaired; let slip the role of *maîtresse de maison* she had previously carried out so diligently, and neglected her appearance in which – the unsatisfactory result notwithstanding – she had previously taken pride.

All these changes in his wife's demeanour went unremarked by the doltish Claude Balard, who had other things on his mind. Not least of these were the changes at

Château de Cluzac, which had spiked his guns in more than one respect.

His feelings about the appropriation of the estate by the Baron's daughter were dumped on to the accommodating bosom of Beatrice Biancarelli, who had her own reasons for wishing Clare de Cluzac had stayed at home.

In view of the unexpected reverses in Balard's fortunes, the villa in Arcachon on which Biancarelli had set her heart, and which she had mentally furnished, would no longer materialise. Even more than she missed the promised villa, however, plans for which were temporarily given up rather than abandoned (there were bigger fish in the Garonne than Claude Balard), Biancarelli missed Charles-Louis.

Deprived, after twenty-six years, of the Baron's daily visits, and unaware how much she had depended on them, she was dumbfounded to discover that, for the second time in her life, she was in love.

Like Charles-Louis' wife Viola, whom Biancarelli had never met (even in her Bordeaux days, the young Baronne de Cluzac had been uninterested in clothes), the boutique owner had not the least illusion about her former lunchtime lover. Like Viola she had made the paradoxical, if not exactly earth-shattering, discovery that, despite his often outrageous behaviour, the Baron was possessed of a considerable amount of charm.

She did not delude herself. Charles-Louis was a playboy and a wastrel. He had fallen out with his mother, squandered his resources, deceived his wife, cheated on his mistresses. Having bootlegged funds out of the country and in so doing dispossessed his sister and his daughter of what was rightfully theirs, he was also a criminal. When it came to the irrationality of the human heart, none of these acts, each one in itself despicable, and some of which were punishable by law, counted for anything. *Il a rendu fades tous les hommes*. He had made all other men seem dull.

Before he had left for Florida and its oranges, with the painted ringmaster, Laura Spray, who could make the present Baron de Cluzac stand on his hind legs at the flick of her Bryn Mawr whip, Charles-Louis had taken his Rolls-Royce Phantom II Continental out of the garage and, in a rare act of folly, driven Biancarelli into the country for dinner.

The Baron's presence at La Belle Epoque, a restaurant not only well worth a detour both for its idyllic setting and its food, but the possessor of three Michelin rosettes, was greeted with much bowing and scraping. This deference was due not only to his haughty demeanour, but to the fact that although the table had been booked by Petronella under his alias, Monsieur Rougemont, the Baron's face was well known.

Sitting opposite him at the most coveted table, her hair piled high and her dress cut low, Biancarelli, suddenly, and utterly without warning, was struck by a sensation of happiness such as she had not experienced for a great many years.

This rapture had nothing to do either with the Baron's pre-prandial conversation, which centred largely and obsessively on his daughter's outrageous behaviour and was neither amorous nor scintillating, or with the manner in which he addressed his food, which was, as far as Biancarelli was concerned, an infallible barometer of the esteem in which a woman was held.

A good trencherman, reared on the offerings of Sidonie, whose culinary skills had been passed down from her mother and her grandmother, Charles-Louis bestowed on his food the seriousness and attention he felt it deserved.

While Biancarelli chattered away like a mynah bird between the *premier plat* and the *entrée*, between the cheese and the dessert, and afterwards over the coffee, the Baron's meal was despatched in virtual silence. There was, as far as Charles-Louis was concerned, no solicitous enquiry as to his companion's preferences, no participation in her selection from the menu, no concern lest her choice turn out not to her liking, and certainly no intimate exchange of food.

Their table was hedged about, at a respectful distance, by a veritable battalion of waiters responsive to the Baron's every move – although the large and elegantly furnished room was full to capacity – but Biancarelli might well, for all the attention she was getting, be dining at La Belle Epoque *femme seule*.

They were waiting for the bill, which Biancarelli would settle – the Baron had never come to terms with credit cards and did not carry any cash – and Charles-Louis was trying to explain to her the delights of Real Tennis, played, as far as she could make out, with wooden balls and a lop-sided racquet on a court with sloping roofs, wooden boards and a cowbell. Her companion was explaining that his weekly game was one of the things he was going to miss most in Florida, when taking a minuscule *tartelette*, from the plate of petits fours on the table, he put the pastry case, which was filled with glazed raspberries, reflectively into his mouth.

'I used to gather raspberries in the woods with my father.' The Baron, his eyes far away, spoke softly, almost as if he were talking to himself. 'I was only six years old . . .'

It was at that moment, moved perhaps by the gentleness of Charles-Louis' voice and by the unguarded expression on his normally controlled face, that Biancarelli felt the unaccustomed stirrings of desire.

Back in her *appartement*, while he sat on the bed and waited for her to disappear into her little dressing-room, no bigger than a cupboard, and don the *guêpière* her lover liked her to wear for his visits, she removed all her clothes and stood naked before him. When he demanded a glass of champagne, she walked naked to the fridge.

Serving him, like an acolyte, she waited for him to

assuage his thirst, then removed his clothes, her eyes taking in, as if for the first time, the shape of the body that in the years in which she had known him had grown from youth to maturity: his still athletic shoulders, his loins, his thick penis, the slight hollow which followed the inner curve of the thigh up to the groin.

If Charles-Louis noticed a difference in the activities that followed, Biancarelli was unaware of it. He did not ask for the *guêpière* but neither did he need it. Drunk with passion, Beatrice acknowledged her Dante. Bathed in perspiration, her soaked hair clinging in red strands to her tanned shoulders, she begged him to stay the night. In an unprecedented gesture, Charles-Louis kissed his mistress on the mouth, before leaving her bed.

When he had gone, back to Laura Spray, back to Florida where he would no doubt forget all about her, Biancarelli, shaking with the force of her discovery, slipped a CD into the hi-fi. Eyes closed, lips pursed, wearing her satin wrapper, she swayed round the room to Sylvie Vartan singing '. . . *C'est fatal, animal*', as if she was the first woman in the world to feel that way.

Obsessed with thoughts of Charles-Louis, distracting her from her business, which demanded total commitment to her clientele, Biancarelli had little time for either Claude Balard or his vendetta against Clare de Cluzac.

Humiliating and degrading Biancarelli during the course of his daily visits – for which privilege he undertook the rent of both boutique and *appartement* – his paranoid and highly embroidered narrative of cancelled contracts and wine sales to the public, advertised by means of a blatant and offensive display, fell on indifferent ears. Preoccupied as usual with his own feelings, Claude Balard was as oblivious of the lack of interest with which Biancarelli greeted his saga of treachery and betrayal, as was Baron de Cluzac to the fact that his mistress was in love with him.

*   *   *

While Claude Balard was able to act out the anger he felt at losing Chateau de Cluzac in Biancarelli's boudoir, Marie-Paule, for whom no such outlet was available, turned her rage at being cheated of the estate upon herself and slid into an unfamiliar depression. It was Harry, whose motives were, as always, self-serving, who had made her go to the doctor. His mother's indisposition was interfering with his life.

When Marie-Paule had observed, two years ago, that some of the housekeeping money Balard gave her was missing from her purse, her suspicions had fallen upon the Balards' long-suffering maid. When an affronted Martine, whom she had challenged with the theft, had packed her bags and left the Cours Xavier-Arnozan for her home in Alsace, and the pilfering went on, Marie-Paule was at a loss. That she did not mention the theft to Balard was due partly to the fact that she harboured a suspicion she was unwilling to confront, and partly to a symptom of the lack of communication between herself and her husband.

When she caught Harry, red-handed, going through her bag when he thought she was in the *salle de bain*, her misgivings were confirmed. Confident that his mother, with whom since his birth he had an unwritten alliance, would not shop him to his father, Harry, who had allowed the innocent Martine to be dismissed without saying a word in her defence, came clean.

Playing to the gallery of Marie-Paule's vicarious aspirations for him – the marriage of her adored son would, she hoped, do much to compensate for the failure of her own – Harry Balard made his confession. While the salary for which he worked extremely hard at Balard et Fils went a long way to supporting his lifestyle (Marie-Paule had never seen a young man with so many electronic 'toys' and so many pairs of cufflinks), it did not stretch to the courtship of his latest girl.

Intrigued, as Harry had calculated that she would be, by the idea that he had at last come to his senses and was thinking of settling down, Marie-Paule chided her son for his lack of trust in her, and asked him how much he would need.

Having been provided with a private income by her father, she settled on a weekly sum which made her blanch – the young lady must be extremely special – but which she could well afford. Strengthening her alliance with Harry, she colluded with him in keeping their arrangement from Balard, and made him promise to come straight to her whenever he was in trouble.

The fact that Harry was already in trouble, and needed the money to support the cocaine habit which accounted for his hyperactivity and his tendency to turn night into day, did not cross her mind.

When Marie-Paule, uncharacteristically, began to regard Harry's demands for money with suspicion, and seemed to have difficulty opening her purse, Harry took her straight to the doctor. While Doctor Hébèque, who had her finger on the pulse of Bordeaux, had a shrewd suspicion of what was bothering her patient, but was unable to do anything about it other than give her an *ordonnance* for pills to elevate her mood, Harry Balard, making an accurate guess at the reason for his mother's indisposition, vowed to avenge himself on her behalf on Clare de Cluzac.

CHAPTER THIRTY-ONE

By the time the grapes on the recently thinned vines began to turn from green to purple, hardware such as was unheard of twenty years ago in Bordeaux, in the form of stainless-steel vats with thermoregulation systems, had replaced the insanitary and time-expired wood in the Château de Cluzac cellars. Pristine and regimented, the two shining lines, their symmetry broken only by the nonchalant incline of the occasional ladder, faced each other beneath the vaulted ceiling. They looked as if they had always been there.

Despite the new installations, the *chais* were still light-years away from the new, architect-designed underground cellars, with their polished marble floors, of Château d'Estaminet, or the giant new vat stores, analytical laboratory, and pneumatic presses of Château Laurent with its ultra-modern bottling chain, which rinsed and treated the bottles with nitrogen and filled them at an astonishing rate, before standing them upright (to allow the cork to expand) and automatically labelling and wrapping them.

Since Clare's return from London to find not only the tyres of the Renault slashed, but the trout with which she had filled the moat of Château de Cluzac floating accusingly on their backs – dead and presumably poisoned – she had not been idle. With her energy levels topped up by her anger at the sabotage, she had never worked so hard in her life.

The fact that she had enemies did not deter her. When obstacles such as the vandalised sign, the slashed tyres, the dead trout were put in her way, she duly reported the crimes to the *gendarmerie*, which had as yet not isolated the perpetrators. On the lookout for further acts of vandalism, she did not allow the incidents to deflect her and, when the blind fury they had provoked had abated, she treated them with the disdain they deserved. She had discussed the matter with Jamie. While obvious names, such as Balard and Van Gelder, presented themselves immediately, she knew that there were others in the Médoc who, for one reason or another, resented her presence. With twenty-four hours in the day not being long enough for all she planned to do, on Jamie's advice she concentrated on buying four new tyres for the Renault and instructing the local fish-farm to restock the moat with trout.

Baron Charles-Louis would not have recognised his recently vacated château and, according to Grandmaman – who was kept up to date with Clare's ventures by the Comtesse de Ribagnac, who no doubt had her own spies – Baron Thibault (fiercely proud of both the agricultural and commercial aspects of the château) would have turned in his grave.

A one-man band, Clare negotiated with builders and supervised the renovations of the Orangerie, which were already well underway, installed toilets in the disused dungeons, made contact with the airlines, to see if she could interest them in her quarter-bottles of Petite Clare, spent two cobwebbed days in the vast underground bottle store with Big Mick, choosing wines suitable to be shipped to London for auction, approached several English supermarket chains – including the formidable Julie Smith of Catesbury's, who had accepted an invitation to Bordeaux – and negotiated with printers for the brochures for distribution to visitors and tour operators. The brochures with their logo, the de Cluzac coat of arms encircled by green and purple grapes, were now piled high in her office.

'Successful wineries must be good at show business.' Without Alain Lamotte at her elbow, she could never have got the show on the road in so short a time.

She had spent days in Alain's office in the Rue Vauban, poring over the layout and wording of her advertising matter, and through Alain she had been invited by Delphine to the annual *fête champêtre* to be held at Le Moulin de la Misère, in two weeks' time.

With Alain's help she had produced an information pack which made public that which for three hundred years the incumbents of Château de Cluzac had taken pride in keeping to themselves. Alain had taken a photograph of her and Rougemont, standing on the steps of Château de Cluzac, for the front cover of the brochure.

As they sat at the desk and hammered out the details of the text, which Alain transferred to his computer – editing and refining it, with reference to the Baron's sale document, the details of which he knew chapter and verse – Clare became aware that the PDG of the Bordeaux branch of Assurance Mondiale was becoming interested in more than protecting his stake in the fortunes of the château.

The first concrete indication she had that Alain's concern was not entirely professional was when he put his proposed wording for an 'Invitation to a château', designed to be sent out independently to journalists and wine-buyers, on his screen.

Alain's spoken English was better than his written and howlers such as '. . . enjoy the vineyards covered with gravels', and '. . . explore the corpse by the lake', brought tears of amusement to Clare's eyes. In an involuntary gesture, she had put her hand over his. Alain's flushed face and the speed with which he had withdrawn his hand with its gold wedding band, as if the contact had burned his skin, confirmed her suspicions.

To create a diversion, Clare had picked up the photograph of Delphine and the children, on holiday on some deserted beach, from his desk, and asked Alain where it had been taken. By the time he had explained that the photograph had been taken early one morning in Brittany, where they had rented a house for the summer, the moment was over, the flush had subsided from Alain's face and he had regained his equilibrium.

The incident, which afterwards was not referred to, was followed by a distinct change in the atmosphere as the relationship, which before had been strictly business, was now overlaid, at least as far as Alain was concerned, by desire.

Watching Alain, as he attempted to keep his mind on the improvements to Château de Cluzac, on working out the feasibility of projects such as letting rooms for 'Château Weekends', and the possibility of opening a wine school such as was up and running at Kilmartin, Clare pitied him.

He was a decent enough chap who was obviously fighting the temptation to deceive his wife and let down his beloved family. When he had difficulty in keeping his eyes on the computer screen, she tried not to let the atmosphere get too heavy, and diverted him with château business – his overriding passion and one that eclipsed any other thought he might have in his head – whenever she could.

Alain was not unattractive. His large frame, which bore tribute to his regular games of tennis and of squash, was running to fat only round his middle, and he exuded a certain dependable appeal. His vapid personality and lack of imagination, however, were a turn-off. Although he was obviously an extremely kind and well-intentioned man, without whose help Clare could not possibly have masterminded the transformation of Château de Cluzac, he could not hold a candle to Jamie. She was not the slightest bit jealous of Delphine.

Many hours which were not passed with Alain were spent supervising the workmen, who now cluttered up the grounds, spreading the word about Château de Cluzac – by telephone and fax – to destinations all over the world, and soothing the ruffled feathers of Monsieur Boniface (out of his element with all the innovations), Albert Rochas, Jean Boyer and Sidonie. She also spent time in the tasting-room with Halliday, who had volunteered to help her with her second wine.

While Big Mick asserted that in the grandest châteaux, where the vines were old and weak, with twisted trunks, stunted rods and pale leaves, the grapes were simply picked and left to get on with it – and Alain Lamotte saw successful wineries in terms of 'show-biz' – Halliday Baines was convinced that the only future for winemaking was in the application of technology.

With no vocational training herself, Clare was fascinated by the oenologist's expertise. Her mind reeled as he boasted of the computer-controlled irrigation systems which he had installed in Australia, and the 'genetically manipulated' yeast with which he turned the time-honoured methods of vinification on their heads.

'We have these huge insulated tanks containing more than five hundred and fifty chemicals . . .'

'Chemicals?'

'Ethanol, acids, esters, sugars, 1,4-dihydroxyphenyl-3-butanone . . . You know it better as wine. Every year, in the desert, we produce seventy million litres – seventy million! – of blended wine, some of it less than a year old, one third of which ends up in the UK where nearly a quarter of a million glasses of the stuff will be filled from a cardboard box with a plastic neoprene tap at the side. "Bag-in-the-box" technology was developed in Australia. Sales of traditional European wines are declining. It's part of the New World revolution. If you're going to make wine, my dear . . .'

'Excuse me?'

'Did I say something?'

'The name's Clare.'

Halliday ignored the admonition.

'It's got to be good wine. Wine that is not oxidised – exposed to the air so that it goes brown and tastes like tea – wine that is not affected by bacterial spoilage . . .'

He moved to the trestle table, covered with a white tablecloth, on which Jean had set out a dozen bottles and glasses. Picking one up he rinsed it in water before holding it up to the light to check that it was perfectly clean.

'So many people have been exposed, for so long, to wine that is technically faulty, that they've forgotten how a good wine should taste.' He handed the glass to Clare. 'OK,' he said arrogantly. 'Let's see what you can do.'

Determined both to improve the tarnished image of Château de Cluzac wine and to take the bumptious oenologist down a peg or two, Clare applied herself to the task in hand.

Ignoring the Australian, but remembering his words that wines, like human beings, must have both personality and character, she concocted a wine in which neither fruit nor oak was dominant, a wine filled with the aroma of plums and blackcurrants, a soft, elegant wine, which, while not for maturing, was easy to drink.

'Not at all bad!' Halliday was clearly impressed. '*Bienvenu à la* "Petite Clare".'

At lunch, served in the *salle-à-manger* by Sidonie, who was somewhat mollified by the present Clare had brought her from London, which was too good to wear and which she had put away, still in its Fortnum and Mason bag, in her drawer, Clare asked after Billy. A look of pleasure he was unable to conceal illuminated Halliday's face as he took out his wallet and removed two well-thumbed sheets of paper, one of which was covered with a childish scrawl.

'I had a letter from Maureen. And one from Billy. Billy's got to have his tonsils operated on. He gets these mega sore throats, all the glands up, can't speak, poor kid, that kind of thing. We've been putting it off.' He referred to the letter on blue airmail paper. 'According to Maureen, the doc says we – she – shouldn't wait any longer. She doesn't want it to interfere with his schooling. I told her to go ahead . . .'

'He'll be all right.'

'You think so?' Halliday's expression was naked with anxiety.

'I had mine out when I was six,' she said. 'All I remember is the ice-cream. Billy will be fine.' Clare tried to reassure him.

'At least he's near a hospital. My father was a wool-grower. I grew up on a farm. Ninety miles from nowhere. One bungalow, two barns and the sheep-shearers' lodge. Eight thousand sheep sharing fifty thousand acres of outback. That was it. In the rainy season, when the road was cut, there was nowhere to go.'

'It sounds romantic.'

'It takes your breath away. A weather-boarded bungalow no more than a speck in a landscape so vast, so empty, that nobody this side of the world can possibly imagine it. There wasn't much in the way of temptation, of course. It's not exactly a social whirl.'

'How did you pass the time?'

'Bushwacking round the countryside with my dad. In his four-wheel drive. He knew every tree, every flower, every animal. There's some pretty strange wildlife. My father could whistle like a kettle.'

'Do your parents still live there?'

'Just the two of them. The next station is six miles up the valley. They read the Bible to each other. It gets pretty lonely.'

'And I think the Médoc is the back of beyond. I miss London. I miss Jamie.'

Halliday raised his wineglass.
'Absent friends. To Jamie!'
'To Billy and his tonsils!'
'To the success of "Petite Clare"!'

CHAPTER THIRTY-TWO

'Claret is a blended wine and each grape variety has its clearly defined role. Cabernet sauvignon, *the* grape of the Médoc, has a blackcurrant flavour which gives the wine its colour and depth, while the merlot is softer and more aromatic. Grapes from different plots in the vineyard – the cabernet sauvignon, the merlot, and in some cases the cabernet franc and the petit verdot' – Clare ticked the varieties off on her fingers three times a day like the beads on her rosary – 'are vinified separately and chronologically according to maturation dates. At Château de Cluzac the grapes arrive here at the winery or *cuvier*, and are then tipped into the *fouloir-égrappoir* . . .'

With a sweep of her hand she indicated a large V-shaped receptacle with a giant screw running along the bottom of it. 'This removes the stalks and gently breaks the skins. The grapes are not so much crushed, as many people imagine, as "broken" just sufficiently to allow the fermentation to begin. Originally the de-stalking was done by hand, on a table with a griddle-top. The bunches were rubbed on the griddle until all the berries were separated from the stalk . . .'

'*Entschuldigen bitte* . . .' The hand of a back-packer in shorts and vest shot up.

'Yes?' She welcomed questions which established that the *visite* was paying attention.

'*Wo sind die Toiletten, bitte?*'

Putting on her best smile, which over the course of the past weeks had begun to wear thin, Clare directed the girl with the sunburned nose to the dungeons, where the toilets were now more or less functioning.

'From the stemmer,' she said, resuming where she had left off, 'the grapes are pumped into the vats' – she led the party along the recently hosed floors – 'where the fermentation process changes the sugar in the grapes to alcohol . . .'

'For how long must they ferment?' A brachycephalic Dutchman blinked at her through his thick lenses.

'About ten to fourteen days. It depends on the year. When the fermentation is underway, the solid matter in the grapes rises to the top and forms what we call the *chapeau*, or cap, which must be kept moist. The act of fermentation releases energy in the form of heat. If the temperature in the vat is allowed to rise too high fermentation can stop and the juice becomes vinegar instead of wine. If the temperature falls too low, the yeasts are inhibited from working.

'These stainless-steel *cuves*,' she continued, indicating the pristine vats still regarded with contempt by Jean Boyer 'have built-in cooling jackets which enable us to control the temperature. The vats used to be made of wood. Some of them were as much as a hundred years old. Wood, of course, does not last for ever . . .'

Keeping an eye on the group, some of whom had wandered off to take flash photographs with their fancy cameras, Clare, wearing her black *directrice*'s trouser-suit relieved by a silk scarf (the Quinconces market rather than Hermès) tied round her neck à la Grandmaman, described the four elements of winemaking – fermentation, maceration, pressing, and malolactic fermentation – as they had been explained to her by Halliday Baines and over which she had burned the midnight oil.

'The first morning of the harvest can sometimes be

cold. If the temperature is less than thirteen or fourteen degrees . . .'

'What's that in fahrenheit?' The up-market accent belonged to a middle-aged Englishwoman with a note-book, wearing an ankle-length skirt over sandals, and an unflattering sunhat. She had already asked how long the *visite* was scheduled to last, if one could leave in the middle, and whether there was anywhere to sit down.

Doubling the centigrade figures to which she added thirty, Clare came up with an approximate answer.

'Roughly fifty-eight degrees . . .' She had now forgotten where she was. 'If the temperature falls below thirteen or fourteen degrees *centigrade*' – she met the Englishwoman's eye – 'fermentation will not start. Four or five days before the harvest begins, a starter vat – *le pied de cuve* – is prepared, and a small quantity of grapes is fermented to produce a "yeast soup". This is placed in the bottom of the first vat to start the fermentation. Using these yeasts, we pump the must . . .' She used the term to see if they were still awake.

'"Must"?'

'The unfermented grape juice. We pump the must over three times a day, and within twenty-four hours fermen-tation will begin. The maximum colour extraction occurs after four to five days and the temperature is carefully maintained . . .'

She explained how the maceration process allowed the pigment to be extracted from the pips and skins to give the characteristic colour to the Médoc wines. The 'marc', or solid matter was pressed, the temperature of the wine increased (encouraging malolactic fermentation, the natural conversion of malic acid to lactic acid), and sulphur dioxide added – to protect against oxidation and bacterial activity – before the wine was racked and put into casks.

Leading the group into the gloom of the first-year cellar, in which each grape variety was kept separately until the *assemblage*, Clare looked with despair at her time-expired barrels which, even at Halliday Baines' conservative estimate of twenty-five per cent, and with the harvest only weeks away, she had little hope of renewing.

Attracting visitors to the château, from which they would hopefully depart having shelled out a few hundred francs on the attractions and purchased a couple of bottles of wine and a T-shirt, was one thing. It enabled her to keep afloat. Ensuring what already promised, according to Albert Rochas, to be a major vintage, one that could make or break the Château, without investing in new oak, was another.

Leading her group through the second-year cellar, she introduced them to the *maître de chai*. Instructed by Sidonie, and for the sake of his job, the blue-overalled Jean Boyer, bung hammer in hand, managed to overcome his embarrassment and pose for the intruders who insisted on taking his photograph (local colour). She amused the group with the cellarmaster's dictum, 'One barrel of wine can work more miracles than a church full of saints' (repeating it for the benefit of the Englishwoman who laboriously wrote it down), before conducting them to the *salle de reception*, which, with its promise of a free drink, was what most of them had been waiting for.

Pouring out samples of Château de Cluzac '92 and '93, she handed the glasses to the *visite*. With the exception of a few wine buffs, they pretended to assess its quality and aroma, about which they had not the first idea (the statutory wit declared it reminded him of his hamster's cage), while wondering whether it was *comme il faut* to ask for refills. Several of them, Clare suspected, would have been equally satisfied had she given them a glass of *vin*, not château-bottled, but extremely *ordinaire*.

'We've got a wine-tasting *machine* in Manchester . . .' The speaker was bearded man who, despite his khaki shorts and sandals, looked, thought Clare – who was getting good at it – like a university lecturer. 'Not in my department, I'm linguistics. In the Institute of Science and Technology.'

'The Aromascan ...' Clare said. Halliday had been thorough in his briefing.

'That will put the wine writers out of business!'

The members of the group were getting friendly with each other.

'Unfortunately,' Clare said, 'the aromascan mistook a Matua Valley Chardonnay for a Drouhin red Beaune. It still has quite a long way to go.'

'Back home we have an aroma *wheel*,' a Californian, who later turned out to be the wine and spirit buyer for a cruise company and an invaluable contact, said. 'It calibrates the experience of wine in the absence of sensory input. The University of California at Davis has identified twelve basic categories and a hundred and twenty-one experimentally distinguishable aromas which have been charted on a wheel. Each of them has a descriptive name. Wet dog is 2-methylbutanol; bell peppers is 2-isobutyl-3-methtoxyprazene, blackcurrant is 2,6,6-trimethyl-2-vinyl-4-acetoxytetrahydropyrane ...'

'They'll be selling wine in the chemist's soon,' Manchester said, saving Clare the job of preventing California from usurping her role and giving a lecture, which would blind the holidaymakers with science as Halliday had blinded her.

'Spinning-cone' technology, developed in the Australian Wine Research Institute, used a fractional column, containing a stack of interlocking spinning cones, to separate out wine compounds and dismantle wine into its component parts. Finely tuned nostrils were then applied to specific aromas, which were graded according to their potency. The highly sophisticated, fractional column of the 'spinning-cone' was being used to remove unwanted flavours from wine, as well as to remove the alcohol for the alcohol-free wine, a contradiction in terms, which was gaining in popularity throughout the world.

'I don't think so,' Clare said, replying to the not-so-far-fetched suggestion that reconstructed wine would eventually be bought over the counter at the *pharmacie*. 'Wine' – she held up her glass – 'is a complex substance. We've not yet succeeded in identifying all the chemical components' (she heard Halliday's voice in her ears) 'which interact with one another in a variety of ways, according to their concentrations, and add up to a great deal more than a flavour. Hopefully – for the wine-producing estates – it will be a very, very long time before a Châteaux de Cluzac ninety-three can be reconstructed in the laboratory!'

On that merry note, she tore the group away from the *salle de reception* and led them out through the courtyard and the formal gardens – where they stopped to take photographs of the geraniums – to the vineyards, where the vines, heavy with black-skinned grapes, were now almost shoulder high and the long hours of sunshine, combined with early-morning dews, presaged the fine harvest anticipated by the *chef de culture*.

Waiting for the photographers to catch up with the others, Clare pointed in the direction of the Gironde.

'You need a lot of water to make a good wine . . .' It was the introduction to her vineyard spiel. 'The wine of Bordeaux is a wine of rivers . . .'

After a brief description of how the third ice age brought pebbles, shifted by the rivers Dordogne and Garonne, to form the terraces and hillocks of deep gravel which accounted for the body and bouquet of the wines assembled in the Médoc, she explained that, according to archaeological excavations, small vineyards had existed in Bordeaux since the time of the Roman occupation. Ending on a lighter note she recounted the story of Dionysus, the Greek god of wine who, according to legend, had first discovered the fruit of the vine and the art of making wine from it, and had spread the gift among mortals.

'Are there any questions?'

'What's the significance of the roses?' A tall American pointed to the pink Lili Marlène, Albert Rochas' pride and joy, which flowered at the end of the rows.

'Rose bushes are traditional in the Médoc. You'll find them in a great many vineyards. Originally they were used to detect the first signs of mildew.'

'The vines look real neat.'

'One metre between them, and one metre between each row. The measurements are precise.'

'You pick by machine?'

'*Certainly not!*' Clare said. 'Because of the *tirage*, the removing of the rotten grapes, the grapes are picked one bunch at a time. It takes two hours to pick one row.'

Although many quality producers in the Médoc still preferred, as had the Baron, to pick by hand, there were, as Halliday Baines had pointed out, several advantages to harvesting by machine, over 1,500 of which were already in use in the undulating landscape of the Gironde. The most important of these was that, by working through the night, the grapes could be got out of the vineyard and into the winery while it was still cool. On a large estate, where the *vendange* could last anything between two and three weeks, this could result in a much higher percentage of the vintage being collected at optimum ripeness, and avoid disappointment should the weather change. Another benefit of the mechanical harvester was that it left unripe grapes behind, which ensured a more effective selection than that made by unskilled hand-pickers.

Leading the group back to the courtyard, which for the past weeks had been filled with cars – coaches were parked in the long drive – Clare directed them to the shop, manned by Petronella, which sold wine and souvenirs.

'I hope you enjoyed your tour of Château de Cluzac,'

she said brightly, and that you'll visit us again. Bring your friends.'

Filing into the shop at the far end of the *chais*, where refreshments were also available, the members of the group thanked her for her guidance. The American who had enquired about the roses thrust a twenty-franc note into her hand.

The first time she had been given a tip, she had handed it back. Now, on the advice of Alain, to whom she related her embarrassment, she accepted the cash gracefully and saved it up to buy petrol for the car.

The unremitting work, the organisation involved in running the château on a commercial basis and the gratuities were not the only things she had had to get used to. Whereas Baron Charles-Louis had usually taken his lunch alone in the dining-room, now, every day, there were visitors from abroad to entertain.

Crossing the courtyard from where she had left the group to Petronella, she went into her office, where there was a fresh bunch of faxes on the desk, put there by Becky Elphinstone, the new secretary from Edinburgh she had taken on. Picking up her diary, she opened it at the day's date.

They were to be six for lunch. She was expecting a Finnish journalist, an Argentinian agent, an important Washington restaurateur, a buyer/broker from Hamburg and the sommelier of a Paris brasserie which served some one hundred covers a day.

Faced with the daily business luncheons, Sidonie had at first rebelled.

'*Ce n'est pas mon travail, Mademoiselle!*' she had snapped. '*Les invitées d'accord, mais pas tous les jours . . .*'

Sitting her down at the kitchen table, Clare had explained, as gently as she could, that her job and her home were on the line, and that if the château wasn't made to pay it could fall into quite the wrong hands. As *directrice*, she needed all the help she could get to keep the estate up and running, and she was relying on Sidonie, whom she not only loved dearly but who was the best cook in the world, to back her up.

Somewhat mollified, and with the promise of extra help in the kitchen, Sidonie, secretly flattered by Clare's remarks, got out her recipe books and arrived at a simple menu which, with only minor variations (*selon le marché*) was served at the working lunches. The meal, of Quiche Lorraine, tournedos, cheese and Sidonie's home-made ice-cream, was accompanied by Château de Cluzac wine (the vintage selected by Jean who had been read the riot act by Sidonie), according to the importance of the guests. Coffee was taken in the salon, where any deal that had been broached over lunch was hopefully clinched.

CHAPTER THIRTY-THREE

Delphine Lamotte, carrying Bijou, and wearing only the narrow towel which she had wrapped round her narrow body after her early-morning swim, stood on the terrace of Le Moulin de la Misère. While Alain, having completed his statutory thirty lengths, frolicked with the children in the pool. She contemplated the leaden sky.

'*Qu'en penses tu, chéri?*'

Alain, who had one child screaming with delight on his broad shoulders and another, whom he held by her outstretched hands, with her skinny legs round his waist, attuned to Delphine's shorthand, knew that what his wife wanted was not only his opinion of the weather, but, more specifically, to know if it was going to rain.

The Lamotte *fête champêtre*, held annually, was an event to which anyone who was anyone in Bordeaux, and who had not gone away for the summer, was invited, together with their children.

Dress was (by Bordeaux standards) informal and the guests were free to roam the spacious grounds, make use of the pool, play tennis or croquet on the lawn, join in the games organised by Alain, and generally make themselves at home. At two o'clock, or two-thirty, depending how things were going, tables of delicious food cooked by Delphine, who held a Cordon Bleu diploma, were set up in the shade of the old mill, rugs and cushions were distributed, and those who could not find deckchairs disposed themselves on the lawn, which ran down to the mill stream. It was a relaxed and popular occasion, the success of which depended to a large extent on the weather.

'Alain!' Delphine rubbed her wet hair on a corner of the towel.

Lifting his younger daughter from his shoulders and depositing her back in the pool where she swam, in her Mickey Mouse armbands, like a tadpole to join her sister, Alain shrugged eloquently. Judging by the appearance of the clouds, it might well rain. He was more concerned about Clare's grapes than the *fête champêtre*. Although Assurance Mondiale now had an appreciable stake in the success of the Château de Cluzac *récolte*, Alain's interest in the estate was more than twenty-six per cent. It concerned its *directrice*, with whom he had, despite himself, fallen passionately in love.

It was a *coup de foudre*. A madness quite beyond his control. From the time that Clare had walked into the Fête de la Fleur at Château Laurent on the arm of Jamie, her image had been imprinted on his retina, from which it refused to budge. From the moment he opened his eyes in the morning, until the time that he closed them at night, no matter what he was doing, how demanding the task on which he was engaged, whether he was slaving away over his computer, clinching a business deal, or making love to Delphine, whose mind was invariably elsewhere, he saw Clare de Cluzac with her luminous skin and lustrous eyes in tantalising proximity. She was even present in his dreams. The folly that possessed him, which was worse than any lunacy, as distressing as an illness, more addictive than any drug – he could not see enough of the object of his desire and turned up at Château de Cluzac on the flimsiest of pretexts – was not of his doing. He had not asked for it. He had not declared his infatuation to the object of it. Alain loved his wife.

Hoping that he would get over whatever it was that possessed him, he had thrown himself with even more vigour than usual into his work and into his leisure pursuits. Slamming the squash ball against the wall, serving one of his legendary aces on the Lamotte tennis court at the far end of the garden – where already he was patiently teaching the little girls to hit the ball over the net – swimming, in his textbook crawl, until he was exhausted, and running, in preparation for the forthcoming marathon, he had tried to expunge Clare de Cluzac from his mind. To no avail.

It was not as if he had never cheated on his marriage. There had been times when Delphine, who was no longer particularly interested in sex, had taken the children to Paris to see their grandparents or when he had travelled abroad on business, when he had indulged in extremely short-lived affairs. They had not been the *grand passion* which now obsessed him, and had been forgotten almost as soon as they were begun. This time there were warning bells. Being a cautious man (which contributed to his success at Assurance Mondiale) he heeded them. He had no intention of losing his wife whom he loved, his children with whom he was besotted, the home which he had created, the job to which he was wedded. His reticence was not without considerable cost to himself.

Now, gazing at his wife's tanned and shapely legs, which never failed to arouse him, as – having put Bijou down on the hammock – she flipped her long hair over her head and rubbed it with the towel, he tried to dispel the mental image of Clare de Cluzac, which was, as usual, superimposed on that of Delphine.

'*Tu as regardé la météo!*' he shouted in answer to Delphine's question. The TV set was at the end of their bed and together, leaning side by side against the square pillows, they had watched the early-morning weather forecast. There had been small puffs of cloud over the area, but no mention of rain.

'*La météo!*' Delphine's voice was scornful. '*Ils se trompent toujours!*'

Lifting the little girls out of the pool, Alain followed them, dripping, to their mother's side.

Wrapping her daughters in their striped bath robes, Delphine despatched them to their room.

Alain opened Delphine's towel and pressed her to him. The Lamottes swam naked.

'Come upstairs.'

'*Alain! J'ai mille choses à faire . . .*'

Listening to the impressive catalogue of domestic tasks she still had to carry out in preparation for the guests, Alain, feeling his disappointment like a pain, as if Delphine had doused his desire with a bucket of cold water, watched his wife snatch her poodle from the hammock and disappear into the house.

To Delphine's relief, the rain, which threatened all day, held off until lunch was almost finished. At which point, suddenly, and without any warning, the heavens opened, deluging guests, rugs and the remains of the buffet alike, and sending the women, fearful for their dresses and their coiffures, clutching whatever they could, and screaming for their children who were enjoying the diversion, scurrying for shelter.

Clare had arrived late. After a flying weekend visit, she had taken Jamie to Mérignac, where she had bought flowers for Delphine in the airport. Alain had been afraid that she was not coming. Aware that he had been on tenterhooks, Clare shook hands formally with her host. She was amused by his agitation. Approaching Delphine, who was fussing over the decimated dishes on the buffet tables, she made her apologies.

'*Je m'excuse de ce retard, Madame . . .*'

'*Delphine!*'

'*Excusez-moi, Delphine.*' Clare handed her the flowers.

'I had to take Jamie to the airport. The traffic was horrendous!'

Delphine kissed her warmly.

'I'm so glad you could come. I understand from Alain that Château de Cluzac is an enormous success.'

'I've left Petronella in charge.' Clare looked up at the sky. 'She's taking the *visite*. Unfortunately there's not much that she can do about the rain.'

'Summer rains . . .' Alain handed her a glass of Laurent Rose, the extremely successful second wine of the Merciers, who sat together with the Balards at a table on the lawn. 'They're usually not too much of a problem . . .'

'Alain is taking a great interest in your harvest.' Delphine, who wore a white trouser-suit which emphasised her tan – if Delphine Lamotte were to fall down a drain, legend had it, she would come up smelling of violets – gave Clare a plate. It was bordered with a pattern of *mignonettes* and held *couverts* wrapped in a matching napkin. '*N'est ce pas, chéri?*' She put a hand, with its delicate gold bracelet, on Alain's shoulder and inclined her face intimately towards his. 'You would think that Assurance Mondiale had a fifty-per-cent interest in the château. This one talks about nothing else.'

Clare, dressed casually in khaki shorts crumpled from the long drive (she thought she had been coming to a picnic) with a taupe vest across which was slung the present Jamie had bought her – a tiny 'coach' bag in soft black leather – and her plimsolls, was oblivious of the stares of Delphine's smart friends in their linen suits, in acid-drop colours, and diaphanous dresses. Escorted by Alain, she carried her plate of little white shrimps (caught in the river and cooked by Delphine with the fennel which grew in abundance in the Médoc), whiskery *langoustines*, frilled batavia leaves, and shining dollop of home-made mayonnaise. Picking at the shrimp as she went, she walked down the sloping garden in the direction of the mill stream.

From her table, where she sat like an overstuffed pink silk cushion, Marie-Paule Balard followed her progress. 'As high-handed as her father,' she remarked in a loud voice. 'Look at the state of her.'

Exhilarated after Jamie's brief visit, Clare had come to the *fête champêtre* only to please Alain, on whose help with the estate she depended. Skirting the Balards, Marie-Paule (fatter than ever) and Harry, with their heads conspiratorially together, Claude, napkin beneath his chin, concentrating on his lunch, Clare cared neither where she sat nor to whom she talked. By the look of it, some of the guests would not be talking to her. She was not bothered.

Jamie, who had been hoping to get away on Friday, had been operating on an osteosarcoma of the femur, a lengthy procedure which entailed putting in a plastic and metal prosthesis. To her disappointment, he had missed his plane and not arrived until Saturday morning. Most of her day had been taken up with paperwork and *visites*, one of which Jamie had joined, mischievously asking unanswerable questions and putting Clare off her stride.

After the last coach had gone, they had strolled down to the fishing-hut, which was silhouetted on its stilts against the river. Beneath the willows, whose winter branches were used by the *vignerons* to tie the trimmed vines to the wires, they lay down side by side.

Jamie caressed Clare's preoccupied face with a blade of the long grass. 'I've been short-listed for the Middlesex job . . .'

'Brilliant! Why didn't you tell me?'

'This is the first moment I've had you to myself.'

'Think you'll get it?'

'I'm up against the Dean's son and a Middlesex senior reg . . . You don't seem very pleased.'

'Sorry Jamie. I keep worrying about where I'm going to get the money for my new barrels.'

'You'll do great with the old ones.'

Laughing, Clare rolled on top of him.

'You don't know the first thing about barrels.'

'It would mean we'd have to live in London . . .'

Clare glanced at the small boats, which brought in the bar, the bass and the lamprey, as they bobbed in the evening breeze. London seemed very far away.

Walking with Alain over the coarse grass (not to be confused with English lawns), of the Lamottes' garden, and thinking still about Jamie and the love they had made by the river, she noticed Christiane Balard sharing a tablecloth (secured by a bottle of champagne in an ice-bucket) with Halliday Baines and surprisingly – a truce must have been called – his sworn enemy Big Mick Bly.

Holding her plate with one hand, and taking her glass of Laurent Rose from Alain, who left her reluctantly, she made her way towards the little group.

'Hi!' Toni Bly, tiny, in a tiny brown dress which clung to her doll-like figure, waved a brown arm. 'Why don't you join us?'

Big Mick, his sport shirt straining over his huge belly, shifted his giant frame a few inches. There was a spare cushion between himself and Christiane Balard. Her flower-trimmed hat matched her voile dress, the skirt of which flowed on to Halliday's lap. She was helping herself, intimately, to the food on the winemaker's plate.

'You couldn't have picked a better moment.' Toni Bly played tennis with the Lamottes whenever she was in Bordeaux. She was a little dervish on the court. She dabbed at her scarlet mouth with her *mignonette* napkin. 'These two' – her wrap-around nails vacillated between Halliday and Big Mick – 'were arguing – for a change.'

'A friendly exchange of views,' Halliday said, looking at Clare. 'What kept you?'

'I had to take Jamie to the airport.'

'It was about the wine . . .' Christiane Balard's English accent was charming.

'Oh that.' Clare pulled the 'coach' bag over her head and put it on the grass beside her. Stretching out her legs, she unwrapped her knife and fork. She wanted to forget about wine.

'The fermentation temperature,' Christiane said, gazing at Halliday adoringly. 'Monsieur Bly keep the vat at twenty-eight degree, and 'Alliday he like to 'ave thirty-three degree . . .'

'Raising the temperature briefly,' Halliday explained to Clare, 'gives you extra dimensions and extract . . .'

'Bullshit.' Big Mick chewed at a herb-encrusted chicken leg. 'Dimensions and extract! You're making wine, boy, not minestrone. A vat temperature of more than thirty degrees is positively dangerous. Any fool will tell you that.'

Reaching across Christiane for the champagne bottle, and meeting Clare's eyes as he did so, Halliday refilled his glass.

'Genius' – he addressed Big Mick – 'sometimes allows one to live dangerously.'

'I'm going to the *bu-fay*,' Toni Bly said, standing up in order to create a diversion. She didn't want a repeat of the Fête de la Fleur episode between her husband and the oenologist. Holding out a hand to Halliday, she pulled him to his feet. 'Why don't you help me get dessert for everyone?'

Clare was playing croquet with Alain, Christiane and Halliday when the rains came, sweeping across the tables, filling the empty coffee cups, and leaving puddles on the parched lawn within seconds.

Handing the remains of Delphine's *Paris Brest*, the bowls of fresh strawberries, and the sodden cheese boards, through the open window of the kitchen as they ran, the guests repaired to the house.

In the long, low '*Maison et Jardin*' salon, with its comfortable sofas, antique tables, and huge fireplace replete with meticulously positioned logs and pine-cones, Harry Balard was sprawled in front of the television. He was watching the Formula One German Grand Prix and had the commentary on at full blast.

Catching the name Barnaby Muirhead, Clare wandered over to the TV. A succession of accidents had eliminated thirteen of the twenty-six starters and the cars that were left in the race were completing their forty-five laps. Barnaby Muirhead was in the lead. Driving brilliantly in his Benetton-Ford, he was cheered on by the roars of the 150,000 spectators at the Hochenheimring, among whom Clare tried to pick out Miranda. The voice of the commentator reached fever pitch as a McLaren Peugeot driven by a Hungarian, and a Lotus Mugen-Honda with an Italian at the wheel, slugged it out for second place. Clare felt her hands break out in a sweat as the two contenders put the pressure on Barnaby.

'I didn't know you were interested in motor-racing.' Alain Lamotte was by her side.

'Really?' Harry Balard's voice was heavy with sarcasm. 'I thought you would have done.'

'What's that supposed to mean?'

'Work it out for yourself.'

Taking her eyes off the TV for a moment and looking at Alain, Clare said, 'Barnaby Muirhead is a friend of mine. Well a friend of a friend of a friend . . .'

A hysterical shriek from the crowd was followed by the frenzied voice of the commentator. '. . . The Italian is acting like a highwayman! He's lost control of the car on the bend . . . Muirhead tries to take avoiding action! I think he's clipped his rear wheel . . .'

Clare's eyes returned to the screen in time to see Barnaby

Muirhead forced off the track at a speed of 144 miles per hour. Rooted to the spot, she watched the Benetton-Ford fly into the air like a red bird, execute a slow-motion somersault and bounce on to the grass verge, where it burst into a ball of orange flame.

CHAPTER THIRTY-FOUR

In the brief respite between the departure of the morning *visite* and her lunchtime guests, Clare stood among the curling leaves and plump grapes in the dusty vineyards and gazed up in bewilderment at the strange overhead sky with its yellow-edged clouds, the implication of which anyone in Bordeaux could tell her.

Since the Lamottes' washed-out *fête champêtre* on the day that Barnaby Muirhead had competed in his last Formula One race, the Médoc had been holding its breath as the effect of the summer rains on the grapes was assessed. According to Albert Rochas, Château de Cluzac had got off lightly.

Although in this respect Clare had been lucky, other things had gone from bad to worse. With the harvest only a few weeks away, she was still no nearer to replacing the requisite twenty-five per cent of her oak, and the news from Florida was that the Baron was returning, to arrange for the transport of his cars and dispose of his stables in which the horses were exercised but no longer ridden.

It was Viola who had told her about the horses. In a long and unexpected letter – Viola hated letter-writing almost as much as she hated the telephone – her mother had explained that she was fed up with Charles-Louis' constant badgering and had finally agreed to a divorce. French law on the matter being vastly different from English, she was coming to Bordeaux to arrange the terms of the settlement

and, at the same time, at the request of Charles-Louis, to
cast her eye over the stables. On her way to France she
planned to spend a few days in London with Declan,
during which she hoped to visit Grandmaman.

Barnaby Muirhead's fatal accident, reported the next
day in the newspapers, with graphic front-page photographs of the inferno at the Hochenheimring (in colour),
was not the only memento of the *fête champêtre*.

Sickened by the tragic death of the thirty-one year-old
Formula One driver, which she had witnessed in the
Lamottes' salon, Clare had turned away from the TV
set, to which Harry Balard was still insensitively glued.
With her eyes full of tears – what was it Grandmaman had
said, 'We weep for ourselves'? – she had looked around
for her coach bag and realised that she had left it in the
garden where the rain was now coming down so hard that
it obscured the windows.

When the storm eased off a little, she had let herself out
on to the terrace. Stepping over the sodden *mignonette*
tablecloths with their now overflowing ice-buckets, she
made her way to the far end of the lawn where she had
left Jamie's present.

She was examining the soaked leather, and hoping that
the bag was not irrevocably ruined, when a clap of thunder,
a sheet of lightening and a deluge of rain, even heavier than
before, sent her running for the nearest shelter.

Bursting into the pool-house, her clothes plastered to
her body, rain dripping off her nose and into her mouth,
she found Halliday Baines *in flagrante delicto* on a pile of
swimming towels, not with Christiane Balard, as might
have been expected, but with little Toni Bly.

In a paroxysm of anger, rather than shock, she slammed
the pool-house door with as much force as she could
muster, and left them to it. She had neither seen nor
heard from Halliday Baines since.

On her return from the *fête champêtre*, which had turned

out to be a great deal more eventful than it had promised, Clare's first thought had been to ring Jamie. His plane had been on time and he had just arrived back in Waterperry to be greeted by a hysterical message from Miranda – who had watched the Formula One race on TV – on his answering machine.

'You just caught me. I was on the doorstep. I'm nipping over to Holland Park . . .'

'Nipping? Jamie, it's fifty miles to Holland Park!'

'I can't leave Miranda on her own.'

Telling Jamie to convey her sympathies to Miranda, Clare, who rarely drank alone, had taken a bottle of claret from the dank and cobwebbed *caveau* and shut herself in the Baron's Room. Working her way steadily through the Château de Cluzac 1943, she tried to expunge the haunting images – the fireball engulfing Barnaby Muirhead and his Benetton-Ford, and Halliday Baines humping Toni Bly in the pool-house – from her mind.

By the time she went to bed, the tray of supper Sidonie had insisted upon bringing to the Baron's Room was still untouched and she had disposed, single-handed, of the entire bottle of wine. Scarcely able to stand, and without undressing, she had flopped on to her four-poster where she had fallen into a profound sleep.

She was woken by the sound of a dog barking. Thinking that she was still dreaming, she had turned over and gone back to sleep. Forcing open her eyelids five minutes later, when the barking persisted, she realised that the bark was Rougemont's, and that it was two o'clock in the morning.

Rougemont was not in his usual place outside the Baron's bedroom. Following the sound of frenzied barking, Clare found him, now almost berserk, jumping up at the door that led to the courtyard, and tearing frantically at it with his claws.

Quivering with excitement, head on one side, he watched

as she struggled with the old iron key. The moment he could squeeze through the doorway, the dog pushed past her, almost knocking her over, and streaked off in the direction of the *chais*, where in the high window a dim light was visible.

Clare followed him into the cellars. Stopping to pick up Jean Boyer's bung hammer and his flashlight from the bureau where the *maître de chai* kept his books, she crept gingerly down the dark stairs to the *chai de conservation*. Reaching the bottom, she stepped, in her bare feet, not on to the beaten-earth floor as expected, but into a cold puddle several inches deep.

'*Merde!*'

She remembered that it had been raining. Heavy as the rain had been, however, she knew – her befuddled mind notwithstanding – that there was no way it could have penetrated the thick roofs of the semi-underground cellars. Bending down and dabbling her fingers, she realised to her horror that the liquid which swirled around her ankles was not water but wine.

Unwilling to venture further without Rougemont, she called softly to the dog.

'*Rougemont, viens ici!*'

She heard him scrambling clumsily over the barrels at the far end of the cellar.

'*Viens ici!*'

Ignored by the dog, who was now yapping excitedly, Clare shone the flashlight from side to side and ventured into the gloom.

'*Qui est là?*' She did not really expect the intruder to respond.

Had she not been so angry she might have been more cautious. Her heart thumped with rage at the loss of her precious claret. As she went deeper into the cellar, the fumes were overpowering and eddies of wine swirled round her feet. Her own safety was far from her mind.

With the hammer held high in one hand and the flashlight in the other, she reached the far corner where Rougement stood guard. Squeezing her way between the barrels, she recognised a cowering figure. She shone the flashlight into his terrified face. It was Harry Balard.

'*Salaud!*' she shrieked in a surge of adrenalin which dispelled the last vestige of her hangover. '*Salaud! Qu'est ce que vous faites ici?*'

Harry did not reply.

'OK. *Vous pourriez raconter votre histoire à la police.*'

Realising that wine was pouring from half a dozen *barriques* and that the bungs had been removed from their sides, Clare's first thought was to save her wine. As she moved towards the barrels, from the corner of her eye she saw Harry Balard heave Rougemont in the chest and scramble past him.

'Don't move!'

Moving swiftly, Clare blocked his path. As he came towards her in the alley between the barrels, she stood her ground and brandished the hammer menacingly. Not wishing to kill him, she was not sure exactly what she was going to do.

She was saved from deciding by Harry. Knocking her roughly and unceremoniously out of his way, so that for a moment she lost her balance, he pushed past her and made for the door.

'*Arrêtez!*'

Rougement, who had been distracted by his discovery of the wine, which he was licking tentatively, was alerted by her scream. Bounding past her and after Harry, he fastened his teeth on the seat of his chinos. There was a sound of tearing fabric as Harry lost his footing and slipped, hitting his head on a barrel and crashing to the sopping floor where he remained, motionless.

Shining her torch into the pale face, now streaked with blood, which seemed to be coming from a cut on his head, Clare thought for a moment that he was dead.

'Harry?'

There was no movement. She wondered what the penalty was for manslaughter.

'Harry?'

Rougemont, head on one side, stood beside her. Putting down the hammer, Clare dropped to her knees and felt for Harry's pulse beneath the slack bracelet of his watch.

At the touch of her hand, he opened his eyes and grinned. Slightly concussed from the blow to his head, and dizzy from the fumes of the wine which assailed his nostrils, he made no effort to get up.

'*Salaud!*' Clare said, as Rougemont put his great paws on the intruder's chest, pinning him to the ground.

Removing Harry's loafers, she flung them to the far side of the cellar where they dropped down among the barrels. She undid his Gucci belt and unzipped his wine-soaked trousers. As she struggled to pull them off, a packet of white substance fell out of the pocket.

'*Tiens, tiens!*' Her eyes widening, she rescued the tiny plastic package from the wine.

She threw the trousers after the shoes.

'That's for slashing my tyres and poisoning my trout . . . !'

She reached for his Calvin Klein underpants.

'*Non!*' Harry grabbed frantically at the elastic.

Rougemont snapped at his hand, leaving toothmarks.

'Ouch! Call that bloody dog off!'

Rougemont growled menacingly.

Clare removed his underpants and flung them disdainfully over her shoulder.

'That's for interfering with my wine.'

Making an inspired guess, she held up the plastic packet.

'And this is for the police, if you so much as come

near Château de Cluzac again. *Alors, foutez le camp!* Get out . . .'

'*Je ne peux pas.*' He clutched the flaccid genitals which Rougement was investigating.

'*Tant pis. Rougemont . . .*'

'*Non, non!*' Harry scrambled up holding his hands before him. '*Je m'en vais.*'

Had she not been so incensed at his sabotage of her irreplaceable wine, every last drop of which she needed if she was going to succeed, she would have found the sight of Harry Balard, limping across the moonlit courtyard in his socks, his soaked tee-shirt flapping above his tight white arse, extremely funny. The fact that the keys to his Porsche were in his trousers' pocket, and that he would have either to hitch a lift or walk home, was small consolation. Unable to stem the purple tide which spread steadily on to the floor, she ran to wake Jean Boyer.

It was four o'clock in the morning before the *maître de chai*, helped by Clare and a young cellar worker, had replaced the *bondes à côté* in the barrels and swept up the wine from the beaten earth floor. Jean Boyer was completely devastated. The wine was his life's blood.

The financial implications of Harry Balard's vicious act were brought home to Clare by Julie Smith, who arrived at Cluzac, as promised, soon afterwards. Finding herself short of claret, the Catesbury's wine buyer tasted the Petite Clare, which she found elegant and full of flavour, and ordered a substantial number of cases. Thanks to Harry Balard, who had cost her several million francs, which there was no way she would be able to recoup, Clare had had, to her chagrin, to cut the shipment down by half.

Even if the forthcoming Christie's sale were to reach the reserve Big Mick had suggested, the money from it would neither be enough, nor soon enough, to replace the all-important barrels on which the success of her harvest depended.

A smart *Bureau d'Acceuil* and a black trouser-suit were one thing. Seeing a wine-producing estate through all its vicissitudes was clearly another. In the Nicola Wade Gallery and Portobello market she had been in control of events. She had been at the mercy of neither saboteurs nor the weather, and knew exactly where she was. She wondered if she had bitten off more than she could chew.

In a bad moment, after the débâcle with Harry Balard, which had shaken her confidence, she had driven to Toulouse to talk to Tante Bernadette.

Although Tante Bernadette had allowed a smile to cross her face at the thought of Harry Balard limping home through the vineyards in his socks, she had looked sternly at Clare, who sat before her desk in the Reverend Mother's room.

'And I thought you were a de Cluzac, Clare. Surely, you're not thinking of giving up?'

'Harry Balard has scuppered wine I was banking on; I can't raise the money for the new barrels . . .'

'Yes?'

She had been about to add that Halliday Baines had been bonking Toni Bly in the pool-house and wondered why it was important.

'I don't know what to do?'

'Have you tried praying?'

'I gave that up long ago.'

'Let me tell you a little story.' The Mother Superior, her elbows on her desk, made a steeple with her fingers. 'In 1571, the Turks were on the rampage in the Middle East. They conquered every land they entered and slaughtered millions on the way. Mustering their galleys, the Turkish navy threatened all the Christian kingdoms of the central Mediterranean. They even menaced Rome herself. The King of Spain, the princes and nobles of Italy, and many other monarchs, hastily assembled a polyglot fleet, but they were far outnumbered by the Turks, who were not only more accomplished sailors but had the added advantage of a common language.

'Pope Pius V, a Dominican devoted to Our Lady, called upon the rosary confraternities of Rome and all over Europe, to undertake special processions and public recitations of the rosary to ask for the prayers of the Blessed Mother.

'On the first Sunday of October, in the Gulf of Lepanto off the Greek coast, the Christian ships found themselves surrounded by the Turkish fleet. As thousands turned to Our Lady through their rosaries, the Christians managed to break through. After a day of fierce fighting, the Turks were either driven back to the shore or drowned, and Europe was saved . . .'

'Why are you telling me this?'

Tante Bernadette dismantled the steeple.

'Take another look at your rosary, my dear. If prayers can turn back the Turkish fleet, just think what they might do for you.'

Walking slowly back from the vineyards, Clare was pondering Tante Bernadette's words. Much as she had enjoyed the parable of the Turkish fleet, enjoyed talking to her aunt, and found pleasure in her company, she had long ago abandoned her rosary and paradoxically did not think that praying was the answer to her prayers.

Crossing the courtyard on her way to the *Bureau d'Acceuil*, she suddenly realised that Rougemont, who now followed her everywhere, as he once had followed the Baron, was no longer by her side.

'Rougemont! Rougemont!'

At the sound of her voice an exceptionally tall and well-built flaxen-haired girl in a pale blue sun-dress, carrying a briefcase, who was approaching the steps of the château, turned round.

'Hi!'

'Are you my lunch?' Clare was surprised. She was expecting a party of sommeliers. 'The Visitor Centre is this way . . .'

The girl shook her head. She seemed amused.

'Rosa Delaware, from Virginia . . .' She held out her hand, large as a man's. 'Mrs Spray's PA. I'm here to help your father. We've just arrived.'

CHAPTER THIRTY-FIVE

The atmosphere at lunch, for which two extra places had been set for the Baron and Rosa Delaware and during the entire course of which Charles-Louis addressed not one word to Clare's guests, was decidedly tepid.

Having got her business lunches down to a fine art, Clare generally had no trouble in breaking the ice. Aided by Sidonie's cooking, and whatever was appropriate by way of wine, she had become adept at making her clients feel so well disposed towards Château de Cluzac that, by the time coffee was served in the salon, she had no difficulty in adding them to her rapidly growing list of customers, impressing them if they happened to be journalists, or clinching the business in hand.

Having been unaware of the date of her father's arrival – typically he had not informed her of it – and already in an apprehensive state of mind, Clare found his presence at the table, heading it as of right, produced in her the familiar feeling that she was no more than three feet tall.

She tried hard to keep a lively conversation going and in particular to make the party of sommeliers feel at home, so that they would leave with memories of Château de Cluzac that would be reflected in the future wine lists of their restaurants. She found her heart as heavy as the leaden sky outside, which made it necessary to put the lights on in the *salle-à-manger* – although the weather forecast had been good – and her tongue inexplicably tied.

If she had been angry with Charles-Louis before, she was now even more so. The Baron was fussed over by Sidonie, who looked comparatively cheerful for the first time in weeks, and indulged by Rosa Delaware – who could not have been more than eighteen and clearly exceeded her role as Laura Spray's PA – who anticipated his every need and never took her large grey eyes off him. Although his presence was clearly welcomed by an overjoyed Rougemont, who did not leave his side, it not only effectively silenced Clare, but cast a pall over the proceedings.

In an effort to draw her father into the conversation, if only for courtesy's sake, Clare had enquired after Laura Spray, who he said was fine, and about the oranges, which were also fine. After that, she had given up.

Rosa Delaware, totally unaware of the undercurrents, took it upon herself to keep the visitors entertained with an account of the goings on of the Palm Beach set, delivered in her Virginian drawl, which the European visitors found mainly incomprehensible (although they smiled politely) and which amused them not at all.

Over coffee, as if they were alone, Charles-Louis made his views known to Clare about the 'improvements' she had carried out, which gave the estate the appearance of a circus rather than a château.

'I met von Graf in New York . . .' He appeared to change the subject. 'The word at Estaminet is that you are planning to sell *my* wine in *screw-top* bottles . . .'

'*My* wine. I've called it . . .'

'I'm not interested in what you call it. It comes from my vineyards. And as for that unspeakable *pancarte* . . .'

'The sign happens to bring people in, Papa . . .' Clare said quietly while Rosa Delaware transfixed the sommeliers with a verbal portrait of the vast tracts of land her people owned in Virginia, which had been in the family since the Civil War, accompanied by vivid descriptions of their old colonial home.

'. . . The château is ticking over nicely and even with the extra staff I've taken on the wages are being paid . . .'

Handing her his empty coffee cup, as if she were a servant, Charles-Louis cut her short.

'As long as you make enough to keep me in the manner to which I am accustomed . . .'

Before Clare had a chance to answer, the Baron had nodded curtly to the visitors, whistled softly to Rougemont, and followed by Rosa Delaware – Clare guessed that despite the official-looking briefcase they were heading for the bedroom – swept from the room.

Furious with herself for once more allowing her father to wrong-foot her, Clare had tried to rescue what remained of the sommeliers' goodwill. Only partially successful – a tour of the cellars had resulted in promises to 'think about it' and to 'let you know' – euphemisms she had used herself to get out of sticky situations, she was glad when they piled into their minibus and left for their next appointment.

Having seen them off, and missing Rougemont – she had in her father's absence grown used to his company – she was reluctant either to confront the pile of paper-work in her office or to return to the château. With no desire to face either the Baron or what was patently his latest mistress (she wondered if Laura Spray knew), she walked disconsolately round the moat and, leaning over the stone wall, watched the hypnotic toing and froing of the darting fish.

She was thinking about Jamie, who was due at the weekend, and wondering if her father and Rosa Delaware would still be in residence – if she questioned Papa about his plans he would merely stare at her blankly – when she felt a glancing blow, as if someone had thrown a stone, on the side of her head. Looking round, she saw that there was no one in sight; the lack of sunshine seemed to have discouraged any afternoon visitors. She was about to put the incident down to her imagination, when there was a further assault on her scalp and a shower of pebbles landed in quick succession to disturb the placid surface of the water. Taken unawares by the suddenness of their appearance, she was amazed to see that the ground at her feet was white, and she had to put up an arm to protect her face from injury, before she realised that what was falling from the heavens were the dreaded giant hailstones which were capable of expunging an entire *récolte* in moments. Her first thought was for her vineyards and for the safety of her crop.

It was Albert Rochas who had impressed upon her the significance of the summer storms, for which he was constantly on the lookout, and which, fortunately only rarely, decimated the Bordeaux vineyards. She remembered his graphic account of the year 1811 when, between eight and nine o'clock in the morning, hail had so badly damaged the communes of Ludon, Macau and Cantenac, that Latour had been left with a mere two-thirds of its harvest; and the tragedy at Yquem, in 1952, when a freak summer storm not only destroyed the entire crop, but had affected the quality of the two succeeding vintages.

Beaten and battered by the hailstones, which now came at her from all sides, scarcely able to see where she was going, and protecting herself as well as she could, Clare lowered her head and made for the safety of the château. Shaking the ice from her hair on to the stone floor, she ran upstairs to the library where the windows, which looked out over the vineyards, were being battered by what looked like a barrage of white cannonballs.

In twenty agonising minutes, each one of which seemed to last an hour, it was all over. With her heart in her boots, Clare left the château and made for the vineyards where Albert Rochas, who had beaten her to it, was already assessing the damage. Walking slowly between the rows, stooping now and then to pick up the bruised and battered bunches torn from their branches, he had difficulty in meeting Clare's eye.

'*Nous avons perdu beaucoup, Albert?*'

'*Enormément!*'

Leading the way through the vineyard, in which each *parcelle* or plot was handed down from father to son, and mother to daughter, and marked with the worker's name, Albert's mud-caked boots mulched the stony soil scattered with grapes and sodden leaves. Like a mother who had lost her baby, he touched his remaining offspring tenderly. Watching his calloused hands as he caressed his 'children' took Clare back to her own childhood when she had watched, fascinated, as the *chef de culture*, more patient then than now, had shown her how to prune. Carefully choosing the branch that would bear the grapes – an intrinsic skill which was by no means as easy as it looked – he would hold the vine in his fingers and, like a surgeon making his first incision, silently prepare for the operation that would 'harmonise' the vine. Bending at the knees, he would caress the bark, hesitate, then, leaving one small spur on the far side so that the vine would not die if the branch bearing the grapes should break, make a swift cut with his pruning-shears to prepare the way for the new buds. A slow pruner, Albert was quickly outdistanced by his workers, whose families, like his own, had been pruning the Château de Cluzac vines for two or three generations.

Muttering as he went, that at a conservative estimate, the hailstones had stripped at least ten hectares of vines, Clare got the distinct impression that Albert Rochas held her directly responsible for the ravages of the storm.

'*C'était la vendange verte* . . .' The old man turned angrily to face her.

Clare couldn't see what the summer pruning she insisted

he carry out in the interests of the quality of the grapes had
to do with the hail.

'*Si nous n'aviez pas bléssé les vignes la perte n'aurait
pas été aussi catastrophique . . .*'

It was her fault. For thinning out her vines. There
was one consolation. Every grower in the Médoc, having
lost ten per cent of the *récolte*, would be in the same
boat. But in this, too, she was wrong. As she was to
learn over the next few days, the hailstorm, isolated
and contained, had, in true Bordeaux fashion, largely
targeted a single area – in this case the Château de
Clauzac vineyards.

Her sense of desolation, as if not only the Balards but
now the gods were after her, was exacerbated by the latest
copy of *Wine Watch*, which had been delivered, along with
the inevitable bills, by the courier.

Bypassing the German and Italian wines and turning
to the French section, she discovered that the Château
de Cluzac, which had been distributed by Balard et Fils,
was now described by Big Mick, albeit regretfully, as
'inconsistent' and 'flabby'.

The buzz on the Place de Bordeaux was to 'forget
Château de Cluzac'. By dint of keeping her eyes and ears
open as she went about her business, and listening to Alain
Lamotte during their late-night sessions in his office (it was
now the only time she had to deal with her complicated
tax returns with which he was helping her), Clare was
in no doubt that, although his vineyards had been kept
impeccably, it was her father's sloppy winemaking over
the past few years that was responsible for Big Mick's
downgrading.

Since his return, her father, together with Rougemont,
the tireless Rosa and a team of advisers, had spent all day
closeted in the garages with his Maserati Bird Cage, his
Dale Earnhardt Chevrolet and his Hudson Sedan. Some
of the cars were to go to Florida and some to Newport

Pagnell, in England, where, shrouded in plastic, they would remain in store.

The Baron was amused by Clare's increasing despondency. The more dispirited she became at the ravages caused by the hailstorm – which turned out to be far more extensive than Albert had at first thought – at the sinking reputation of the estate wine, at the fact that Jamie, busy now with the Medical Research Council grant applications for which he was responsible, found it hard to get away, the more it seemed to please Charles-Louis and it occurred to her suddenly that he was jealous of her.

Coming back from his morning ride with Rosa, the Baron buttonholed Clare over breakfast.

'Rumour has it that Van Gelder – not to mention the Balards . . .'

'I suggest you don't mention the Balards!' Clare had said nothing to her father, with whom she communicated only when necessary, about Harry Balard and his efforts to unseat her.

'The South African, *évidement*, despite all his huffing and puffing, is still sniffing around.'

'Then let him sniff.'

'I warned you that there's a great deal more to running an estate than selling junk from a barrow . . .'

Clare ignored the insult.

'If you're asking do I want to turn it in, the answer is no. I have to get my harvest in . . .' Clare finished her coffee and rose from the table.

'Is there anything left to get in?'

'According to Albert, a fine September could compensate for the hail. From the look of the grapes, this year could be another sixty-one.'

'Provided you know when to pick . . .' Charles-Louis' voice was cynical.

'You are not the only one with knowledge of the world,

Papa,' Clare said, with a great deal more confidence than she felt.

When her father wished to assert his superiority he always reiterated what he had said, as if the repetition, not to mention the authoritative voice in which it was delivered, made it right.

'Provided you know when to pick!'

By the time Viola arrived at Château de Cluzac, Charles-Louis had finished with the cars and turned his attentions to the stables.

Taking out his Plymouth Impala for the last time, he drove to Mérignac to meet his estranged wife, who was coming to Bordeaux not only to advise about selling the horses but to put a legal end to their marriage.

Divorce in France, for which the major criterion was *le caractère intolérable du maintien de la vie conjugale* (the unbearable nature of marital ties), was still considered a crime, not only against one's spouse but against society. It was an offence for which the 'guilty' were punished and the 'innocent' indemnified, and it was not uncommon for substantial damages to be awarded, by way of compensation, by the highly specialised *juges des affaires matrimoniales*.

Viola who, after twenty years, was still smarting from the cavalier treatment meted out by Charles-Louis to both herself and her daughter, had come to Bordeaux to exact her pound of flesh.

The fact that Charles-Louis greeted her in the arrivals hall at Mérignac with a bouquet of gladioli impressed her not at all. She had never been one either for flowers, which she considered it a sin to cut, or for the Baron's transparent attempts at flattery, to which she was immune.

After pleasantries had been exchanged, the Baron, still her husband in name only, had relapsed into silence. For the greater part of the drive to St Julien he revelled in the sheer beauty of his classic automobile in motion, while Viola, who would have been equally happy in the front of a horse-box and was never at a loss for words, chattered away about a filly she had just bought and the shows she had seen during her few days in London. She didn't mention Declan. Not until after the divorce.

'I called on your mother, Charlie . . .'

The Baron's face was impassive.

'Baronne Gertrude's not eating a thing. She doesn't look at all well.'

'What am I supposed to do?'

'There's nothing you can do. I'm just telling you. I think the old lady misses Clare.'

In the courtyard at Château de Cluzac, the Plymouth Impala skirted a group of scantily dressed holidaymakers accompanied by children and laden with picnic baskets, who made their way over the cobbles towards the bouncy castle and the park. At the Baron's imperious hoot they melted in the path of the car.

'I wouldn't know the place,' Viola said, staring at two men, stripped to their vests, fishing in the moat.

'You've got your daughter to thank for that.'

Opening the door for Viola, Charles-Louis, his manners irreproachable as always, helped her out of the car. Seeing him smile his charming smile at the tall, bare-legged woman with the large grey eyes who, at the sound of the horn, had run out of the château to greet him, Viola held out her hand.

'Viola Fitzpatrick. You must be Mrs Spray. I didn't think you were so young.'

'This is Rosa Delaware . . .'

Viola looked from the strapping girl to the Baron, making an accurate assessment of the situation. Charles-Louis hadn't changed.

CHAPTER THIRTY-SIX

Laura Spray had not only set the date for the wedding, which was to be the biggest three-ring circus Palm Beach had ever seen, but put caterers, couturiers, hairdressers, beauticians, builders and decorators, tent-makers, landscape gardeners, photographers and musicians from all over the world on red alert. The prospective bridegroom was relying on a divorce from Viola by *requête conjointe* (mutual consent), to which, as he had informed the *juge des affaires matrimoniales*, he could foresee no objection. He and Viola had been married for a great deal longer than the requisite six months (twenty-eight years to be precise). Both of them had agreed to the divorce. They had agreed *how* to divorce. And promised to remain in agreement throughout the proceedings.

Before the court hearing, the Baron, terrified of Laura Spray, who rang him daily to see how things were going, ran over the proceedings with Viola in the stables, where she was admiring a black mare.

'There was a filly like her just now at Ballybrit,' Viola said. 'An old friend of mine, a retired colonel, waited twelve months, certain she would lift the Plate . . .'

'We need to talk . . .' Charles-Louis said.

'She was balloted out at the last moment without even a run.'

'About the divorce . . .' The Baron was not interested in the Galway Races.

'It was unbelievable! This is a great mare, Charlie. I could ask the Colonel would he know someone who'd be interested.'

'There must be no disagreement between us.'

'Why should there be?'

'If there is any disagreement between the parties, the divorce is invalid. We'd have to start all over again.'

'You're the one wants to get married.'

'And you are the one who must agree.'

'And so I will, Charlie . . .' Taking a saddle and bridle from the stable door, Viola, standing ankle-deep in straw, faced the Baron. 'For a consideration.'

'Consideration?'

Soothing the mare as she did so, Viola put the saddle on her glossy back and expertly bridled her.

'You didn't imagine, Charlie, that after those eight years at Château de Cluzac, not to mention leaving me to bring up your daughter . . .'

'I rather thought it was you who left me.'

'Indeed I did. What good would it have done to her to stay here and see her father . . .'

'What is it you want?'

'I want a million francs.'

'Don't be ridiculous.'

'What's ridiculous?'

'I don't have that sort of money.'

'This Rosa Delaware. Clare tells me you're sleeping with her . . .'

'That has nothing to do with it.'

'The judge might take an altogether different view. It's called "entrapment". I've spoken to Clare. She's willing to back me up.'

'That's blackmail!'

'Call it what you like.' Viola led the horse out of the stable. 'I'll ride her to Kilmartin. Like old times.'

Charles-Louis smiled. Thrown off guard for a nanosecond, Viola re-experienced the potent spell of the charm which had once been her undoing on the banks of the Gironde. The memory of the long humiliation she had afterwards endured brought her to her senses.

'A million francs, Charlie. Cash, mind . . .' The mare's hooves clattered on the cobbles, as Viola expertly mounted her, dug in her heel, about faced, and made for the archway. 'Before the end of the week.'

Clare sat in the North room at Christie's as the squeaky-clean auctioneer, flanked by his two female acolytes, mounted the rostrum. She opened her catalogue, *Claret and White Bordeaux*, and flicked through the pages as the young man quickly ran over the rules of the sale.

Satisfied to leave her enterprise in the hands of David Markham, she had not planned to attend the sale, in which several lots from Château de Cluzac were included. It was Viola, sensing how despondent she was at the fact that it would be another three weeks before she would see Jamie, who had persuaded her to take a break. While she was gone her mother would keep an eye on things at the château. She had not needed much persuading. Viola, who had just spent a few days in London with Declan, had a poor opinion of the capital.

'It gets worse and worse. Filthy dirty it is, and like bedlam! There were a hundred thousand people in Oxford Street if there was one. And begging in the doorways – I've never seen anything like it. I was in Harrods for Eau de Toilette. The old lady likes her Elizabeth Arden. "Can I help you, Madam?" A bit of a girl at the cosmetics counter. "Can I help *you*?" I told her. "If you scraped some of that stuff off your face and gave it a good scrub with soap and water you'd look a far sight prettier." If she was more than sixteen years of age I'd be amazed.'

Catching the early flight to Heathrow, Clare had gone

straight to Christie's. When the sale was over she would take the bus to Hyde Park to visit Grandmaman, then get the train to Oxford and spend the night with Jamie. She had told neither of them that she was coming.

She had not informed her father about the sale. When she had looked for him, to tell him she was going to London, she had been informed by Petronella that he had left for Switzerland with Rosa. He had not indicated when he would be back.

'There are two withdrawals this morning, ladies and gentlemen, lot one-six-two and lot four-or-five . . .'

The auctioneer's crisp voice brought her back from her reverie.

'We start the sale with lot one, six magnums of Ducru-Beaucaillou sixty-four, which is available in bond. I start the bidding at two hundred and eighty. Two eighty, two ninety, three hundred and ten . . .'

Concentrating on the business in hand, Clare sat through the swiftly moving 'dozens' of First Growths (Lafite, Margaux, and Pétrus '70s), names with which she had grown up, the large-format clarets (jeroboams and *impériales*), the Private Stocks of Le Pin and Trotanoy (in large wooden cases), and magnums of Giscours '85 (offered duty-paid and lying in Wiltshire).

It was Big Mick who had advised her that the best prices would be realised by releasing vintages that were no longer around. To offer what was still available at the wine merchants would only antagonise the trade. The '75 was ready for drinking, and anyone but a fool would be happy to drink the '79 . . .

'Lot two twenty. Top quality claret of the seventy-five, seventy-nine and eighty-one vintages.' Hearing the name Château de Cluzac, Clare felt her hands grow moist.

'Three hundred and fifty, four hundred I'm bid, four hundred and fifty, five hundred . . . all done at five hundred? At the back. Lot two-two-one, one dozen bottles . . . Three hundred and fifty I'm bid, four hundred, four hundred and fifty, five hundred, five hundred and fifty – in the front – all done at five hundred and fifty . . .' Like a mantra the voice droned on disposing in seconds of the cellarmasters' consummate art. What was it Nicola had said? A great picture could be hung on the wall and looked at; a great wine was finished the moment you opened the bottle.

Several thousand pounds richer (a drop in the ocean when it came to replacing her barrels), to the tune now of Château Chasse-Spleen, Château Haut-Bailly, and Château Cos d'Estournel, excusing herself as she went, Clare pushed her way, with her two large duffle bags, along the tightly packed row of wine buffs, onlookers and serious bidders clutching their numbered paddles.

Although it was almost one o'clock by the time she got to Hyde Park, Grandmaman, wearing a lace peignoir and sitting in the armchair in her bedroom, reading the obituaries in *The Times*, was still in *deshabillé*. She was as dismayed by the fact that her granddaughter had found her not yet dressed, as was Clare at seeing the Baronne anything but immaculately turned out.

'*Es-tu malade, Grandmaman*?' Remembering what Viola had said about the Baronne's lack of appetite, Clare kissed the papery cheeks and enquired if she was ill.

'Certainly not. The sun is so warm through the window, I thought I'd be a little lazy.'

'Lazy' did not feature in her grandmother's vocabulary; Clare had never heard her use the word.

It was not until after lunch, during which she had merely pushed her food around her plate, that Baronne Gertrude, dressed now in black crepe with sparkling white collar and cuffs, confessed that she had gone to see the doctor concerning a symptom which she did not wish to disclose.

'He would like me to attend the hospital for some further investigations.'

'Who will go with you?' Clare was worried – Grandmaman was never ill.

'I am not going to the hospital. I do not care for hospitals.'

'Then why did you go to the doctor?'

'I wanted to be sure. When Lydia Fermoy was in St George's, God rest her poor soul . . .' the Baronne crossed herself, 'the women were walking round the ward in their *chemises de nuits!* No sign of a gown. Poor Lydia. They took blood from her veins, aspirated her chest, injected her with pain-killers, stuck tubes . . . everywhere. And expected her to eat food I wouldn't give to my cat.'

'You haven't got a cat, Grandmaman.'

'I have not the slightest intention of being subjected to such indignities.'

'They only want to *investigate.*'

'The moment I was baptised, my body became the temple of the Holy Spirit. It is going to rise again to everlasting life. I intend to treat it with respect.'

'There are drugs . . .'

'Drugs! They pumped Lydia Fermoy full of antibiotics. Each time she went towards her Maker they called her back again. "Our body is a machine for living. That is what it's made for, and that is its nature. Leave life to take care of itself, and don't interfere . . ." Why are you crying?'

'I don't want you to go . . .'

'I'm not going anywhere. Read your Bible. John, Chapter Eleven. On the immortality of the soul. I'm not afraid, you see. Jesus Christ went through the whole cycle himself so that we would know ahead of time exactly how things would work.'

'You've probably got something perfectly straightforward which can be treated.'

' "Old men must die. Or the world would grow moldy, would only breed the past again." '

The Baronne, who was getting tired, did not protest when it was time for Clare to leave. Realising that time was probably of the essence, she made up her mind to get Jamie, who hadn't seen her for a few weeks, as well as her father, to speak to Grandmaman, who had always been obdurate.

'See you soon.' She put her arms round the old lady.

'I rely on you,' Baronne Gertrude said, 'to keep our *petite conversation* to yourself. I'd rather you did not discuss the matter with Jamie, and I shall be particularly angry if you mention it to my son. Charles-Louis has shown no indication of caring whether I am alive or dead.'

'I'll come again . . .' Clare avoided the issue. 'As soon as I've got my harvest in.'

'"And God who made shall gather them."'

'That's if the weather holds!'

'I was not referring to the grapes.'

Looking out of the window of the train on the way to Oxford, at the English fields and hedges – how strange it seemed that there were no vines – Clare thought about the Baronne's obduracy. They didn't seem to make people like that any more. People with minds of their own, who accepted responsibility for their actions and who were not at the mercy of bureaucracy or of the State. She thought of her own mortality, of which she had been made disturbingly aware at school. If you died with your sins forgiven and your atonement made in full sacramental communion with the Church, with a bit of luck you would go straight to Heaven, to enjoy for ever the presence of God. If you died unrepentant, with unforgiven sins so serious that they imperilled your soul, you could look forward to hell and everlasting torment. It was this dire threat that kept the girls at St Mary's repenting every day. Sometimes they turned the need for penance to good account, giving up a meal during Lent, or sending their pocket money to foreign missions to feed the truly hungry. Steeped in the fear of the ultimate personal judgement, which could be rescinded only at the end of time, when the last trumpet sounded and the dead were to be raised, they had compared the divine revelation to a package deal, paid for with Christ's suffering and death, to which nothing could be added and from which nothing would be taken away.

Although she had lost her conviction in Catholic tenets at school, where she had sprinkled rose petals in the paths of priests and always been picked to play Mary in the Nativity play, her lack of *absolute* certainty about the absence of an afterlife, the possibility that she might be turned back at the Pearly Gates and punished for ever, acted occasionally as a constraint on her behaviour.

In the taxi to Waterperry, she decided that she would take her chance and figure it all out when she got there. St Augustine himself had problems explaining it. Turning her thoughts to Jamie, and reminded by the strange odour which emanated from her duffle bag and pervaded the cab, she remembered the melon from Cavaillon, the Reblochon cheese, and Sidonie's *tarte tatin* which would form part of the meal with which she planned to welcome him home from the hospital.

Pushing open the wooden gate, with its warning 'Beware of the Dog' (although Jamie had no dog), she stood for a few moments in the overgrown front garden. The cottage, with its dipping roof and missing tiles, was a far cry from the austere façade of Château de Cluzac. She automatically dead-headed a few time-expired roses. The petals fell, like confetti, on the path.

Opening the front door with her key, she stopped dead and wrinkled her nostrils. Even the smell of the Reblochon, now decidedly overripe, could not disguise the aroma of stale cigars.

On the wooden draining-board in the kitchen there was an empty panatella packet and two coffee mugs, one with a crescent of orange lipstick. On the bentwood coatstand (she had bought it at a country fair) next to Jamie's running gear, hung a shocking-pink PVC raincoat, and an outsize Hervé Chapelier bag.

Upstairs in the bedroom, with its sloping ceiling, a pair of discarded black tights danced by themselves on the duvet. In place of her scarlet kimono with its dragon motif, a black satin housecoat hung from the hook behind the bathroom door. Feeling her way, like a blind person, she touched an unfamiliar hairbrush laced with red hairs, green nail lacquer, an underwired bra. Almost falling in her haste to get down the steep and narrow stairs, she picked up her malodorous duffle bag and left the cottage, slamming the front door behind her.

CHAPTER THIRTY-SEVEN

With his Australian bush hat pushed to the back of his head, Halliday Baines squatted on the parched earth of Château de Cluzac. He was measuring the maturation of the grapes, now bunched so tightly that there were no air spaces between them.

'How are they doing?' Clare watched the progress of his hydrometer.

'Should be OK.'

'Not long to go now.'

'Not long.'

'Albert says it could be the best year since sixty-one.'

'What's left of it!'

'The hail wasn't my fault . . .'

'And the green harvest?'

'Everyone else was doing it.'

'Everyone else could afford to. You should have left it to Albert.'

'He says it should be all right.'

'If it doesn't rain.'

'Albert says the conditions are perfect . . .'

Halliday straightened up and walked on along the rows ahead of Clare.

'The trick is knowing when to pick,' he said. 'Pick too soon and your wine won't be fruity; wait too long, the balance and development is affected. Quality comes from concentration. Each of these old vines yields one bottle of wine. That's your château wine. Your money in the bank. You wait until there's a good balance, then start picking while the weather holds. Twenty vats of wine and the livelihoods of twenty families will depend on your decision. You need strong nerves.' Halliday glanced at his watch. 'I'm due at Estaminet.'

'We were expecting you for lunch. Sidonie made your favourite . . .'

'Some other time.'

Clare was disappointed.

'Haven't seen much of you recently.'

'No.'

'Where have you been?'

'Around.'

'Have you heard from Billy?'

'Billy's in good shape.'

'Look, Halliday, it was hardly my fault it chose to hail on my vineyards . . .'

'Did I say it was?'

'Then what's wrong?'

'Nothing. Nothing's wrong.'

Walking him to the courtyard, Clare was discomfited by the oenologist's uncharacteristic silence. He jumped lightly into the jeep.

'See you!' His voice was flat.

'Are you ill or something?'

'Nope.' Reaching for the seat-belt, he looked at her for the first time. 'If you really want to know, Clare, I saw you coming out of Assurance Mondiale . . .'

'So?'

He switched on the ignition.

'It was two o'clock in the morning.'

After leaving Waterperry, Clare could not even remember how she had got back to Bordeaux. The shock of discovering that Miranda was shacked up with Jamie, coming hard on the heels of the gloomy conversation with Grandmaman, had completely thrown her. Downing two straight vodkas at the airport bar, she had presumably boarded the plane, where they were followed by two more.

What prompted her to drive to the Rue Vauban rather than branching off at Blanquefort on to the Route des Châteaux, she could only guess.

To her relief, Alain Lamotte was still working. He opened the door to her himself. Switching off the computer in his office, he motioned her to a seat on the sofa as he collected up his papers and put them into his briefcase.

'Lucky you caught me. I was just going home. What brings you here so late? Problems?'

'You could say that.'

'Messieurs Huchez and Combe been bothering you?'

'*Donne moi un cigarette, Alain!*'

He looked up sharply.

'You don't smoke.'

'*Donne quand même . . .*'

Alain picked up the pack from his desk and proffered them, lighting her cigarette for her.

'It's not the *fisc*.' Clare inhaled deeply. Jamie would kill her. 'It has nothing to do with the château.'

Lighting his own cigarette, Alain came to sit beside her, his hands between his knees.

'Want to talk?'

Outside it was still warm. Clare was surprised to find that she was cold and that her hands were shaking.

Getting up from the sofa, Alain stubbed out his cigarette, lowered the blind on the door and picked up the telephone.

'*Qu'est ce que tu fais?*'

'I am calling Delphine. She worries if I am late.'

While Alain told Delphine that she was not to delay dinner, that some urgent business had cropped up, Clare

took the bottle of Château de Cluzac she had brought for
Jamie from her duffle bag and put it on the table in front
of the sofa.

'You don't happen to have a corkscrew?'

Alain brought a corkscrew and two glasses and sat down
beside her. As he opened the bottle, she noticed for the first
time that his eyes were green and that there were yellow
flecks in them.

'Jamie's fucking Miranda.'

'Who's Miranda?' Alain handed her a glass of wine.

'Does it matter?'

By the time she had recounted her story, by the time
she had given Alain a blow-by-blow account of her day,
forgetting neither the rose petals nor the tell-tale red
hairs in the brush, the ashtray was full, the Château
de Cluzac empty, and they had made inroads into the
cognac, which was kept for the Assurance Mondiale
clients.

Sitting so close to Alain that she could feel the warmth
of his body, Clare put her head on his shoulder.

'It's so nice to have friends.'

The room was revolving.

'Maybe you have made a mistake.'

'I'm not s-s-stupid.'

Alain touched her hair, breathing the scent of it.

'Hold me tight, Alain.'

He could hardly believe he held Clare de Cluzac in
his arms.

'Tighter.' Clare fastened her mouth over his.

Alain thought of Delphine, then, dismissing her image
from his mind, removed his 'Galleon' tie.

Clare closed her eyes. She did not want to look at him,
did not want him to speak.

'*Que je t'aime . . .*'

She did not want to be loved. She wanted to be
ravaged, annihilated, brutalised, until the image of Jamie

and Miranda Pugh was expunged from her head. She tore at Alain's shirt.

'Fuck me, Alain. Fuck me!'

Sobbing, she let go of her anger, channelling it into her pelvis until it flowed out between her legs.

There was no more conversation. Rolling off the sofa, scattering the papers from Alain's briefcase, biting and scratching at each other, they made love until they were exhausted.

'*Mon Dieu, Clare . . .*'

She stopped his lips with her finger, as he covered her body with kisses before taking her tenderly in his arms. When he felt the slow drops damp on his skin, he imagined that her tears were for him.

Clare awoke with her head on Alain's knees. Trying not to disturb him – he was sleeping like a baby – she disentangled herself. Picking up her clothes, and taking the key to the washroom from his desk, she slipped out of the office.

When she returned, Alain was dressed. He was picking up his papers from the floor, trying to collate them.

She let him hold her, but turned her head when he attempted to kiss her.

'*Qu'est ce que ne va pas?*'

'Nothing's the matter. I'm hungry.' She had eaten nothing since lunch.

Alain reached for his jacket.

'I'll take you for dinner . . .'

'*Non.*'

Clare extricated Sidonie's *tarte tatin* and the over-ripe cheese from her duffle bag and set them on the table.

'You are a strange girl!'

It was two o'clock by the time they left Assurance Mondiale. Going down in the lift, Alain pressed her to the wall with his body and kissed her gently.

'When will I see you?'

'See me?'

In the mirror she noticed the dark circles that ringed her eyes.

'I'll call you.' She meant about château business.

'Soon?'

She was tired and needed to sleep.

'Soon.'

She slept for two days. Viola thought that she was ill. Petronella, who was coping with the *visites*, needed some time off; the paperwork was piling up on the desk of the *Bureau d'Acceuil*; Monsieur Boniface wanted an urgent meeting.

'Jamie's rung twice,' Viola said, when Clare finally appeared for breakfast. 'I told him you were exhausted . . .'

Clare looked up sharply as if her one-night stand with Alain were written on her face.

'He was worried about you.'

'If he calls again I'm out.'

'Out . . .?'

'I'd rather not discuss it.'

'Suit yourself.'

Taking several bulky manilla envelopes from the chair beside her, Viola handed them to Clare.

'This is for you.'

'What is it?'

'Open it, you'll find out.'

Opening one of the envelopes, Clare removed a bundle of 500-franc notes. She stared at Viola.

'It's for your barrels.'

'Where did you get it?'

'From Charles-Louis.'

'Papa giving me money to buy new oak!'

'In a manner of speaking.'

'Mother! What exactly have you been up to?'

'Give me another cup of coffee and I'll tell you.'

Smiling broadly, for it was the best thing that had

happened to her in years, Viola repeated the story – now heavily embroidered – of what had passed between herself and Charles-Louis and how she had held him to ransom over the divorce.

When Clare had stopped laughing, her own troubles temporarily forgotten, she said, 'This money belongs to you.'

'I don't need it. The Fitzpatrick Equine Centre is turning over nicely. I don't owe anything on the house. I rarely move from the place. I've got Declan. What more do I want?'

'I can't take it.'

'You've no choice. There's one condition. Don't tell your father. He'd kill me!'

By the time Clare called unannounced on Halliday, Jamie had rung a dozen times, and there was a stack of unanswered faxes from the John Radcliffe on her desk.

Wearing shorts and trainers – he had just returned from his marathon training – Halliday seemed neither pleased nor displeased to see her.

Wandering round his apartment while he was in the shower, Clare looked at the framed photographs on the buffet. She picked one up to examine it more closely.

'Is this your wife?'

Halliday, his long hair still wet, had changed into a bush shirt and clean jeans.

'That's Maureen.'

'She's pretty.'

He nodded.

'You miss her.'

'What do you think? You didn't come here to talk about Maureen.'

'You said you'd help me with new barrels.'

'I *said* you need a million francs . . .'

'I've got a million francs.'

'Where from?'

'Is that any of your business?'

'It doesn't matter. I can take a pretty shrewd guess.'

'Look, Halliday, I've had enough of your innuendoes. I welcome your opinion as an oenologist; I'm willing to take your advice about my grapes. Keep out of my private life! It has nothing whatever to do with you.'

'Sit down, I'll show you a card trick.'

Apologising in the only way he knew, Halliday took a deck of cards from the buffet and, laying them on the coffee table, deftly sorted out the four aces, four kings, four queens and four knaves, which he removed from the pack.

'There were once four queens, whose countries bordered upon each other. The four countries met at a point marked by a dense forest where the four kings – their husbands – hunted deer. One day, these four royal ladies' – he laid the four queens side by side – 'decided to take a country ramble without guards or attendants. They hadn't gone very far when a great storm arose. Convinced that the weather would soon clear, each queen hurried as fast as possible to the shelter of the forest where they found a woodcutter's cottage. The good woman who owned the cottage, who was much flattered by the royal favour, ushered each queen into one of her four rooms. Then she went into the kitchen to brew them some tea . . .'

He slid the four queens across the coffee table into four imaginary rooms.

'Now it so happened that the four kings missed their wives and went out looking for them. They were also caught in the storm and went to the woodcutter's hut, where the old woman begged them to make themselves at home under her poor roof. One by one the kings found their wives and joined them, while they waited for more favourable weather . . .'

As Clare watched, fascinated, Halliday placed the kings,

according to suit, beside their queens in the four imaginary rooms.

'Scarcely were the kings settled, than four young officers arrived at the cottage demanding shelter. "Please accommodate yourselves where you can, your excellencies," said the old woman, and the four young officers each went to a different room . . .'

He placed the knaves, indiscriminately, together with the matched kings and queens in each of the four rooms.

'The quiet of the cottage was disturbed once more by the arrival of four Secret Service agents who believed that the young officers were spies. Ordering the old woman aside, they marched into the four rooms . . .'

Without regard to suit, he put the aces one in each room.

'Finding that their suspicions were groundless, the Secret Service agents grew restless. They wandered around from room to room, as did the rest of the party, all of whom were getting bored with waiting for the storm to end . . .'

Halliday mixed up the occupants of the various rooms thoroughly, before gathering up all sixteen of the cards.

'After a while, the four young officers thought they would like to join forces again; the four kings and queens got fed up with each other – as husbands and wives do . . .'

Glancing at Clare he dealt the cards one by one – one card into each room and then another card into each room – into four packs of four, as if for a rubber of whist.

'When the old woman, bearing her best tray filled with cups of tea, knocked on the doors of the rooms later on, what do you think she found? In one room she found the four queens discussing the latest court scandal . . .'

He turned up the four queens.

'In another room the four kings were playing piquet . . .'

He turned up the four kings.

'In the third room the four young officers were boasting about their conquests . . .'

He turned up the four knaves.

'And in the last the Secret Service officers were discussing the latest bugging devices . . .'

Beating him to it, Clare turned up the four aces.

'Brilliant!'

'Billy used to like that one.'

'About Alain Lamotte . . .'

'I didn't ask you about Alain.'

'I had a terrible a shock. It's about Jamie . . . I was just *using* poor Alain.'

'A pain-killer.' Halliday put the cards back on the buffet and picked up the photograph of Maureen. 'I know all about that.'

CHAPTER THIRTY-EIGHT

Halliday Baines was not the only one to have seen Clare coming out of the offices of Assurance Mondiale at two o'clock in the morning. Harry Balard had been cruising the streets in search of one of the rent boys who hung out in the Place Ste Croix, when he had caught sight of Clare embracing Alain Lamotte beneath the streetlight on the pavement, and jammed on the brakes of his Porsche.

Harry was not one to keep anything to himself. Certainly not such a succulent morsel of gossip. He had passed on the tid-bit to Marie-Paule, while at the same time storing it in his head to be put to good use at some future date.

Since the information sounded highly unlikely – everyone in Bordeaux knew that Clare de Cluzac was engaged to be married – Marie-Paule wondered if Harry, who lately had been acting decidedly strangely, could possibly have invented the story.

It was several weeks now since, in the early hours of the morning, she had heard the patter of pebbles against the tightly shut *volets* of the marital bedroom. No matter what the temperature, Claude was opposed to fresh air. Putting the sound down to hailstones – accounts of the freak storm at Château de Cluzac were still circulating in the Médoc – Marie-Paule had taken no notice. When the noise persisted, she had heaved herself off the bed – it was far too hot for covers – released the catch and pushed open the purple-painted shutters, which matched the purple *couvre-lit*. Had she not witnessed the sight with her very own eyes, she would not have believed it. Her beloved Harry, his hair dishevelled, his forehead encrusted with what looked very much like dried blood, was standing woefully beneath a chestnut tree on the deserted pavement, without a stitch on below his waist, his hands modestly shielding his *sexe*.

Taking care not to wake Balard, Marie-Paule put on her peignoir and let Harry into the apartment.

Gathering him into her arms, she cooed at him as she had when he was six years old.

'*Mon petit chou!*'

Pushing his mother aside roughly, and without a word of apology for waking her, Harry had gone straight to his room, where Marie-Paule, who followed him, found the door shut in her face.

Since there had been no explanation from Harry, either at the time or since, Marie-Paule wondered if he was perfectly well. She did not dare discuss the matter with Balard, who was more bad-tempered than usual, and Christiane's head was permanently in the clouds as she day-dreamed of Halliday Baines. The only person she confided in was Biancarelli who, although she had hidden it from Harry's mother, had been highly amused.

Marie-Paule's other piece of gossip, concerning Clare and Alain Lamotte, had amused Biancarelli considerably less. If the story was true, however, and considering her discussion with Clare before the looking-glass in her showroom she would be very much surprised, it was Clare's problem. Biancarelli had her own.

The return of the Baron to the Médoc had put the boutique owner into a flat spin. She had not wanted to fall in love with her benefactor, she had not asked for it; but ever since he had gone back to Florida she had been acting like a lovesick girl. She was unable to eat, unable to sleep, and had lost interest in her clients, whose requirements had previously been paramount. Shooting herself in the foot – business was bad and rents were going up – she had given even Claude Balard and her other *petits amis* their marching orders.

The fact that Charles-Louis had returned to Bordeaux with Rosa Delaware, rather than Laura Spray, was neither here nor there. Biancarelli saw neither of them as a competitor for the Baron's heart. Alone of all the women who came and went in his life, she knew that he did not have one. All that she asked was to be able, unequivocally, to love him. Her Corsican heart was big enough for two.

Making no excuse to Rosa Delaware, the Baron had been to see Biancarelli; she knew all about the divorce and Viola's blackmail (a woman after her own heart). Distraught at the thought of losing her lover permanently to his orange groves – she did not see the uptight Laura Spray as a rival – on the last occasion she had seen him, Biancarelli had grappled him to her side.

Slipping on a gown when the business of the afternoon was over, she had shyly approached the Baron, put her arms round him, and pressed his mouth to her own. If he was surprised, he did not show it. Releasing himself from her grasp, he sat down on the Louis-XV-style *fauteuil* in her boudoir to put on his monogrammed socks.

'*La prochaine fois qu'on se verra, je serai marié . . .*'

Next time he would be married. Biancarelli's face fell. Installing herself on his lap, she pulled his face to her magnificent breast.

'*Ne t'inquiétes pas, Bianca . . .*'

She was always Bianca after they had made love.

'. . . I'll be back.'

'What would you do if I were no longer here?'

Charles-Louis looked at her blankly. The thought of his long-term mistress being no longer around was as farcical as the idea of returning to Château de Cluzac to discover that it had vanished into a hole in the ground.

'You'll be here.' Tipping Biancarelli unceremoniously off his lap, the Baron reached for his trousers, as she lit a cigarette. He was right, of course. Like the Trojan women, she would be around, awaiting his pleasure.

'*Je t'aime.*' I love you. There was nothing to lose.

Putting on his tie, the Baron laughed his deep-throated laugh. It was like a dagger in Biancarelli's heart. Picking up his jacket and caressing his mistress's dimpled *derrière*, in much the same way as he patted the rump of his horse, Baron de Cluzac, whom she had served for so many years as concubine and confessor, without a backward glance, took his customary leave.

Having passed on the latest gossip about Clare and Alain Lamotte, Marie-Paule Balard, who had ostensibly come to choose another evening gown, this time for the *Ban de Vendange* to celebrate the gathering of the harvest, decided to confide in her further.

'Shall I tell you a secret?'

Heavy of heart, Biancarelli automatically selected an only moderately *moche* size forty-eight, and held it out for her approval to the wife of the negociant.

'I pray for rain, at harvest time.' Marie-Paule crossed herself. 'On Clare de Cluzac's grapes!'

Clare de Cluzac was in her *Bureau d'Acceuil*. She was putting the finishing touches to the arrangements for a banquet, booked by a group of psychiatrists who were touring the Médoc, which was to take place in the newly renovated *Orangerie*.

Together with Jean Boyer, she had already chosen the wine (the cases were *in situ*), and she was working out with Petronella what might be required by way of liqueurs to follow the dinner, which was being catered for by two of Bordeaux's most reliable *traiteurs*.

Hearing a car draw up, the slam of a door, and determined footsteps approaching the *Bureau d'Acceuil*,

she looked up to see a gaunt and dishevelled Alain
Lamotte – whose repeated telephone calls she had, like
Jamie's, refused to answer – standing in the doorway with
a beribboned bouquet of red roses.

Dismissing Petronella, Clare held out her hand.

Ignoring the gesture, Alain leaned across the desk to
kiss her. Clare averted her face.

'I've been telephoning you.' Handing her the flowers,
Alain hung his jacket proprietorially on the back of
the chair.

'*Oui.*'

'I can't sleep . . .'

'I had a call from Cathay Pacific. They want three
thousand dozen quarter-bottles of Petite Clare . . .'

'I didn't come here to talk about Petite Clare. When
will I see you?'

'You're seeing me. Look, I'm really busy Alain . . .'

'Busy!'

'I have to finalise the arrangements for tonight. My
first conference dinner – what if it all goes wrong? – and
then there are the pickers to be sorted out with Monsieur
Boniface . . .'

'Why didn't you answer my calls?'

'I was too ashamed.'

'Ashamed?'

'If you really want to know, I've a confession to
make. I was just using you, Alain. I'm not proud of
it. I hate myself. I didn't know how to tell you. I'm
really sorry.'

'I don't understand.'

'It's about Jamie. It's hard to explain. I should never
have come to your office. I don't want to break up your
marriage. *You* don't want to break up your marriage.
Can't we just forget about what happened?'

'Forget about it!' A vein stood out on Alain's forehead.
'*Je suis fou de toi.* How can I forget about it?'

'I was upset. I had too much to drink. I'd like us to be friends . . .'

Flushing to the roots of his hair as the message finally got home, Alain snatched his jacket from the chair and made for the door.

'Alain!'

A few moments later, standing awkwardly in the office, holding the roses, not sure what to do with them, she heard the car door slam.

It had been an eventful week. Hurting Alain, the last thing she wanted to do, had been its culmination. With the divorce proceedings completed, and his cars loaded on to transporters, Charles-Louis, and Rosa Delaware, had departed. Still furious with Clare, the Baron, who addressed his daughter only when strictly necessary, had not invited her to his forthcoming wedding. He had not even said goodbye.

After the transporters, a succession of horse-boxes supervised by Viola had left Château de Cluzac for the Fitzpatrick Equine Centre. Viola had returned to Ireland, leaving Clare alone to handle the imminent harvest.

She was standing with her clipboard in the *Orangerie*, making a last-minute check of the tables and thinking about Alain, whose stunned face was still haunting her, when Petronella, who had instructions not to disturb her, bleeped her to say that she was wanted urgently in the office.

With her mind buzzing with plates and glasses, and wondering what she had forgotten and whether she had ordered enough food, she crossed the courtyard, followed by Rougemont, and went angrily into the *Bureau d'Acceuil* to give Petronella a piece of her mind. In her office she found Jamie, his arms folded, wearing his dark suit and hospital tie, leaning grimly against the filing-cabinet.

'Jamie!'

'Clare. What the hell is going on?'

'I might ask you that.'

'Shall I bring some coffee?' Petronella, programmed to entertain clients, put her head round the door.

'No. Thank you. Just hold the calls.'

Putting her clipboard on the desk, Clare sat down behind it. This was a new Jamie. His eyes were cold. She had never seen him so angry.

'I left an extremely important meeting to come here. You haven't answered my faxes. I must have called you a dozen times. Perhaps you'd be good enough to tell me what you're playing at.'

'You've been fucking Miranda . . .'

'I've been what!' Pulling the visitor's chair towards him and turning it around, Jamie straddled it and sat facing her. He waited for her to go on.

'I came to Waterperry. Miranda's bag was on the coat stand. The cottage stank of cigars . . .'

'Miranda has been *staying* with me.'

'You've never really got over her . . .'

'I can't believe I'm hearing this.'

'Now that Barnaby's dead, I suppose . . .'

'Hang on a minute. Miranda OD'd on temazepam. She nearly died. When she came out of hospital there was no one to keep an eye on her . . .'

'Did I, or did I not, see her tights on *our* bed?'

'Highly likely.'

'Well then?'

'I gave Miranda the bed. I've been sleeping on the sofa. You don't really think . . . ?'

'You mean you and Miranda haven't . . . ?'

'Miranda's sick. She's devastated. She's taken Barnaby's death extremely badly . . .'

'You mean you would have if she wasn't?'

'If she wasn't what?'

'Sick.'

'What I mean is that she needs looking after. She's a human being, Clare. She's my friend.'

'How can I be sure?'

'If you have to ask, you can't.'

'God. I've been so bloody miserable.'

'Wouldn't it have been easier . . .'

'You can't imagine what I've gone through.'

'. . . to have told me you came to the cottage . . .'

'I've been a total idiot!'

'. . . to have given me a chance to explain?'

'I just jumped to conclusions.'

'It would have been so simple . . .'

'My formative years were spent at Château de Cluzac, Jamie, where – as Viola so neatly put it – my father "bonked everything that moved". Where are you going?' There was panic in her voice.

'I'm going to the airport.'

'You can't.'

'Any reason why not?'

'You've missed the last flight. There's no plane until tomorrow morning. Jamie, I'm really sorry . . .' She seemed to have spent her day apologising. 'I wish I could put back the clock.'

'I've been out of my mind with worry.'

'I don't know how I could have been so stupid.'

'It's your bloody grapes.'

'What have grapes to do with it?'

'Grapes and barrels. That's all you think about these days. We're out of touch. I need to think for a bit. I'll take Rougemont for a walk.'

Clare looked anxiously at her watch. The conference bus was due in less than an hour. She had to get changed.

'There's one thing I want you to understand, Clare.' Jamie turned at the door. 'I am not your father.'

CHAPTER THIRTY-NINE

Keeping a weather eye out for Jamie, Clare, wearing a Biancarelli suit and playing the part of chatelaine as if to the manner born (which she was), greeted the psychiatrists as they stepped down from the bus.

Unaccustomed to the heat, the male members of the party struggled to put on their dinner-jackets over the motley assortment of shirts, which, with typical English aplomb, they imagined would pass for dress-shirts. Tidying their hair with their hands, they straightened their made-up bowties. The ladies, ambassadors for Jaeger and Liberty in floppy prints which stopped short at the ankle, fanned themselves with their invitations ('9.00 p.m. Gala Dinner, Château de Cluzac') and adjusted the leather bags slung from their shoulders.

Welcoming each of her guests personally, Clare allowed them to practise their French, which varied in proficiency from school to fluent, before leading them up to the salon for *apéritifs*, whereupon she let them off the hook and revealed that she was, to all intents and purposes, English.

While snippets of conversation buzzed around her head, she longed for the evening, to which she had been looking forward, to end, so that she could make her peace with Jamie. Overtaken by a sudden bout of homesickness amid talk of 'neuroleptic drugs', 'functional psychosis', the amenities (or lack of) in respective hotels (the luck of the draw), and the forthcoming boat trip on the Gironde, she longed suddenly for Nicola and Neal Street where, among the dustbins and the diesel, rain was a welcome diversion, and she need never see another vine.

Silenced by the grandeur of their surroundings, by the family portraits on the staircase, by the bleached courtyard, and the formal gardens reminiscent of Villandry, through which she escorted them, answering their many questions on the way, the party crowded round the seating plan, which she had pinned on to a board in the Orangerie. Stooping to decipher Petronella's writing, the conference members and their spouses disposed themselves at the round tables, perusing the menus and unfolding their napkins as they decorously waited to be served.

Hoping there was going to be sufficient room for everyone, Clare watched anxiously as the few stragglers table-hopped, chatting to friends from whom they had been separated, before finding their own place names and settling down.

In direct proportion to the rate at which the Château de Cluzac '87 (followed by the '79), which Jean Boyer had had sent up from the *chais*, was appreciatively downed, the noise level proliferated. By the time the special *marc* made its appearance, the wheels were well oiled and the fact that – owing to serious miscalculations – there was not enough cherry *clafoutis* to go round was good-naturedly overlooked.

It was after midnight, and Clare's feet were aching, by the time the psychiatrists followed her into the candlelit *chais*, where several of the group – regular attenders at the Lay and Wheeler tastings, and members of the Wine Society – who knew a great deal more than she about winemaking, kept her talking long after the allotted time.

She led the way into the first-year cellar, where the women shivered in their flimsy dresses as their heels sank into the beaten earth floor, and the air was scented by the unmistakable aroma of new wood. The ancient, red-bellied barrels were now abutted by an entire section of pale and pristine casks.

Clare gathered her group around her.

'The casks are made of oak. Before the war the best oak came from Lithuania. Today we use oak from the forests of Nevers, Vosges and Allier. 'Each year at Château de Cluzac we aim to renew at least twenty-five per cent of our barrels . . .'

The purchase of the casks had been entrusted to Halliday. They came from Séguin-Moreau in Cognac, where he had a friend he could trust. Wearing his baseball cap, Halliday had walked into the *Bureau d'Acceuil* with the invoice, which would be settled with Viola's divorce money.

'The deed is done. Two hundred nicely charred barrels. Just the right degree of toastiness. I can rely on Geoff.' He put the invoice down on the desk, where Clare sat amid a sea of paperwork. 'You work too hard.'

'How else do you suggest I get everything done?'

'You have to give yourself a break sometimes. How does the idea of a picnic by the lake grab you?'

Clare, who had been working non-stop, didn't need much persuading. Leaving Petronella to man the office and deal with any callers, she had given herself a few hours off.

Stopping in a sleepy village where the dank *alimenterie* was just about to close for lunch, they bought the last solitary chicken browning on the spit, some bread, some cheese and some fruit. Anxious for them to go, and wishing them a '*bonne après-midi*', the *patronne* locked the door behind them.

Driving due west until they reached the Lac d'Hourtin-Carcans, with the midday sun overhead, Halliday suddenly turned the jeep off the road and, while Clare hung on for dear life, he brought it to a halt by the side of the lake.

Jumping out of the jeep, Halliday took a bottle of wine from the back seat, wrapped it in his handkerchief and, hanging on to the branches of an overhanging tree, lowered it into the dank water to cool.

'Cabernet Sauvignon! From Chile. My dad used to take me to the creek when I was little.' Straightening up, he flopped down on the grass beside Clare. 'He taught me to swim. It's the time to learn things. I tried to teach Billy. Swimming, running, tennis. About the solar system, what goes on on the sea bed. All the things a kid should know.'

'He's lucky to have such a good father.'

'Chance would be a fine thing!'

Wanting to steer him away from the painful subject of Billy, Clare started to unwrap the picnic, which was already being investigated by the ants.

'Hungry?'

'The thought of that *poulet* is burning a hole in my mouth.'

By the time they had eaten, they were not only invaded by ants, but covered with bites and surrounded by inquisitive flies. Brushing them away from his forehead, Halliday poured the last of the wine.

'Why is it that picnic spots always look better from a distance? Did you know there were vines in Chile as long ago as 1548?'

'Can't say I'd really thought about it.'

'The climate's near perfect for grape growing. Thanks to General Pinochet, Chile was left for dead as far as wine producing was concerned. Hundreds of thousands of hectares of vines were given over to kiwi fruit. Now they've replanted four thousand hectares – mostly with Cabernet – and sixty million US dollars have been invested in the industry. To make Bordeaux-style wine is the target of all

Chilean winemakers. I wish you could see my vineyard, Clare . . .'

While Halliday was talking – it was difficult to keep him off the subject of wine, or of Chile, for long – Clare rescued the scattered food papers from the ants and stuffed them into the plastic bags. Noticing that it had suddenly become silent, except for the buzzing of the wildlife in the long grass, she glanced up.

Halliday had removed his clothes. His long hair lay loose on his naked shoulders. His slight body, with its demarcation where his swimmers had been, had the deceptive smoothness of a girl's.

'Coming for a dip?'

Hesitating for only a moment, Clare slipped out of her clothes and followed him, gasping, into the icy water where they swam swiftly side by side.

'Not bad for a sheila!' Halliday admired her steady crawl.

Dowsing the cocky Australian with water, Clare veered away from him and dived suddenly beneath the reeds.

'Clare! Clare? Where are you?' There was panic in his voice. 'You OK, Clare?'

Silently she slid past his legs and emerged laughing, as she scrambled up the bank.

'You had me worried there.' Following her, Halliday bent his head sideways to shake the water from his ears.

Clare dried herself on her handkerchief aware that he was appraising her. She watched him become aroused.

'You're very beautiful.'

'You think so . . . ?' Her voice was unsteady. She quickly put on her clothes.

'Jamie's a lucky guy.'

Hearing the bitterness return to his voice as he pulled on his trousers and belted them firmly round his taut waist, Clare flopped down in the long grass.

'Why don't you show me a card trick?'

'What makes you think I've got any cards?'

Clare produced a pack from her pocket.

'They fell out of your pants.'

Grinning, he came to lie beside her.

'What'll it be? Ups and Downs? The Twin-Card Trick?'

'Anything to make me laugh.'

To keep her thoughts from Jamie and Miranda.

'OK.' He fixed his cobalt-blue eyes, with their clear whites, on her. 'I'm going to read your mind. Ready?'

'Ready.'

Shuffling the cards, as if they were an extension of his arms, he handed the pack to Clare.

'Cut.'

She split the pack in two.

'Now look at the card on top of *one* of the packs, any one you like, and memorise it.'

Noting the three of spades, Clare replaced the card and returned both packs to Halliday. Placing one on top of the other, he shuffled them once again.

'OK. Here comes the mind reading.'

He spread the cards over the grass so that every one was visible.

'Now, hold my wrist. Right here.'

Clare put her fingers round the strong slim wrist.

Moving his hand slowly, the index finger extended, Halliday pointed one by one to the cards. Over the three of spades his hand faltered, then stopped.

'Three of spades!'

'How did you do it?'

'Read your mind. I got a message through my pulse.'

'You expect me to believe that?'

'Sure.'

'OK . . .' She could hear the crickets in the grass. 'Tell me what I'm thinking?'

Halliday folded her fingers over his wrist until she could

feel his steady pulse, sense the electric charge of his skin.
He was silent for a long time.

'Well?'

Halliday pulled his hand away abruptly.

'We'd better be making a move.'

'How many bottles of wine do you get out of each
barrel . . . ?'

'Sorry?'

Coming back to her psychiatrists in the cellar, Clare
returned to château mode.

'The shape, circumference, and even the number of iron
bands of the *barrique bordelaise* is strictly controlled. Each
barrel will provide three hundred bottles of point-seven-
five litres of wine apiece . . .'

Jamie was in bed, reading.

'Thanks for waiting up for me.'

He put his book down.

'I'll always wait up for you.'

'That's such a nice thing to say.'

'I love you.'

'I thought they'd never go home. Jamie . . .'

'Come to bed.'

'When I came back. From Waterperry. When I thought
that you and Miranda . . .'

'It's finished. I must have walked for fifteen miles.
Rougemont was exhausted. I've got it out of my system.'

Clare removed her jacket. She wore nothing underneath. 'I didn't come straight home, Jamie. I drove into
Bordeaux . . .'

'*Tais toi!*'

She loved it when he spoke French.

'I was so angry . . . !'

'It was a misunderstanding. Does it matter?'

She wanted to explain to Jamie how she had felt, but he was not into feelings. She got into bed.

'No.'

'How long until the harvest?'

Sunlight was filtering through the curtains. Recapturing their old closeness, they had had very little sleep.

'It's usually the last week in September. Most growers settle for an average level of alcohol and pick while the weather's in their favour. The gamblers wait just that little bit longer to get the last drops of *surmaturité* out of the grapes . . .'

'There are so many things I wanted to talk to you about. For starters, I didn't get the job at the Middlesex.'

'Oh, Jamie!'

'It's OK. I wasn't that keen on living in London. There might be a consultant job coming up in Oxford.'

'What else?'

'What else what?'

'Did you want to talk to me about?'

'I went to see Grandmaman.'

'I'm worried about Grandmaman. Did she say anything to you?'

'She didn't have to. She's as thin as a stick. I tried to get her to go back to her GP.'

'What did she say?'

' "Leave life to take care of itself, young man, and don't interfere!" '

'She said that?'

'Well, actually it was Tolstoy. According to Grandmaman, the body will fight its own battles a great deal better if you don't paralyse it with remedies. My guess is that if she doesn't go into hospital PDQ she'll be dead before Christmas. From what she let slip I think she could have cancer of the colon.'

'I think she *wants* to die. I think she's looking forward

to it. Grandmaman has always believed that people should think things out for themselves, take charge of their own lives. She likes to have everything under control. If it was me I'd be scared witless. I'm terrified of dying.'

' "If you don't know how to die, don't worry; Nature will tell you what to do on the spot, fully and adequately. She will do this job perfectly for you, don't bother your head about it." '

'Tolstoy, I suppose.'

'Montaigne. He didn't share Socrates' sense of the immortality of the soul. Your grandmother has simply chosen her own way to "get out of it".'

'Montaigne?'

'Thomas Browne.'

'Do you have to go home today?'

'I'll be back in a couple of weeks for the marathon.'

Clare looked at Jamie's watch; waterproof, shockproof, accurate to a millionth of a second. Never late for anything, he wore the chronometer even in bed. The coarse black hairs on his thick wrist curled themselves round the brown leather strap. Unbidden images flashed into her mind.

'We've only got another hour . . .' She dismissed the unwanted thoughts from her head.

'Fifty minutes actually . . .' Jamie took her in his arms.

'Don't tell me. Freud!'

CHAPTER FORTY

By the morning of the Bordeaux marathon, as runners from the United States and Europe as well as from all over France, converged on St-Estèphe, *chefs de culture* were looking anxiously to both their grapes and the sky. As the annual tensions which accompanied the run-up to the *vendange* were beginning to be felt, preparations for the forthcoming harvest were being completed throughout the Médoc.

In the wineries, century-old vats in outmoded pressing houses had been hosed down and dried out; stainless-steel *cuves* scrubbed clean as saucepans; cement vats scraped; mechanical harvesters taken to pieces, cleaned and reassembled. Everything in the cellars, from mechanical stemmers to electric wiring, had been meticulously checked out, and in a thousand châteaux the casks and vats that would receive the pressed juice lay waiting.

At Château de Cluzac, Albert Rochas had begun to take regular samples of grapes to the laboratory in Bordeaux, where Halliday Baines assessed them for acidity level and sugar content; with letters piled high on his desk, Monsieur Boniface dealt with applications from the hundreds of pickers (many of them regulars) from all over the world, who were soon to descend on the château; while in the kitchens, together with the wives of the estate workers, Sidonie made preparations to feed them.

The ingredients for Harvesters' Stew, almost obliterated

by time and spilled grease, from her tattered recipe book, had remained unaltered since the days of Baron Thibault: 50 kilos of beef (cut into 4 cm squares), 50 fine onions, 60 small pieces of garlic and 40 peeled cloves, 160 carrots, 4 fistfuls of cooking salt, 2 fistfuls of pepper, celery and ground cloves.

Larding the pieces of beef with the garlic and cloves, Sidonie would put them into giant iron cooking pots, add cold water, bring it to the boil several times, and painstakingly remove the foam before throwing in the chopped vegetables, reducing the heat, and letting the stew simmer, so that only a bubble broke the surface, for several hours.

Placing a slice of *gros pain* into the soup plate of each weary harvester at the end of the first day's picking, she would ladle the very hot stew over the bread. Eaten with thickly sliced tomatoes from the château gardens, accompanied by fiery mustard, and washed down with young wine, it was a meal fit for the gods.

As the annual drama drew nearer, the tourists returned home, the *visites* to the *chais* tailed off, and the protagonists prepared for countdown, Clare felt increasingly isolated and alone. She was not short of expert advice. Jean Boyer, Albert Rochas and Monsieur Boniface had lived through a great many more *vendanges* than she, but as harvest time drew nearer none of them seemed to have time for her.

Monsieur Boniface was busy with his applications in the estate office; Sidonie was up to her eyeballs counting out piles of plates and sacks of potatoes; and in the vineyards Albert Rochas paced anxiously up and down the rows of vines like a mother hen.

Halliday Baines was equally preoccupied. He not only had his vineyards to look after, but had stepped up his marathon training. This year he was determined to be accepted into the Commanderie du Bontemps de Médoc, a privilege awarded to the winner who would, in addition,

receive the equivalent of his weight in wine. Apart from
providing Clare with the address of a winemaker in Spain,
who would give her a reasonable price for her old barrels,
his one flying visit had been spent in the vineyards in
the company of Albert Rochas. He had declined Clare's
invitation to stay for lunch.

'Maureen's filing for divorce,' he said, as she walked
him to the jeep. 'She wants to marry Chris.'

'It was on the cards.'

They laughed, remembering the mind reading.

'It's different when it actually comes to it. Billy's settling
into his new school.'

'About the harvest. Is it true that I have to start picking
on a Monday?'

'That's the calendar of men . . .' Halliday switched on
the ignition. 'The calendar of nature is something else.
Don't worry about the harvest. I'll tell you when to start
picking.'

'When will that be?'

'When your grapes are ripe.'

While Halliday was physically absent, Alain Lamotte was
mentally remote. Although they had resumed their business
dealings and the incident at Assurance Mondiale was not
directly referred to, Clare was aware that she had treated
Alain extremely badly and that he was still wounded in
his pride. Knowing only too well what it was like to feel
rejected, she had bought him a tie with butterflies on it
and tried to put things right.

'Look Alain, I've told you how sorry I am about what
happened. Can't we be friends?'

'I thought we were friends.'

'It doesn't feel like it.'

'What do you want me to do?'

Since the night in his office, Alain had been more
obsessed with Clare than ever. Despite his humiliation,

and against his better judgement, he knew that he would continue to help her with the château until she was on her feet.

Delphine had remarked his preoccupation – which she had attributed to the demands of Assurance Mondiale – for which she had suggested a week's holiday in Morocco. Alain had turned down the idea on the grounds of commitments in Bordeaux, but which were in fact at Château de Cluzac. Even the two little girls had noticed.

'*Papa est toujours faché avec nous,*' Amélie had complained, when Alain had curtly refused to play tennis with her.

'Papa doesn't mean to be angry with you.' Delphine was in the garden preparing a barbecue over which Alain would preside. 'Sometimes your papa works too hard.'

She was not entirely convinced by her own explanation for Alain's unaccustomedly short fuse and his moroseness. There were days when she could scarcely get a word out of him. When Harry Balard – with whom she had played a mixed doubles at the Primrose – had suggested that she keep a closer eye on her husband, she had reported the conversation to Alain, who had immediately passed it on to Clare.

'If Delphine ever found out about us, she'd go straight back to Paris with the children. I know my wife.'

'There's nothing to find out,' Clare said briskly.

'*Malheureusement . . .*'

'Come on Alain. You love Delphine. Delphine loves you. Leave Harry Balard to me.'

Careful not to go anywhere near Alain's office, they held their frequent meetings in the *Bureau d'Acceuil*, where the agenda was strictly business.

'I saw Philip Van Gelder.' Alain lit a cigarette. 'I was coming out of the Cité Administrative . . .'

'The tax office?'

Alain nodded.

'Van Gelder was just going in.'

'*Et alors?*'

'Afterwards I had lunch at La Tupina. Van Gelder was at the next table . . .'

Clare waited.

'He was talking to Monsieur Huchez and Monsieur Combe!'

'What about?' Clare wondered what the South African wine-grower had to do with the *fisc*.

'Unfortunately I couldn't hear what they were saying.'

Clare had other things to think about. Not only was she worried about the harvest but about Grandmaman. She had been to Notre Dame de la Consolation to discuss the matter with Tante Bernadette.

'I thought perhaps that you could have a word with her . . .' Clare had walked round the convent gardens with the Reverend Mother, who stopped to chide a sister as she hoed the dry beds.

'*Vous devez ramasser les courgettes quand elles sont encore petites. Elles ont plus de gout.*'

'*Entendu ma Mère.*'

Clare hadn't come to talk about the optimum size of courgettes.

'Grandmaman is *your* mother.'

'Maman abdicated that role long ago,' Tante Bernadette said.

Recalling the fateful day of her wedding, when she had left her bridegroom at the altar, Bernadette took Clare's arm. 'She has not spoken to me in nearly forty years.'

'Grandmaman is sick. She needs urgent medical attention. Is there nothing you can do?'

'I shall pray for her.'

'That's not quite what I meant.'

'"More things are wrought by prayer . . ."'

'You sound like Grandmaman.'

'I am her daughter. A fact your grandmother seems to have forgotten.'

'Grandmaman doesn't talk to Papa either.'

'The de Cluzacs are a law unto themselves, Clare. I am surprised you haven't found that out.'

Stopping for a moment as they paused at a gate in the stone wall at the end of the vegetable garden, Bernadette looked up at the autumnal sky. 'When I was a small girl, Maman used to take me to the harvest festival at St-Emilion – I think about it every year – that was where *my* grandmother lived . . .'

Passing into the Contemplative Garden, she led Clare to a wooden bench in an alcove formed by a yew hedge, and lowered her voice.

'Every year, on the Sunday before the *vendange*, the people of St-Emilion would gather in the church on the hill. There was a very old Abbé . . . Abbé . . . His name escapes me. It's not important. He was the parish priest. One Sunday, I must have been about ten years old, he told us about the wedding at Canaan, at which Jesus turned the water into wine: "The wedding guests were all assembled when the mother of Jesus said to Him, 'They have no wine . . .'" At which point of course everybody laughed.

'After the sermon, the Abbé blessed the congregation, the choir from the Cathédral Saint-André in Bordeaux sang a Gloria by Monteverdi, the church doors were flung open and we poured out into the sunshine. The *Jurade* of St-Emilion, in their cardinal-red robes, preceded by pipes, drums, trumpets and heraldic banners, led the way down the steep cobbled streets to the monolithic church . . .'

'Monolithic church?'

'An old stone monument with subterranean passages. It was used by the *Jurade* for their induction ceremony. The stage was lit by torches, and as each new applicant arrived the leader of the *Jurade* asked his *Jurats*, "Are you willing to open the doors of your cellars and your houses to our new candidate?" Of course they replied, "We are."

'When the ceremony was over, the *Jurade* left the church and climbed to the top of the King's Tower where the *Procureur* proclaimed the new harvest. The trumpets were sounded, the *Jurade* cried out "Allelujah!", and the rest of the day was spent eating, drinking and telling stories to go with the wine. I remember it as if it were yesterday.'

Bernadette turned to Clare.

'I will pray for Maman. And for your harvest.'

Although Clare had little faith that Tante Bernadette's prayers could influence either Baronne Gertrude's intestines or the Château de Cluzac grapes, there was always the niggling suspicion that lurked in the mind of the unbeliever, that in the next world – should it of course turn out that there was such a thing – she might just be proved wrong.

The imminent harvest had for weeks now provided *le tout* Bordeaux with its sole topic of conversation. The marathon, which many of the Bordelais would turn out to watch, provided a little light relief.

Every year, as Madame la Présidente de *l'Equipe Tendresse de l'Association des Joyeux Tartineurs* (the Association of Happy Sandwich Makers), Marie-Paule Balard manned the buffet at the finishing line. This year she was assisted by Christiane.

Things at the Balard residence had gone from bad to worse. The thwarted Claude, whose temper had not improved, had not given up for a moment his ambition to own Château de Cluzac; Harry was still importuning Marie-Paule at regular intervals for funds and had become increasingly secretive; and Christiane was even more besotted with Halliday Baines, for whose benefit it was that she had volunteered to help her mother with the sandwiches.

While Halliday, an élite runner who had spent nine

months training for the marathon, looked upon it as a personal measuring post, and Alain Lamotte aimed annually at improving his time, Jamie, who started in the back row and made a game out of passing as many people as possible, joined in purely for enjoyment.

Refusing to agonise over what he ate on the night before the big race, he had refused to let Clare sign him up for the high-carbohydrate *Diner de Pâtes* which was given by Baronne Philippine de Rothschild at Château d'Armailhacq and attended by two thousand runners. Instead he took her to dinner at Le Chapon Fin – an erstwhile haunt both of Edward VII and Toulouse-Lautrec – where they could be alone.

'I've been short-listed for the Oxford job,' he told Clare as, waiting to be served, they caught up with the news.

'The Oxford job?'

'The one I told you about. It's a blue-chip job.'

'Great.'

'I went to see Grandmaman last night; I knew you'd want an up-to-date report. If anything, she seemed slightly better.'

'Perhaps Grandmaman's right after all. About the body fighting its own battles.'

'Miranda's gone back to her flat. She's organising a memorial service for Barnaby . . .' Jamie leaned back as the white-aproned waiter approached with their order.

Clare did not want to talk about Miranda. She looked at Jamie's plate with its thick tournedos on a bed of fried bread and foie gras.

'Are you sure that's wise?'

'I'm only running to St-Estèphe, not Sparta. I'm not in good nick anyway. I was up nearly all night doing emergency surgery. A group of schoolkids ran in front of a bus in the High. You've never seen such a mess. Fortunately no one was killed. One poor little girl had several fractured ribs, her humerus poking into the brachial artery, and the bone right through the skin in her forearm. Compartment syndrome. By the time I got to her the pressure had risen and the blood supply to the muscle was almost cut off. I had to do a fasciotomy – separate the fibrous layer – before the muscle died . . . Am I boring you?'

Clare picked up her knife and fork. 'Sorry Jamie.' She seemed to spend her life apologising lately. 'I was thinking about my grapes.'

CHAPTER FORTY-ONE

The marathon of the Châteaux of the Médoc and the Graves, routed through the Bordeaux vineyards, was rated among the ten most beautiful of the world. Unlike any other marathon, it was a three-day affair, marked by celebrations both before and after the race, which ended where it began, at the port of St-Estèphe.

The festivities included a gastronomic Great Trade Fair at La Chapelle, a photographic exhibition (to entice people to the Maison du Vin), aeroplane rides and boat trips, boutiques, side shows and amusements set up in Les Allées Marines along the banks of the Gironde, fancy dress and entertainments, jazz bands and bungee jumping, buffet suppers by the dozen, and wine-tastings along the route. By the time the runners had assembled on the quayside on the second day, excitement had reached fever pitch. The entire Médoc was *en fête*.

Halliday Baines' technique, which he had put into practice in marathons from Sydney to Fukoka, had been learned the hard way. Scorning the idea of a running coach, he had worked out for himself the best way to optimise his performance. Aware that, as the heart muscle became stronger, the oxygen delivery became more efficient and the blood flow through the muscle fibres was increased, he knew that it was important not to overdo it. The more you overdid it, the more likely you were to crash, and, even if you didn't actually injure yourself, you'd find that you were actually running more slowly instead of faster. The stronger the muscles, the more effectively they contracted, the faster it was possible to run (using the same amount of energy) before hitting the pain threshold.

While Halliday's method entailed distinguishing between what the mind perceived and the body perceived, Jamie's game plan was to put one leg in front of the other for 42.2 kilometres, until he was presented with the T-shirt awarded to all finishers.

With his number, 24, fastened to his singlet with safety pins (courtesy of Sidonie), Jamie was directed to the far reaches of the colourful field, while Halliday was pampered with a private dressing area and given a privileged position near the starting line. Oblivious of the buzz of excitement around him and the broadcast music, interrupted from time to time by announcements – 'Time spent in wine-tasting will not be deducted from the running time!' – he concentrated on his strategy. Although ability, training and experience were major factors in the race, and temperature and wind factors also had to be taken into consideration, what distinguished the good runner from the not-so-good was the ability to focus his attention for long periods. While 'disassociating' was not advised for beginners, it was recommended for those determined to run fast. Allowing the mind to wander slowed one down. Staying focused concentrated the body systems so that a steady pace could be sustained, energy conserved and running-form maintained.

Dividing the 42.2 kilometres of the race into four, Halliday had worked out exactly how long to spend on each segment and estimated his finishing time. His calibrated 'pace table', written on a piece of paper and covered with clingfilm, was taped to the back of his number (7) for easy reference.

Unlike Halliday, Jamie chatted amiably to his running-mates, a practice frowned upon by serious runners, while waiting for the Président du Conseil General to fire the gun. He was concentrating not so much on concentrating as on keeping cool.

For every litre of fluid lost, the heartrate increased by eight beats and the temperature rose accordingly. In the interests of proper hydration, it was recommended that sixteen ounces of water an hour be drunk before the race. For several days now, to the amusement of his students in the hospital, Mr Spence-Jones had been unable to pass a water fountain in the corridor without stopping for a quick drink.

He had downed a litre of Perrier at breakfast, after which, for obvious reasons, he had had nothing to drink until five minutes ago, when he had polished off a can of Fanta which would be absorbed by the body before it reached the kidneys. After that, it was a question of avoiding dehydration by stopping frequently to refuel.

Notwithstanding the physical discomfort of drinking such large quantities, he would replenish his fluids every hour from the refreshment stands, manned by the local population and set up every two kilometres along the route. Remembering his physiology, he knew that it took thirty minutes for the air-conditioning effects of fluids to migrate through the system and be released as sweat. In the unlikely event that he would get as far as the closing stages of the race, it would be a case of fluids 'on', rather than fluids 'in', and he would use his sunhat as a vessel from which to douse himself with water.

At eleven o'clock sharp, to the accompaniment of martial music, the several-thousand-strong column, serious runners interspersed with clowns, pyramids of balloons and a variety of fancy dress (from cave men to South Sea islanders in grass skirts), moved towards Pauillac via Château Phélan-Ségur and Châteaux Haut-Marbuzet and Marbuzet.

Following the race on her bicycle, for which there

were parallel lanes, Clare cycled her way from Jamie in the back row, to Alain Lamotte, who had positioned himself as close to the starting line as possible without blocking faster runners, until she drew level with the élite runners, in whose midst she picked out Halliday, where the punishing pace was rapidly separating the men from the boys.

Two hours into the race, many of the competitors, their faces contorted with pain, had hit the 'wall' and dropped out. Having made sure that number 24 was not among them, she cycled to the Maison du Vin, in search of refreshment which was laid on by the Rugby Club.

Delphine Lamotte was queuing up with her two children at the buffet, while at the long bar Harry Balard – who registered Clare's appearance in the mirror – was buying a drink for his sister Christiane, who had taken a break from the Happy Sandwich Makers.

Making her way towards the food, Clare noticed Harry Balard leave Christiane, whose eyes were glued to the TV screen, presumably for a sight of Halliday, and elbow his way determinedly through the throng in the direction of Delphine Lamotte.

Guessing that Harry was up to no good, Clare intercepted him. Blocking his path she opened Jamie's coach bag, which was slung across her body, and removed a white plastic packet. She held it in front of her so that it was visible to no one but Harry.

'*Un mot à Delphine Lamotte et vous êtes mort*,' she warned him.

'*Salope!*'

Harry Balard turned on his heel, but not before several shocked Médocains almost dropped their loaded trays as they heard him insult Clare de Cluzac.

'What was all that about?' Delphine asked innocently at the table where Clare had joined her and the children.

'It was nothing.'

She was not about to tell blonde Delphine Lamotte, in her blonde designer shorts, her Ray-Bans resting nonchalantly on her streaked hair, that she had stopped Harry Balard from denouncing her husband and thereby saved her marriage.

'*Peu importe* . . .' Shrugging her shoulders, Delphine removed the paper from two drinking straws and stuck them into the children's Coca-Cola. 'Harry Balard is not my favourite person.'

'*Papa! Papa!*'

Amélie and Joséphine Lamotte jumped up and down excitedly as they caught sight of their father on the TV screen.

Following their gaze, Clare saw Alain Lamotte, teeth gritted, running as if he had glue on his shoes, and looking as if he were about to drop from exhaustion.

'Alain won't give up,' Delphine said proudly. 'When he wants something he goes for it.'

Leaving the Maison du Vin, Clare rescued her bicycle and joined the other cyclists, one of whom was dressed as a penguin, pedalling slowly in the midday heat.

Happy to have saved Delphine Lamotte from having her illusions about her husband shattered by Harry Balard, she made her torpid way through the parched countryside; past refreshment stands selling oranges, biscuits and dried fruit; past First Aid stations offering massage and anti-blister blocks; through village squares, criss-crossed with bunting, where brass bands played, runners massaged their cramped limbs, and refreshed themselves in the fountains.

Leaving her bicycle near the finishing point, she pushed through the crowd and found herself standing beside Biancarelli, who had closed her shop for three days.

'What number is your Jamie?' Biancarelli shouted above the blaring speakers, which were broadcasting a continuous commentary on the race.

'Twenty-four!' Clare yelled.

'*Je vous envie.*'

Biancarelli looked different somehow. As if the bounce had gone out of her.

'I thought you had a poor opinion of men. And marriage.'

'*J'ai changé d'avis.*'

'Anyone in particular?'

'*Oui.*'

'*Félicitations.*'

'*Félicitations, pfui!*' Biancarelli shouted to the amusement of those around her. 'I have as much chance of marrying him as marrying the President of France.'

'He's already married?'

'I think so. I don't know. It's out of the question.'

The voice of the commentator reached fever pitch as the first runners came within two kilometres of the port. Clare pricked up her ears as the number seven was repeated over and over.

As Halliday Baines, ahead of the field, approached the finishing line, and the crowd behind them surged forward to get a better view, Clare took Biancarelli's arm.

'Am I allowed to know who it is?'

'You would be the last person . . .'

Having mastered concentration on the fast track, Halliday, looking straight ahead like a blinkered horse, had transferred it to his road runs. For the past forty-one kilometres it had stood him in good stead.

Ignoring his blistered feet, concentrating on overtaking the dozen or so competitors he had strategically allowed to overtake him earlier on in the race (no sooner had he outstripped one of them than with grim determination he concentrated on reeling in the next), managing to convince himself that the world would end immediately after the race, disregarding his sore muscles, matching his thoughts to his pace, straining to think positively, to block out his mind drift, he had passed one runner after another.

He told himself how tough he was. That he had trained hard. That he was nearly through. That he was the greatest. That he deserved to win. How tough he was. That he had trained hard. That he was nearly through. That he was the greatest. That he deserved to win. How tough he was. That he had trained hard. That he was nearly through. That he was the greatest. That he deserved to win. Running steadily, having managed to shake off all but one of his challengers, he was followed at only a very few paces by a six-foot Dane with flaxen hair.

'Numéro sept. 'Alliday Baines d'Australie. Et numéro quarante-six. Lars Pedersen de Danemark . . . !' The voice through the loudspeaker was hoarse with excitement.

Saving his best mental image until last, Halliday thought of Billy. I'm doing this for you, kid. He was half a training shoe in front. I've always told you you've got to be the best. Half a stride now ahead of the Dane. You want me to teach you the Three Kings, Billy? You've got to concentrate on the cards. If you want to get on in life, Billy, you've got to give it all you've got. Don't let yourself be pipped at the post, Billy. Never look round. Never check the scenery. It's where you're going that's important, not where you've been. Keep going, Billy. Keep going. Billy. Billy. Billy. Billy . . . Billy!

''Alliday! 'Alliday!'

Christiane Balard's voice came from somewhere in the crowd as Halliday Baines, looking neither to right nor to left, came into view. As he advanced towards the finishing line, where TV cameras, race directors and Red Cross workers with drinks and aluminium blankets waited, Clare willed him to win.

''Alliday! 'Alliday!'

Christiane's voice reached a crescendo.

'Vite! Vite!'

Cheered on by the crowd, the two finalists, their legs seeming to intermingle, their bodies strained to the limit after forty-two kilometres on the road, scraping the very bottom of their physical barrels, summoned up the final vestiges of their reserves.

Halliday, his legs going like pistons, breasted the tape first. Ignoring Christiane who appeared with his bush hat, ignoring well-wishers with cups of water, ignoring TV interviewers with microphones, looking neither to right nor to left, not slowing his pace, he continued to run.

CHAPTER FORTY-TWO

Two weeks after the marathon, after consultation with their *maîtres de chais* and their *chefs de culture*, most of the wine-growers in the Médoc had made their decisions. Picking, at the majority of châteaux, had begun.

With her *récolte* already decimated by the hailstorm – damage exacerbated by her ill-advised decision to carry out the green harvest – Clare, who inherited her gambling spirit from her father, was determined not to be proved a failure once more by him. Aware of the risk she took by waiting, she stubbornly refused to be browbeaten into picking her grapes in anything but peak condition.

Jean Boyer and Albert Rochas monitored the vines several times daily. They were glued to the *météo* reports on their TV sets at night. They implored her to get in at least the Merlot, which ripened earlier than the Cabernet, before there was a change in the weather.

The opinion of the cellarmaster and the *chef de culture* was backed by Halliday Baines. Although the oenologist had been regularly checking the Château de Cluzac grapes in his laboratory, Clare had not seen him since he had run the Marathon des Châteaux du Médoc et des Graves in a record three hours, fifteen minutes and twenty-four seconds.

While Christiane Balard had chased after Halliday, who had beaten the Dane by fifteen seconds, Clare had waited more than an hour for Jamie. Looking anxiously at each runner in turn as they limped up to the finishing line, she had recognised only the anguished face of Alain Lamotte. Leaving Delphine to minister to Alain, who despite his exhaustion had looked at Clare in triumph, as if seeking her approval, as if he had run the race for her, Clare had joined the slow-moving traffic to look for Jamie. She found him guzzling oysters at the thirty-seventh kilometre, where finally beaten by the heat, he had abandoned the race.

Back at the château, he had lain naked on the bed, giving instructions to Clare as she massaged his sore muscles.

'Begin with the lower back and buttocks to get intra-muscular fluids flowing . . .'

'Oh yes?'

'. . . then work gently on the legs with long, flowing movements towards the heart . . . Ouch!'

'Sorry.'

'If the massage hurts, ask the therapist to be more gentle.'

'Like so?'

'Like so.'

'If it still hurts, thank the therapist graciously and get off the table. Or alternatively' – he pulled Clare down on top of him – 'suggest that the therapist gets *on* to the table . . .'

Squatting in the Cluzac vineyards, among the beautiful black grapes, which were now almost bursting their skins with sugar, Halliday, who had finally found time to visit the château, narrowed his eyes against the sun, which had been shining constantly on the Médoc for the past six weeks. He squinted up at Clare.

'These grapes are ninety-five per cent, Clare. You don't want them *over*ripe.'

'No.'

'Then what the fuck are you waiting for?'

Bullied as a child by her father, Clare had been indoctrinated by him with the belief that nothing but the best was good enough.

'One hundred per cent. I thought winemakers were supposed to take risks?

Halliday straightened up.

'We're not stupid! What if it rains?'

'The thermometer hit the roof today, Halliday. The highest September temperature on record . . .'

'This is not Spain, Clare. It's not California. Bordeaux is like England – the weather can change overnight.'

Clare had done her homework. Alone at night in the Baron's Room, the old records spread out about her, she had studied the history of past Bordeaux vintages. She knew that an extra half per cent of alcohol in her Cabernet grapes could make all the difference between a decent wine and a sensational one. The vintage of 1961, which now fetched astronomical prices at auction, had been made from 'perfectly mature grapes'; the weather in the Médoc, prior to picking, had been as hot as it was now, and the size of the récolte reflected her own decimated vineyards as did the average age of the vines. Pitting weather patterns and laboratory reports against her instincts, she had made up her mind to wait.

'This vintage . . .' she said slowly, 'my vintage, is going to be better than the eighty-two, better than the seventy, better even than the sixty-one . . .'

'You're taking a big, big chance.'

'That's my problem.'

'Don't say I didn't warn you.'

Halliday, in shorts and dusty walking boots, moved away from her towards the end of the row of vines with their brown and curling leaves.

'Where are you going?'

'I've got work to do. I get paid for my advice. Pick your

grapes, Mademoiselle de Cluzac!' He patted Rougemont
who had followed him. 'Don't keep a dog and bark.'

Taking into account the fact that some of the pickers,
who were cooling their heels on the estate, not only had
to be housed and fed but paid for doing nothing, and that
the oenologist was concerned with guiding and controlling
natural phenomena in order to avoid damaging mistakes,
Clare was not as sanguine as she seemed.

At Médaillac and Ribagnac troupes of pickers worked
their way methodically along the vines, cutting the bunches
and placing them in the light wooden *panniers* to be
collected and tipped into the larger *hottes* on the backs of
the stronger workers. At Kilmartin and Estaminet, costly
mechanical harvesters, with their containers of inert gas,
which would prevent the grapes from oxidising before they
reached the vats, flailed noisily and effectively between
the rows.

While both Jean Boyer and Albert Rochas, like Halliday
Baines, had made it clear to Clare that they thought she
was making a big mistake, it was left to Sidonie, who was
tired of providing for the bored and disgruntled harvesters,
to tell Clare exactly what she thought of her.

'You are as pig-headed as Madame la Baronne,' the old
cook said as she sweated over the iron pots in the kitchens.
'As obstinate as your father. What experience have you
had with the harvest? Don't you think Jean and Albert,
who have grapes in their bones, who have claret instead
of blood in their veins, who imbibed wine-wisdom with
their mother's milk, who live, eat and breathe Château de
Cluzac and its vineyards, know better than you?'

'I told Papa . . .'

'And your *oenologue*, with his fancy *laboratoire*. I don't
see you taking his advice.'

'I told Papa, I would . . .'

'Told Papa, told Papa! I regret the day I took you
to the Baron's Room, that I showed you the *Mémo*

de Chasse. Château de Cluzac would have been better off with Monsieur Balard, better sold to that Monsieur Lamotte – don't think I haven't seen the two of you with your heads together in your office – better off with the South African and his bonsai trees, than with someone who doesn't know a grape from a gooseberry. Look around you, Mademoiselle! Ribagnac is picking, Estaminet is picking, Gélise-Rose has nearly finished picking, even your cousins at Kilmartin . . .'

'*Sois patiente,*' Clare said.

'*Vous dites que je dois patienter? C'est bien ça. C'est tellement drôle.* If you wait any longer the rain will come. And if the rains come . . . *Bonté Divine, Mademoiselle Clare* . . .' Sidonie crossed herself. 'We will all be out of a job!'

'They're all gunning for me,' Clare told Jamie on the phone.

'I'm on your side.'

'I wish the harvest was over.'

'So do I. There's a trauma meeting in Brazil in October. You've always wanted to see Rio. You can go on the spouse tours . . .'

'Jamie I can't.'

'Can't what?'

'Come to the conference.'

'Nonsense!'

'Nonsense? You sound like . . .'

'I thought that after the harvest . . .'

'After the harvest I have to watch the fermentation.'

'. . . it was all over bar the shouting.'

It was Halliday who had explained to her that her constant presence in the *chais* was crucial, not only until the grapes were in, but until after she had made her wine.

'I have to make sure that the vats are heated, that there are no glitches before the *assemblage* . . .'

'No sweat.' Jamie's voice was breezy but she knew that he was hurt. 'I'll go by myself.'

Ten days later, the neighbouring châteaux were making a start on their cabernets sauvignon. Although they had papered over the cracks, Clare was still feeling guilty about Jamie, as Albert Rochas, Jean Boyer and Monsieur Boniface, who had been holding a council of war in the cellars, made their way in a disgruntled posse to the *Bureau d'Acceuil* where they confronted her.

'The report from the *laboratoire*!' Albert banged a sheet of paper triumphantly in front of her. 'Thirteen degrees for the merlots, and a full twelve degrees for the cabernets!'

'*La météo!*' Monsieur Boniface waved a fax in her face. 'The long-range forecast is for rain.'

Out of the habit of praying, Clare yearned suddenly and unaccountably for the comfort of her rosary. Beseeching inwardly that her one small vintage, like that of Palmer in 1961, which had created unparalleled excitement in the Gironde, would produce an exceptional claret, she recalled the promise made by Our Lady to St Dominic that you shall obtain all you ask of me by recitation of the rosary.

Glancing at the three grim faces, at the sun, which still bathed the courtyard in golden light, although the temperature had dropped dramatically and there was a distinct hint of autumn in the air, she asked Jean Boyer, Albert Rochas and Monsieur Boniface to accompany her to the cellars.

In the *chais*, aware of the glum looks, the mutterings and the puzzled glances behind her, she drew four glasses of last year's wine, still tannic from the wood.

Albert Rochas exchanged glances with Jean Boyer who rolled his long-suffering eyes towards the ceiling. She heard the impatient click of Monsieur Boniface's false teeth.

Clare raised her glass.

'*A la vendange!* We start picking tomorrow!'

'*Finalement!*' A smile of pure joy illuminated Albert Rochas' face.

'*La vendange!*' Even Monsieur Boniface was smiling.

'*La vendange!*' Putting down his glass on an upturned barrel, Jean limped towards the door.

'*Ou vas tu, Jean?*' Albert looked surprised.

'I'm going to tell them in the château!'

Scarcely able to contain her excitement that her harvest – Clare de Cluzac's harvest – was actually going to begin, Clare was anxious to pass the good news on to Halliday.

After a long time, the telephone was answered by a female Australian voice.

Clare was puzzled. 'I'd like to speak to Halliday Baines . . .'

'Halliday's not here; this is Jenny speaking.'

'Jenny?'

'Jennifer Patterson. Can I give Halliday a message?'

'Not really. What time are you expecting him?'

'It's anybody's guess. He's bringing in the harvest. This is his busy time. Who shall I say called?'

'Nobody. It doesn't matter.'

'Cheers then.'

'Cheers.'

Two days later, the motley troupe of pickers – Spaniards from Andalusia, Portuguese and gypsies, students from Holland and Germany, Rambos and Tarzans – each of whom had been assigned a particular position by Albert Rochas, made their methodical way along the rows cutting the ripe bunches of grapes. As they worked the muscular 'carrier', who had been allotted to them, emptied their baskets into the heavy plastic *hotte* strapped to his back. When the *hotte* was full, he dumped his load into the trailer on the sandy path at the end of the rows, to be collected by the tractor.

Clare watched the stooped shoulders, the agile fingers,

the arms executing the ritualistic movements of some ancient ballet. As each picker made obeisance at the foot of the vine, before making his cut and holding out the swollen bunch like some votive offering, she realised suddenly that throughout her childhood the responsibility of getting the grapes from vineyard to vat in the shortest possible interval had always been her father's. This time, terrifyingly, it was down to her.

As she walked along the rows among the curses directed at blisters and at aching backs, among the snatches of song and the ribaldry, among the camaraderie forged in previous vintages, she caught sight of Halliday Baines, in his familiar bush hat, stopping now and then to take the secateurs from the hands of a slow picker, making his way towards her.

'You're a gutsy sheila!' He looked up at the sky in which there was no sign of cloud. There was grudging admiration in his voice. 'Where's your *chef de culture*?'

'What's the problem?'

'I just came from Ribagnac. There's a trailer load of your grapes standing by the roadside.'

'*Merde!*'

Once the grapes were mature, it was not only speed of picking that was essential. A trailer load of grapes left standing in the midday sun, with the attendant risk of oxidation, could spell disaster. Nothing that would detract from the final quality of the wine could be left to chance.

Clare had been up since five supervising the freshly sluiced pressing house where the sight of the previous day's skins and bits of twig left in the giant screw of the *égrappoir* had sent her baying for blood. Later on she had had to give the women at the sorting table, who were so busy laughing and joking – using language that would make a publican blush – that they were letting rotten grapes into the *égrappoir*, the sharp end of her tongue.

Trembling with rage at the thought of an entire load of her precious grapes being left in the sun to rot; and, screaming as she went at a 'carrier' with a dirty *hotte* to replace it with a clean one, she returned to the château with Halliday in search of her *chef de culture*, who was responsible for the tractors.

'Who's Jenny?'

'A mate.'

'Is that it?'

'What more do you want, her shoe size?'

'Sorry.'

'I'm sorry. I was over at Kilmartin last night. I had too much too drink.'

The atmosphere of carnival that pervaded the vineyards by day continued in the châteaux at night. Last night at Cluzac, when a weary Jean had finally closed the heavy doors of the pressing house, the sunburned pickers had trailed back through the vineyards to the château. Over dinner at the long tables, at the end of their first day, the wine had flowed freely.

It was midnight, by the bonfire they had made, by the time the gypsies got out their accordians and the Spaniards their guitars. Singing until they could sing no more, dancing to music which crossed the boundaries of language, clapping their calloused hands, the troupe made their own entertainment, until even the most stout-hearted gave in, and, one by one, they drifted off to bed.

When they had all gone Clare strolled across the lawns in the moonlight, listening to cries of the crickets and the croaking of the frogs. In the distance she thought she heard a rumble of thunder. Then that she had imagined it. Calling to Rougemont who, still pining for the Baron, slept outside her door, she had fallen, fully clothed, into bed.

Recalling that she had woken three hours later with a splitting headache the remnants of which still hovered behind her eyes, Clare acknowledged the oenologist's apology.

'We're all a bit the worse for wear.'

'You ain't seen nothing.' Halliday grinned. 'Wait till the end of your second week.'

They found Albert Rochas in the far corner of the vineyard, where he was supervising a group of inexperienced pickers. While the *chef de culture*, purple with rage, drove off in search of the culprit who had left the loaded trailer by the roadside, Halliday went with Clare to the cellars, where the supervision of the vats was as fundamental to the harvest as was the picking of the grapes.

Jean Boyer, faced not with an inept troupe, but with gleaming and hostile inox in place of his familiar and unsanitary wooden vats, greeted them gruffly.

'Need any help?' Halliday cast an expert eye over the temperature on the inox as above them the grapes were pumped into the vats.

The old cellarmaster shook his head. He was not as baffled by the calibrated thermostats and electronic mysteries of the new technology as he made out. Adept at priming a hand grenade and at wiring a detonator, he had made it his business to understand it.

Following Halliday's glance, he took his glasses, one side held on with sticking plaster, from the pocket of his overalls and peered at the thermometer on the side of the vat. '*Trente-deux degrés.*'

As Halliday turned on the cold water, Clare noticed a load of grapes which was about to be pumped into the vat currently being filled.

'Hey! Hold it a minute.'

'*Il y a encore de la place.*' Jean didn't welcome the interference.

'I don't care how much room there is. Those grapes come from a different *parcelle*. They must go into a separate vat.'

Muttering that it had been good enough for the Baron, Jean reluctantly directed the gum-booted loaders to the adjoining vat.

'Good on you, girl.'

Picking up a glass, Halliday opened the tap and drew the must from an earlier vat. He held it to the light.

'*Quelle couleur, Monsieur!*'

There was grudging admiration in Jean's voice. He had never known the wine to run so clear after only one day.

Clare smiled triumphantly.

It was a Pyhrric victory.

Twenty-four hours later, the rain, forecast for the Pyrenees and the Massif Central, fell in slanting sheets, dousing the grapes in the deserted vineyards.

CHAPTER FORTY-THREE

The sun that streamed into Marie-Paule Balard's bedroom as she flung open the shutters caused her, uncharacteristically, to swear.

'*Merde!*'

'*Qu'est ce que tu as dis?*' Claude Balard sat up in bed. He could not believe what he was hearing.

'*Merde.*'

'*Pourquoi merde?*'

'*Il ne pleut plus.*'

'*Et alors?*'

Wrapping her *robe de chambre* around her, Marie-Paule did not reply. How could she explain that with the downpour of the past twenty-four hours, which had flooded the Bordeaux gutters and swelled the murky waters of the Garonne, had come renewed hope that Clare's harvest would fail and she would yet be mistress of Château de Cluzac.

'*Je vais regarder le télévision.*'

Trotting down to the salon in which the TV set sat oddly among the Louis XV chairs and *canapés*, she kicked off her pink slippers and settled down to watch the weather forecast, which she hoped would contradict what she had seen out of the bedroom window with her own eyes.

The news on the Pavé des Chartrons, confirmed by the sexy weather girl on TF1, was welcomed with relief at

Château de Cluzac. After a day of enforced idleness the pickers streamed out towards the vineyards where the grapes, saved in the nick of time from destruction, were already drying in the breeze that came tenderly from the south. The *chef de culture* had spent a few early-morning moments in the chapel, acknowledging the small miracle that had left his grapes none the worse for their wash.

Albert Rochas was not the only one to express his gratitude. Clare was scarcely able to believe that what she saw as her punishment – for defying her father, for thinking that she knew better than Halliday, for not following the lead of the other châteaux, for pushing her luck – had been averted. She offered up, to a God with whom she was unfamiliar, a brief litany of thanks.

For the next two back-breaking weeks, as the tractors, piled high with purple grapes, bumped their way once more along the paths towards the pressing house, and the troupe set about the vines with renewed vigour, filling their *panniers* in record time, she kept a weather eye on the sky.

Somewhat subdued, after the humiliating episode of the rain, and breaking her back to get her harvest in on time, she kept up the morale of the pickers as they systematically denuded the vines, watched as the bunches were sorted, scrutinised the *fouloir-égrappoir*, and supervised the cellars in which the skins of the grapes rose slowly to form a *chapeau* in the new vats. Dashing from vineyard to *chais*, and *chais* to vineyard, she brought in the last of the cabernet sauvignon, which were already fermenting in the neighbouring cellars.

In the winery she found Halliday, eyes everywhere as usual, at the top of a ladder. He was wielding an aluminium pole with which he broke up the purple crust of grape skins which had formed at the top of the vat.

'This cap should have been pierced, Clare. I suggest you have a word with your cellarmaster.'

Jean's years under the *laissez-faire* attitude of the Baron had made him lazy. Hoarse and utterly exhausted, Clare exhorted the cellarmaster to greater vigilance.

The last day of the harvest was traditionally celebrated with a wild party, at the conclusion of which the regular pickers, swearing undying friendship, would take emotional leave of each other for another year. As the preparations were being completed, Baron de Cluzac arrived, unexpectedly, back at his château.

The first intimation Clare had of her father's return was when Rougemont, who had been at her side all day as the last of the grapes were gleaned, went suddenly berserk.

She followed the dog, who scampered, falling over himself, all the way from the vineyards to the château. In the courtyard, she found her father shouting, at the top of his voice, for Monsieur Boniface to pay the driver of his taxi.

'Papa!'

'Clare.'

Clare recognised the familiar look of disapproval in her father's eyes as he took in her grape-stained hands, her dishevelled appearance.

'It's the last day of the harvest,' she said defensively, then realised that her father was alone. 'Where's Laura?'

'In Florida.'

'Getting the big top ready for the wedding?'

'There will be no wedding.'

'Changed your mind?' Clare thought of the money he had paid Viola for the divorce, with which she had bought the new casks now waiting to be filled.

'Not exactly.'

'Are you going to tell me?' She had no time to play games.

Charles-Louis hesitated.

All had been going well in Florida. The orange groves

needed less attention and were more predictable than his vineyards, and much of his summer had been spent cruising on the *Laura Dear*.

Back at the mansion, where the giant marquee was already under construction, Laura had entered the Baron's quarters to ask him about some last-minute preparations. Although it was not yet noon, she had found her prospective bridegroom in the arms of Rosa Delaware.

Laura had been doing her best for some time to ignore the rumours that had been circulating about Charles-Louis' proclivity for women, many of whom she suspected were her close friends. Had she not felt that she was rapidly becoming a laughing stock, she might have overlooked what might, in other circumstances, have been regarded as an indiscretion.

Coming as it did hard on the heels of his seduction of her New York decorator, who had been unable to keep what she saw as her double triumph at the Spray mansion to herself, Laura flipped her lid.

Emptying a large Chinese flower vase (*famille rose*) of contract lilies over the copulating couple – so that the brass and mahogany bed resembled a lily pond – and shrieking like a harridan, she hurled everything in sight that was not battened down at the lovers, and told Charles-Louis Eugène Bertrand, Baron de Cluzac, to get the hell out.

The Baron's subsequent remorse – he knew on which side his wheat-toast was buttered – got him nowhere. Before she had signed the pre-nuptial contract on which they had agreed, and which would get Charles-Louis out of his financial difficulties, Laura Spray had had her butler pack his valise, and ordered the immediate dismantling of the marquee.

In reply to Clare's question as to why there was now to be no wedding, Charles-Louis shrugged. He stepped over the pile of battered leather suitcases which the taxi driver, displeased with his meagre tip, had abandoned in the courtyard.

'*Changement d'avis*. Send somebody out for my things.'

The end-of-the-harvest party took place in one of the disused cellars which had been festively decorated for the occasion.

That there was something to celebrate, that Clare's gamble to wait until the grapes were fully mature before she brought them in had paid off, was in no doubt. Albert Rochas, tired as he was – as they all were – had been heard to express his satisfaction at the culmination of his year's work, and even Jean Boyer who had finally come to terms with both Clare and the inox, in which the new wine was fermenting, allowed himself a smile.

Only the Baron refused to join in the festivities. Despite Clare's invitation, he insisted on taking his solitary dinner in the *salle-à-manger* as usual.

'Will you be going back to Florida, Papa?' Clare was curious.

'I have thirty orange groves in Florida.'

The sarcasm of his tone, which had once succeeded in diminishing her, left Clare unmoved.

'I thought that Laura Spray . . . ?'

'Laura Spray is neither here nor there.'

From the contempt in his voice, Clare deduced that the woman he had been about to marry had been erased from his mind as if she had never existed. Her father's ability to turn his back on women, as Baronne Gertrude had once turned her back on him, never to give another thought to those he wished to strike from his mental agenda, had not changed.

One person who had been delighted with the news that the wedding would not now take place was Biancarelli, in whom the Baron detected a subtle change which he was at a loss to explain.

When Charles-Louis had told her, almost as an after-thought, during his afternoon visit, that he had been thrown out of the Palm Beach mansion and that the wedding was cancelled, Biancarelli had, to his surprise, put affectionate arms round his neck.

'*Ce n'est pas la fin du monde, Bianca!*' he said, sub-mitting to her embrace.

'I didn't say it was the end of the world, Charles. *Je suis tellement heureuse.*'

'Happy?'

'*La reine de Palm Beach* was not for you.'

Biancarelli's concern was reflected in their lovemaking. Dressed as usual in her *guêpière*, she had, with all the little tricks at her disposal, convinced him that he was the great lover, reassured him of his manhood, dispelled any lurking doubts that he was unloved. Her ministrations were marked by a new tenderness towards him which took him by surprise. He asked her if anything were wrong.

'*Je suis malade.*'

'Ill?' Charles-Louis was impotent in the face of illness. 'Have you seen a doctor?'

'There is no cure.'

'Rubbish. What is the matter?'

'You would not understand, Charles.'

'Ah, a woman's complaint.' There was relief in his voice.

'Men can suffer from it too.'

'Now you are talking in riddles.' He was not into innuendo.

Watched speculatively by his mistress from the depths of her lace-trimmed pillows, the Baron left her bed and put on his clothes.

'*A demain, Bianca.*'

'*A demain.*'

Although Charles-Louis could not quite put his finger on it, something about Biancarelli was different. At a loss to explain it, he decided to ignore it. Unable to live without women, he had never tried to understand them. It was not worth the effort. There didn't seem to be much point.

Clare left the Baron, whose every movement was watched by Rougemont, to his solitary dinner. In the cellars, where the rowdy pickers were already assembled at long tables beneath the giant bunches of black balloons, symbolising the black grapes, which hung from the low ceiling, she took her place at the top table. Flanked by her *chef de culture* and her *maître de chai*, surrounded by the exhilarated troupe, who had worked so hard to bring in the Château de Cluzac grapes, she gave herself up to the merriment and allowed herself to become exceedingly drunk on her own wine.

Sidonie and her kitchen staff had excelled themselves. A triumphant version of her *potage aux légumes*, heavily impregnated with chives and basil from Monsieur Louchemain's herb garden, preceded a *Gigot Brayaude*, local lamb cooked until it could be eaten with a spoon, accompanied by blackberry jam. This was followed by Clare's favourite *tarte aux mirabelles*, served with great bowls of yellow cream, whipped together with icing-sugar, over crushed ice, until it was thick.

The intervals between the courses were enlivened by enthusiastic songs from a dozen different countries accompanied by improvised music played on guitars and accordians. It was hardly surprising that the meal took four hours to consume.

When at last it was finished, the youngest of the harvesters, a boy from Andalusia, noisily egged on by his companions, approached the top table. Red in the face with embarrassment, to the accompaniment of wolf-whistles, he handed over the *gerbaude*, the traditional bouquet of flowers presented annually to the château owner by the pickers.

Kissing the boy on both cheeks, amid ribaldry and cat-calls, Clare accepted the bouquet. Overcome with emotion, she rose, with some difficulty, to her feet.

'So many countries are represented here . . .' She wondered why the room appeared to be unsteady. 'So many countries are represented here, that I shall stick to English, and hope that most of you will understand. First of all I would like to say how much I appreciate your patience and understanding . . .'

She waited for the mocking cheers to die down.

'. . . in waiting for the grapes to become completely mature, and for working so very hard to make this such a wonderful harvest. As most of you who have been coming regularly to pick the Château de Cluzac grapes will know, this is my very first *vendange*. Thank you for making it what promises to be an outstanding one. I am sure you would like to show your appreciation to my *maître de chai*, Monsieur Jean Boyer . . .'

The applause reverberated round the cellars.

'And my *chef de culture*, Monsieur Albert Rochas . . .'

Albert stood up bowing. It was the moment that made all the pruning and the spraying the fertilising and the ploughing worthwhile.

'. . . who are the real stars of this evening. *Merci, danke schön, danke, gracie, muchas grazias* to all of you, and a special thank you for these wonderful, wonderful flowers.'

The cheering grew frantic. Clare held up her hand.

'Before you leave Château de Cluzac, before you go back to your own countries and your day jobs, I would like you to join me in a toast to the spent *vignobles* of Château de Cluzac, which have performed so extraordinarily well. This will be followed by "Auld Lang Syne" with the words of which, I have it on the most reliable authority, you are all familiar.'

Clare filled her glass from the bottle on the table.

'The vineyards of Château de Cluzac!'

The toast, accompanied by tears and laughter, echoed round the cellars. Glasses were filled and emptied, instruments struck up, and two hundred white table napkins were waved above the heads of the troupe as 'Auld Lang Syne', in a variety of strange accents, hit the rafters.

As Clare linked arms with Jean on her left, and Albert on her right, she caught sight of Halliday Baines, who had been called away to deal with a faulty temperature gauge at Kilmartin, pushing his way between the tables towards her.

'Clare . . . !'

'"Should old acquaintance be forgot . . ."' Singing enthusiastically, Clare smiled as he approached.

'Clare!'

'What is it?'

Leaning across the trestle table, Halliday shouted to make himself heard above the noise.

'Sidonie wants you . . .'

'Now!'

Halliday nodded.

'What does she want?'

'Search me. She says it's urgent.'

Disengaging her arms from the cellarmaster and the *chef de culture* and imagining some domestic disaster, Clare made her way through the chains of swaying bodies to the kitchens, where Sidonie, surrounded by a mountain of empty pots and dirty dishes, was cradling the telephone receiver.

'*C'est Monsieur Jamie* . . .'

'Jamie? At this hour!'

Jamie should have been at the party, but the flights had all been fully booked. Clare took the receiver from Sidonie.

'Jamie?'

'Sorry to drag you away from the celebrations . . .'

Clare was overtaken by a giant hiccup.

'Whoops! I'm afraid I've had too much to drink.'

'Look, I do not really quite know how to put this . . .'

In a moment of drunken clarity, and feeling her heart sink, Clare said, 'It's Grandmaman, isn't it?'

'How did you know?'

'We're very close. I'll come at once.'

'There's no need. Baronne Gertrude died at ten o'clock this evening. Louise rang me. It was very peaceful. Father Aloysius was there.'

'Poor Grandmaman. I've been so busy . . . I've been meaning to call her.'

'Sorry to be the bearer of bad tidings. It was what Baronne Gertrude wanted. I'll speak to you tomorrow, darling. Try to get some sleep.'

As she replaced the receiver, suddenly grown heavy, an Australian voice broke into her thoughts.

'Thought you might want these . . .'

Halliday gave her the *gerbaude*, long roses and Arum lilies.

'My grandmother is dead.'

'I'm so sorry. Anything I can do?'

Clare shook her head.

The flowers were trembling.

Taking the bouquet from her, and putting his arms round her, Halliday kissed her on the lips. His mouth was warm and concerned. She drew away from him reluctantly.

'I'd better tell Papa.'

CHAPTER FORTY-FOUR

The funeral service of Baronne Gertrude de Cluzac was the first of the family funerals to be held in the chapel of Château de Cluzac since that of Baron Thibault, twenty-six years previously. Although it was to be a private affair, a few of the Bordelais closely aligned to the estate had come along to pay their respects to Baron de Cluzac and his daughter.

Entering the little chapel behind Charles-Louis and Tante Bernadette, who had returned to Château de Cluzac for the first time since she had fled from it to Notre Dame de Consolation, Clare had noticed, through the gloom of the traditional black veil Sidonie had insisted she wear, Jean Boyer with a red-eyed Sidonie, an ill-at-ease Albert Rochas and his family, Claude Balard with his wife Marie-Paule, the notary Maître Long, Halliday Baines, whom she scarcely recognised constrained in a suit, Alain Lamotte paying exaggerated court to Delphine in designer black, which was sculpted to reveal her early pregnancy, and, to her surprise, a heavily veiled Biancarelli.

Settling into the front pew, together with Jamie, who had come to Bordeaux for the day, Viola, who had been fond of Grandmaman, and Nicola and Hannah, who had insisted on accompanying Jamie, Clare thought that, although it was some time since she had been in a church, a funeral, like a wedding or a baptism, was one of the few occasions when the Christianity in which she had been raised came bobbing, uninvited, to the surface. It was as if what was happening to Grandmaman today was what the Church had been banging on about ever since she had been little.

It had been a week of turmoil. Grandmaman, who had been growing increasingly weak, had finally and uncomplainingly succumbed to acute intestinal obstruction. Only Louise, who had spent a night-long vigil on her knees, had been by her bedside together with the priest and the doctor who, unable to talk his patient into any treatment, had at least ensured that her exit from the world was painless.

Charles-Louis, who had not spoken more than a few words to his mother in twenty-five years, had travelled to London to collect her body (managing at the same time to fit in a visit to his tailor), and, while Clare was busy overseeing her new vintage in the cellars, had dealt with the formalities and made the arrangements for the funeral.

In the little room off the chapel in which Grandmaman's coffin lay surrounded by flowers, the estate workers and the neighbouring château owners – including the old Comtesse de Ribagnac, who had had to be assisted from the room – had come to pay their respects. By the light of the guttering candles, Clare had read the letter which Baronne Gertrude had left for her.

Ma chère petite Clare,

That 'machine for living', my tired old body, has finally given up. You thought that I was sanguine about what I knew very well to be the gravity of my condition. Like any human being, I was apprehensive at times, but I learned as a child how to control my thoughts in the face of danger.

Since I have been going downhill, unable to play bridge any more, or even to go out, I have had plenty of time to think. Life, Clare, is very much like the

Cours Albert le Grand. You are sent to school at an early age without being consulted. You get a great deal of work assigned to you (which helps you to grow) and are tested on it at frequent intervals. At the end of it all is the final examination, at which it will be decided whether you graduate or fail. This pattern is reflected everywhere, not just in life but in literature, from the Bible to the *Odyssey* of Homer, through Hindu and Buddhist scriptures to the Koran.

From the Church's point of view, the journey through life is governed by God's plan of creation, sanctification, and salvation: birth, sin, reconciliation, death, judgement, and verdict, the so-called 'cycle of redemption'. Christ went through it all himself and took his mother through it, so we know about it ahead of time and there is no need to be afraid.

As I write this, my sins have been forgiven and my atonement made, and I look forward to going straight to Heaven to enjoy for ever the presence of God. Put flowers on my grave for a while if you will, but from my point of view, outside of time, my body, the temple of the Holy Spirit at baptism destined for everlasting life, has already risen, and here I am.

I am so sad not to be here to witness your marriage. Jamie has been a rock. He never misses a Tuesday. It's a long way for him to come, although I believe that he has friends in Holland Park. The more I talk to Jamie, the more I care for him. He reminds me so much of your grandfather, and not only in build. Jamie is as strong-minded as Thibault. He knows exactly where he is going. Thibault and I were always a team, but there was never any doubt who was team leader. Jamie has shown me nothing but kindness and respect and I know that, given his head, he will make a princely husband.

Though you will lay me to rest in the chapel at

Cluzac where my coffin will be placed beside that of my beloved Thibault, you and I will not be parted (remember the resurrection of the dead). A person does not cease to exist or lose identity (immortality of the soul), death will never break the bonds that exist between us (communion of the saints), and the living Church will be there to comfort and embrace you (unity of the faithful). If bodily death separates us, then Christianity makes no sense at all.

As I enter into everlasting life, I pray that yours on earth will be as blessed as the happiness you have given to your Grandmaman. *Je pense à toi.*

Gertrude (Baronne de Cluzac).

As the funeral liturgy was completed – by the order of the Baron they would not celebrate the Mass – the young priest from Pauillac, who had not known Grandmaman, adjusted his cassock and took his place at the lectern to deliver his homily. There would be no eulogy, no dwelling on past glories or on achievements in the face of the great equaliser, death.

'"Men fear Death, as children fear to go in the dark: and as that natural fear in children is increased with tales, so is the other. Certainly the contemplation of Death as the wages of sin and passage to another world is Holy and religious: but the fear of it, as a tribute unto nature, is weak . . ."'

'Francis Bacon,' Jamie whispered.

As the young priest went on to speak, in suitably muted tones, of God's compassion and love and of his promise of resurrection and of everlasting life, Clare looked at the coffin girded by the book of Gospels, a few fresh flowers, and a cross, which lay before the altar. The white pall beneath it, like the square of starched linen used at Mass to cover the paten and chalice – the Body and the Blood of Christ – was a sign of life; an echo of the mantle worn by the French monarchs which demonstrated that the office did not die with the incumbent.

On occasions such as this, she wished she could go along with it all. It would be nice to believe that she and Grandmaman would not be parted, and that when she went back to London, everything would be as it had been; that they would sit over a gigot and a bottle of Château de Cluzac in the Hyde Park flat, while Grandmaman and Jamie pitted their literary wits against each other.

Glancing at Viola, wearing a skirt rather than her habitual jodhpurs, who had done her limited best as far as Clare was concerned, she thought that it was Grandmaman who had been her real mother and that, notwithstanding all the crap about everlasting life, Grandmaman was now dead.

Looking round the congregation, Tante Bernadette in her grey coif praying silently, Charles-Louis stony-faced, she realised that she was the only one weeping.

Picking up a worn, gold-embossed book for his final recitation, the young priest at the lectern removed a leather marker from it and lowered both his eyes and his voice:

' "The world was all before them, where to choose their place of rest, and Providence their guide: they hand in hand, with wandering steps and slow, through Eden took their solitary way . . ." '

'*Paradise Lost*,' Jamie whispered.

Baronne Gertrude had stipulated the readings, as she had the 'March of the Hebrew Slaves', which would accompany her to her last resting place.

Sprinkling the coffin with holy water in a final commendation, the priest bade farewell to the deceased. With a nod to her only son, Charles-Louis Eugène Bertrand, he signalled the mourners to escort the body to the private cemetery behind the chapel, the last resting place of the de Cluzacs.

Thinking afterwards about the rite of committal, the

sight of the coffin being lowered into the chasm, which she had found especially distressing, Clare wondered about the two black-clad figures she had noticed as she had laid her tribute of miniature roses – 'to Grandmaman from her Petite Clare' – on the grave. They had stood, their hats in their hands, at a respectful distance at the edge of the cemetery. She wondered what business Monsieur Huchez and Monsieur Combe had at her grandmother's funeral.

Caught up with the cold collation, which Sidonie had laid out in the *salle-à-manger* for the mourners, she had thought no more about the *fisc*. After exchanging a few words with the Baron, they had disappeared as silently as they had come.

After lunch she took Hannah and Nicola, stumbling in their city shoes, for a tour of the denuded vineyards. As she related to them the near disaster of her *vendange verte*, she saw them exchange glances.

'Zoffany's getting on my nerves,' Nicola said. 'And I'm missing Portobello. When are you coming home?'

'When I've made my wine.'

Nicola took her arm, hardly glancing at the vines. 'We'll have a big rave-up.'

'We're having one,' Clare said. 'It's called a wedding.'

'I've got the consultant job at the John Radcliffe.' Jamie was exultant. 'From next week I'll be flying solo.'

'*Félicitations* . . . I mean congratulations! That's terrific. Why didn't you tell me?'

'I waited until after the funeral.'

He spread some architectural drawings out on the floor of the library.

'That means we'll be staying in Waterperry. I brought the preliminary plans. What the architect wants to do is to extend the cottage at the side and back and add an extra floor over what is now the sitting-room but which,

rather cleverly I think, he is turning into the kitchen . . .
Clare, you're not listening!'

'I'm listening.'

Rolling up the drawings, Jamie thrust them into their
cardboard tube. 'I think we need to talk.'

'I thought that's what we were doing.'

'There are things we have to discuss, arrangements for
the wedding. Sebastian's agreed to be my best man, and
I've made a list of the ushers . . .'

'It won't be the same without Grandmaman.'

'I get the impression you're not interested in the
wedding . . .'

'I've got so much on my mind.'

'I'm sorry, darling.' Jamie put his arm round her and
drew her to him. 'You're upset about Grandmaman. This
wasn't the day to talk about Waterperry. Cheer up. I
love you. Grandmaman wouldn't have wanted you to be
sad . . .'

Nicola's voice, preceded by a discreet cough, came from
the corridor.

'Jamie! We're going to miss the plane!'

Petronella took them to the airport. Waving to the back
window of the station wagon as it left the yard, Clare
made disconsolately for the obscurity of the *chais*. Bereft
of Grandmaman, bereft of Jamie who had solicitously put
her reluctance to discuss the wedding down to her grief,
bereft of her friends, bereft of the funeral guests, bereft
even of Rougemont who had now deserted her for the
Baron, the cellars suited her dark mood.

'Are you going to show me the "divorce" barrels,
Clare?'

Viola's voice in the courtyard broke into her gloomy
thoughts. Slipping her hand into Clare's in an unfamiliar
gesture, Viola accompanied her daughter into the first-year
cellars in which the aroma of the new oak was coupled
with the aroma of the newly fermented wine.

'Grandmaman would have been so happy to see you actually making wine. What was it she used to say? *Toot passe . . .*'

'*Tout passe, tout lasse, tout casse.*' Shivering, Clare took her mother's arm. 'Let's get out of here.'

Alone in the château – Viola was visiting Kilmartin and the Baron had gone out – Clare sat in the solitary *salle-à-manger*, where a disapproving Sidonie removed her untouched dinner plate.

Wishing that Grandmaman were not lying silent and unreachable in the dank vault, trying to make sense of death and of non-being, never mind all that life eternal, she drifted disconsolately out into the grounds.

Pulling her black cardigan around her – the nights were drawing in – she leaned against the parapet of the moat in a halo of evening midges, and stared unseeingly at the trout making small ripples in the murky water. Noticing a few drops of water fall on to the stone of the balustrade, she thought that it was raining. Realising that her face too was wet, she wiped away her tears on her sleeve.

'Want to see the ace of diamonds vanish?' a gentle voice asked as a pack of cards appeared before her on the parapet.

'Halliday!'

Holding the three cards like a small fan, Halliday showed Clare the ace of spades, the ace of clubs, and the ace of diamonds. Closing the fan, he placed the three cards in different parts of the pack.

'OK, here we go.' He handed the cards to Clare. 'Find the ace of diamonds.'

Clare sifted unenthusiastically through the pack.

'It isn't here.'

'You saw me put it back.'

'Where is it then?'

'How about in that urn?' Halliday indicated the moss-covered urn several yards away at the edge of the parapet.

Putting her hand into its cobwebbed cavity, Clare removed the ace of diamonds.

'Why did you come?'

'I thought you might be lonely. I thought I'd drive you back to Bordeaux. I've been saving a bottle of champagne. One of the last of Krug's private *cuvée* . . .'

While Halliday was in the kitchenette, Clare, unable to settle after her traumatic day, wandered round the sitting-room. On the buffet, next to the photograph of Billy, was a neatly ironed woman's handkerchief embroidered with an ornate 'C'.

'Christiane Balard?'

Coming in with the champagne in an ice-bucket and two glasses on a tray, Halliday followed her gaze.

'How did you guess?'

Taking the Krug from the bucket, he clasped the cork firmly and, concentrating hard, twisted the bottle.

Pouring out two glasses, he handed one to Clare.

'To your grandmother.' He touched Clare's glass with his own. 'May she rest in peace.'

They sat side by side on the sofa.

When the champagne was almost finished, Clare said, 'Have you ever thought that the bliss of the saved in heaven is more difficult to imagine than the torments of the damned in hell?'

'It's only in this world that life can be hell. What do you think of it?'

'Hell?'

'The Krug.'

Clare held her glass by the foot. 'The apotheosis of elegance. Rich but well mannered, perfectly balanced and beautifully textured, with an understated bouquet and long finish, dry . . . fruity . . . smoky . . . meaty . . .' Her voice wavered unsteadily as a tear fell into the champagne.

'Hang on there.' He removed the glass from her hand. 'This was meant to cheer you up . . .'

Sobbing unashamedly, Clare let all the misery of the past week come out.

Halliday fetched the incriminating handkerchief from the buffet. Sitting close to her, he dried her face gently. 'Christiane Balard *lent* it to me,' he said softly. 'When Big Mick chucked the claret over me at the Fête de la Fleur.'

Feeling the warmth of his body leeching into her own, conscious of strange and jangled feelings in her head, Clare turned to face him. Meeting her eyes for no more than a moment, Halliday got to his feet.

'What you need is some fresh air.' His voice was brusque. 'Why don't we take a walk? I'll buy you a plate of oysters at the Bistrot des Quinconces.'

CHAPTER FORTY-FIVE

By the time of the trial *assemblage*, Clare had spent an entire week painstakingly tasting every single barrel of new wine in the first-year cellar.

Ever since Baronne Gertrude's funeral, she had not been herself. At first she had thought she was ill. Sidonie had made her stay in bed and brought up tisanes made from fennel and from lemon-balm from the herb garden. Later Clare had put it down to the unseasonably cold weather, which had kept her for long nights in the damp cellars, making sure that the vats were adequately heated and that, because of the drop in temperature, the fermentation did not suddenly stop.

She had not seen Halliday, who had spent Christmas in Australia, since the night they had disposed of the Krug. That night, heading back along the river after leaving the oyster bar – the Quai Louis XVIII and the Quai Richelieu, as far as the Place de la Bourse illuminated like a giant opera set – Clare, still in her funeral black, had slipped her arm into his.

'It's all very well for Grandmaman, comfortably settled in her pew in her church in heaven. Do you believe in God?'

'Bacchus.'

'Dionysus.' Clare gave the god of wine his Greek name.

'On the island of Naxos, Bacchus . . .'

'Dionysus!'

'. . . found a young woman lying asleep on the shore.'

'Ariadne.'

'The very same.'

'Daughter of Minos, whom Theseus had brought with him from Crete and abandoned.'

'When she awoke, she realised that Theseus had left her. She gave way to uncontrollable tears. The arrival of Bacchus . . .'

'Dionysus!'

'Have it your own way. The arrival of Bacchus-stroke-Dionysus consoled her . . .'

'And shortly afterwards . . .'

'Shortly afterwards' – Halliday turned to face her beneath the light of the street lamp – 'they were solemnly married.'

Clare pointed an astonished arm over his shoulder, as a well-built man and a woman with hennaed hair, strolling close to each other with the matched steps of lovers, appeared on the quayside.

'Isn't that my father?'

'It certainly looks like the Baron.'

'He's with Biancarelli!'

In the courtyard of Château de Cluzac where, as dawn broke over the vineyards, Halliday dropped her off, Clare had put grateful arms around the Australian.

'You saved my life.'

'Any time.'

She had not seen her oenologist since, and it was over a month since she had seen Jamie, although she had been back to England twice. On the first occasion she had discussed her wedding dress – a simple sheath of oyster satin worn with Grandmaman's veil – with Hannah, and before Jamie left for his conference in Barbados they had finalised the guest list. Next week the invitations were going out.

On the day following Grandmaman's obsequies, Monsieur Huchez and Monsieur Combe had presented themselves in the *Bureau d'Acceuil* and asked for the Baron on a matter of some urgency. They refused to budge until he was found.

Having just seen her father leave the château with his shotgun, presumably to pot rabbits, Clare had set out along the drive to find him. A large saloon car, coming towards her at what seemed to be an immoderate speed, made her hop smartly on to the safety of the grass verge.

As she did so, Rougemont, who had been running alongside the Baron, on the opposite side of the park, caught sight of her. With a yelp of excitement, he bounded across the drive.

'*Attention!*'

Charles-Louis' anguished yell came at the same moment as the screech of brakes, the squeal of skidding tyres, and a sickening thud, as the bumper of the oncoming car caught Rougement's flank. In apparent slow motion, the heavy red setter was tossed high into the air, before crashing, spreadeagled and immobile, like a burnished hearthrug, into the road.

Thinking about it afterwards, Clare was unable to recall the precise sequence of events.

As the Baron belted between the trees like one possessed, an appalled and ashen-faced Claude Balard climbed out of his BMW. Dropping to his knees, Charles-Louis gazed in disbelief at his dog, whose fixed eyes were staring into space and whose blood was leaving his body at an alarming rate.

'*Va cherchez la voiture,*' he ordered Clare.

'*Ma voiture est à votre disposition.*' Claude Balard offered his car to Charles-Louis.

'*Allez-vous en, Balard!*' the Baron roared. 'This is the last time you set foot on this estate . . .'

'*Mais* . . . I have come about the château. We set up a meeting . . .'

'*Foutez le camp!*' Raising the shotgun, Charles-Louis pointed it at the petrified Balard as the overweight negociant stumbled towards his car.

As the wheels clumsily mounted the grass verge, and the BMW disappeared in a cloud of dust towards the gates, Clare tried, and failed, to find the pulse in Rougemont's neck.

'*Il est mort, Papa.*'

'*Non.*'

'*Regarde-le!*'

'Get the car.'

'What for?'

'I'm taking him to the vet. Hurry!'

'Rougemont is *dead*.'

Fondling the dog's silken ear, his eyes strangely moist, Charles-Louis shook his head.

'*Va vite!*' His voice was numb.

By the time Clare got back with the Renault, her father, in an unbelievable act of strength, was standing, like some blood-stained Colossus, splay-legged in the middle of the drive with Rougemont, limp and inert, in his arms. Helping him to manoeuvre the dead weight on to the back seat of the car, an exercise that left them both breathless, she watched with disbelief as he climbed, like a robot, into the driving seat and motioned her imperiously out of the way.

Left staring at the puddle of blood seeping into the gravel, Clare could scarcely credit what, in the space of just a few moments, had taken place. The dog was Charles-Louis' immortal beloved: the only thing in the world for which he truly cared. Clare would not have put it past her father to kill the perpetrator of the crime, Claude Balard, with his own hands.

Remembering Monsieur Huchez and Monsieur Combe, she had made her slow way back to her office.

'*Ou est votre père?*'
'*Il n'est pas ici.*'

Judging by the look on their faces, Monsieur Huchez and Monsieur Combe were up to no good. Clare guessed that Philip Van Gelder had shopped her father to the *fisc*. She told the inspectors, in her best château owner's manner, that she had no idea when the Baron would be back.

'*Nous l'attenderons.*'

Clare left them in the *Bureau d'Acceuil*. This was not going to be her father's day.

'Did your father go back to Florida?'

True to his word, Halliday had come to Château de Cluzac to help Clare with the *assemblage*. They were in the tasting-room.

'My father is in Monte Carlo . . .'

'I thought I hadn't seen Rougemont.'

'Rougemont is dead. *Tout passe, tout lasse, tout casse . . .*'

'Sorry?'

'Nothing.'

Clare had been to visit the Baron in the Avenue Princesse Grace, where he lived with a devoted Biancarelli, leaving the orange groves to tick over by themselves. His time was spent at the blackjack tables. He was no longer interested either in oranges or in vines.

'He is awaiting trial for fraud. In connection with his profits. I felt quite sorry for him. Fortunately Papa doesn't believe that any judge in the land would dare to find him guilty.'

With her yield low, Clare's first decision was how much of her wine she was going to declassify. Bearing in mind that her Petite Clare would realise little more than quarter as much per bottle as her *grand vin*, it was a decision that could cost the château up to half a million pounds in badly needed cash.

Watched by her cynical *chef de culture*, who stood,

with his arms folded, by the door, Clare began tasting and mixing from the carefully racked bottles and calibrated measuring-cylinders on the table. As she silently practised her alchemist's art, Jean Boyer and Halliday Baines, making frequent journeys to the sink in the corner, concentrated on their own selections.

Noticing that Clare had discarded a vat sample he had put to the fore, Jean, who was watching her every move, protested:

'C'est un des Merlots!'

'It's too soft.'

'Don't forget your yield is low,' Halliday said, backing up the cellarmaster. 'You're going to need the merlot for volume.'

Clare replaced the cylinder of merlot in the reject rack. 'Remember forty-five? Great vintage. Very little merlot. Did you hear anyone complain?'

They spent the rest of day arguing, lining up, as possibles, mixtures which they all agreed had balance, spurning others which were short. When Clare dismissed out of hand a sample of cabernet, which Jean was convinced should be added to the final blend, it was as if she had slapped the cellarmaster's face.

'It's an adequate luncheon claret, Jean. That's all that can be said.'

'C'était assez bon pour Monsieur le Baron . . .'

'It may well have been good enough for my father, but it is thin and unconcentrated. It is not going anywhere near my grand vin.'

Another sample, this time recommended by Halliday, was rejected on the grounds of its not having the 'class' which Clare was determined from now on must be synonymous with the Château de Cluzac label.

Refusing to give up until she was satified, choosing only from the finest casks, and working on the premiss that a wine that would please her would please everyone, and

have a common language which could be enjoyed anywhere, she produced a plummy, seductive claret with the
elegance of a woman, the potential body of a prize fighter,
and the insouciance of a courtesan. Even Jean Boyer, who
had recovered from his pique, was impressed.

'*Félicitations, Mademoiselle Clare!*' He raised his glass
of deep ruby Château de Cluzac, which he tasted appreciatively and swallowed.

'A bloody beauty! And it has your handwriting!' There
was admiration in Halliday's voice as he savoured the
final blend.

'Let's get out of here.' Clare pushed her hair out of her
eyes. 'I'm bushed.'

Making her way with Halliday to the cheerless vineyards, where the few remaining leaves on the resting vines
were yellow and curling, she picked up a handful of gravel
and ran it slowly through her fingers.

'I'm going to miss this place.'

'You've made a pretty good job of things. The vintage
was great. You've vinified *brilliantly*.'

'More by good luck than good management . . .'

'Only the ignorant make good wine by chance.'

'Have you ever thought that, when you do things to
"show people", they're either dead or they no longer
care?'

'Why don't you stick around?' Halliday said casually.
'In three years, based on today's showing, the château
should be making a profit. Big Mick will be licking your
boots. You could replace the dead wood. Plant new vines.
Computerise the *chais* . . .'

'Aren't you forgetting something?'

'An A-one bottling plant?'

'Alain Lamotte's loan has to be paid off. The château
has to be sold.'

Picking up a quartz pebble, Halliday made it appear, a
second later, from Clare's ear.

'Did you know that pieces of quartz from the vineyards of Latour were once polished and presented to King Louis XVI as buttons for his waistcoat? What if *I* paid off the loan?'

'You? Since when have you got so much money?'

'I could sell my vineyard in Chile . . .'

'You'd do that!'

'We'd make a great team, Clare . . .'

A great team. She could recite Grandmaman's last letter by heart. '. . . Jamie is as strong-minded as Thibault. He knows exactly where he is going. Thibault and I were always a team, but there was never any doubt who was team leader . . .'

'Your flair . . .' Halliday was saying.

'And your expertise.' Any partnership with Halliday would be a partnership of equals.

'We could turn this place into a showpiece.'

'Château de Cluzac would be known all over the world.'

Halliday took his cards from his pocket. 'When I was about twelve, I was taken to see a magic show. I helped my dad round the place and saved up enough to buy my first book of card tricks. By the age of fourteen I was hooked. You can't expect every trick in the book to suit your style, but find the right ones and they can fill your life, bring you riches you've never imagined . . .'

'I'm getting married in four weeks.' Clare glanced involuntarily at the ring from Butler's Wharf. 'You're leaving Jamie out of all this.'

'Not me. You.'

Touching the wooden pickets with her fingertips as they walked along the rows, Clare examined the thoughts she had been suppressing. She tried to picture herself walking down the aisle in the little church in Scotland, supervising the extension to the cottage in Waterperry, working her butt off in the Nicola Wade Gallery, selling her wares in

Portobello, joining the spouse tours at conferences, waiting for Jamie as he reduced fractures and pinned bones.

She wanted to see the vines beneath their blanket of snow in winter, to be there when the sap rose, to witness the first buds of spring.

Halliday had stopped. His eyes were level with her own.

'There are things that must be confronted,' he said.

'Are you trying to tell me something?'

'Nothing that you don't already know.'

'What if it's a mistake?'

'If you don't make decisions, you can't make mistakes.'

Clare glanced up at the crenellated château, which stood, as it had for three hundred years, severe, rigorous, rational, silhouetted against the Médoc sky; she looked down at the arid earth which would shortly build up its deep reserves of water on which the success of next year's vintage would depend. She could hear Baronne Gertrude's voice.

'You have de Cluzac roots, Clare. Like the roots of the vines, they are planted deep.'

'You belong here, Clare.' Halliday spoke softly, reading her mind.

Unaware who made the first move, she found herself in his arms.

After twenty-eight years, Clare de Cluzac had come home.

ENVOI

[Extract from *Wine Watch*]

Cluzac 1994 The most dramatic improvement in a single vintage since Ch Margaux in 1978. After more than a decade of thin, unconcentrated wines this one is not only the best Cluzac in a generation, it is also fully the equal of other great wines of the appellation. Rich, firm, fruity, well-balanced, with tannins that are firm without being harsh. 91